LOVE Park

For Cyndi —
In friendship, and
in the spirit of Philadelphia,

J.

LOVE Park

by Jim Zervanos

CABLE PUBLISHING

Brule, Wisconsin

LOVE Park

First Edition

Published by:
Cable Publishing
14090 E Keinenen Rd
Brule, WI 54820

Website: www.cablepublishing.com
E-mail: nan@cablepublishing.com

This is a work of fiction. Any resemblance to actual people, living or dead, is purely coincidental.

Hardcover: ISBN 13: 978-1-934980-62-0
              ISBN 10: 1-934980-62-5

Soft cover: ISBN 13: 978-1-934980-63-7
              ISBN 10: 1-934980-63-3

Library of Congress Control Number: 2009921595

Printed in the United States of America

For Vana

Jesus said, "If those who lead you say to you, 'Look, the kingdom is in the sky,' then the birds of the sky will get there before you.... If they say to you, 'It is in the sea,' then the fish will get there before you."
    —The Gospel of Thomas

Painting is no problem. The problem is what to do when you're not painting.
    —Jackson Pollock

1
Nice Greek Girl

At twenty-one, I believed I was going to write a book that would immortalize Philadelphia. I thought of my hometown as a museum without walls, harboring future relics—the sky-blue buildings reaching ever higher into the clouds, the Art Museum, another artifact, atop the city's own Acropolis, the boulevard leading to LOVE Park, fountains gushing pink water before City Hall's blunt, pale tower. The opening line came to me just as Dorothy Maloney snapped a picture of the two of us, author and photographer, posing for the dustcover, side by side at the base of the LOVE sculpture, bound together for eternity. This is love, I thought. Then: *This is LOVE.*

I had met Dorothy Maloney in an Eastern Religion seminar our junior year at Temple University, just after she'd vowed to purify herself by abstaining from alcohol, drugs, and sex. She was *re-virginizing*, she explained to me, and I sympathized with her spiritual crisis. I was picking up a Religion minor in hopes of making my Greek Orthodoxy seem an informed choice, not just something I was born into. Each of us felt safe dry-humping incessantly, without fear of the other's expectations. As she saw it, she was abstaining; as I saw it, I was enjoying a virtual sex life. She envied my apparent detachment from the need to have intercourse and told me how she admired my restraint and trusted my discipline. I made sure to wear shirts long enough to hide the proof that she overestimated me.

As a kid I'd had my heart set on Tori Williams, who used to tease and call me virgin, either predicting my permanent sexual state or offering to put an end to it, I was never sure, though for a long time I imagined she'd be my first. I liked that I was the priest's son while she was the WASPy girl from around the block who had a backyard pool and looked great in her pink bikini. Almost as great as her older sister, Bridget, whose looks won her a contract with a suntan-lotion company and with whom my big brother got naked under an afghan right on the living-room couch at least once before she took off for California. I'd run in through the kitchen and frozen at the sight of Andrew's pale ribs and her golden thighs sunken into red leather cushions. While my brother moved obliviously above her, Bridget curled her arm above her head and smiled at me, her legs tangled in a red-white-and-blue crocheted blanket.

At sixteen, in my newly purchased pickup, I was driving Tori home from McDonald's the day she opened the Velcro fly of my bathing suit and, for about three fantastic seconds, rubbed me through my damp, chlorinated briefs. When at first she saw my underwear and asked why I wore it under my bathing suit, I shrugged, never having considered going without it. Mercifully, she didn't ask about my subsequent flinching. I sealed up my surfer shorts, trying to appear cool, though tiny explosions were going off even as I entered her driveway.

During the next two years, my condition, or affliction—disability? *curse?*—was confirmed and, as far I knew, kept secret from the ranks at Plymouth High School, thanks to insufficient lighting and my own practiced non-reaction. As a junior at a youth-group retreat in the woods along the Susquehanna, I shuddered discreetly in a pair of thick blue camper shorts when Stella Mavroutsis, as if hefting melons, clenched my buttocks only seconds after our lips had met. As a senior I found myself still inept, this time in a dark-brown suit at the Homecoming dance, in the shadows of the lockers, kissing the Mennonite girl, Donna Fisher, who I'd assumed was inexperienced, until she plunged her tongue into my ear and grabbed my crotch.

*

At twenty-six, another summer spread out before me, I broke out a small stack of blank note cards and finally wrote those three words down. *This is LOVE.* Day after day I carried that stack, secured with a rubber band, in the big front pocket of the army shorts I wore while painting the interiors of empty apartments white.

*

On the third Saturday in June, my father came down to the base-ment to wake me up. Every weekday for the past five years I'd been waking up at six—before anyone else—and painting houses till dusk, yet on Saturday mornings my father, the priest playing Domestic Dad, still wanted me to play apprentice, to steady the dowel rods while he tied the tomato vines, to pull back the thorny rose branches while he reached for weeds, to follow with a broom while he groomed the hemlocks along the walkway. The basement walls almost completely muted the distant buzz of the lawn mower, but my father's heavy foot-falls across the kitchen floor achieved their purpose, penetrating my cocoon. It wasn't until the old man sat down on the bed that I antici-pated hearing some sacred father-to-son speech, instead of a list of chores. When your priest-father tells you it's time you started dating and found your own place, it's official: your life has become a joke. You might even consider taking his advice for once. "A nice Greek girl…your own apartment…a job you can be proud of…" It must have pained the old man to say these things to his grown son. "You've got the whole summer. Enough is enough."

The next Saturday, when I finally tackled the stairs up to the kitchen, my mother announced I'd risen just in time for lamb sandwiches on the good rolls. Instead, I stepped onto the back patio, still in pajama bottoms, cradling a bowl of Lucky Charms, while my father trudged across the lawn in old Nikes, gripping a bursting Hefty bag in each fist and glaring at me: *Why do you still eat that stuff?* He'd told my mother not to buy the fruity-marshmallow junk anymore, so I'd gone to the grocery store myself and paid nearly five bucks for the small box.

Making her way across the final strip of uncut grass, my sister, Sophia, tipped the Toro onto its hind wheels and glowered at me, reminding me that this was the last time she'd be mowing this lawn. I couldn't believe she was really leaving tomorrow, off to California—just out of high school and already a woman. Tomorrow she would be gone, and I would be home alone—with my parents, my uncle, and my grandmother—twenty-six years old and asserting my independence by going to the Acme to buy my own Lucky Charms and Tastykakes.

Not even an hour later, I was staring at the red glow of the traffic light two blocks from home, having just picked up four cases of soda and beer for the name-day party that night. Sitting there, I thought, I'm still running errands like a teenager, and then: *Forget about Dorothy Maloney.* Thinking of Dorothy always made me feel not just sad but ashamed, not because I'd allowed my inadequacy to seem like abstinence, not even because I'd turned her down the night before graduation when she asked me once and for all to go south with her to some kind of commune, but because I'd never had the guts to bring her home to meet my parents.

The light turned to green, and I turned left into my neighborhood, and left again onto Birch Hill. Even up here, the pollen-sticky air, through the window of my pickup, smelled of cut grass. I would wear a smile for the party, I decided, but secretly I'd be packing. Enough *was* enough. I was already imagining myself lounging poolside at Stone Bridge Apartments, where for the last five years I'd been rolling fresh coats of paint for the incoming tenants.

I swore to God right then and there: this summer I was going to change my life, come hell or high water. As it turned out, it would take Him less than a week to make it clear that He had heard me.

I slammed the brakes and gasped when Freddy West, at first a blur of denim and tie-dyed T-shirt, shot out from his driveway and barreled down the hill on his skateboard. The weekend before, the kid, while hammering two-by-fours in his yard, had explained to me how he was not allowed to take the center-city train to LOVE Park anymore, because his parents had heard the cops were cracking down on skateboarders ruining the sidewalks and steps. "That stinks," I'd offered. In high school, I, too, had gone to LOVE Park now and then, though I'd never amounted to much of a skateboarder. Still, I missed those days. "Whatever," Freddy had said, and I'd admired his indifference. Now, I admired his initiative: against the Wests' garage door, a wooden ramp—an upraised, bright-yellow plank, bordered with giant silver nail heads—was shining in the sun. I exhaled, finally, as Freddy, with knees bent and hands out surfer-style, swooped and disappeared at the bottom of the hill, where the road came to a T at our freshly mown front yard.

All of a sudden my engine died, just as I spotted my family gathering on the driveway down below. I loved my truck, which I'd bought in high school with lawn money. The engine restarted, no problem. Still, I pictured my truck sputtering into the driveway and dying once and for all behind my brother's red Porsche. I pressed the gas gingerly and lingered at the top of the hill.

My brother was offering our father the keys to a new green car— evidently Andrew's latest toy. The old man seemed to be declining a test drive, hands folded and head bowed, faithful to his old black Nissan, which was usually—as it was now—awaiting new parts at the local Exxon service station. When Melanie, Andrew's girlfriend, facing the waxy hood, pointed toward the rear of the car, the old man stepped around back, as if to inspect the bumper. Melanie clapped, while my mother rushed from the grass to see what the fuss was about. A bumper sticker? All the while, Sophia couldn't have cared less, hosing down the mower, her back to everyone.

I was too far away to see anyone's expression, but I could imagine the scene: Andrew hoping for a pat on the back from the old man, who was contemplating how a priest should respond to such extravagance, not to mention a priest who was determined to drive his old Nissan over the two-hundred-thousand-mile mark; Melanie silently urging the old man to go ahead, pat Andrew on the back, despite the ethical implications of endorsing the purchase of a second luxury car; my mother, torn, beaming proudly, offering an ambiguous "Oh, Andrew," while trying to shake the thought of tithing, reminding herself that as a doctor Andrew gave much more than ten percent of himself to people every day; and Sophia, her boots stained green, listening to our brother's chatter—anti-lock brakes, side air bags, satellite tracking system, Such-and-Such sound system—wanting to turn the water gun on all of them, angry for having spent the last four hours mowing this goddamn three-acre yard, angrier for having to wash a lawn mower.

Halfway down Birch Hill, tucked on the right side of the street in the shade of overhanging pine branches, a dark-haired woman hunched at the steering wheel of a maroon Chevrolet. Drifting, pulling alongside, I leaned over, cranked down the passenger window, and heard the familiar plucky whine of *bouzouki* music seeping out through the sealed windows. Verifying the woman's Greekness was a laminated postcard-sized icon of a distinctly Byzantine Jesus tucked into the near corner of the dashboard. When the woman glanced up from the purse on her lap, I was struck by her dark beauty, the severe, shadowy angles of her eyes and nose, the bulk of hair that fell, suddenly, over her face. I thought I recognized her from church, though I hadn't been there in years.

After a moment her door opened, and I backed up to make room. Engine problems? We had something in common. She took a step toward me and hesitated, her eyes aimed on me in a deadly squint. It was only when her hand rose to block the sun that I realized she couldn't see me through the glare on the windshield. Her apologetic, closed-lipped smile vanished as she turned toward the front of the car, her red heels clicking on the pavement, her dress, white with red polka dots, flirting just below her knees. Nice Greek girl, I thought. If she turned out to be a second cousin or a distant aunt, I'd pay for my gawking.

Her fingers danced at the lip of the car's hood.

I stepped out of my truck and leaned on my door.

"Need a jump?" I asked.

She lowered her eyes.

"I've got cables." I aimed my thumb at the truck bed.

"I'm fine," she said, and turned to face the pine trees, which blocked the view to my family on the driveway.

"Can I help you somehow?" I called out.

She tapped her fingers on the hood, turning slightly toward me. "No no," she said, the two syllables rolling together, the o's sounding short and vaguely accented.

I enunciated carefully: "Are you here for the par-tee?"

"Party?" She gazed down at my house.

My truck spluttered and groaned.

Should I invite her home? Or ask if she needed a phone? She was too young, wasn't she, to be one of those destitute widows who needed my father—or my mother? My mother wouldn't hesitate to invite some lonesome Greek woman into our home—especially today, the name day honoring Saints Peter and Paul, the founders of the church.

Suddenly the woman stumbled.

"Jesus." I rushed around the front of my truck.

"I'm a little off balance." Hobbling, she slipped off her shoe and held it out toward me, the heel jutting like a broken finger. Her smile startled me almost as much as her reaching for my ponytail. "Your hair—it's so long. The artist, right?"

I wasn't sure what or whom she was remembering. Apparently, it had been a long time since I'd seen this woman—or since *she'd* seen *me*. For years now, my hair had been long enough to be the subject of more than a few domestic disputes, overshadowed only by battles over Sophia's latest piercings and, more recently, her unwashed twists of hair, which were finally, after months of painstaking disregard, beginning to assert themselves as dreadlocks.

"I just paint apartments. I was an Art *History* major."

"Oh." A frown formed between the woman's eyebrows.

Instantly I was as disappointed as she seemed to be. I could explain that there was an art to painting houses, even to whitewashing apartments. I could explain that I had an idea for my own art history book, about Philadelphia, about the Calders, the Clothespin, and the LOVE sculpture, about outdoor art and its relationship with the people. But nobody wanted to hear my analysis of it all, not even Sophia, who'd said recently that if my book idea had anything going for it, it was my uncanny ability to analyze a thing to death.

"Are you here for my father?" I asked, finally.

The woman reached for my shoulder, and for a moment I expected her to whisper something into my ear. I leaned forward, anticipating, as she lowered her eyes. Tiny crystals of blue eye shadow flashed beneath the perfectly shaped black arcs that were her eyebrows. She leaned back against the car, her bare foot hovering. Injured shoe in her hands, she pressed the nearly severed heel into its joint and let it droop from a leathery thread.

"Ruined," she said, just as a navy-blue Volvo, Mrs. West's, sidled up to my truck.

Mrs. West's fleshy strawberry face and orange hair, which rose into an ice-cream swirl, appeared behind the descending passenger window. She waved, in no hurry.

"Everything all right?" she said.

I rushed back to my truck. "I'll get out of the way."

"You want me to get Barry?"

"Barry? Mr. West? *Dr.* West?" I corrected myself, not that Mrs. West seemed offended, though her husband, who taught anthropology at the local women's college, had corrected me more than once when I was a kid. Whenever my eyes had met the cynical squint of Dr. West, whether I was peeling the papery bark off the birches in the front yard or popping wheelies on my banana-seated Schwinn in the driveway, I would imagine the professor reading deep meanings into my actions, dark meanings I was not yet capable of comprehending.

The Greek woman had opened her door and tossed her shoes inside.

"Is your car all right?" Mrs. West called out.

"It's fine," I blurted.

The Greek woman flashed a smirk at me and rummaged through her car's front seat.

I suspected the professor's wife had adopted her husband's eye for hidden motivations, for the secret truths of the human condition, or at least *my* condition.

With a lop-sided skip—though both shoes were off now—the Greek woman hurried toward my truck, dismissing Mrs. West with a wave and carrying a glossy black purse.

The blue Volvo coasted slowly downhill and finally turned at the corner.

"You don't recognize me, do you, Peter?" The Greek woman set her purse on the hood of my truck. Her hair fell in thick black swoops that framed her face.

"You look familiar."

"Daisy Diamond."

The name was unfamiliar and anything but Greek, yet I was sure I remembered this woman from church. She'd had long, curly hair then... She was the one who would go on standing after my father gestured for the congregation to sit down during Communion. Once, as a thirteen-year-old altar boy, I failed to disguise my laughter by coughing in the direction of the stained-glass windows. I'd be defrocked, I thought, as the other altar boys bowed their heads and this exotic, curvy woman with the wild mane went on crossing herself, hand sailing from belly to forehead, shoulder to shoulder, with a passion I'd considered unique to shrunken old widows in black sacks. "Genuflecting," my father explained after the service. "A beautiful young woman who lost her husband—you find that funny?" The next Sunday, happily robed, I spied her through the carved wooden gaps of the altar screen, secretly undressing her, imagining myself her new husband, lost in the deep shadow at the lip of her neckline, as I was right now, my memory of her returning, thinking she must have kept her American husband's last name, wondering what Greek name could be anglicized into *Daisy*...

"I'd come by your house to pick grape leaves with your mother." She touched her throat. "You remember?"

"I remember my mom picking grape leaves."

"She was a saint when I lost my husband." She wiped her damp cheek and added in a gravelly whisper, "Poor woman."

"*Poor woman?*" I crossed my arms, as Daisy Diamond began digging through her purse. I hated people pitying my mother, let alone thinking her a martyr. "She *is* a saint," I said, getting the woman's attention and asking, once and for all, "What are you *doing* here?"

"I need you to take me home, Peter." She dipped her head toward the passenger door, looked up, and said, "I'm not well."

"Mrs. *Diamond*—"

"*Daisy*. Please." The door latch clicked, and she lifted herself into the truck.

Through the windshield I saw her, this unlikely Daisy, wrestling with her dress as she twisted to get comfortable. I opened the door and leaned in. "You're *sick?*"

"I'm depressed." She set her purse at her feet. "I'm in no condition to drive." Her hand rose to her forehead, poised, it seemed, to descend to her navel and proceed to make the cross.

I stared into the pine trees beyond her car. I felt cruel for not asking, "Why are you depressed?" but I didn't want the full confession.

Instead, I stood outside the truck, hoping that she'd find her bearings, or that *I* would.

I didn't know how my father did it. This woman, and people like her, were the reason I'd always known, deep down, that I wasn't cut out for the priesthood—I could never handle surprise visits by depressed parishioners, each certain she was the sole miserable person on the planet. No matter how beautiful she was.

I leaned into the truck. "I think you should talk to my father."

"I don't need your father." She flattened the wrinkles on her thighs.

I glared at Daisy Diamond's bare feet. "Don't you need anything from your car? Your *shoes?*"

She lifted her purse onto her lap. "My keys," she said, displaying them on a finger, "are all I need." She put them back into her purse and in one motion pulled out an orange prescription bottle, unscrewed the cap, cupped her hand to her mouth, and swallowed. "And these."

I got in. I rode the brake down the hill, biding my time, trying to think of a plan, now that this woman was refusing to see my father, opting for pills over spiritual counsel. Should I just drive her home and leave her there *alone?* What if she really *was* sick, or even as sick as my uncle Theo, who, when he cracked up in his twenties, couldn't have seemed to anyone like a prime suspect for manic depression, let alone suicidal tendencies?

At the bottom of the hill I turned right and paused before my driveway. "I have to drop this stuff off."

Daisy reached for my arm. "Peter, I'm sorry. I've been horrible." She scanned the yard.

Between the hemlocks that lined the sidewalk along the front of the house, my father, in a white undershirt, emerged from the garage, the corrugated door rising behind him.

"Stop," Daisy said. "Please."

My father bent down, behind bushes, to pick up a piece of trash or a leaf or an unswept blade of grass.

"It's okay," I assured her, but kept my foot on the brake.

Daisy sighed.

I took a deep breath, wishing the old man would rise up, spot his son hovering desperately at the edge of the yard, and rescue me from the impending mission. Still, I was trying to be patient. I understood that people from the church weren't used to seeing the priest out of his gold vestment, or at least a black suit coat—as if my father weren't an ordinary man, made of flesh and blood. Once, as a kid, I swiped the collar right from the slit in my father's black shirt, right from his neck, ripped it like a Band-Aid—relishing the secret of the thing's ordinariness. I waved it in the faces of Sunday-school girls, who shrieked with fear and delight, not knowing that the Holy Collar was just a plastic strip, nicked and scratched, made from the same stuff as dog bowls and Frisbees. In church-picnic softball games, my father used to strike out intentionally just to appear ordinary. The old man had played for Holy Cross, and he could hit, all right. After the park cleared out, Andrew would lob pitches while Sophia and I would hurl our gloves at long drives being launched over our heads. That was our father's style. Teach through example. Walk softly and carry a big stick, he would say. There was nothing humble about striking out in front of a crowd if you couldn't hit in the first place.

"Mrs. Diamond…" I tried again. "People come by all the time. Even on Saturdays."

Daisy went on staring straight ahead, as I accelerated, gingerly, over the concrete gutter and into the driveway.

"Damn it, Peter!" She braced herself against the dashboard, just as my father stood and disappeared into the garage.

What the hell was the matter with this woman? The situation called for a professional—a priest or a doctor, either of which was inside the house right now. The garage door began to close, and Daisy's arms relaxed.

Or maybe I could pawn her off on my mother, by inviting her in for something to drink, telling her how happy Saint Olympia would be to see her.

"Take me home," Daisy whispered.

It was official: I would play the taxi driver.

"The beer needs time to get cold," I announced, and when she didn't protest, I got out, dumped all the drinks—two cases of Coke, one of

7-Up, and one of Heineken—into the front yard, and got back into the truck. "That'll look pretty strange," I huffed, as the truck whined in reverse. I made my way back up the hill and out of the neighborhood. "Where do you live?"

"In the city."

As I jerked the wheel right and headed toward Lincoln Drive, the bags of ice tumbled across the ridged floor of the truck bed. "God damn it," I spat, imagining my father lugging the drinks and figuring I'd bungled the task and had to go back. "I forgot the ice."

Daisy didn't flinch, even as I picked up speed away from home. Wind whipped through my open window and curled behind me. When Daisy's dress fluttered at her knees, she gripped her thighs, letting her hair fly.

I raised my window, leaving an inch for warm air to blow against my moist forehead. Daisy wiped stray hairs from her eyes and scanned the trees of Fairmount Park.

For four years of college I had traveled this path—Lincoln to Kelly to Broad—in spite of more direct routes that cut through North Philly. I'd always thought it must be the most beautiful drive in the country. Beyond lush green leaves, the arches of old stone bridges soared high above Wissahickon Creek. At times like these, I imagined the limitlessness of the art book I intended to write. I could include the bridges and even the trees themselves. I could examine the very notion of beauty and explain what defined a thing as art, as opposed to, say, architecture or nature, and, how, when you really started thinking about all forms of beauty around you, everything started to blur together and definitions became purely subjective. Feeling inspired, I wondered if Daisy Diamond's peaceful expression was due to the beautiful landscape or just her pill taking effect.

"I've lived in the city my whole life," Daisy said, as if I had insisted otherwise. "You know Saint George's?"

I shook my head no.

"The Greek church, *vreh*. Eighth and Pine."

I was pretty sure she'd just called me idiot. In my mind I could hear my grandmother barking Greek aspersions behind her closed door.

"It's a term of endearment." Daisy smirked.

She was a mind reader. Or I must have appeared insulted.

"You don't know *Greek?*" she said.

"*To milo eineh kokino*"—The apple is red—I heard myself say.

"Oh, very good... *Hah!*" Her eyes widened as though she were as surprised as I was by my sudden willingness to please, let alone by her strange, delayed laugh. She swallowed intently and shifted to face me, smiling.

The miracle of Xanax—or whatever she'd taken—I thought. The breeze had brought some of the old curl I remembered back to her hair. She lifted a knee onto the cushion between us and folded her hands in her lap, anticipating more of my botched-up Greek. Looking forward to it, it seemed. Okay. I'd play the charming fool.

"That's it, my one sentence," I said. "The apple is red."

"I know what it means, *vreh*." She paused. "Let's try again. *Ti kaneis?*"—How are you?

"*Kala*"—Good—I said.

"See!" she beamed. "You *know...*" She reached over and poked my thigh, then turned toward the trees whipping past. To my surprise—and disappointment—she rested her head against the glass and closed her eyes, grinning, uninterested, apparently, in a conversation in either language.

I couldn't help the swelling in my jeans.

As my truck hugged the curving concrete barrier lining the Schuylkill River, I imagined pulling over into some boathouse parking lot up ahead, lifting Daisy Diamond's polka-dotted dress above her waist, and sinking between her legs.

The Philadelphia skyline—pristine, angled shapes of cool blue—emerged from behind the tree line of Fairmount Park, as the truck motored along winding Kelly Drive and past the Art Museum. City Hall punched the shallow sky with its tower, atop which stood the largest cast-bronze statue in the world: thirty-six-foot-tall, twenty-seven-ton William Penn, facing the Great Northeast, his right hand, gesturing from a ballooning sleeve and frilled cuff, appearing, as it always did from this angle, as a drooping erection.

Up ahead was LOVE Park, clean and desolate. The newly laid stone slabs shone white-gray in the sun. Robert Indiana's LOVE sculpture, its stacked red letters and funky tilted O, stood beyond the fountain, which gushed pink water, dyed for some women's-cause parade this weekend, I had heard on the radio earlier. Breast Cancer or Pro-Choice. A policewoman, in dark hat and light-blue shirt, stood guard, perched on the concrete barrier surrounding the pool. Three shifty-eyed boys sauntered down the sidewalk with skateboards under their arms. I remembered, as a kid, standing tiptoe in my black-and-white checkered Chuck Taylors, Magic Markered in my own hand to match the Vans the real punks wore, framing what I could within the inner circle of the tilted O, while skateboards looped and skidded all around me.

The LOVE sculpture also made me think of Dorothy Maloney. It was her favorite thing in the city—*our* favorite thing. At its base was where we'd envisioned our future together. I wondered if she'd stayed in North Carolina, or if she'd ever come back to Philadelphia. If she'd found a Hare Krishna to marry or gone off to a convent. Anything was possible. That's what I'd both loved and feared about her.

Times like these made me wonder if maybe my mother was right—if I, not Sophia, was the one who was depressed, who needed therapy or even medication. When my sister had demanded treatment recently, the therapist insisted she wasn't depressed and certainly didn't need to be medicated—a diagnosis, or *lack* of one, she'd found not just incompetent but insulting. My mother had suggested to me that I simply "talk to someone," in lieu of going to church—not that she'd given up on church for me. My father must have considered all this psychotherapy business blasphemous, what with Sophia's considering it the salvation her parents and idiotic doctors were depriving her of, though the old man wasn't against Theo taking his medication.

I came to a red light on Market Street. In the window of a corner store, bright rows of yellow and blue plastic bottles taunted me—Cheer and Glad. Inches from my thigh Daisy Diamond's hand, ringless and white, lay flat on the ridged plastic seat. I had the strange desire to clench her fingers and say something comforting—or for her to say something comforting to me.

"Eighth and Pine," she said again.

When I approached the corner of Eighth and Pine, she pointed beyond the pole that marked the last legal parking space. I pulled in toward the curb at an angle.

"You're kind." Eyes lowered, Daisy clutched the purse on her lap. "I insulted you earlier."

"It's okay."

Digging the keys from her purse, she looked up. "You have a right to know why I came to your house today."

"I assume you came for my dad and then changed your mind," I said.

"You're the smart one." She touched my cheek and smiled gently. I wasn't sure if she would laugh or cry. "I want to give you something." She hooked her finger on the door handle. "Come in for a minute."

"Well…" I wasn't sure what I was feeling. The Greeks had a thousand words for love—*eros, agape…* I pointed with my thumb. "I've got the ice."

"I have something for your father," she said.

I rested my hand on the vinyl between us.

Maybe I should go in, I thought. Maybe she really did have something for my father—a name-day gift, a basket stuffed with cheese and a bottle of olive oil. The old man was always bringing home bags filled with tomatoes from parishioners' backyard gardens. *Sit down,* she would say. *Let me get you some iced tea.* I glanced at the melting ice.

"No reason to rush home, I guess," I said.

Daisy got out and made her way around to the sidewalk.

I turned the engine off and sealed the cracked window, then followed her toward the wrought-iron railing of her four-step walk-up. A French-windowed door opened into a small tile-floored vestibule. She swept aside with her bare foot a small mountain of mail, her name—Mrs. Ms. Miss Daisy Diamond, Dionysia Diamond, Dionysia Diamonides—flashing in the plastic windows of the envelopes, and unlocked a second door that swung into a dim, carpeted foyer. Immediately to the right, her apartment door opened onto a salmon-pink Oriental rug covering most of the living room's hardwood floor, which extended back through a dining room and bordered the kitchen.

"Just a minute," she said, and headed toward the kitchen. She returned with a brown paper bag and started up the stairway that rose from the dining room. "I'm going to gather some things."

Three white doilies hung over the curved back of the couch against the far wall of the living room. On corner tables, thick-framed photographs surrounded light-green marble lamps. I saw, in one picture near the window, the black suit and white collar of a priest. I stepped into the corner to confirm: my father, flanked by Daisy Diamond and five other devotees at the church bazaar, reaching his arms out over the shoulders of these aproned women cradling Styrofoam to-go boxes. I held the picture in the light of the window. Through the translucent drapes, I could see the bags of melting ice, glimmering like beached jellyfish.

Daisy came down the steps, cradling the paper bag in her arms, her gaze calm as she made her way toward me and set the bag on the coffee table. She took the framed photograph from my hands and tucked it into the bag, then stood and without any apparent hesitation looked into my eyes.

"You're a good man." She took my hand.

She reached up and with both hands brought my face toward hers. Her cool, thin lips pressed against mine, thick and dry. My fingertips touched her dress. Her kiss was firm, and I swelled up again instantly. I closed my eyes and in a flash recalled Bernini's *Ecstasy of St. Theresa*: the angel thrusting his golden spear into swooning Theresa's heart, the spiritual and sensual worlds colliding.

When my hand landed on her hip, she withdrew.

"Go," she said. "Before I go too far." She picked up the shopping bag and handed it to me. "I finally figured something out today. Tell your father I'm finished with all of it."

"What is this?" I cradled the bag in one arm.

Lying on top of a folded pair of jeans was another framed picture; this one, of my father with Andrew, Sophia, and me in our back yard. I dug past the jeans to find a gray T-shirt with purple-block, collegiate-style letters that I recognized: Holy Cross. And a pair of grass-stained, red-striped Adidas tennis sneakers.

"Your father's been trapped for years. Give it back or keep it yourself. I don't care anymore."

She put her hand on my shoulder, but I stepped away into the foyer, looking down at the picture—at my own little-boy body in a red-and-yellow T-shirt with a decal of Speedy Gonzalez grinning in a sombrero.

She was following me, saying how these things had found their home here, saying something that made no sense to me. I was envisioning in a bed upstairs my father's humped back, her pink legs angled out. It was as impossible as my mother beneath another man.

"I've never told a soul," she said.

I backed into the vestibule and stopped. Light poured down on her gray-streaked face.

"You're crazy," I said.

"Go back to your family, Peter. *Please.*" She closed the big, heavy door.

Outside the sky was flat white and infinite. The leaves on the trees merged into a green blur.

I froze and bowed my head, as the stink of smashed gingko fruit rose from the sidewalk. In my arms, Andrew was smiling up at me, beneath a nest of brown hair, wearing striped tube socks up to his knees and pounding a baseball mitt. With two fists my sister, barely standing on her own, was tugging at the seam of her pink T-shirt, displaying her name, *Sophia*, in glittery cursive from armpit to armpit. My father, rosy-faced, was reaching out, one hand on Andrew's shoulder, the other on my head, his suit jacket rising beneath his arms—like a superhero's cape. My mother must have been seeing all of this from the other side of the camera, out there on the sun-drenched green grass of our East Birch house, the ancient wrought-iron fence rising up into young pine trees.

2
And Now the Moment We've All Been Waiting For

On the night before I drove Daisy Diamond home, I picked up my parents at the hospital, where they'd been visiting with a parishioner whose wife was dying of cancer. As the man walked with my parents to the curb, his glistening bald head shone. He wore a wrinkled corduroy sport coat, despite the heat, and loosely tied sneakers that shuffled like slippers on the concrete. He was hunched over, less from old age, it seemed, than from grief. But when he came into the light of the streetlamp overhead, I could see that he was smiling gloriously. The man hugged my mother and took my father's hand. After my mother settled into the front seat of the truck and my father followed, the man held my father's hand through the open window. He pressed his moist lips to my father's knuckles and politely wiped them dry. "Your parents give us peace," the man said to me, "more than the doctors." I was nodding, speechless, as the man reached for my mother's hand and brought it to his lips. "I love your mother and father," he said. His eyes were brimming with liquid light. "I do too," I choked out. The man brought my parents' hands together and stepped back from the curb. My parents' fingers stayed intertwined in my mother's lap, even as the truck entered our driveway and came to rest under the basketball hoop.

Years ago, on the day my father installed that hoop, Andrew dribbled a basketball and shot at the stone wall above the garage door, announcing buzzer-beaters, while I straddled the gray metal pole in the grass, raised my worshipping fists, and cheered my big brother's heroics. The old man was bare-chested, jabbing his shovel into the stubborn earth just off the lip of the macadam, while Stavros, the always-reliable church custodian, stirred cement with a broom handle in a red, rusted wheelbarrow. The old man's shoulders rippled when he muscled the shovel's tip into the growing hole. That night, under the floodlight, the old man and Andrew played HORSE, while I caught their shots before they hit the ground. The old man sank baskets from the sidewalk and back yard, calling out *swish!*

Today, when I got back from Daisy Diamond's house, I wanted to chain the pole to my truck's front end and back up until I heaved it out of the ground and off the property. I wanted to take the stuffed paper bag from under the dashboard and set fire to it in the front yard.

I couldn't stay here—*home*. At the moment, I couldn't even get out of the truck, let alone go inside the house, this great house we lived in only because my rich grandfather had left my grandmother so he could live happily ever after with a cocktail waitress in Atlantic City. I wondered if my father, growing up, had known about *his* father, if he had lain awake in bed, picturing him sipping martinis and eyeing girls in fishnet stockings strutting past the blackjack table. Even before today, I'd wondered if I was the only one in the family, including Yiayia herself, who had any proper sense of justice—not that I hoped Papou was burning in Hell for what he'd done, but you'd think the woman would take down his photographs or at least stop wearing black like some widow whose husband deserved to be mourned. What used to drive me nuts was less that my grandparents had never bothered to get a divorce than that, for years, my *yiayia* pretended the old bastard had never left her for another woman—pretended he was coming back, until the day she got word he'd keeled over on a Carnival cruise ship in the middle of the Caribbean. Yiayia's most recent self-quarantining, in fact, had been triggered by my prankish removal of Papou's large black-and-white portrait outside her bedroom, the absence of which had gone unnoticed only until I got to the kitchen, where I was too far away to make out the curses coming from the third-floor landing.

When I stepped down from the truck, finally, I felt lightheaded. I bent over, hands on my knees, and inhaled thick humid air. I would make it through the party, I decided, but I'd slept in this house for the last time. On Monday I would take the cheapest apartment I could find. Until then—tonight, tomorrow night—I would slip out of the house and stay in one of the motels up by the turnpike exit. Hell, for two nights I could survive in a sleeping bag on the truck bed.

I pulled the rubber band from my ponytail, scratched my damp scalp, and shook my hair out. The drinks still sat on the lawn. No doubt, my mother was worried—it didn't take three hours to go to the Brew Mall.

It was time to go inside, but I was paralyzed on the driveway.

In the bedroom window above the floodlight, the black figure of my grandmother passed by. At the apex of the roof, a satellite dish the size of a dinner plate pulled in Greek soap operas. The old woman was content to fill the rest of her days with stories of Mediterranean lovers, whom she cursed at and cried for, sometimes taking part in the dialogues, sometimes even dressing up for her role. More than once I'd caught her in a bright-colored dress—out of her mourning garb— her door mistakenly left unlocked; setting her tray on the night table, rather than on the floor in the hallway, I'd asked if she was going to a cocktail party or just dressing up for afternoon tea. There had been a time when she and Papou would go downtown for dinner off Broad Street and to the Academy of Music to see the orchestra or the ballet. In certain pictures it was obvious the old bastard was showing off his exotically beautiful and sophisticated Greek wife, who must have added some class to the lifestyle he'd attained through construction. My father had tried to make a lesson of Yiayia's sad saga. We weren't to think ill of the cocktail waitress. She'd loved Papou. We weren't to think ill even of Papou. The devil homed in on you in slick ways. He wanted only to steer you away from the church. You had to be careful.

A legacy of betrayal, I thought. At least my grandfather had had the decency to be a public louse. At least his whole life wasn't a lie.

My shoulders sank, and my lungs seemed to shrink, as I realized that Daisy Diamond had dumped the secret onto me, perhaps for the same reason I wanted, now, to tell Andrew, Sophia, or anyone: to free myself from being the only one who knew. On the way home something had kept me from pulling over and dumping the clothes and pictures into the river. Maybe I should carry the brown paper bag inside and calmly set it on the kitchen table. My mother would ask what else I'd picked up for dinner—corn on the cob? Andrew and Sophia would spread the contents on the table. Where did you get this stuff? I would keep my eyes on the old man.

First things first, I told myself. For now the bag would stay tucked under the dashboard. No need for dramatics. I didn't want to be the one responsible for my mother's heart stopping. I would bide my time until I got Andrew and Sophia alone, and then together we could decide what to do.

Beyond Andrew's red Porsche was the new green car, a Lexus. As it turned out, it had been not a bumper sticker that had drawn my family's attention earlier, but a license plate—four blue letters: ZEUS. I considered the chances—hoping—that fate had picked out these letters at random. Then I accepted the fact that Andrew had actually chosen these letters for himself; at the same moment, I accepted, too, that I could never tell my brother what had happened today because Andrew would simply shoot the story down—even if he were shown the bag. I would end up the unforgivable asshole, not to mention idiot, for having considered some clothes and a couple of pictures evidence of anything. Come to think of it, Andrew would have refused to believe Daisy Diamond's story even if he had been the one to take her home. He would have laughed it off, left the bag on the woman's coffee table, driven away, and never mentioned it. Andrew never would have given it a second thought, because some things you just don't think about.

I envied my brother's ability to simplify, or even to ignore, things— and then to remain sane, or even perfectly happy.

I leaned back on the new car, remembering Andrew in his Mark Spitz Speedo at the local pool, doing gainers and two-and-a-halfs off the high dive. As a kid I'd believed that my big brother might actually be some kind of god. An audience would form along the gutter, as I sat on a towel in the grass, munching a frozen Snickers bar, overhearing high-school girls saying, "He's a Greek god." Even when Andrew's tucked body opened too early on a dive and his belly or back smacked, he would rise from the water with a smile so beguiling you were convinced he'd landed it exactly as he'd intended. He didn't acknowledge failure. That was the trick: he didn't even *recognize* it. Andrew was handsome and talented, but most enviable was his ability to transform everything he did into something golden. He seemed to *will* his life into good form.

Such was the case six years ago when Andrew started dating Melanie Winklestein. Early on in their relationship she made it clear to Andrew—and to the whole Pappas family, boldly, one Sunday afternoon at the dinner table—that she would never convert to Christianity, out of respect. She could never lie about believing in something that was supposed to be sacred, least of all the whole Jesus story. Cross that bridge when you get there, was Andrew's philosophy.

I had my own theories: here was Andrew, the eldest son of a Greek Orthodox priest, dating this girl he would never marry—not in his father's church, anyway, and so, presumably, not anywhere; Melanie must have imagined them eloping or somehow evading marriage indefinitely. Before long, though, no one talked about anyone being Jewish anymore, not even my parents, who came to love the girl. Andrew's optimism was not only contagious, but blinding. I was still carrying around the secret of the Winklesteins' dog, who died years ago, the night Andrew threw a blowout party while Melanie and her family were on vacation. What people don't know won't hurt them, Andrew told me. A dead dog was a dead dog no matter how it died— no matter where it was buried. As for marriage—why worry now? Enjoy the moment. The guy made it all look easy. What was worse: for him it *was* easy.

Okay, so I wouldn't tell Andrew about the old man.

In Sophia, on the other hand, I knew I had an ally. Unlike Andrew, she would believe my story, if only because she was drawn to Tragedy, which validated what she saw as her own and everyone else's miserable existence. Sophia was no nihilist, though she dressed like the club president—that is, when she wasn't dressed for a peace rally or a Free Mumia! march. I knew that if I showed her the bag, she would grit her teeth and set her eyes on justice. The real danger in telling her, however, was that she might actually crack up—or, at least she had me convinced she might. Then she would get her therapy and medication after all, and I would be blamed for the consummation of my sister's decline as a human being.

Earlier in the day, over lunch, the old man had shot me the familiar look that meant Sophia had gone off the deep end her senior year only because her long-haired brother still lived in the basement and had turned their double-car garage into a storage room for paint buckets and drop cloths. Sophia had been marching back and forth from oven to kitchen table, boots smelling of cut grass, reminding us all of the evils of meat-eating and announcing for the last time that her ticket to California was one-way, that she wouldn't be coming back any time soon, and that this family, me included, didn't understand her— *lacked the capacity* to understand her. By now, I had changed out of my pajama bottoms and into my army shorts; I had agreed to run to the Brew Mall and was rushing through my lamb sandwich when my father shot me the look. When the old man told Sophia to eat her lunch and then go wash the lawn mower, she disappeared out the back screen door. Now the ancient white Toyota, which she'd taken for an angry spin, was back, aimed at the garage door, and boxed in by her brothers' two cars and truck.

For the time being, I would keep the secret to myself, I concluded. More than that, I would try to be like Andrew and just not think about it. I took a deep breath and headed for the back porch, planning my surreptitious descent into the basement.

As I skulked toward the sliding screen door, tip-toeing in the mulch, I could hear Sophia continuing a conversation that apparently had no end. I sidestepped Theo's untamed pink roses and leaned against the stone wall outside the kitchen.

"It's not just some *idea*, Dad. It's a real program that Veronica's totally doing, and you don't have to be a student. I told you at Christmas, and you've known this is my plan. I never said I'm *not* going to college—just not right away."

Sophia wasn't going to college right away because she'd spent her senior year doing God knew what with her friend Veronica, instead of meeting application deadlines. Actually, I had a good idea of what she'd been doing with Veronica, but I told myself she was going through a phase. She just wanted what everyone else wanted, she would say. Did they have to *name* it? They'd kissed, all right? She admitted that much to me, after swearing me to secrecy. A crush, I'd figured, until they went to the prom together. Meanwhile, Veronica's dysfunctional life, unlike Sophia's, hadn't foiled *her* academic success: she'd already moved out to Berkeley—Sophia's dream school.

Through the window above my head, I could hear the kitchen-sink spigot's perpetual hum, my mother making dinner or clearing up from lunch—cleaning raw chicken or rinsing sauce from plates—while reviewing in her mind Sophia's flight itinerary. I imagined my father, standing there, perplexed, wondering when, if ever, he'd actually approved his daughter's one-way trip to California. Over the sound of rushing water, Andrew made a joke about Sophia's need for the heaviest-duty suntan lotion—SPF forty—lest she make herself so dark that our mother, assuming Sophia might ever return home, would once and for all mistake her daughter for an Albanian or even African refugee from one of the church's missions, as if such racial blurring weren't precisely what Sophia had in mind. Theo blurted that she was better off not going to Berkeley after all, that she should stay home and hold out for the Ivy League.

Apparently, Sophia had rounded up everyone to hear her final complaints before her departure the next morning. Amid all the interruptions, she was trying to explain that she just wanted to explore for a year.

"Explore *what?*" my father said.

"*Life.* The *world*," Sophia said, as if introducing new words to her audience. "And I really don't appreciate that you think I'm going out there just because Veronica's out there. I'm the one who told *her* about Berkeley—"

"Nothing's been decided yet," my father said. "I don't want you flying."

"*Flying?* I have the *ticket*, Dad! It's a *summer program!* I'm leaving *tomorrow!* Where have you *been?!*"

"Mom's already got a care package assembled," Andrew added.

At last, with a deep breath, I shoved the screen door in its dry groove and stepped into the kitchen.

"Peter, you *made* it!" Theo sat in the old-fashioned schoolhouse desk next to the basement door, his string of gray worry beads twirling perpetually at his fingers. His blue eyes appeared magnified by the thick glasses he wore only when he didn't want to miss something.

"How long does it take to go to the Brew Hall?" my father asked.

"Brew *Mall*," Sophia corrected him.

I froze, wanting to lash out: *You don't get to question me anymore!* My heart was pounding. I glanced into the foyer, the sun-drenched hallway leading to the front door and beyond.

My mother stood off to my left, frozen for the moment, looking up from a white-capped blue bottle she'd just plucked from a cabinet converted for vitamin and medicine storage. They all seemed to be scowling at me, except Melanie, who stood by the refrigerator in an ocean-colored dress, smiling sweetly. Sophia and my father were in opposite corners, in standoff position, each head-to-toe in black, with a touch of silver jewelry: against the icon-littered backdrop of the kitchen wall stood my father, in black shoes, slacks, and short-sleeve shirt open to the first button, along with his silver wedding band; to my left, between my mother and me, stood my sister, in black calf-high lace-up Doc Martens, fishnet stockings, mid-thigh skirt, and tank top, along with her silver rings pierced through the brow and both ears, a virtual Slinky of bands along the forearms, and a stud through the belly button, in full view, like an evil eye aimed at the old man.

Andrew broke the silence. "Why don't you just take some classes?"

I stepped around the kitchen table toward the basement door, where Theo's worry beads clicked and smacked, vanishing in his grip and reemerging, a nervous gray blur.

"I'm not taking classes to make anybody happy. No class can make you an *artist*." Sophia glanced at me, to acknowledge the source of her wisdom, though I wanted no credit for the effect I'd had on her.

"You see?" my father said. "I don't believe this. Peter put this idea into your head. *Theo—!*" The old man glared at Theo's hands.

Theo silenced his beads, and I stopped cold.

"Don't blame Peter, Dad! You can't even give me credit for the stuff I do that pisses you off!"

"*Honey*," my mother said. "That *word*." She handed Sophia the bottle from the cabinet. "Put this with the other things."

"*Pisses?* Jesus, Mom, stop *censoring* me. You don't need school to be a poet. You just need to live life!" Sophia examined the label on the bottle. "*Petroleum suppositories?*"

I wanted to call out the Truth. Good News, Sophia! Dad's a fraud! We're all free! Then I remembered Daisy Diamond's words—*your father's been trapped for years*—and I thought, we're all trapped.

"You'll be eating different foods, honey," my mother said. "You never know how the change in diet will affect your bowels."

"*Mom!*" Sophia looked, horrified, at Melanie, who pretended, mercifully, to be distracted by the church calendar pinned to the refrigerator.

"If you're not going to college," my father said, "you can stay home until you're ready. Even Peter went to college."

"Look what it got *him*." Andrew grinned. "Just kidding, Doc."

"What does *Peter* have to do with anything?" Sophia said. "This is so humiliating..."

My theory was that this kind of verbal abuse had replaced the physical abuse we'd inflicted on each other as kids—and that all of it, then and now, disguised our brotherly, and sisterly, love. Andrew used to seal his mouth around my little nose and exhale his hot, wet breath, which poured through my nasal passage and back out my mouth. I would laugh and spit at the same time, in horror, then lie back on the carpet. When Sophia was old enough to endure such torture, both Andrew and I would pin her down and tickle her until her laughing turned to crying and, at least a few times, peeing—she wet her little cotton pants and ran screaming into the kitchen. Minutes later she would return in fresh pants, tears dried up, and spread herself on the carpet like an X. No more, Andrew would tell her, and eventually her giggling would once again turn to sobbing.

Sophia set the blue bottle next to a white surgical mask on the kitchen table, among the vitamins and first-aid items my mother had already collected. I recognized the red letters on the packet of iOSAT tablets—"to be used only as directed by state or local public health authorities in the event of a radiation emergency." Months ago, Andrew had brought home a bag of surgical masks, along with the iOSAT tablets, from the hospital, announcing that he'd finally managed to confiscate the highly coveted antidote for anthrax poisoning. His teasing had been evident to everyone but my mother, who promptly arranged the packets in prominent locations throughout the house, but only after pleading with me to wear a mask at work and inquiring if the tablets might also protect against asbestos and lead poisoning, this in spite of the countless times I'd explained that I worked only with water-based paint.

Sophia was going on: "I want to *go* somewhere. And *do* something *interesting* and *good* for people. Help homeless people. *He* hasn't gone anywhere or done anything for *anyone!* He lives in the *basement!*"

As she went on, referring to me as a third-person pronoun as if I were not standing there in the room, I thought: we keep coming back for more abuse. Then I realized, it isn't so bad to be invisible, and side-stepped toward the basement door.

"Peter," Melanie said.

I looked up, my hand on the doorknob.

"Andrew and I still have our announcement."

Melanie was painfully lovely, her sandy-blond hair already, in late June, streaked with gold from the summer sun. When Andrew had first brought her home, I'd looked up from art history books and gone dumbstruck. By the end of the night she'd made her way back into the dimly lit kitchen, sat, and paged through one of my books, asking me about Ionic versus Doric, Impressionist versus Expressionist, and why I didn't have a girlfriend.

"Remember," Andrew said, "Melanie and I called everyone in here for a reason before Sophia hijacked everything with her impassioned little diatribe—"

"Fuck you, Andrew."

A dish slipped from my mother's hands, and, as she reached out to save it, another followed, each crashing on the cold tile floor.

"Enough with the language!" my father yelled.

"It's just a *word!*" Sophia hollered.

My mother stooped, and Melanie bent down to help.

I crouched toward the mess, but when my mother glanced up, I stepped back, curling my hair behind my ears and searching my pockets for a rubber band. I picked up a ceramic chip near my foot and set it on the table.

Theo tucked his worry beads delicately into his pants pocket.

Sophia paced in short steps by the sink, her eyes wild, her stiff, infant dreadlocks tumbling and jutting like spasmodic fingers.

Suddenly I became sad at the sight and sound of her—of this unceasing rant—and wondered if maybe she *was* going crazy, as she often claimed to be.

"…You don't say anything to Andrew and he completely insults me. That's so American, to care more about language than common human decency…"

Maybe this is how it happened, I thought: your brain can't keep it all together anymore; you've gotten too smart for your own good, and you snap, right here in the kitchen, eighteen years old, the people who love you witnessing the whole fitful breakdown, your brain splintering in as many directions as there are family members; or, as I imagined Theo decades ago, you're trekking through Athens in the prime of your life, knapsack filled with your next batch of books, your mind like a diamond, perfectly carved and sizzling with condensed energy, entire histories of civilizations and whole novels and epic poems you hadn't known you'd memorized firing out from your skull into your blood and muscles and nerves and into the sun-scorched world, while your sandaled feet mount the same rocks Socrates walked upon when he envisioned his fate, and you fall to your knees and scurry like a bug to a crack, crawling, in your mind, to the nearest safe place where you can rest and gather your thoughts.

Or maybe Sophia was the only sane one in the room—perhaps along with Theo—barely keeping it together while she watched everything around her falling apart.

"That's deep, Sophia." Andrew clapped.

"I hate you." She stormed off toward the stairs.

We all waited for the heavy footfalls above us to stop.

"Okay, let's hear this announcement," Theo said.

"Sophia has to be here," Melanie said.

"No she doesn't."Andrew sighed and stuffed his hands into his pockets.

"Yes she does," Melanie said. "We have to wait."

I turned for the basement again.

"Peter." My mother was still holding white ceramic triangles, like pita, in each hand.

"What took you so long?" my father said.

"Everything's in the yard," I said, opening the basement door.

"We've been worried about you," my mother said.

"Everything's fine, Mom."

"We agreed you'd wear a rubber band," my father said.

The fucking rubber band!—as if wearing it were the last thing I could do to maintain some dignity. I closed the basement door and took a single deliberate step toward my father. *We* didn't agree to anything, I thought, gripping my hair in a fist and then letting it fall. The shadowy grooves in the old man's forehead deepened. Andrew crossed his arms, offering his little brother a rare moment of deferential curiosity. I imagined destroying all they knew of family dignity, making my own announcement, loud enough so that even Sophia could hear me up in her bedroom: *Our Father…!*

"I'm twenty-six," I said instead, and I meant what being twenty-six implied: I was on my own now.

My mother placed the ceramic pieces on the counter and wiped her hands on her apron. "What *is* it, Peter?"

"Nothing."

Daisy Diamond, I wanted to say. Just her name, to see what the old man would do.

Sophia's silhouette—mini-skirted Medusa in combat boots—suddenly appeared in the foyer, before the Plexiglas storm door. She'd come quietly down the stairs, I realized, and now she stood staring into the front yard, perhaps envisioning her new life in California.

"I'm not your servant," I said to my father.

When Sophia turned around, hearing me, I signaled to her with a squint: Everything's cool. I'm not insane.

Just then the old man called out, "Sophia!" but she was already making her way into the kitchen.

"What?" she said.

Theo clapped and rubbed his hands together. "And now the moment we've all been waiting for!"

My father snapped, "Theo, *skaseh!"*—Shut up!

Sophia glanced at Theo, who was securing his glasses over his ears, and then she grinned at me: We're *all* crazy.

I nodded anxiously.

Melanie said, "We wanted to tell immediate family before anyone else showed up."

I slid my hands into my pockets.

My mother leaned against the kitchen counter. "I don't think I can handle any big announcements today."

"It's okay, Mom." Andrew smiled. "It's good news."

I crossed my arms. My mother folded her hands over the apron knot at her waist.

"Melanie and I wanted to announce this together," Andrew said. "We haven't even told her parents yet—"

"But we're telling them later tonight, *so…*" Melanie cupped her left hand with her right—hiding the evidence, I assumed.

My brother had finally done it…

"Well…" Andrew inhaled dramatically. "Melanie decided she's willing to convert."

Andrew had finally won her over to our side—not that there had ever been a real contest, not that he'd ever considered donning the *yarmulke.* Of course, Melanie's conversion meant *marriage*—a detail that, at least for Andrew, went without saying, though the look on Melanie's face suggested that the announcement had stopped short, too soon before my parents were rushing in toward the soon-to-be-converted Jew.

"Wait—" Melanie squirmed free from my mother's hug. "Mrs. Pappas, that's just the beginning…"

My mother stepped back. "Oh?" She glanced at Melanie's belly.

"*Jesus*, Mom." Andrew laughed through his teeth.

"*Olympia*—" my father gasped, as if my mother had just suggested something impossible.

"Well, I don't *know*," she said.

Melanie tucked her hands into her armpits. "Andrew, *tell* them."

My mother reached out and took Melanie's wrist gently. "Oh, Andrew," she whispered.

The diamond flickered like a Christmas light.

Melanie stared at Andrew, who gave a tiny shake of his head: *Not now...*

"Will the wedding be this summer?" my mother added, Melanie's hand docile in hers.

"Ma, it's almost *July*," Andrew said.

"Mrs. Pappas, there's something *else*," Melanie said.

"Melanie—" Andrew took Melanie's hand from my mother's hand.

"Don't *grab* me!" Melanie snapped.

"What's the matter, honey?" my mother said. "This is beautiful news."

"This is what I *hate!*" Sophia cried out. "Why is this such good news to everyone?"

Melanie's resistance to her conversion had secretly represented, for Sophia, humanity's, or at least this family's, last hope for salvation.

"Your brother's getting *married*, honey."

"Nobody's even *said* that! You're just glad she's *converting!*"

"*No*, Sophia," my mother said.

"It's not just *that*, Sophia." Melanie crossed her arms. "But apparently Andrew's having second thoughts."

"About *what?*" my mother said.

I had no idea. No way was she pregnant.

"All right, look," Andrew said. "We're engaged. That's what the ring means. That's it."

"I can't believe you." Melanie backed up toward the refrigerator. "You are such a coward," she huffed, and turned toward the garage.

"Let's talk about this in private," my father said. "Why don't you take a walk, Peter."

"*Me?*"

"With your sister."

"No!" Sophia cried out. "This isn't what God wants! Melanie should not have to do this! God loves *everyone!*"

"Of course He does, honey," my mother said.

"Melanie, don't *do* it! Jesus was a *Jew!*" Sophia marched back into the foyer and slammed the storm door behind her. Through the Plexiglas, I could see her black boots trudging in the grass toward the driveway, her dark-brown, braceleted arms flailing.

"Don't let her spoil this," my father said, but Melanie had already gone into the garage through the door beyond the refrigerator.

"Honey…" my mother said.

"Let her go." Andrew brought his hands to his waist.

"Go talk to her," my mother said. "This is an emotional time."

"Trust me," Andrew said. "She'll be right back."

My father went into the dining room and stared out the bay window. Instead of Melanie or Sophia, four colorful figures were making their way across the front lawn. They appeared, framed in Plexiglas, as the bell rang.

In poked the pink pocked face and grinning bald head of Uncle Mike from Havertown. He extended a clear bottle of booze into the foyer. "Happy name days, Peters and Pauls!"

"Hey-ay!" my father boomed, entering the foyer from the dining room. He held the door and ushered them in. "*Ela, ela!*"—Come, come! He kissed and shooed them one by one into the kitchen, where I anticipated the roar of celebration, my mother's brothers, Uncle Mike and Uncle Joe, and their wives, Aunt Bess and Aunt Flo, forming a small mob of thick-strapped sundresses, bright green and orange handbags, white leather shoes and belts. "We've got wonderful news."

"Oh!" The aunts shuffled over to hug Andrew.

I lamented the predictability of the good news around here.

"Melanie's going to convert to Greek Orthodoxy!" My mother glowed, though her beautiful, sandy-haired daughter-in-law-to-be, who would become the mother of her grandchildren—likely her *only* grandchildren, if one considered how the lives of Sophia and me were taking shape—was nowhere in sight, a detail that didn't distract anyone from celebrating.

Uncle Mike raised his gift bottle of ouzo toward the ceiling like celebration champagne. "Let's have a drink! Glasses!" Glasses hung from

Aunt Bess's clenched fingers. "Ice, Paul, ice! Let's have it!" He waved everyone toward the table. "Peter! Take this."

I took the bottle, wanting, suddenly, to be oblivious, drunk, along with Uncle Mike, in the colorful noise of his company.

Uncle Mike looked around. "Where's Sophia? Theo! *Ela!* Get us more ice!"

I pictured the watery plastic bags in my truck bed.

Theo was reaching out into the air before him like a blind man, his wine-colored slippers shuffling toward the freezer.

"Theo, put your *glasses* on!" the old man called out.

"Peter, what's the matter, honey?" Aunt Bess said. "You're quiet. You look pale. Look at your hair." She set the small glasses down on the table and took my face into her warm, damp hands.

"He's got beautiful hair," Aunt Flo said.

I gripped the ouzo bottle's neck.

"You feel hot, honey," Aunt Bess said. "Drink something. A little ouzo maybe."

She pulled the chair out, and I sat down.

Theo set the shoebox-size ice container on the table and stooped to see his own hand plucking one cube and dropping it into a glass.

"Ice, ice!" Uncle Mike's thick fingers scraped the inside of the container. He called out, "Ice, Paul!" and swiped the bottle from my hand.

My father stared into the open freezer.

Uncle Mike plopped a filled glass into Theo's eager hand. "Okay, Theo, wait for the toast."

Theo jiggled his glass near his nose, watching the ice cube bouncing and turning the clear liquid cloudy.

My father twisted a half-empty plastic ice tray above the container.

"Ahh, bravo." Uncle Mike scooped a handful.

My father displayed the empty tray to me.

"I told you," I said. "Everything's outside."

"What good is it melting in the grass?"

"It's not *in* the grass," I said.

"Okay, okay," Uncle Mike said. "We have plenty of ice. Drink, Paul, come on."

Aunt Flo poked her arm through Andrew's, rehearsing for the aisle.

I folded my arms on the table.

My father handed me a glass.

"I took home one of your parishioners," I said.

"Everybody have a drink?" Uncle Mike called out.

"Who?" my father said.

Glasses rose, clanging amid audible smiles—"Hey-ay! *Yiasou!*"

"That's what took me so long." I was still sitting.

My father waited, arm raised with the rest of them.

"Daisy Diamond." I watched the old man's stony face.

"To Andrew and Melanie!" Aunt Flo called out.

My father turned his eyes to the ceiling, where clinking glasses hovered. They all awaited the priest's blessing.

"Stand up, Peter," Aunt Bess said.

For a moment I made the old man wait for his apathetic, atheist son; then I inched off my chair and reached toward the chandelier of glasses—"'Atta boy," Uncle Joe said—all our necks poised to receive the drink.

"*Hronia polah!*"—Many years!—Aunt Flo cheered.

I knew the toast, which was heard at every holiday. They all glanced at Andrew, who smiled back gratefully.

My father pronounced joyfully, "*Keh stah thikah sou!*"

I knew *this* one, too: And to yours! As in, *your* engagement—*my* engagement. I couldn't believe my ears—or eyes: the old man was grinning down at me, as the roomful of Greeks relished their blood-connection to Tragedy, spotlighting the poor soul whose story was most pathetic, just as they always turned their attention to the unmarried older sisters of young mothers with newborn babies, singing, "And to *yours!*" reminding them of their dried-up, disappointing lives, just as they were reminding me now that I was the only one in the room still unhitched, that I still hadn't found a nice Greek girl, or any girl at all.

They all sighed, "Ahhh," and displayed their hopeful smiles. With a unified tip of their glasses, they all leaned back, my father never flinching, and cooled their throats with sweet liquor.

3
Modern People

Tonight when Uncle George referred to the "towel-heads," as he had on Memorial Day, Sophia—to exactly no one's dismay—wouldn't be there to explain the difference between Arabs and Persians, between Islam and militant fundamentalism. When Aunt Irene used the term "sexual relations," Sophia wouldn't be there to enlighten her on the fine-pointed distinction between intercourse and "a blow job." The family would be content eating dinner without Sophia, wherever she was. And later, with the twin cousins in the basement, rummaging angrily through the old game closet, the elders would be happy in the living room, eating pastries and rehashing the old debates, without fear of inciting Sophia's anarchic rebuttals: Uncle George, leading the Coatesville coalition, rallying to nuke the Middle East; Aunt Irene maintaining that impeachment alone was insufficient punishment for a president who'd shamed the country; their audience of self-proclaimed moderates straining to articulate an argument that didn't make them out to be terrorist-loving perverts—the whole evening swallowed up in no time at all.

For years now, Sophia relished designing whole scenarios that left her victims squirming in the blare of her tirades, wishing they'd seen it coming. When she was thirteen—when her disappointment in the world had only begun to taint her sense of wonder—she'd tucked into the tangle of Theo's backyard garden what she'd just recently come to appreciate as a reproduction of a beautiful *statue*, of a certain black boy holding a lantern. Her sole purpose was to enlighten the first innocent soul who dared to call it a "lawn jockey" and who, in doing so, revealed himself to be an unwitting conspirator in the same insidious tradition of racist American folklore that had turned honorable Aunt Jemima into a laughing stock—a tidbit she'd picked up recently while doing a research paper for Civics class. Days before, she had bicycled into the driveway, calling out for me to feast my eyes on the lawn ornament under her arm. "Can you believe this?" Racism in broad daylight. "Have we made no progress?" She went on to express deep empathy, as well as admiration, for the African Americans who, on their daily walk to the SEPTA station to catch the R-12, right there on Stone Bridge Road, restrained themselves as they passed the home of those shameless racists. "You stole it," I reminded her, and went on to explain how people had displayed these lawn "sculptures" during the times of the Underground Railroad, right here in this region, in fact, to identify their homes as safe havens for runaway slaves. Rapt—by both my knowledge and the unfailing capacity of courageous people to move her—Sophia instantly restored the jockey's dignity—and her own—by displaying him in the front yard, until the old man came home and insisted, despite Sophia's reasonable defense, that what mattered more than historical fact was people's perception. By the time Uncle George, biting into a hot July Fourth hotdog, spotted someone lurking in the tomatoes, Sophia had done further research. Poor Uncle George no sooner pointed and howled with delight, announcing he hadn't seen a "lawn jockey" in ages, than Sophia described how on Christmas, 1776, a boy had frozen to death, looking after George Washington's horses the night he crossed the Delaware. With bookish pride, she regaled her audience with a brief history of the Underground Railroad, highlighting the heroism of Harriet Tubman, and saving the story's missing link for last: George Washington had honored Jocko Graves by memorializing him with a statue at Mount Vernon, his Virginia estate—"the first lawn jockey." Repeating the dubious term that had given rise to her speech in the first place, she couldn't resist her own cleverness—but then neither could anyone else—her intelligence and inadvertent charm, not to mention mock curtsy and literal wink at Uncle George, drawing applause, even from the twins, the sum total of whose grade point averages would never amount to hers.

For years Sophia's nature had seemed elevated by a certain benevolent eagerness—not spiked with bitterness as it was now.

I cupped my hands against the garage-door windows, hoping to find my sister comforting Melanie, but the garage was empty except for my painting equipment. Melanie must have gone back inside, prepared to smile for the camera. A single chirp from some invisible bird came from the white sky. The world around me seemed infinite. I imagined Sophia hitchhiking west, the rust-crusted Toyota—what might have been her getaway car—blocked on the driveway. She could be anywhere by now, riding shotgun on some eighteen-wheeler.

Still, I was determined to find her.

Beyond the stone wall extending from the garage, Uncle George's gold Dodge skittered nervously over the curb and into the driveway. I peered through the hemlocks as my aunt and uncle rushed toward the house, their nearly indistinguishable twin sons, trailing along in collared shirts hanging over striped mesh basketball shorts, each lanky and scowling, their lopsided pimpled faces already victims of a ruthless adolescence.

Uncle George snapped, "You don't *have* to like them. It's *family*."

"Peter's boring," the one twin said. Tony, the little prick. His nose bone jutted like a knuckle.

"*Enough*," Uncle George huffed. "Now *move* it—"

"You said yourself he's fat and lazy," said bigger-nosed Dean.

"I said that's *enough!*"

"All he does is play board games in the basement—"

"—and she's a total freak."

"She's very smart." Aunt Irene took an earnest drag of her cigarette and paused before the white concrete walkway.

Uncle George and the boys waited for her to exhale.

She tamped the butt out on the blacktop and toed it into the edge of the grass. Smoke rose from her mouth as she spoke. "Just be nice, is all. She's a troubled girl."

"Oh, don't start with the troubled-girl stuff, Irene," Uncle George growled. "*Look* at this place. She has nothing to be troubled about."

The boys looked up at the house, which was four times the size of theirs in Coatesville.

Aunt Irene whispered, "There's depression in the family, George. A child doesn't just go piercing herself all over."

"*Everyone's* got tattoos," Tony said.

Dean smacked his brother's ribs.

Uncle George twisted Dean's collar with a fist. "*Who's* got tattoos?"

Dean went docile in his father's grip.

"Sophia has *tattoos* now?" Aunt Irene stopped before the front step.

"*You* don't have tattoos!" Uncle George said to his sons. "Your *mother* doesn't have tattoos."

"Shh—George!"

The suck of the storm door was followed by the gleeful howl of reunion.

I headed for the streets. In the grass along the driveway, the Heineken case's cardboard lid had been torn open. A shattered bottle lay at the curb by the mailbox. I pictured Sophia chugging through the hills of the neighborhood, leaving a trail of broken green glass. I circled the yard, following the strip of thick grass between the street and wrought-iron fence, which wrapped around the property and stopped at the cluster of giant pines where our yard's back corner met the neighbors'.

Splotches of Melanie's turquoise dress appeared through branches. Sophia's black shirt blended with the shadows. They were sitting on white Adirondack chairs, which they must have dragged from the front yard, through the neighbors' property and into this pocket of grass. Through the trees they stared at the house down below, their backs to the street, each gripping a Heineken on the flat armrest of her chair.

Sophia dipped her head and squinted, as I stepped around jutting branches.

"Hey," I said.

Sophia plucked an unlit cigarette from her lips. A cardboard six-pack container sat in the patch of grass between them. Melanie's tan legs extended into the brown bed of needles, her hair draped like tinsel on her bare shoulders. Her sea-green eyes matched her dress, thin silk held up by orange spaghetti straps and splashed with white foamy arcs. She swigged, uncrossed her legs briefly, and re-crossed them.

"Not much of a hiding place," I said.

"We're not *hiding*." Sophia hammered her fist at the edge of the armrest, popping the cap off a Heineken and offering the bottle to me.

I folded my arms on my chest. Sophia shrugged and lit her cigarette.

In the uncomfortable silence, Melanie put the six-pack container on the other side of her chair, making space. All the while Sophia enjoyed her cigarette, holding out the Heineken that I refused to take.

Melanie patted the grass, and, finally, I sat.

Sophia blew smoke and put the bottle into my hand.

"We were having a bitch session," she said.

"Does that mean I can't be here?" I said.

"Don't try to be funny."

I sipped.

"I shouldn't be talking about this anyway," Melanie said.

"Peter gives good advice," Sophia said.

"You're on my side again?" I said.

"I was never on your side."

Melanie seemed reluctant to speak.

"Don't mind him," Sophia said.

"Okay." Melanie looked at me. "Here's the deal—I was just telling Sophia. I always knew I'd be the one to convert, because it only made sense. That's not the issue. Andrew agreed that if I converted, he'd live with me for a year before we got married."

"Whoa," I said. "You were going to *announce* that?"

"Give me a break," Sophia said. "That's the point, Peter. That's what he was supposed to do, but he pussied out."

"Nice language, Sophia," I said.

"Fuck yourself, Peter."

"We already got our own apartment," Melanie said. "We both gave up our old apartments."

"He gave up his old apartment?" I said.

"We're not kids," Melanie said. "I'm thirty."

"*You're thirty?*" It was as if, in my mind, I'd kept her from aging, since the night I'd first met her—as if I'd thought I would one day catch up with her.

Melanie fluttered her eyelashes, in mock, flirtatious embarrassment, reaching for my hand. Instantly I understood how Andrew must have given in to her demands in a rush of romantic instinct. Today in the kitchen, though, Andrew must have locked up when he looked into our parents' eyes and another, more deeply rooted instinct took over. He must have taken to heart that to the Greeks—at least to our parents, whose family should serve as a model—living in sin was grounds for excommunication, even if Melanie were a nice Greek girl (though how nice could she be, after all, if she were having sex before marriage?).

"So *now* what?" I said.

Melanie revealed her naked fingers.

"You're not *engaged?*" I said.

"There's a ring." She displayed it in her hand. "I always wanted to live with Andrew, but he never would, and that was fine." She slid the ring onto her pinkie and examined it. "But then if my cousin Heidi wouldn't have lived with this guy, she wouldn't have known he was psycho. So now my parents feel really strong about living with someone first."

"Your parents *want* you to live with someone first?" Sophia couldn't conceal her admiration. "That is *so* cool."

"You think Andrew might be psycho?" I said.

"Of course not," Melanie said. "That's not *why* I want to live together first. It's just different for us."

"For who?" I said.

Melanie hesitated.

"Jewish people?" I said.

"No." Melanie peered from under soft brown eyebrows. "Modern people. Living together's not a big deal."

"*Modern* people?" I grabbed my beer from the grass.

"Don't act like you don't *know*, Peter," Sophia said. "We're completely backwards. Jews aren't hung up on all the bullshit."

"I'm giving up my *religion*." Melanie was gazing reminiscently at her bare, bronze fingers splayed on her thigh. "I can't wear it now. It's not even about living together anymore. It's about trust. I mean, proof."

"Proof?" I said.

"Proof, Peter," Sophia said. "It's what Melanie and I were talking about before you got here. If you're willing to give something up for someone, I mean, women want *proof*."

"Of how it's going to be." Melanie's fingers curled into a fist.

"We're tired of *words*," Sophia said. "We want to see *action*. Right, Melanie?"

Sophia shifted anxiously in her seat. I waited for her to say more. She puffed her cigarette and looked away.

"Your parents are such good people," Melanie said. "I don't want them to be upset. I just want to know that we're on our own, you know? That we can do what we want."

"It's not easy being raised by such good people," I said.

"Don't be a dick, Peter," Sophia said.

"I don't want to feel trapped," Melanie said.

"Welcome to the family," I said.

"*I'm* not trapped." Sophia pulled a cigarette out from somewhere and a lighter from her bootlaces. "Think what you want." She lit up, pinching her cigarette between two knuckles. Smoke rose before her clenched eye.

"That's why you started dressing like a hippie-vampire," I said. "And got a tattoo."

"What about it?" Sophia faced me with open eyes.

"First of all, you got it where no one can see it," I said.

"That's where I *wanted* it," she said.

"A *cross*? Please," I said.

Melanie sat up. "Can I see?"

Sophia smirked at me, twisted out of her chair, and knelt in the grass. Melanie leaned forward, her thin dress straps drooping from her shoulders. Sophia peeled down her skirt, her fleshy brown hip in my face. I leaned back on both hands, legs crossed Indian-style. I imagined Melanie crouched over a bench in the downtown gym where she'd met Andrew, pulling a dumbbell toward her chest.

Melanie dragged a fingertip over Sophia's dyed skin. "I've always wondered what I'd get if I got one."

Sophia grinned in triumph and twisted her ass toward me, pulling her skirt down farther, making sure I got a full view, her thumb nudging the black-lace waistband of her panties and settling into the shadowy dimple just north of her pale buttocks. The cross, with its four Orthodox-style triple-rounded tips, just like the heavy silver one the old man held out for parishioners to kiss, hovered in the tan skin just above the stark horizon. She'd shown it to me the night she got home from the South Street parlor last winter, only then she was crying in my bedroom, twisting to see in the mirror, jimmying her jeans as I gently peeled the cloth tape and pulled away the gauze. We were speechless together, in awe of its purplish permanence, its still-fuzzy perimeter, bloody and glazed with Vaseline. "What were you *thinking?*" I said, and followed with, "It's okay—*okay, okay,*" when, sobbing, Sophia swore she'd kill me if I said another word about it to her or anyone. Her swollen red flesh had relaxed as I blew cool air and wiped her skin with a soft, white tube sock.

"Jews can't get them," Melanie said.

"What do you mean?" Sophia said.

"We're not allowed to permanently scar our bodies. It's like you've ruined your body before God. You can't get a proper burial if you have one."

"No way," Sophia said.

"We encourage them," I said. "Especially the ol' cross on the ass."

"You're such an asshole." Sophia coughed, and a fresh cigarette appeared in her fingers.

"How many of those have you smoked?" I said.

"Why don't you just stop talking." She cleared her throat and flicked her lighter.

The sky was turning gray. I wanted it to rain, to cool everything off. In the kitchen windows down below, ghostly silhouettes passed through yellow light. The screen door opened, and Andrew stepped out, one hand holding his cell phone to his ear, the other holding something in a pink paper napkin. Melanie put her bottle in the six-pack box and wiped her hands. Sophia puffed. We all sat silently, watching Andrew stepping up to the patio's concrete edge and looking out at the sky. Melanie twisted her ring on the appropriate finger.

Andrew's phone snapped shut, a silver flash. He twisted his torso left and right, hands on his waist, eyeing up the stretch of grass before him. His fingers flickered at the wide mouths of long unbuttoned sleeves, his purple-paisley shirttail un-tucked now from stretching. The back yard might have been the exact size of an Olympic pool. He still had the swimmer's shoulders and the perpetual twitchy athletic movements, which made him seem to be always loosening up, shaking out last-second kinks. Andrew's times in freestyle, back, butterfly, and breast—still the district records—had long been fastened to the high-school natatorium wall by the time I, in my sixth-grade gym class, had to prove I could tread water for twenty minutes. The crew-cut, pink-skinned teacher, also the Varsity coach, a barrel-chested seventy-year-old in a navy Speedo, had barked at me, stocky and desperately paddling, to keep my eyes glued to my brother's last name, which—impossible as it seemed—I shared. Now, at thirty-two, Andrew still had the same mop of loose, light-brown curls he'd stubbornly kept despite all of his coach's lamentations that the resistance was costing him God-knew-how-many tenths of a second. At the concrete ledge of the porch Andrew's arms fluttered; his legs rose and fell, his knees winking at the white-threaded holes in his jeans, his bare feet slipping elegantly out of, and back into, his rubber-soled clogs, a pair of which he'd been encouraging me to wear while painting, as he did while operating. Andrew bit into whatever was inside the pink napkin, stepped into the grass, and walked toward the Lexus in the driveway.

"I think your dad's embarrassed by it," Melanie said.

"The car?" Sophia said.

"Not just the car but the license plate. Andrew thought it would be fun. He really wanted to do something nice."

I sat up.

"A priest with a sense of humor, you know?" Melanie's eyes stayed on Andrew down below. "I mean, some people have no idea. They don't know what Greek Orthodox is. They think you worship Zeus or something."

"That car's for *Dad?*" I was incredulous.

Andrew tapped his fingertips on the hood.

"He surprised them," Melanie said. "He brought them both out to the driveway and then handed your father the keys. There was a Mercedes I liked, but Andrew said it was pretentious."

"I'm gonna puke." I had gotten to my feet and, hunched over, was peering through the trees.

"What is it?" Melanie asked.

I was already twisting into the dense wall of trees, backing into snapping branches.

"What are you *doing?*" Sophia said.

I backpedaled on the brown bed of needles toward the yard, slipping into the crackling thickness. I closed my eyes and rushed backwards. The quicker the flogging, the less painful, I figured. I erupted through the trees, sneakers skidding, and fell back, riding the grass on my rear end and wrists. At the bottom of the hill I spun and got myself to my feet in one swift motion. I rushed toward the driveway, where Andrew held a square piece of our mother's *spanakopita*. He'd just taken a bite and was mid-chew. His face was contorted as if I'd just fallen from the sky.

The smell of spicy cheese and *philo* dough reminded me that I hadn't eaten a thing since my lamb sandwich. Andrew crumpled the pink napkin into a ball.

"What's up, Doc?"

"I can't believe you," I said, approaching.

"What are you talking about, Doc?"

"Stop calling me that. Seriously." I squared my stance, hands on my hips.

Melanie and Sophia came up from behind.

Andrew frowned at Melanie. "Where have you been?"

"I'm *talking* to you," I said.

"What's your problem, *Peter?*" Andrew swallowed and tossed the remaining *spanakopita* into the grass.

"You were buttering him up," I said. "Before telling them your plan—about living together."

Andrew wiped his hands, tucked the napkin into his pocket, and stepped casually toward me.

"It's a bribe," I said, crossing my arms.

"Watch it." Andrew raised a finger.

I swiped at Andrew's hand.

"What *is* this?" Andrew looked at Melanie. "What did you *tell* them?"

Melanie shrugged. "I said you bought your parents a car."

"Where's your ring?" Andrew said.

Melanie displayed it on her pinkie, playing tough.

"Why don't you tell the truth?" I said. I thought of the Winklesteins' dead dog and added, "For once."

Grinning, Andrew shoved his finger into my face. "Don't make me embarrass you."

"What are you gonna do?" I punched Andrew's forearm out of the way.

"He needs a new *car*, Peter." Andrew grabbed my cheeks, thumb and fingers gouging, pushing me back onto my heels. "Are you *jealous?*"

"Stop it!" Sophia cried. "Andrew!"

I stumbled off the edge of the driveway, swinging at Andrew's head and catching his eye. I made loose fists as I stood up straight.

"You fucking nut." Andrew cupped his eye and adjusted a foot in a clog.

"Peter, what's the *matter* with you?" Sophia cried.

Andrew sat back against the hood of the car. "Put your fists down, idiot. Here comes Mom."

"Sophia!" Our mother came from the patio, wiping her hands on her apron. Her children and her future daughter-in-law stood paralyzed in the grass.

Tony and Dean gripped the wrought-iron railing bordering the patio.

Sophia looked at our mother, then back at Andrew and me.

Andrew pulled keys from his pocket.

"What's going on, honey?" our mother said, making her way across the lawn.

"We're leaving," Andrew said.

"Why? What's the matter?" She sidled up to me.

"Nothing, Mom," Andrew said.

"Peter, what happened?" my mother said.

My chest was heaving. I stepped back farther into the grass.

"Mom!" one of the twins shouted, though Aunt Irene was already standing behind her sons, lighting a cigarette.

Andrew pressed his key-chain button, his Porsche beeped, and the locks thumped.

"Andrew…" my mother said.

"You need us to move the car?" Aunt Irene called out. "George!"

"Everything's fine," Andrew said. "We gotta go."

Shielding her eyes, Melanie said, "I'm sorry," and rushed toward the Porsche.

The engine moaned as Andrew inched by the Toyota and backed up past my truck. At the end of the driveway, he paused between Uncle George's gold Dodge and the mailbox.

"Whoa, whoa, watch it, watch it." Uncle George came running, keys jangling, as Andrew squeezed through and buzzed off.

"Poor Andrew," my mother said. "They're having a hard time."

Poor Andrew. I kept my mouth shut.

Heading for the patio, my mother paused. "Peter, come and play with your cousins."

On their knees, the twins gripped the railing, white knuckles at their cheeks.

"Sophia, you too," my mother said. "The boys want to spend time with you."

"I have to finish packing," Sophia said.

"Just for a while," my mother said.

Sophia groaned.

My mother, Aunt Irene, and Uncle George went back inside. The twins stayed where they were.

"It's okay, guys," I called out. "We were just messing around. Like brothers. You know."

They nodded.

"Go ahead inside," I said. "We'll be in in a sec. Go downstairs and pick out a game."

They walked inside obediently.

"What's the *matter* with you, Peter?" Sophia said.

"Nothing," I said.

"Why do you care so much about the car?"

"I don't give a shit about the car."

"You never hit anyone in your life," she said.

"I overreacted, all right?"

Sophia offered her sad scowl and turned for the house.

I bowed my head, ashamed. On the tips of grass a delicate pale chip of *philo* crust sat like bread raised on fingertips. Nearby was Andrew's discarded lump of *spanakopita*. I remembered my mother carrying a basket wedged at her hip, snipping fresh spinach from narrow beds, and plucking grape leaves from vines tangled in lattice wood. It was sacrilegious to waste my mother's cooking. Years ago, on some past name day, our mother had caught Andrew and me leaping out from the pine trees with handfuls of her *dolmades*. We'd been gunning the mini green grenades at the rear windows of passing cars, wet grape leaves splaying against glass, ground beef and rice spraying like fine shrapnel. We'd bowed our heads in shame, not for recklessly endangering the lives of the drivers but for forsaking the *dolmades* she'd folded and caressed in her loving hands.

White streaks in the sky—all that remained of the sun—vanished above the tall pines. I headed for the screen door, hoping that they wouldn't notice me entering, or, better yet, that they would all be exiting through the front door as I entered through the back. I would make myself a plate and sneak into the basement.

In the kitchen, the coast was clear except for Theo, who was huddled over his schoolhouse desk in the corner, quietly massaging his worry beads. In the living room Uncle Mike was telling a story to an enraptured audience, circling the coffee table, as if at the base of an amphitheater.

The kitchen counter was covered with serving trays and glass bowls, still half-full with salad, rice, pork and lamb. I bit into a hunk of dark meat and eyed my options. My mother had circled the main stairwell and was homing in on me from the dining room. A unified belly laugh from the living room glided to a satisfied moan. My mother handed me a plate filled with powdered cookies and *baklava*.

I displayed my greasy handful, indicating I wasn't ready for dessert.

"It's not for you," my mother said. "Take it up to Yiayia."

"I haven't eaten all day," I said.

She set the dessert plate on the stove. "Go. I'll make you a plate. See if you can say a few words to your grandmother if you won't speak to anyone else today."

"*Mom.*"

"Peter!" Theo reached a pencil towards the ceiling. "Let me show you something."

My mother pushed the dessert plate into my belly. "When you come back, you can sit with Theo."

"I'm ready to eat again!" Theo called out. "Who's up for Scrabble!"

"You've had enough meat, Theo. Eat some tomatoes." My mother was already heading for the dining room, where the table was speckled with desserts—*baklava, kourampiedes*—in pastel-colored paper cupcake containers.

"Peter, one game," Theo said, as I turned away. "No Greek, just English, I promise."

All at once Theo spun from his desk, slapped down onto the kitchen table his composition-style notebook with marbleized-black-and-white cover, and cleared away the Scrabble board as well as the tiny wooden squares that slid in its wake, terminating the game he must have been playing with himself, unless, earlier, my mother, or some other merciful soul, submitted to a challenge and managed to escape by forfeiting.

I passed my mother in the dining room and turned up the steps. Uncle Mike's audience in the living room was still catching its breath between acts.

The banister came to a landing on the second floor. A shiny red sticker portraying the silhouette of a helmeted fireman saving a boy had never been scraped from the door of my bedroom, where Theo had been sleeping for over a decade. I used to imagine myself the little boy in the sticker, Jesus the fireman. Flames skipped off Jesus, who gathered me in his arms and leapt over the railing, white robe flapping.

Years later, in college, longhaired and bearded, I posed for a photograph, just outside my old bedroom, where an icon of Jesus seemed like a mirror I was gazing into. For a while, until I stopped going to church, my parents, even the old man, seemed to *like* the long hair, as if mine were the look of holy men or at least the look of someone considering the seminary. Now, on the wall just outside my old bedroom, the framed snapshot was a relic hanging next to the icon that inspired it.

On the third floor, a plate with uneaten chicken sat on the hardwood floor outside Yiayia's room. I knocked and waited, then stooped and swapped plates. "Yiayia! Dessert!" A man's voice was reporting the news from the Old Country. I knocked again, this time trying to get a response by charming her with some Greek: "*Baklava*, Yiayia! *Thelis cafeh?*"—You want coffee? For days, sometimes, soiled plates were all you got as evidence that she was okay in there. "Yiayia! Tastykake?" She would wait until I was gone before she came out for her dessert. I faked footsteps fading away on the hardwood, but the door stayed shut. "C'mon, Yiayia. *Signomey*"—I'm sorry. The black-and-white portrait I'd taken down had been restored to its place in the hallway. I stood face-to-face with the old bastard, trying to remember my grandfather in the flesh, but the pictures on the walls were all I'd ever really known of him. Up close, the ancient man's eyes turned to gray dust.

At the bottom of the stairs my mother was looking up at me, laughing, and for a moment I imagined her charmed by my teasing Yiayia in Greek, offering her desserts and an apology. Then I heard Uncle Mike, going on about the Greek kids in the old neighborhood sledding on garbage bags, my mother egging him on, "Tell about the pool, Mike, when you hit your teeth on the diving board." As I made my way toward the living room, my mother leaned against the front door, arms crossed, and winked at me, gesturing toward Uncle Mike, who with his thumb and forefinger plucked out his incisors and started again, lisping up a storm.

I slipped through the dining room and into the kitchen. Awaiting me, on the table, was a plate filled with assorted meats and *dolmades*. On a small white dessert dish four *kourampiedes* in their pink paper cupcake containers appeared as a snowy mound of confectioners' sugar. Theo nudged his bowl of freshly salted tomato slices to make room for the Scrabble board.

"No thanks, Theo." I picked up the plate intended for me and took one step toward the basement.

"Wait till I show you this," Theo said, finger-tipping his notebook.

I reached for a fork on the table. "Not now, Theo."

"No, no, no, not now, not now, when you have time, when you have time." Theo scooted out on his chair, blocking me. "I'm almost done with my research."

Theo had been almost done with his research for all the years I could remember. He believed that as soon as he finished his life's work—*The History of the Greeks in America*—the University of Pennsylvania would be pining for his return.

"That's great, Theo. I have to go downstairs now."

I chewed, waiting for Theo to let me pass. In the living room the conversation had shifted from Uncle Mike's prosthetic teeth to a parishioner's less-easily-replaceable body part, a heart or a liver. "They say it's worse…oh nohh…it doesn't look good…they're talking transplant…well, whatdya gonna do?" Arms folded, my mother gestured with her chin toward the empty chair next to Theo, who was studying the beads in his hand.

"These were your *papou's kompoloi*. Here—" The milky gems dangled from Theo's fingers. "*You* should have them."

I sat down finally.

Theo set the beads next to my plate. The chain of silvery spheres spread out in the space between us.

Theo squinted slightly, his glasses off; his severe near-sightedness suited most of the activities that filled his days. He lowered his face into his notebook. "I'm almost up to date. My mother's side hasn't taken as long as my father's. Your *yiayia's* not much help, but she gave me some new names. A lot of the local Greeks have helpful information."

Theo had notebooks filled with family trees, vertical and horizontal lines, pressed into their pages in dark pencil, immaculate diagrams, like an engineer's blueprint for plumbing and wiring, sprawling across the pages, which were crinkled like ancient documents. His up-to-the-minute research—stories and biographies—were printed in all capitals, thick and black, with complete disregard for the pages' blue and red guide lines, nonetheless written in perfectly straight rows, edge to binding, binding to edge, each letter uniform in height as if produced by a mad comic-book artist who no longer bothered drawing his characters and instead wrote only their bubbled dialogue. In my old bedroom closet Theo had collected scrapbooks and shoeboxes filled with archives of ancient paraphernalia—passports, birth certificates, bankbooks, boat tickets, postcards, letters—my grandfather's *kompoloi*—and only God knew what else. On the backs of photographs he'd penned names, dates and anecdotes. You could give him the name of any Philadelphia Greek, and Theo would identify the grandfathers of the grandfathers and explain where in Greece they originated and who set out when for America.

"So last week I finished the Havertowners—your mom's side. I've been working on your brother. Tonight I made a few notes on Melanie, now that it's official. You think Sophia will stay in California?"

"Yes." I pressed the prongs of my fork into bits of ground beef.

A bar of light from under the basement door glowed onto the kitchen floor. Between bursts of living-room conversation, sounds of Sophia and the twins searching my bedroom made me nervous, not that there was anything interesting to find, unless—would the twins be suspicious of the hand lotion on my night table? They were old enough to make the connection. I heard the sound of crunching hard plastic, Legos being crushed by hammers, Tony and Dean cackling, letting out guttural howls.

"Have you been to California, Peter?" Theo eyed my plate.

"No." I gestured toward the lamb with my fork.

Theo pinched a drenched piece and devoured it, encouraged. "I know I'm jumping ahead, but I'm almost done with the histories. I'm getting it all on the computer upstairs. It's old but it works." The computer had already been obsolete when the old man had brought it home from the church, when I'd begun writing longer papers in high school. "It's all there in your bedroom. I'll show you. Whenever you have time. Family trees, old slides. At this point I've got every detail you could imagine about my great-grandfather. I've thought about putting the bigger project on hold just to write his biography. He was a Panayiotis, you know, like you, like your grandfather—my father." Theo seized every opportunity to remind me I was named after my grandfather, my supposed namesake, though the truth was that my birth certificate read "Peter," not "Panayiotis"—I'd verified the fact with my mother years ago—so technically my name was my own. I didn't bother disputing the issue with Theo anymore. Right now I wanted to ask him if a certain cocktail waitress appeared anywhere in that family tree of his. I wanted to offer him a ride to Atlantic City to get *her* story. Instead, I silenced myself with another bite.

Theo went on: "I've told you about him, right?" Countless times. My great-great-grandfather, the one who... "escaped the Turks by hiding in the north. He was an *Ikodomakis*—a great name. Not like *Pappas*, which is like *Smith*." Theo nearly spit—*Smithh*. "A lot of the Greeks changed their names so the Turks couldn't identify them, but your great-great-grandfather, Panayiotis Ikodomakis, was *proud* of his name—and what it *meant*." Here it came, the sad, etymologically complete saga of how Ikodomakis became Pappas: "*Ikodomi* means 'the structure of the house,' from *Ikia*, the ancient-Greek word for 'house,' which is where they get IKEA, the store. And where we get the Greek words for 'family,' *ikoghenia;* 'resident,' *katikos;* 'residence,' *katikia;* 'apartment building,' *polikatikia*—you know *poli* means 'many,' and then *katikia*—'many residences'; and *apikia*, 'colony'—*apo*, 'from,' and *ikia*—'where you come from'—*colony*. Your great-great-grandfather—your *pro-pro-papou*—was the last Ikodomakis." Theo helped himself to the last chunk of lamb. "They were builders of houses—for generations before him. So when your grandfather came here, it was still in his blood. He looked at the farmland, and he had a vision to build *neighborhoods,* like this one, as his grandfathers had built entire *villages* in Crete. That's *destiny*, Peter. You think it's a coincidence you paint houses? Someday you'll *build* them and pay someone *else* to paint them."

Theo reached for his glass of water but didn't interrupt himself to sip. "You can thank your great-great-grandfather. Without him, we wouldn't exist. You know the story, right? His brothers were all wiped out by the Turks. Dimitrios, Achileas, and Paulos—none of them had sons. But then Panayiotis had a son he named Paulos, after his brother. And this Paulos—your *great*-grandfather—is the reason we're not Ikodomakis anymore, because he decided he didn't want to be a builder; he wanted to be a *priest*—" Theo said the word with a certain undisguised scorn, then set the glass down and licked his stained fingertips. "So we became *Papapaulos* instead—*Papa*, 'Father,' and *Paulos*. That's what they used to do when a priest came into your family—they changed your name. *Papa* plus the priest's name. That's why you have Papayiannis, Papadimitrios, Papandreou—the old prime minister of Greece—Papa-you-name-it. And now we have all these Pappases, because, like your grandfather, when they came here, to the United States, they dropped the Paulos, or the Yiannis, and made it Pappas. More American, I guess. Maybe Papapaulos wouldn't have been good for business. I don't know." He paused and then, as if in a rush of insight, burst, "Ikodomakis was good enough for your great-*great-grandfather*..." When the story circled back, I reached for Theo's arm. Theo blinked and took a deep breath. "It's important to know what the words mean, Peter. Everyone has a story. You remember what Socrates said?"

"I do."

"*Think* about it. Incredible stories. And this is *real history*."

"It *is* incredible, Theo."

"Can you imagine the stories I'd collect in Greece? *Firsthand?* You know I haven't been there since the sixties? Can you imagine that? I'm sixty-five years old."

I nodded.

Theo sighed. "'A life unexamined is not worth living'"—he could not resist. Orange sauce circled his lips. "Did I tell you where the *akis* in Ikodom*akis* comes from?"

"Not today, Theo."

"Paz*akis*, Kreon*akis*, Leftherou*dakis*, Mavro*dakis*—local Greeks, all from Crete. We're all from the same island. Ikodom*akis*. Like

Kazant*zakis*, the greatest of all the modern authors, who wrote *Zorba the Greek, The Last Temptation of Christ, Report to Greco*. The greatest writer since Euripides—you know what they did to him?"

"Yes."

"They kicked him out, just like they did Euripides."

Not exactly true, I suspected. The author had *left*, on his own, gone to Russia, traveled through Europe—at least according to biographical tidbits imparted by Theo himself, in past lectures meant to inspire exploration and adventure.

Theo kicked a chair leg under the table. "That's what they do when you write what people don't want to read, Peter."

This was a warning, or a challenge. I nodded.

"You know what he says on his gravestone? *I expect nothing. I fear nothing. I am free.* Understand? They could have exiled him to the moon. But they could not beat him. Not even death could beat him."

His appetite whetted, Theo contemplated, and then reached for, the bowl of tomato slices, his hand quivering at the wrist, one of the old-man traits he'd recently acquired. Only nine months older than my father, Theo was sporting hair that had recently turned from ash gray to silver, a wooly clump that he stubbornly combed forward but that puffed out inches from his forehead like a cloud. Theo's recent transformation had seemed freakish and sudden—a delayed reaction to years of taking tranquilizers, or, more likely, to a decade of refusing them. My father, on the other hand, maintained a thick black hairdo that combed over and waxed down easily; a few glassy hairs had sprung up but none you'd call gray. And though he hadn't seen a weight room since college, he could have passed for an Eagles tight end, if not for the grooves that sloped from the corners of his eyes, the only feature that marked him as over fifty. You couldn't blame the old man for seeing a young man staring back in the mirror.

Perhaps today I had discovered the old man's fountain of youth.

A red sliver, glazed with olive oil, slipped from Theo's indifferent fingers. "Don't wait to go to Greece, Peter." He shoved the bowl away. "Take a vacation and just go, now. You're at the perfect age. You'll be twenty-seven in less than one week. Time doesn't slow down as you get older. Trust me."

Of course Theo had my birthday-countdown at his fingertips, though generally the family didn't make much of birthdays, what with name days getting so much attention. At some point in the next few days, before July Fourth—my birthday—Theo the Hellenophile would transform into Theo the American patriot. In the silver slot fastened to a column on the front porch, the American flag would replace the Greek flag, which had been flying since March 25th, Greece's Independence Day. My mother would play along, baking an apple pie and poking it with the appropriate number of candles. She might sneak a wrapped box or two onto my bed—a collared shirt and a pair of pleated slacks—less a birthday present than an invitation to don some decent clothes and join them for church one of these days. Theo would sing "*Hronia polah*" to the tune of *Happy Birthday* and then start in on the National Anthem or one of the others—*America the Beautiful; My Country, 'Tis of Thee*—nailing the opening line and then humming what he could. The image of Theo and my parents standing over a candlelit apple pie reawakened in me the desire to go to California with Sophia, or at least to a local motel until I found my own place.

Theo bit into a cookie, his eyes, all the while, locked into mine. He might have been seeing my imagined escape: "I tell you, I wouldn't mind going to California myself." He wiped his chin, goateed with powder.

I licked my fork and went to the sink.

"Whenever you want to take a look at this, Peter..." Theo flipped a page.

I glanced over my shoulder. "Soon, Theo."

"I really appreciate you giving up your bedroom for me. I couldn't be doing this project without it."

"It's your room now, Theo."

As I headed for the basement door, Theo shoveled the gray beads into his hand and reached for my arm.

"Whenever you want it back, Peter. I've kept everything exactly the same."

"I know, Theo, thank you. I appreciate it."

When he held out the worry beads for me to take, I refused them, closing my hand into a soft fist.

Theo went right on, "I may get back into teaching, you know, when I'm finished with all of this." All at once, he let go of my arm and turned back to his notebook, the pages crackling, the *kompoloi* clicking.

In the living room, Uncle George pressed his hands to his knees and raised himself from a cushioned chair. He tucked his thumbs inside his terry-cloth waistband, his puff of a belch announcing he'd had enough. Aunt Irene rubbed Uncle George's belly and entered the kitchen to gather her sons from the basement. "We haven't had a chance to talk to you much today, Peter." The twins' sneakered feet pounded their way upstairs. She pulled her hand back from the door as her boys burst into the kitchen.

"Are we *leaving?!*" They might have been bound for Disneyland.

The remaining Havertown uncles and aunts, melded into chairs, groaned and straightened themselves, as if being slowly cranked. Gone were the days of endless visits. They'd be back in their own living rooms by nine o'clock.

Tony and Dean scampered through the living room, escaping reaching arms, and disappeared into the darkening front yard. Aunt Irene, in the doorway, one-arm hugged everyone, while digging elbow-deep into her purse for her Newports. My father, his cheeks flushed and unshaven, stood from the wing-backed chair before the bay window and fingertipped the marble lamp table, where empty Heinekens encircled a bottle of ouzo, the scent of licorice blending with the piney outside air. My mother guided the old man by the elbow.

"I have to give a sermon tomorrow, Irene," he said.

My mother laughed.

"Too much fun, Paul." Aunt Irene spewed smoke.

"It's *your* fault." My father's eyes gleamed, as he walked out into the yard. Shrinking pastel figures blinked out as car doors thumped. The porch light seemed to ignite my father's sunburned neck. Headlights flickered and rose up Birch Hill. Red brake lights pulsed. My father stared into the quickly darkening night, as my eyes met my mother's in the reflection of the storm door.

"*Talk* to him, Peter," she said quietly. "I think he's depressed."

"He's not depressed, Mom. We've talked about this." I was more certain than ever; the old man's past silences had reflected not exhaustion or some mysterious grief, as my mother had theorized, but pent-up longing.

My father entered the middle of the yard.

My mother went on, "Andrew bought him that beautiful car, and he barely smiled."

"That's because he's happy with *any* car."

"Peter, you can talk to him. He needs to talk, man to man. Maybe you do, too." She touched my cheek. "You know how *his* father drank…"

"Dad is nothing like Papou, Mom." The lie sickened me, like the truth itself.

"I'm worried about you, too, Peter."

"Mom, *please.*"

My father turned to us and called out something. My mother opened the storm door, and the old man said, "Where'd the Adirondack chairs go?"

My mother poked her head out. "I don't know, Paul. Around back maybe."

She turned to me. "I'm going to help your father with the chairs." She stared at me, waiting for me to take the cue, to go help the old man lug the chairs from wherever they were.

Lamb and wet salad rose into my throat.

My mother nodded forgivingly and went outside.

As I turned for the basement, the phone rang—once. Sophia must have picked up downstairs. Maybe the call was for my father: a woman from church had overdosed or hanged herself and was found sprawled on the bedroom carpet or dangling from electrical wire in the cellar. The suicide would be traced to me. Like an idiot, I'd taken her home and left her alone.

At the top of the steps I heard my sister's voice drop an octave. I bent over the banister. The heavy base of my ancient olive-green phone sat on the bed behind Sophia, who was sprawled out, her back to me, knees pulled in toward her belly. Another agonizing call to California. Figures. Veronica. Even now, the night before her flight, Sophia was still torn up about her plans, as she had been all year. She muffled her whisper, the coiled cord winding up her side, the receiver resting on her neck like a sympathetic hand. I had been her counselor through it all, or so I liked to think; deep down I knew that all I really did was listen while she danced around the truth.

The dark-purple tip of her cross tattoo peeked out over her black waistband.

Maybe the news of our father's fallibility would free her finally. Throughout high school she'd been defining herself by resisting the old man's commands. God knew she pierced and scarred herself just to spite him.

When I reached the floor, Sophia said bye in a rushed whisper and hung up. She flipped over, smearing mascara with her wrist.

"What's the matter?" I said.

"Nothing."

I accidentally kicked the game at my feet—Rock'Em Sock'Em Robots—a solid yellow base with two muscley figures on top: the loser, with extended, Pez-dispenser-like neck; the winner, with big-fisted punch, frozen in mid-air, cannonball shoulders, and crazy grin. Sophia must have witnessed her cousins' testosterone-driven competition. They might have been reenacting the backyard battle between Andrew and me. When I knocked the game, the victorious boxer's head unhinged with a zing.

"I *hate* them." She grinned, propping herself on an elbow.

"Well, they're gone now."

"No, I mean *them*." She pointed to the little plastic men at my shins. "I've wanted to kill them for the last hour. My *God*. Blam, blam. They could have played Yahtzee or something."

"Or *Twister*." I pulled my desk chair out and sat. "Then *you* could have played with them."

"Oh, yeah," she laughed. "That's what I want more than anything, to get tangled up on the floor with those two."

"You wish they weren't your cousins."

"I know." She moaned, "Mmm, Dean and Tony, I want to get it on with both of them…"

"Okay, stop."

She peeled her shirt up slightly, leaning back onto my bed. "I just couldn't take my eyes off them, beating on each other like that on the rug, all that manliness."

"Seriously, don't make me barf. C'mon."

She pulled her shirt down.

"That's why I was crying, Peter," she said. "It's something I never told you, but now you know. I'm in love with my twin cousins. I'm so *confused*."

She gazed up, longing for counsel. I would play along. Unloading my own secret would have to wait a minute.

"Okay, I see…" I reached for a pen from my desk. "Do they know? These cousins of yours?" I crossed my legs and faked a notepad on my thigh.

"I don't see how they *can't* know, Doctor. I just—" She buried her face in her hands, whimpering.

"Very interesting."

Her quivering hand and sniffle were impressively acted. I leaned back onto the chair's hind legs, biting the pen. When her cry turned real, I dragged my chair closer.

"What happened?" I said.

"I don't know. She's an asshole. Right now I don't even want to go."

I bent down to see into her face. "What'd she say? What about the homeless people?"

She shrugged. "Don't make fun."

"I'm not. Would you—?" I stopped myself. "Don't get pissed off at me now, I'm just asking…"

She peered at me through her fingers. "Don't say *pissed*, Peter."

"Would you be going out there if *she* wasn't out there, or…?"

"*Or…?*" She dropped her hands.

"What if she was in North Dakota? Would you be going *there?* Be honest."

She swung her legs off the bed, planted her elbows on her knees, and dropped her chin into her hands, appearing contemplative. I wasn't sure if this was the dramatic Sophia, playing patient, or the real Sophia. And then she looked straight into my eyes: she would follow Veronica to the North Pole.

"So why's she an asshole?"

Sophia licked a dark tear from her lip. Then she huffed, suddenly, and sat up straight, newly composed, as if she'd just changed her mind about Veronica, or about something. "I'm so full of shit. I just want to throw up." She bowed her head and stared at her boots. "Seriously, I feel nauseous. I just need to go out there and get it over with. I don't want to talk about it anymore."

Of course I couldn't tell her not to go.

"I wish I was going with you," I said.

She stared at the ceiling. "What do you think Dad would do if he knew?"

"He'd never believe it."

"I guess." She seemed disappointed.

Now was my chance: let me tell you something about the old man...

"I smell like grass," Sophia said. She sniffed her sleeve. "I haven't showered."

Scattered and nervous, she didn't seem fit to bathe herself, much less travel alone.

My sister's keeper, I would keep my secret to myself.

I patted her thigh. "I'll visit," I offered.

Sophia stared off past me, already gone. "You want to play that?" she said.

I looked over my shoulder, then back at Sophia. My eyebrows rose. Hers mimicked mine. I understood that it couldn't be easy for Sophia, holding so much in. We glided onto the floor, fingers combing the thick orange rug as we laid ourselves down before the yellow ring. We gripped the control handles, getting a feel for our respective few square inches of space, slammed the plastic heads back into their torsos, grinning, thumbing our buttons, taking a few practice punches. With a nod, we went at each other, arms in a frenzy, fists crunching against hard-shelled chests. I glanced up to see my sister's merciless eyes, her jutting tongue and wild smile. I felt the zing! of my internal spring and looked down to see my own knocked-out head.

Fists raised, Sophia announced herself champion.

Our mother's vacuum sounded just above us.

As Sophia made her way to the banister, I stood with the yellow boxing ring in my arms.

"I'll see about flights," I said.

"Happy birthday ahead of time," she said, and went upstairs.

I put the game back into the game closet.

The walls thumped, and the pipes hissed—Sophia in the shower. I had never been shocked by the thought of my sister with Veronica, who was flirty and confident and wore heels with her jeans, bright-pink lip gloss, and big hoopy earrings. Hell, I might have known what was going on between the two of them before the girls themselves knew, seeing how Veronica dipped her head for Sophia, who smiled and petted her like a cat, right there in the kitchen, while our mother set the table. God knew no one else suspected a thing. The old man worried too much about how Sophia might ruin her life with a boy to be worried about how she might ruin her life with a girl. Besides, why would my parents be suspicious of teenage girls grooming and swaddling each other in compliments?

Not long before Veronica came along, it seemed that Sophia was on a mission to skateboard off into the sunset with Freddy West, or at least to torture the old man with the possibility of such a fate for his daughter. Then Freddy West quietly vanished from her life after years of making pit stops in the driveway, disguising his visits as innocent flybys. In the meantime, my mother was proud of Sophia for being so sweet to Veronica, who informed us all bluntly at a dinnertime therapy session this past spring that she'd survived a sexually abusive father and a drug-addicted mother. "I'm done with boys," she announced. "You're too young for boys anyway," the old man said, a message that was familiar to Sophia, who, having dropped Freddy, explained that she wasn't about to let her best friend go to the prom alone, or, God forbid, not go at all.

I shed my shirt and jeans, swiped my trusty bottle of hand lotion from the night table, and went into the bathroom, where I made the shower so hot it stung.

I pictured Veronica just outside the shower doors, where she unzipped her pink prom dress. She braced herself on the toilet, her smooth thighs and round ass all a white fleshy blur through the steaming swirled glass, her jet-black hair draped on her arms. Sophia appeared, one hand on the sink, the other on her hip, rolling her eyes and shaking her head, with her I-can't-believe-you-are-such-a-loser face. Is this what you've been keeping from me? That you're in love with my girlfriend?

I turned my back and finished quickly against the slippery wall, fighting off images of my sister's face between Veronica's legs, my father's between Daisy's.

Her car was still at the top of the hill.

I toweled off, stuffed my legs back into my jeans, and slipped into rubber flip-flops. Maybe the shoes she'd tossed into the front seat would be the first in a series of clues to prove something one way or the other. I would dig around for handwritten notes, slips of paper with scribbled numbers and cryptic phrases, or gift receipts in the glove compartment.

Bare-chested, I stepped softly up the stairs and into the dark kitchen. A dim lamp in the living room shined an orange half-moon onto the bay window. The front door's bolt slid unlocked with a click, and I made my way into the yard. Floodlights at my back, I followed my stretched-out shadow across the lawn. Her chrome bumper gleamed in the trees on the hill.

"Hey!"

I turned. Near the corner of the house, in the shadows of the hemlocks, my father sat just off the sidewalk in an Adirondack chair, which, along with the one next to him, he must have found among Heineken bottles and cigarette butts. A glass of water sat in the grass by his ankles. A legal-style notepad lay in his lap, pages curled over his knees.

"What are you doing?" he asked me.

The blinding floodlight above the gutter of the garage drenched the old man. I folded my arms, not about to answer his questions, and stood at the edge of his long shadow.

"What are *you* doing?" I said.

"Reviewing my sermon."

Water dripped from my hair, down my back. I shielded my eyes, glancing up at the top-floor windows. When my grandmother wanted to be alone, no one bothered her, even on holidays. I wondered if I could pull off such a feat in the basement.

"Going for a walk?" the old man said.

I hiked my jeans at my belt loops. "Couldn't sleep." I swiped a hand over my damp belly.

"We didn't see you much today."

I crossed my arms. I scrunched my naked toes away from the grass.

"Have a seat." My father tapped the arm of the chair next to him.

I stepped toward the garage, skirting my father's shadow.

"Come and keep your old man company."

I turned away from the smell of the musky suit coat, lifting my face toward the spicy scent of hemlocks along the house. A dark-green silhouette—the Lexus, pulled in for safekeeping—was barely visible through the garage window.

"Your brother should save his money." My father flattened his notepad pages and clicked his pen. "So you met Daisy Diamond today…"

I marveled at the old man's audacity.

"She's a very sad lady," my father said.

Tomorrow the old man would read from the torn-out pages of his notepad to a flock of innocents who would hear his words as God's.

"Did she invite you in?"

I dragged a berry beneath my flip-flop. Its tiny-pebble pit rolled beneath my rubber sole, a thin red stain extending from my toes.

"She's always been a lonely person. She came here after high school. She wanted to be an actress, or singer, some kind of performer, I don't know. Her father had died young. Her mother was sick in Greece. When her husband died, she became very depressed. You have to be careful, Peter. Did she upset you?"

The fragile son.

"It's hard with people like her," the old man went on, "for people like *us*, to know how God wants us to love sometimes. It's hard to say no when someone's really hurting. Where did you find her?"

Find her—a stray cat the old man had taken home how many times.

"Up the street," I said, almost pointing. "Her car died."

The old man puffed, "You see? That car's fine. Trust me." He knew. "Your mother got angry with me when I gave her some church money for repairs. You know the boy who cried wolf? I won't lie to you—it's not easy ignoring those cries. Years ago she managed to get me to do some housework for her. Imagine that? Your mother would have a fit if she knew. Did you go inside?"

I nodded. The old man knew her whole routine.

He nodded sympathetically, with stiffened bottom lip. "She keeps a picture of your old man in the living room. Did you see it? Your mother and I decided years ago we had to set boundaries with her. She would come over to the house. We'd have to start turning off lights for her to get the message."

"*Jesus*," I whispered. My father had no idea just how delusional she was. Suddenly I wanted to blurt the whole story, to say I'd seen *two* pictures, both of which I had in my truck, along with some other things she'd dumped on me. For a moment I imagined digging the bag out from the truck and, together with my father, destroying it, burning it, right now. The old man had no idea what a fool his son was. I would never admit what I'd been led to believe. Tomorrow I would get rid of the bag myself.

The old man looked up at me, understanding, forgiving, it seemed.

"My sermon tomorrow is on Saint Peter," he announced. "Even *he* couldn't deny the church for too long."

I grimaced, ashamed. Maybe it *was* time to return.

"Her car's still up there." I gestured with my chin.

"Try not to think about it." My father handed me his notepad. "Help your old man up."

4
Wisdom! Arise!

Sunday Morning. No one bothered waking me for church anymore.

A few miles west, at St. Peter's Greek Orthodox Church, my father was calling out, "Wisdom! Arise!" while, east, Sophia was rising into the sky, heading for San Francisco, my mother at the terminal bay window, praying her daughter would discover out there the beauty that, here, she pierced and obscured in strange clothes.

The night before, after my rendezvous with the old man out on the front lawn, I was fraught with guilt and couldn't sleep. I'd bought into Daisy's lie as if I'd been *looking* for a reason to turn against my father. For the first time, I understood Sophia's urge to punish herself, as dreams of penance lulled me to sleep: I imagined going to the gym, where I was smothered under weights; I imagined running a marathon—lugging a tarp filled with rocks—collapsing on the road-side, and being delivered home. Deep down, I knew my father was right: it was time to return to church.

Five years ago I'd stopped going to church at the same time I stopped exercising—not that I'd ever been a sportsman. Last winter, as a belated Christmas present, my brother bought me a six-month membership to the Philadelphia Gym Club, which, Andrew empha-sized, was a great place to meet women—the downtown location was where he'd met Melanie. When Andrew announced the gift at dinner on New Year's Day—"in the spirit of New Year's resolutions"—the whole family encouraged me delicately as if I were a drug addict and this were an intervention. At the time, even the name of the place, *Gym Club*, conjured intimidating images of men and women chatting it up in some common social area over Powerbars and Gatorade. Since then, Andrew's monthly payments, whatever their amount, were more like donations. In the first week of membership, back in January, I went twice, after work, and strolled on a treadmill for an hour, my eyes glued to MTV. Except for the strolling, the hour at the gym was not unlike a typical hour after work at home, where I dozed on the couch, flipping through channels while waiting for dinner.

For me, exercise and religion required the same kind of all-or-nothing commitment from which I had been retreating for years but to which I was feeling drawn now, even in my sleep. And so the instant I woke up, the thought occurred to me to go back to the gym and do it right.

It was 10:01. The alarm clock, set for weekday mornings, droned away on the night table like a dying lamb. I dozed off, then shot up, half-dreaming, tugging my wrists free from grasping hands, blood-red polka dots pulsing on the backs of my eyelids. And yet I couldn't deny what was pushing against my boxers, as I kicked off the sheet and got dressed quickly.

What I needed was to repent, not to exercise.

Heading upstairs, I pictured my father spooning Communion. In the kitchen the dessert plate of *kourampiedes* reminded me to take things one step at a time—you didn't just waltz in off the streets and take Communion, the most sacred of sacraments; you mentally prepared yourself, even fasted. I grabbed the three powdered cookies, in their pink paper containers, and shuffled out to the driveway.

In my truck I stared at the brown paper bag under the dashboard. No need to destroy it, I thought, or even to get rid of it. Why not prop the photos on corner tables in the living room and not say a word? Put the jeans and Holy Cross T-shirt into the old man's drawers, the sneakers by the lawn mower.

The pictures, I figured, would have been easy to stuff into her purse. The rest she could have swept up on her way out through the garage. Or maybe she'd insisted on washing the old man's clothes the time he helped her with housework—mowing the lawn?—hoping to lure him back, then hoarding the stuff like keepsakes. She'd turned her fantasy into reality by surrounding herself with stolen trinkets.

The day was gray, neither warm nor cool. I set the cookies on the passenger seat and backed out of the driveway. I already felt a weight lifted, picturing myself entering the narthex. I popped a cookie into my mouth and worked it into a thick gum. On Birch Hill, the maroon Chevrolet seemed abandoned, the owner unknown, rusting away under a canopy of branches. Daisy's red shoes flashed in the glare of the window, and again I imagined setting fire to the bag, this time at the corner of Eighth and Pine. Loneliness—or even *insanity*, I thought—was no excuse: I wanted an explanation from her, or an apology—or *something*. I imagined the townspeople rushing into the street to lay their eyes on the woman who had borne false witness against my father.

Halfway down Provincetown Avenue, I pulled over in front of the McDonald's, having second thoughts. Even Saint Peter couldn't deny the church for too long, my father had said. Little did the old man know that *he* had been the reason I jumped ship in the first place. I had never openly blamed my father, perhaps because my return to church had always felt imminent. Then, somehow, five years had blown past. Yet today felt too soon. Or maybe I just wasn't ready for St. Peter's, my father's church—*my* church. The inquisition from the congregation would be unbearable—as would the celebration: Peter Pappas had come to see the light! Hallelujah!

There was a place downtown—not church exactly. The old Quaker meetinghouse. Since college I had wanted to go but had lacked the proper motivation. As a student I'd skipped Religion Department-sponsored group trips to the meetinghouse—and to synagogues, mosques, and churches—on the grounds that I would start going as soon as I was certain I wanted to be a Quaker—or a Jew, Muslim, or Christian of whatever denomination. Now it seemed that God was finally guiding me.

I stared up at the Golden Arches, as the third and final cookie expanded in my cheek like warm dough. I considered pulling into the drive-thru for an orange drink—and maybe an Egg McMuffin—but finally managed to swallow.

I sped out of East Birch—took Lincoln to Kelly to Broad—and raced down Market Street. I parked on Third Street, where the corner building's royal-blue brick facade announced SUITS in giant red letters. In my jeans and sneakers, I hoped the Quakers didn't have a dress code.

Inside the brick wall of the churchyard—meetinghouse yard—I listened for clues of parishioners—people meeting—but there was only silence. Of course. Black wrought-iron S-shaped clamps were bolted into tall yellow doors and shutters. A man wearing an open-collared shirt and carrying a briefcase entered the courtyard under a red-brick arch on the opposite side. I was relieved to be following a man who seemed to be dropping by on his way to the office. We nodded to each other at the concrete steps.

At the doorway a woman in a navy-blue dress greeted us, offering a quiet nod and a small sheet of paper. I licked my caked lips and smacked my denim thighs, streaking them with sugary lines. She said in a soft voice, "Your first time at meeting?" The open-collared man said, "First time in a long time." I bowed slightly and with a tinge of penitence said, "Me, too," then wondered if she, or any Quaker, gave a damn about my guilt.

In the meeting room, rows of pews, parallel with each of the four walls, extended toward the empty lime-green carpet in the center. A dozen or so men were spaced out evenly. I sat in the nearest pew, and the woman sat behind me. A bench creaked. I glanced down at the pink piece of paper the woman had handed me: "Be still and know that I am God," the top line read. It went on to explain that what we were doing here was submitting to the Divine Spirit. There was no human leader, no planned program. We were all trying to live by the example of Christ. I looked up, at the blank white ceiling, and then around, at the virtually empty room. How anticlimactic it would be for my father, after preparing a sermon, to look down from the pulpit at only twelve faces. But no priest would be disappointed here.

I didn't want to stare at the others, so instead I stared straight ahead at the empty pew against the far wall. The wood's deep finish had been worn away to a pale circle. The benches might have been the originals. Some early-American Ben Franklin type in a black hat and white-bibbed shirt might have sat there every week for God-knew-how-many years. This was one of the first meetinghouses in the country—1804, boasted an iron sign out on the sidewalk. My father would remind me that the Orthodox Church was the first church, the

one true church, which began with the disciples on the first
Pentecost and remained the living continuation of that primitive
church in Jerusalem. I imagined the fat Quaker squinting back at me,
asking what I was doing here, why I wasn't where I belonged. For all
those years, in my father's church, each symbolic gesture had been no
more or less meaningful to me than the still air of the Quaker meetinghouse today. But now I longed to hear anything, even a black-robed
psalti droning hymns in the corner, or my father plodding along in his
gold-laced vestments.

The little sheet of paper said, "Sometimes speaking arises out of
silence." I looked for signs of anyone on the brink. A bearded man in a
golf shirt yawned. The open-collared man propped his elbow on his
briefcase and stretched his neck, leaning his head back. A thin twenty-something fellow, whom I admired instantly just for being young
and here alone, closed his eyes. What was everyone thinking about? I
couldn't remember from my religion classes just how Christian, technically, the Quakers were. What did that mean, anyway—Christian—
technically?

What was I doing here? Should I be thinking of *Jesus?*

At my own church, the Divine Liturgy would at least be providing
some opportunity for exercise, as I would be standing, sitting, and
kneeling in an endless routine of rising and falling. My father might
explain to the Sunday-school kids that "liturgy"—*leitourghia*—meant
"work," so that their exhaustion would seem all part of the master
plan. As a kid I got lost in the maze of stories, of vibrant-robed martyrs,
immortalized on the walls, which intersected, tunneled, and vaulted.
Inhaling the sweet incense—not to mention swallowing warm wine
on an empty stomach—put me in a daze, inside a kaleidoscope of
icons, made all the more brilliant by sunlight through stained glass.
Here, in the meetinghouse, I stared at the white walls, white ceiling,
white light at the windows, and at the darkness behind my own shut
eyelids, while I tried to concentrate on the silence. Here, the point
was simplicity.

Meanwhile, my father was jangling the *thimiatoh*, spreading
incense, or raising the Eucharist above his head—*this is my body,*

which is broken for you... Maybe some altar boy was eyeing faces through the carved wooden holes of the *iconostasis*, while boiling water in a little green electric teapot on the back corner table. When my father poured the water into the chalice, it would transform into the very water that poured out from Christ's pierced side. Maybe the Quakers just imagined Communion or contemplated the Last Supper, His passing the bread around, asking to be remembered...

Here we all were, two thousand years later, remembering. Was this sufficient, just sitting around thinking? Did the Greeks overdo it? Maybe actual wine and bread made no difference. If you could believe that these modern ingredients could be transubstantiated (I could hear my father: "I believe that this is in truth Your sacred Body and that this is in truth Your precious Blood"), altered from bread and wine (a hard loaf from your own mother's oven and wine from Martini and Rossi) into the *actual Body and Blood;* if you could believe that Jesus himself was being mixed into a chalice held in the hands of your own father and spooned into your own body—then why couldn't you just as well believe that the whole transaction, from Jesus to you, could occur without anyone or anything at all?

It was all in your mind.

I swallowed, peaceful faces surrounding me. This was where men of real faith came. No robed leader would be spoon-feeding them. I would try to be still, to submit to the Divine Spirit, as the little pink sheet instructed. I leaned my head back and stared into the dull ceiling. Should I recite the Jesus prayer? *Lord Jesus Christ, Son of God, have mercy on me, a sinner...* The prayer had no place here, conjuring guilt; it was the equivalent of a giant Christ looming on the ceiling, inspiring fear. Where would the Christians be without their guilt and fear?

Here, I thought.

I should try to think of nothing. For a split second I managed to think of nothing. At least I thought I did; but then I found myself thinking about thinking of nothing.

That's why I'd come here today, I realized, to learn from the Quakers. Here, there was no need for absolution, formal ceremonies, or even spoken words. All I needed was to let go, to admit the truth about turning my back on him—not just yesterday but five years ago—to let the old man off the hook.

The last time I'd been in church, I was holding the Communion cloth up to old ladies' devoted dribbling lips, shoulder to shoulder with my father, who spooned from the chalice and uttered, "Servant of God," and then the parishioner's name. I was twenty-one at the time, a junior at Temple, and hadn't yet counted out the seminary; in fact, I was still considering the priesthood more seriously than any other profession. For the time being I was getting a liberal arts education, just as my father had done at Holy Cross, in Boston, where he'd gone on to become a priest. My father had always encouraged me to study with an open mind and to take my time before committing to a career. "*Sigah, sigah*"—slowly, slowly—the old man would say, whenever I would express doubt, looking for some kind of sign. "Most of us aren't so lucky to have a vision, or even to hear Him calling..."

It had been a cold November day, the unstained windowpanes ice blue in their wrought-iron frames. An old lady, swathed in black, blotted her lips and turned away. I lifted the red cloth to the next reaching hand—Theo's. He wore his rumpled, gray, pinstripe suit. When he opened his mouth, both Theo and I waited for my father to say, "Servant of God..." But my father turned the gold spoon upside down, wine dribbling into the chalice, and gestured, flicking the spoon's handle, toward the side aisle. Theo glared at my father, whose face remained unchanged, and turned away.

After church I'd waited, in the sanctuary, for some explanation, as my father shifted out of his robe. Then, in the back office, my father explained, finally, "He's a grown man who's never held a job. What business does he have being with a woman? He didn't confess, exactly, so I'm not breaching confidence telling you this. I want you to understand." When Theo revealed he'd been seeing a woman, my father assumed he'd come for the sacrament of Confession. No, for Godsakes, Theo said, as my father retrieved his Bible and gestured toward the office door, he just wanted to talk to his brother. "I advised him to confess. He said he'd never confessed before and he didn't plan to start now, especially since he wasn't committing any sin. And he said"—I assumed Theo must have let this slip—"he didn't believe in such a formal ceremony anyway, and he certainly didn't need a priest to play middleman, least of all his own brother."

My father told me, "As a priest, you have to draw the line somewhere. Even if it's your brother. I'm not just a man in the world you come to chat with about your extra-marital affairs—or your *pre*-marital affairs. I don't know what he expected me to tell him—that what he was doing was okay? The church does not condone sex outside of marriage. Period. When I asked him if he was going to stop seeing this woman, he looked at me like I was crazy. Then he comes up for Communion today and expects to receive the Body and Blood of Christ, no questions asked? I'm sorry. He knows better. I can't make an exception because he's my brother. You can't just leave the church doors open for anyone to walk in off the streets, stamp out his cigarette, and expect to participate in the holy sacrament of Communion. This is a holy place. This is the most holy of all the sacraments."

I had never considered my father's burden. To be the one who had to draw the line. Sitting there in the old man's office, I began to share his resentment; after all, I had been holding the cloth. "How could he put you in that position?" I asked. "Like he was *testing* you!" I strained to imitate my father's stoic calmness as we walked downstairs into the gymnasium, where we joined parishioners for coffee and pastries.

Staring at the ceiling of the meetinghouse, I wondered if this rush of memory was an indication of having successfully submitted to the Divine Spirit, or of failing to keep the channel clear so that the Divine Spirit could make its way to me.

On the night my father had turned Theo away I couldn't sleep. In the basement, in the black space between my eyes and the ceiling, a rugged-faced but sorrowful Jesus sat in a circle of his beloved friends and broke the news of what would be happening in the next twenty-four hours. They were all sitting on pale dirt, around a small fire, surrounded by trees, their leader tearing pieces of thin bread, like pita, his hands reaching in both directions, and sipping from a wooden cup. Theo, lost, in his gray, pinstripe suit, emerged from the trees. Of course, Jesus knew where he had been. Theo had accidentally stumbled upon them, nervously rushing home in the dark. Jesus stood and gestured at his own place in the dirt. Theo sat down, ate, and drank.

Jesus paced around the circle toward Judas. Theo, along with me, looked on, as Jesus stopped behind Judas and informed him of his role. His had been the one unforgivable sin, my father had once explained, echoing the church's refusal to give someone who killed himself a proper funeral. Judas pleaded, then bowed his head and sobbed. How was he to go on after this?

The next day I asked my father if he thought Judas had gone to Hell. "If not for the betrayal..." my father started, then paused. "I think when a human being takes his own life, he's already *in* Hell. We stand in judgment of ourselves first. God didn't have to condemn him—he condemned himself. But," my father said, perhaps leaving room for some other possibility, "who knows what was going on in Judas' head when he hung that noose from the dogwood tree? God offers salvation, and the rest is up to us. If Judas had rage in his heart, if he was spitting in God's face, if he felt betrayed by God, thinking Him already dead on the cross, well, then, my guess is that Judas went straight to Hell and stayed there."

I had felt tremendous sympathy for Judas, though I didn't admit it out loud. Judas must have been in a horrible hell already. In my own church there had been a girl I knew from Sunday school who'd taken pills. Her family threatened to leave the church if their daughter didn't get a proper funeral. My father explained to the family that this was church policy, not *his* policy. The girl's father was a banker and was on the church's board of directors. Eventually the old man conceded that there was no way they could know for sure what the girl's intention had been. So the girl got her funeral, and the family stayed in the church.

But what if she *hadn't* gotten her funeral? I had overheard conversations about the distraught parents, who'd found their daughter on her bedroom floor. Did they think that without the church's approval, she had no chance at Heaven? That until the church acknowledged her death, she would remain in purgatory? Did the church think a proper funeral pointless because she'd already gone to Hell? Was the church reluctant to usurp God's judgment by presuming the girl's qualifications for His Kingdom? Maybe giving her a proper funeral would send the dangerous message that the church condoned suicide. As if not having the church's permission were the one thing keeping everyone from slitting his own throat.

That night, in the dark basement, five years ago, I decided my father couldn't deprive a girl of Heaven, or even a man of Communion. I was convinced that Theo would never go back to church and considered tiptoeing upstairs to talk with him. I wanted to tell him that the church made no difference. Nothing could interfere with what was between you and God. All that week I kept silent around my father. I kept thinking about Theo, who went about his business of spending all day in the East Birch public library. All week Theo ate dinner in his bedroom, never uttering a complaint, resigned, as it turned out, simply not to return to church—or to confide ever again in a priest, or anyone else, it seemed. The old man had cast him out. One less sinner in the Garden. The next Sunday, wrapping my tie around my neck, I felt like a hypocrite. I felt that if I went back myself, I'd be betraying not only my uncle but also something deep in myself.

In the meetinghouse, I was enraptured, my neck stiff, having projected the whole reverie onto the blank ceiling, when, suddenly, a thin man in a checkered flannel shirt stood up and sounded his voice in what seemed for a moment to be utter nonsense, a slurring of vowels trying to find their way; at last, the silence had been broken by this apparent lunatic, who must have thought he'd received a message worth sharing but whose transmitter had then betrayed him. The man's mouth pinched and quivered. This is what happens when you let anyone in off the streets, I heard my father say. The church needs structure, needs someone to serve as God's agent.

The man's vowels formed into coherent syllables. "The words of John..." The man's neck twitched. Maybe the woman behind me would ask the man to sit down. His eyelids shut tight, the man went on, "...speak to us today." He paused, then finished, "just as the words of Peter did two thousand years ago at Pentecost." The man sighed, satisfied. Mission accomplished. All the other men sat still with their eyes closed. I was shocked at the man's fully articulated sentence, particularly the appropriate reference to Pentecost, about which my father might be expounding at this very moment. The man's incomprehensible start might have been the equivalent of radio static as he tuned in to my father's frequency.

I imagined my father at the pulpit and inhaled deeply, feeling forgiven. Yesterday the old man must have detected my wrestling with horrible thoughts. It was as if he'd been waiting for me out on the lawn. I'd stomped and pouted, ready to crush the old man and crusade against hypocrisy. For all I knew, my father regretted what he'd done to his brother that day, regretted what he'd taken from him—that act might be the single greatest regret of his life. Or maybe my father apologized to Theo a long time ago and they'd come to peace with their differences. I'd never asked my father about any of it afterward. I'd just stopped going to church, waiting for the old man to raise hell. Instead, my father had said, many times, come back when you're ready. Meanwhile, I'd hardly started a crusade. Even my cynical sister had continued to go dutifully, albeit scowling and appearing more and more like an insurgent biding time; even my brother went now and then, when he wasn't on call, usually with Melanie, whose transformation had already begun. After a while my mother had stopped knocking on the basement door on Sunday mornings, respecting one's faith as his own business.

I sat up, at the edge of the bench, wanting to leap to my feet. Friends! The bearded man, the twenty-something, and the short, black-haired man with the briefcase—they would all open their eyes. I would tell them, I felt His presence! We're forgiven! And then I remembered: these people weren't consumed with guilt; they wanted *peace*, not forgiveness for their sins. My unspoken words hung dreadfully in my mind. I sat back. The bench creaked. Blood pounded at my temples.

These Quakers knew the secret. The secret was in the silence. Strange Christians, but Christians nonetheless. East meets West. Jesus shaking hands with the Buddha. William Penn shaking hands with the

Indians. That painting of the treaty by Benjamin West. No common language. No words required. A peaceful exchange. They weren't just peace *seekers*, the Quakers; they were peace*makers*. That was the Christian element: you don't just seek peace in the desert and then stay out there; you return to the world...

Maybe I was a Quaker deep down and my spiritual journey had just begun. I would hand Daisy Diamond the brown paper bag as a peace offering. I wouldn't say a thing. She would be home from church today, stranded without a car—unless she'd gone to the Greek church on Eighth Street. Come to think of it, why had she ever driven all the way out to the East Birch church in the first place? I had to stop being so suspicious of people, I thought. She must have had her reasons. After all, you couldn't blame her for preferring cheerful St. Peter's to dreary St. George's, which might have conjured morbid thoughts of her mother or empty feelings about her father, long-buried in Greece. You could never know the whole story. Maybe yesterday she hadn't even been *lying*, exactly; you're not lying if you believe what you're saying. Or maybe I'd read too deeply into what she'd said. Already her exact words were hard to recall. *Your father's been trapped for years, I'm finished with all of it,* et cetera. None of it, now, seemed patently false. The search for Truth was a vain mission. Besides, Jesus didn't preach about Truth. He preached about Love.

The secret was to think of nothing—or nothing but peace and love.

When the blond woman put her hand on my shoulder, I turned to see her standing. She held out her hand, and I took it. Did she want me to rise up and speak? Saint Peter had been a great orator. The woman released me and shuffled into the aisle, where the others were gathering. The meeting was over.

5
The Pink Slip

The drapes hung like gauze in the windows of Daisy Diamond's apartment. The contents of the brown paper bag, soft and heavy on my thighs, felt like rotting vegetables about to break through. My knuckles nicked the steering wheel as I clenched and rolled the thick brown paper, envisioning our awkward reunion on the stoop, her stepping outside and glaring at the bag clutched against my chest. I wasn't here for an apology or an explanation. I would be cool, like the Quakers, who had no planned program. If I needed guidance I would clutch the pink slip of paper in my right-hand pocket, submit to the Divine Sprit, and trust that sometimes speaking arose out of silence.

I got out and set the bag in the truck bed behind the steel storage box built in beneath the rear window. I placed the bag inside the box and secured the lock. A satisfied feeling came over me, just as a tapping came from the window behind me, where Daisy Diamond's fingers, at the end of a green sleeve, moved the drape and disappeared. Starting up the steps, I decided to appear as though I'd come—as I *had*, I told myself—to pay her an innocent visit. Through the window of the outside door, I could see, on the vestibule floor, that the mail had been swept up, perhaps trashed by a neighbor. Inside, a bolt clicked, thumped, and the heavy black door swung open.

A tight-fitting green shirt hugged Daisy's arms, her waist, her breasts—her body so robust she seemed almost cartoonishly womanly. Yesterday's polka-dotted dress had somehow disguised her figure, which now seemed both petite and voluptuous. Thick damp curls, apparently just towel-dried, fell across her shoulders as she reached for the outer door. She tilted her head to meet my gaze, offering a silly, open-mouthed smile.

"I'm surprised to see you, *too*," she said, opening the door. "Come in."

Stepping into the vestibule, I realized, as I sealed my lips, that she'd been mirroring my hanging jaw, a habit from childhood I'd consciously tried to break, tongue out when I was thoughtless or thoughtful. My amazement grew, as almost every vivid detail of her, even her especially wide, cotton-white smile, distinguished her from the weary woman I'd brought home the day before—the garden-sharp scent of rose shampoo; the milky skin peeking out above her jeans; the jeans themselves, well-worn Levi's, taut against her hips and thighs. When she took my left hand, leading me into her apartment, my right hand sank into my pocket.

"Well, look at you," Daisy said. Her eyes were clear and alive. "You look so…"

I bowed my head to see myself.

The sounds of violins flickered like moths at the high ceiling, cracked with sprawling piss-yellow water stains. The music dipped into a low, vibrating bawl—felt hammers against drums—a man cried, and I turned toward the tall black speakers on each side of the door. Next to the speakers were bookshelves packed with short stacks of paperbacks on top of rows of hardbacks. On the coffee table a plate of sliced red apple and a golden puddle of what appeared to be honey sat beside a pile of mail. Steam rose from a yellow mug.

"You like Puccini?" she said, reaching for the mug.

I shook my head, no thank you, not sure what I was turning down.

"Pavarotti." She grinned, sipping.

I nodded, realizing.

"Aren't *we* quiet today." She set the mug down and headed for the kitchen. "Tea?"

A roll of stamps, a pile of envelopes, a checkbook, and flattened-out bills were all arranged neatly on the light-orange marble tabletop. Two thick candles burned in shallow black bowls. Catalogues and discarded paper jutted from a brown paper bag on the rug.

Daisy returned, handing me a steaming-hot blue mug. "I didn't expect to see you again."

"Ahhh—" I moaned, shifting the mug, hooking the handle with two fingers. "I, uh…"

"Careful," she laughed. "Here—" She scooped the tea bag with a spoon, wrung it with the string, and set it on an envelope.

On the mug was a stark-white dome topped with a Byzantine cross, a Matisse-like cutout of a church, floating in the familiar cobalt blue that seemed exclusive to the Greek skies I knew only from photographs in coffee-table books at home. On the wall above the couch, a poster of *The Kiss* hung in a golden metal frame. Having failed on Puccini, I wanted to redeem my knowledge of the fine arts by uttering "Klimt," or—I lifted the mug to my lips, pensively—by noting the two Corinthian columns that marked the entranceway into the dining room. Instead, I nodded approvingly, though to me the couple had always seemed strangely wrapped in a metallic shroud, mummified in gold, the woman's head crooked in the man's grip.

"Let it cool," she said.

I blew, and said, "Your hair."

"He speaks." Daisy grinned and wriggled her fingers through her curls. "This is what happens when I don't spend an hour with a brush and dryer. Sit." We went around opposite sides of the coffee table and sat on the couch. "Oh my." She reached for my ponytail, twisting it as if to get a better view of some foul growth on my neck. "When was the last time you got a haircut?"

"Couple years."

She gestured with scissoring fingers toward my hair. I flinched, holding the hot tea out from my knees.

"You need to take care of yourself," she said. "Let me trim it."

I inched away. "I didn't come here for a haircut."

"Oh. Of course."

I hadn't meant to sound so blunt. "But thanks."

She grinned. "I'm a professional. You have too nice a face."

I sipped. She didn't seem depressed—and certainly not crazy.

"I'll do it right now. If you come where I work, it costs you fifty dollars. Plus tip."

"You're really a hairdresser?"

"That's what I'm saying, *vreh*. Just a trim. If you want a good style, whatever."

I jiggled my ponytail. "This took too long."

She put her mug down and swiped my arm away. "It looks like a squirrel." She removed the rubber band and combed my hair with her fingers. "You're like a big Jesus. You're too old not to have a man's haircut."

"Jesus was older than I am."

"That was the style." She tugged me by the wrist toward the dining room. "Come."

I stood, slouching. "Mrs. Diamond, I—"

"Peter!" She whipped around and with both hands pinched my cheeks, her eyes darkening.

In a flash I braced myself for the manic explosion.

"If you call me that again— How would you like it if I called you Mister Pappas?" Her voice softened. "Now, your hair is damaged, and I can help." She led me up the stairs. "You'll just sit there like a good boy, and I'll fix everything." She grinned over her shoulder.

I looked back into the living room at nothing in particular, feeling something like relief.

Just beyond the upstairs landing, the bathroom door opened inward against a yellow tub. In the window above the toilet, telephone wires crisscrossed before a background of leafy green trees. A corrugated silver roof jutted out just below, blocking the view of the back yard, except for a narrow brick path inside a wall of tall shrubs and wooden fence. I imagined my father on a Sunday afternoon, one-fisting a motorless mower pulled out from the cellar, rusty old blades slashing and spitting thick city grass, mystified, as I was now, by this woman's ability to ensnare me, by my own submission. A brief hiss came from behind the tile walls, and water exploded into the tub. Daisy Diamond shut the door and tested the water with her fingertips.

"On your knees," she said.

"Mrs.—"

Her mouth opened in amused shock, her hand poised to smack. "Repeat after me. *Day*— Say it." She gripped my face with her wet fingers and moved my chin. "Day...*zeee*."

"Daisy."

"Very good, now get your head down there."

I knelt at the tub's ledge, hunched over the cool porcelain, hands splayed on the tub floor. Water gushed at my ear. Daisy kicked her green plastic sandals into the corner, rolled her jeans up to her calves, stepped over the tub wall, and sat with her hip at my shoulder. Her hand on my neck guided me under the metal edge of the faucet. A lid clicked. A bottle spit. Her toes scrunched in the water. Her painted toenails glimmered like pink stones.

"How long have you cut hair?" I turned my head, and water rushed into my ear.

"Too long. It's not exactly my dream come true." She fingertipped my cheek back toward the water.

"You don't like it?" Warmth enveloped my head.

"I didn't say that," she said.

"Are you *good?*"

"Leave it to me." Daisy nudged my head out from the faucet. Fingers and foam filled my hair.

"What was your dream?" I asked.

"I don't remember," she said.

"*C'mon*. I'm curious."

"I was an actress."

My father's story confirmed—some kind of performer.

"Why didn't you—or *don't* you…?" I said.

"Well, I *didn't* for a few reasons. And I *don't* because I got old."

"You're not *old*," I said.

"For some things I am, I'm afraid."

When Daisy's hands stopped, I wiped foam from my eyes and squinted up at her. She gripped my head like a melon, moved it back under the water. I palmed the tub floor. Suds swirled toward the drain, like clouds above my fingers.

"So what were the reasons?"

She sighed. "Well, to begin with, I came here when I was eighteen and got married when I was twenty-one. When my husband got sick, I took care of him, and when he died, my mother got sick. So for ten years I was back and forth to Greece, taking care of her. Three months here, three months there. I didn't know if I was coming home or leaving home. Then she died, I woke up, and I was forty-three. That's it. I wanted to act and sing on Broadway, and I ended up in my own little Greek tragedy. My good friend with a hair salon said, hey, you need to make a living, you're artistic, it's not brain science, so I learned—and now here we are in America."

"Why haven't you remarried?"

Daisy's hands stopped.

I hadn't meant to conduct an interview. But I was intrigued. I wanted to know more.

She guided my head out from under the pounding water, which cooled and stopped. The pipes thumped. She stepped toward the corner closet for a towel, and snickered, finally, "Maybe if I were ten years younger, Peter." Instantly, her words, thrilling and provocative, moved deep into me and boiled, welling up in my belly, as I waited on hands and knees. Eyes clenched, I imagined her grinning, as she sat back down. With her fingers she combed my slick hair forward, a black drape drizzling before my eyes, the waxy remnants of conditioner, mint or menthol, tingling as the air met my scalp.

I dreaded what was bound to happen next. Daisy would tell me to sit up, and, throbbing, I would pretend to have something in my eye, just as I had in high school when my prayers not to be called to the chalkboard had been denied. Even then I'd known I was too old to be aching like this in the middle of calculus class—but I'd been left to the mercy of the girl who sat right behind me, Becky McDermott. She, too, knew what she was doing, when she slid her polished fingernails over my shoulders and pulled me back so she could see my notebook, which I lifted a little higher. She would whisper in her smoker's breath that we would make a great couple if only I weren't too smart for her. "You're the type of guy I'm going to marry." I knew what she meant—it was what I'd been coming to realize: that I would have to wait for girls, or at least girls like Becky, that whatever they wanted now I didn't have to offer, and whatever I had to offer now they wouldn't need for a while. In the meantime, I pretended that the reason she never had her homework on Mondays had nothing to do with the well-known fact that she spent the weekends with her college boyfriend.

"On the toilet."

My head was swathed in a thick white towel. I twisted, hunched over, as Daisy took a comb and scissors from the mirrored cabinet above the sink. She parted my hair in the middle, girlish strands falling past my cheeks. On her pale belly, a line of hair, like faint brown zipper teeth, zigzagged into her jeans. With my wrist I nudged myself between my legs.

"I need to tell you, Peter. I was at the lowest point of my life yesterday, and I can't thank you enough."

"What'd I do?"

Daisy lifted my chin in her hands, leaned and kissed my forehead. "You gave me what I needed. You didn't need to hear those things."

I was shocked to hear her speak at all of yesterday.

And yet perhaps Daisy's lies were no less embarrassing than the ones I told myself: I was a tireless romantic, prepared to endure a life of celibacy; a mystic, whose beliefs had not yet crystallized; an observer of the world, prepared to endure manual labor as long as my aesthetic philosophy remained not fully formed. The lies we told ourselves to survive. She was the alienated mistress of a beloved priest, whose world she'd selflessly protected from their secret for years; she'd sacrificed Broadway glory to be the tragic hero of her own drama.

Who could say who was crazy?

As quickly as I'd swelled up, I shrank into a wrinkled balloon pinched in my jeans. I tugged discreetly at the denim at my thigh, adjusting my keys, feeling for the pink slip.

"Let's start with the ends." Daisy squeezed hair near my shoulder. "You won't even notice."

Her thick curls dangling at my eyes, I breathed in the cool detergent scent of her shirt. A wet clump of hair, the length of a finger, dropped onto my thigh.

"Jesus," I said.

"Trust me."

She pressed my head down with her fingertips. I bowed.

This was it, time to let go.

She loosened my collar, drawing the comb over the ridges of my spine. Water drops slipped into the nest of hair on my chest. Shears closed down on the thick mass against my neck, the cool, smooth edge gliding across my skin until the grinding ceased. A limp black clump—a nest or a small animal—in her hand, she paused, and stared out the window.

"I've never been good with endings." She offered an embarrassed laugh, and glanced down at me. "I should be by now."

I smiled sympathetically. I knew a bit about holding on to the past. I picked hairs from my jeans, and, leaning forward, rubbed my fingers above a yellow plastic trashcan beneath the sink. Daisy reached down to lay my severed ponytail inside it, a plastic tomb for this dead black thing.

The air was light and cool against my neck.

She wiped her hand on her thigh.

"Have you ever thought of getting a pet?" I regretted the question instantly. As if a cat could fill the void. I anticipated the scissors plunging into my idiotic neck.

Instead, with her comb she gently carved a line in my scalp. Inches of hair fell like chipped bark onto my hands and jeans.

"I had a fat little dachshund," Daisy said. "I can't even throw out his bowl and leash. I like it hanging there in the kitchen, as if we're going for a walk later. Sometimes I even put a bowl of water on the back steps. I'm not crazy—I just think maybe some bird or squirrel will come."

The bowl, the leash, like the old man's jeans and sneakers—and like a certain kept letter from Dorothy Maloney: all relics of a harmless myth.

Minutes later I was standing before the mirror, not prepared to see the overgrown Beaver Cleaver returning my horrified stare. Damp jags of hair that wouldn't stay back drooped onto my forehead. The part, on the side of my head, appeared silvery—not gray, I was relieved to realize, but glowing, my scalp exposed. Over my ears were bluish arcs, smooth skin where hair had never sprouted.

"Cary Grant," Daisy said.

Be silent, I reminded myself. My stomach sank, and I looked away from my reflection. From this angle, out the window, through a gap in the aluminum roofing just below, I saw that there was no grass at all. No lawn to mow. What I'd thought was a brick border along the perimeter of the property was in fact the edge of a brick courtyard.

"I should go," I said.

When I reached for the doorknob, Daisy took hold of my wrist.

"You look very handsome," she said.

"Thanks." I opened the door as far as her hip.

She stood in the doorway. "I enjoyed doing that for you."

I nodded. "I'm glad you're okay now."

Daisy folded her arms and leaned against the doorframe. "What do you mean?"

I put my hand on the sink. "You *know*..."

"No, I *don't* know." Her posture inflated. "But I'm interested to know how it is you think I'm suddenly okay after all I've told you."

"Just— that everything's behind you now."

"Nothing is *behind* me, Peter. I'm shocked. That's not how it works. Maybe for *you*—"

"Mrs. *Diamond*—"

Her hand flashed from her armpit and smacked my cheek. "Don't *mock* me." She stood, legs spread.

I held my jaw. "*Sorry*— I have to go. I didn't mean anything." As I stepped, a stiff finger jabbed into my chest.

"Listen to me, *Mister Pappas*. I am not whatever you think I am. I'm not some whore that goes to bed with anyone off the street—"

"*What?*"

"You think my life is somehow better than it was yesterday? I want you to know, I am *not* okay, and you, Peter, have nothing to do with anything..."

"Fine."

"You think you're doing me a favor coming here today?"

"I'm sorry I came." I broke through her arm and started down the steps.

"You came here to make your*self* feel better."

I stopped, halfway down. "You need help, Mrs. Diamond."

"How *dare* you?"

I looked up, leaning against the wall, arms crossed.

"Leave, Peter."

She stepped into the shadows of the hallway.

"I just wanted to *help*. I mean…" I climbed a step, her pale ankles visible between the columns of the banister, her feet settled into the rug. "I wanted to make sure you were okay." I climbed the stairwell until my eyes met hers in the shadows.

She gazed down at me through the railing. Behind her at the end of the hallway an inch of light came from under a bedroom door. Her face was gray, her whisper gravelly: "I promise I won't mention you in my suicide note."

I grasped a post of the banister and lowered a knee toward the steps.

"You're safe," she said. "It won't be your fault. Isn't that what you're worried about? That I'm some kind of maniac you'll feel responsible for? Please go. I feel less alone when I'm here by myself." She flicked her hand, shooing me.

I stood my ground.

"Before you got here, I was fine," she said. "I was playing my music, drinking my tea." The music had stopped. "I don't need your help." She raised her eyebrows, apparently amused by my mute paralysis. "I've got my own toys to play with."

I shoved my fist, along with the pink piece of paper, into the depths of my pocket.

"Why don't you act anymore?" I said.

"I preferred you silent."

"I'm serious."

"My time is up, Peter. You're a *boy*. Plus, you have biology on your side."

"What about adoption?"

"*What?* Oh, Peter, you are something else. You think I want to be a single *mother*? I said I missed my window of opportunity—as an *actress*."

"I mean your opportunity with a *man*."

She shook her head. "You're very sweet, but you might take your own advice."

"What's *that* supposed to mean?"

She laughed, approaching me. "Nothing." She took my arm and directed me down the steps. "I appreciate what you're doing. You're young, you're kind, smart, handsome. You should be out there with a young, smart, beautiful girl."

In the dining room she nudged me, teasingly, it seemed, toward the door. "You should walk up to Walnut Street," she said, "right now. Go. That's where the action is. The cafés. Go shopping. Treat yourself."

"You should come with me," I heard myself say.

"Don't be silly. Believe it or not, I have things to do." She gestured toward the coffee table. "Please, Peter, I don't need your pity."

"I don't pity you." I faced her abruptly.

She looked up at me with darkening eyes.

I thought of her kiss, yesterday, in this same spot, and now *I* wanted to kiss *her*. I wanted to shovel her into me. My thumbs remained hooked in my pockets, as her hands rose to my head. With her fingernails she combed the short hair above my ears. You're beautiful, I thought. I wanted to say it. I should have told her earlier when I'd had the chance, instead of suggesting she get a pet, or adopt. Only the faint spidery lines at the sides of her eyes indicated her age. Her fingertips arched over my ears to examine the bristly back of my neck. She fluffed the sides, flicked tiny hairs from my cheek. "Okay," she said. "Time's up." I imagined my fingers climbing her back, my nose sinking into her hair as we embraced. "If you want another haircut, you'll have to come to the salon." You're beautiful, I would whisper into her ear. Or I would ask her to the movies. "It's right around the corner," she added. My thumbs had unhooked from my pockets, and my hands hovered at her waist.

When she hugged me and said, "Goodbye, Peter," rising to kiss my cheek, she must have felt my blood pulsing. "Let's not be foolish," she said.

She reached for the door, through which I obediently stepped, feeling ridiculous, until I realized, gazing back from the sidewalk and remembering Becky McDermott from calculus class, that "foolish" only meant wanting a girl who said she wasn't right for you but who knew deep down that, come Monday, you were the one she needed.

6
Like Zorba

For years, on Pentecost, Bishop Manopoulos, who was also a Paul, had been coming to the East Birch church to assist in the service and then to our house for Sunday dinner—a June 29th-name-day tradition shared by old friends. Among the reasons I had always liked the bishop was that his visits meant grilled sirloins and mashed potatoes, the bishop's favorite. As a boy I was fascinated by the bishop, who entered the house laughing at nothing, his grin tucked into his soft white beard, his eyes dark slits full of magic, his hands stuffed into his long, dark-blue robe as if about to emerge with candy and toys. When my mother hugged the bishop, I imagined him lonely at home, understanding that a bishop could never be married. Instead of gifts, the bishop brought new jokes, just one or two, which he told after dinner as we ate ice cream. When he delivered the punch line he leaned back, patting his belly, and howled silently with surprised delight, as if having heard the joke for the first time. My father and Andrew roared till they teared up, while my mother rolled her eyes at me—I didn't get the joke either. As I got older I wondered how this man who seemed more like a monk, or Santa Claus, could be in charge of all the churches, a job that seemed better suited for my father, who could never be the bishop because he'd made the decision, before becoming a priest, to get married and have a family.

When I returned home from the city, entering the driveway and pulling up alongside the bishop's black Buick, a little boy on the old Big Wheel braked where the concrete floor of the garage met macadam. The boy's eyes stayed glued on me as I approached. He might have sensed that I was the Big Wheel's rightful owner, in spite of the generous spirit of whoever had hauled it down from the attic. Still, the boy's expression seemed less one of fear than of determination. He gripped the handles, elbows rising and dipping, gassing it, as if taking aim at me.

"It's okay," I said. "You can ride it."

In blue and white striped T-shirt, tan camper shorts, and black, hard-soled lace-up shoes, the boy stared, single-minded, heels hooked onto the pedals, even as I stepped into the garage toward the door into the kitchen.

"Let's see ya do it." I pointed to the driveway.

The boy blinked.

"What's your name?" I asked.

Maybe the kid was deaf. I turned the doorknob. The boy pedaled an inch, the plastic tire scraping the concrete. I pushed the door in, and the boy pedaled some more. Finally, I stepped inside and closed the door, and outside the plastic wheels ground slowly and got their traction. I cracked the door to see the boy riding into the driveway, knees bobbing like pistons. Suddenly a little pale leg locked up against the pedal, and the boy skidded to a stop. He stared up at what must have seemed like a great big truck, not the lame piece of shit that had stalled twice on the way home.

"What's going on over there?" my mother said, before erupting with joyful surprise, her hands rising to her cheeks, as I turned into the kitchen. "Look at you!" She dashed with arms outstretched toward my newly shaped head. "What is it?" the old man called from the living room. "Peter cut his hair!" My mother, geared up for her afternoon walk, in her powder-blue, terry-cloth sweat suit, gripped my head like a volleyball. "You look wonderful. Sandy, you met Peter. Look at this handsome guy." At the kitchen table the wife of the new assistant priest was spoon-feeding her baby. "Looks great," she said. Another son, a couple years older than the one on the Big Wheel, held two fistfuls of Star Wars action figures—mine—and, frozen like his little brother, seemed to be both proclaiming ownership and waiting for permission to resume playing.

"Come in, let's see!" the old man called out. I walked to the living-room entranceway. "Holy—!" My father shot up from the corner chair. "Bravo! Look at that!" He reached for my hand to shake and turned around to introduce me, as if for the first time, to the bishop and the assistant priest, who simultaneously stood from their chairs. "You remember Father Chris, Peter..."

That my having got a haircut could give my parents such a sense of pride made me feel pathetic, as if I were the source of a long-lost joy, as if I were a recovered drug addict, home after months of rehab, tracks on my arms gone, everyone mixed up with feelings of relief— that I was better now—and regret—that I'd lived so much of my life in that sad old condition. The bishop put his arms out for a hug. His smooth, silvery nest of a beard smelled of incense and talcum powder.

My mother rubbed the tender back of my neck. "Like a movie star. Who do you look like?"

"Cary Grant," I said.

"Hah!" she said. "That's right."

"Who was open on a Sunday?" my father said.

"Alan Bates," the bishop said.

We all looked at the bishop. Alan Bates?

"From *Zorba*," the bishop said. "The other guy."

"We should be going," Father Chris said.

Sandy had stepped into the living room with the baby tucked into a stroller.

"Are you sure?" my father said. "You're welcome to stay as long as you like."

"If you don't mind," Father Chris said.

"Of course not," my father said. "We'll get you home."

I anticipated playing chauffeur.

Since Father Chris and his family had returned from Africa last month, they hadn't bought a car, and, I assumed, considering the salary of a missionary and, now, of an assistant priest, they weren't about to. They were living, indefinitely—"for as long as he wants, as long as they can stand it," the old man had said to me—on the property adjacent to the church, a cottage-style house that ordinarily served as additional office and storage space. This past spring, once it was official that Father Chris had chosen the East Birch assistantship, I helped my father make way for the new family, clearing out desks, filing cabinets, and unsold stuff from the annual bazaar—books, clothes, jewelry—hauling it all across the church parking lot and into

Sunday-school classrooms. My father bragged, "He could have gone *anywhere*," quoting Temple University's familiar ad campaign, "but he chose…" I humored the old man, substituting "St. Peter's Greek Orthodox Church" for "Temple." My father mused, "It'll be nice to have such a competent guy by my side."

A few weeks ago on a weeknight, after the old man fell asleep in his chair and the new assistant politely endured a history lesson from Theo, the two of them riffling through books from the living-room shelves, I drove Father Chris home, his long, black-slacked legs cramped in the foot space of the pickup. I learned that Father Chris had been a high-school basketball star in the suburbs north of New York City, and, like my father, had gone on to play his sport at the Division One level at Holy Cross. After a year doing missionary work in Africa, he said, he couldn't wait to get settled and have a normal life, to have a driveway with a basketball hoop. He loved East Birch, what a great parish, a perfect area to raise a family, a lot like where he'd grown up, and, he said, the timing of your father's retirement couldn't be better. At the time I didn't break the news to Father Chris that the old man might not be relinquishing the lead role anytime soon, that on a daily basis he second-guessed his decision to retire. Of course— no regrets—getting Father Chris to be his assistant had been a great victory. "Everyone wants this guy," my father had said that day, lugging a box filled with Crop Walk posters across the hot asphalt.

In the kitchen Sandy was gathering up the baby's things—the food, the bib, the spoon—into a bag strapped over her shoulder. "C'mon, Kimon," she said mildly to her son, who mournfully tucked Darth Vader into the collector's carrying case. Sandy, a small, lovely girl, who seemed no older than me, was gathering up her kids to head home with the guy who'd been selected to follow in the old man's footsteps. "He's a rising star in the church," my father had said, as if it were possible that I still hadn't gotten the point. "His wife is sweet, a beautiful family. He's bright, athletic. You think I want just *anyone* taking over?"

Father Chris took the baby from his wife, who took the older son's hand and led the way toward the front door.

"We'll take the Lexus," the old man said, twirling a single giant key on a finger. "Keep Bishop Manopoulos company, Peter." The old man opened the storm door as the little boy on the Big Wheel rolled up the sidewalk and into the grass.

I followed the bishop. His blue robe fell so perfectly flush with the glossy surface of the hardwood that he appeared to be gliding. He turned into the bathroom.

In the kitchen my mother bent over to tighten her laces. "Help yourself. A couple steaks left, mashed potatoes, and salad. You all right?"

I nodded.

She smiled and slipped out through the screen door.

A few weeks before, my mother had, amazingly, hit the magic forty mark—forty pounds—reaching her goal two months early. In less than a year she had transformed herself, slimming down to a size four, once again able to squeeze into her wedding dress—"if I were so inclined," she'd joked at dinner recently, winking at the old man. Still, she was sticking to her routine, happy, she'd added, to be walking without a particular goal in mind. Late last August she and my father had gone, for the first time in years, to the Jersey shore. Andrew had, for their anniversary, bought them a bed-and-breakfast weekend, not in Wildwood, where we'd vacationed as a family, but north, in a town east of New Hope, right on the beach, where, Andrew had explained, you don't eat pizza and *gyros*. On Saturday evening, in a scene that threatened to end prematurely their romantic getaway, my mother yanked her old lemon-yellow one-piece only as high as mid-thigh before announcing she felt sick from something they had eaten and did not want to leave the room. They had hobnobbed in town during the day—in antique stores, galleries, cafés—and now she'd just persuaded the old man to don his trunks and go for a swim. Eventually they made their way downstairs to the back deck for their dinner reservation, which was part of the package deal, and, already on a mission, she ate only the apple slices and lettuce in her salad.

It was not until two months later, after she'd lost a recognizable amount of weight—it was on the Sunday night of the Crop Walk, in October, after she and Sophia had just walked twenty miles to help stop world hunger—that she told the whole story, at the dinner table, eating peaches and cottage cheese, while everyone else ate *spanako-pita*. When the elastic of the thigh hole had stretched to its limit, she said, she had braced herself for a nervous breakdown, just as the number forty—*pounds*, she'd realized—had come into her head. It had seemed outrageous—*forty*—she admitted; after all, if she lost only ten pounds she would fit into the bathing suit—but it had seemed like a calling, a vision. And that was that. She went on to reveal, with a kind of flirty air, which was as surprising to me as it must have been to my father and everyone else sitting there, that before they left the bed-and-breakfast on Sunday afternoon, she'd not only made a reservation for the same weekend the following August but tossed the lemon-yellow one-piece into the trash can in the bathroom, promising herself that, come hell or high water, in one year she would wear a brand-new size-four bikini on an evening swim with her husband. "Bravo!" Theo had called out, and everyone applauded. She reassured everyone—particularly Theo, who suddenly stopped clapping, struck dumb by the fear we all shared—that her diet would not affect the cooking around here, a promise already fulfilled, she pointed out, by the *spanakopita* we were all eating.

Three grilled steaks lay in brown juice under Saran wrap on a giant ceramic platter next to the sink. I pressed a finger to the warm plastic. I ate at the kitchen table.

"You never see *Zorba?*" the bishop said, startling me.

I choked down a mouthful of mashed potatoes, as the bishop sat down across from me.

"You working hard?" the bishop said.

I wasn't sure what he meant exactly—right now, eating? "Painting houses?"

"It's a good job?"

I nodded, cutting my steak.

"This man wants your father's job. Now your father doesn't want to give it to him." The bishop folded his hands on the table. "What are you gonna do?" My steak lodged briefly in my throat, until the bishop shrugged and I realized he'd meant the question only rhetorically.

"Your work is important. This Chris, he has a family..." The bishop tossed his fingers. "Wife, kids. The full catastrophe." The bishop grinned; his shoulders bounced. He raised his eyebrows, anticipating a response from me; I'd stopped chewing, missing the joke. "*Ela, vreh*"—C'mon—"*Zorba the Greek*. You have to see this movie. Anthony Quinn." The bishop reached for the bowl of peanuts. "I don't know. Don't ask me..."

I offered a quizzical smile, then realized the bishop was still contemplating the issue of the old man's job.

"What would Zorba do?" the bishop asked, and then answered, "He would dance. That's what he would do. What does that tell you?"

I was curious. "I don't know."

"Nothing. I can't help your father. He needs to decide for himself. Do I want him to retire? Of course not. Why should I? I'm seventy-five myself. What do I know about retiring? But now this young man is here with his family..." The bishop separated a peanut and looked at its insides. Chewing half the peanut, he held the other half between his thumb and fingertip, lifting it for me to see. "You know the *papou* inside the peanut?"

This was a riddle, I thought, or the after-dinner joke. The bishop handed me the peanut half, and I examined what my *yiayia* had first revealed to me as a boy: the tiny wrinkled head at the knotted tip, where the peanut divided, the little old Greek man's deep bushy brow and walrusy mustache. Maybe the bishop was about to reveal its hidden meaning.

"He looks like a sailor," the bishop said.

"Looks like a bishop." I handed it back. "The hat."

The bishop squinted. "Or the pope."

"*So...?*"

The bishop looked up. "*Ti thelis?*"—What do you want?

"What does it mean?" I asked.

"*Mean?*" The bishop popped the peanut into his mouth, his mustache curling over his silvery smile. "Don't think. Just eat."

I nodded, slightly disappointed, and then said, "Like Zorba."

"Ahh, 'at's a boy." The bishop laughed.

I was pleased to have made the connection.

"So what do you think?" the bishop said. "Maybe in five years your father is ready to give up his job?"

"Maybe ten," I quipped.

"Maybe never, eh? Like me. If you go to the seminary now, when you finish—it's not too late—you take your father's job. Find a nice Greek girl to be *presvytera*, like your mother."

Et tu, Bishop?

I shook my head, no, I don't think so, waiting for the wink: *just kidding*.

Instead, the bishop said, "You like painting houses?"

"It's not my dream come true." I swept up the last of the mashed potatoes with my fork.

"How much longer will you do it?"

I shrugged and took my dish to the sink. I dug through the freezer, my back to the bishop. Had my parents put the bishop up to this, recruited him to counsel their floundering son, to pick my brain, feel me out, and enlist me for the seminary? With a spoon I scraped at the insides of a carton of mint-chocolate-chip ice cream, lingering in the cold cloud drifting past my face. Come to think of it, no sooner had I gotten home than my parents had rushed out, leaving me alone with the bishop.

Did my father still have dreams of my taking over the reins? In spite of my five-year hiatus from the church? Maybe the old man was determined to retire after all, but only if I were the one, and not Father Chris, to be following in his footsteps. Standing there with my back to the bishop, I was surprised to feel a long-lost sense of excitement mixing with the more familiar sense of dread. Still, no way was I going down my father's path.

I was used to being badgered about finding a nice Greek girl, but it had been years since anyone had bugged me about becoming a priest, a job option I hadn't openly humored since college. Even then, it hadn't taken long for my faith—or at least my aspiration to follow the old man's lead—to begin to crumble. It had taken only an Introduction to Theology course for me to lose my conviction to campaign for the one Lord, Jesus Christ, the only-begotten Son of God, as my Creed proclaimed. When I announced once and for all that my religion studies would probably never lead to more than a college major—and only a minor, as it turned out—my father encouraged me passionately, revealing in so many words that I represented his last hope. After all, Andrew was officially a doctor and Sophia was, and, presumably, would remain, female, a biological fact that, to my great envy, left her off the hook, though, ironically, the rule excluding her from the priesthood had inspired the first of her many church boycotts, her complete lack of interest in the priesthood notwithstanding. Hedging his bets, the old man encouraged me at least to continue my religion studies, hailing theologians as scholars. And when I settled on an irrelevant major, still the old man did not give up hope, pointing out that a doctorate, even in Art History, with the right focus—say, the Byzantine period—could still land you a good job—you could be a professor—maybe even at the seminary—certainly at a school like Holy Cross. To this day, my golden-starred *Summa Cum Laude* sticker drew looks of curious admiration, the framed diploma hanging in the living room next to the senior portrait of a much fairer-skinned Sophia.

After a year of painting houses I had been recruited to give the church walls a fresh coat of light peach. Why hire expensive professionals when your gifted son could do it, with some help from Stavros, the versatile custodian? While I was taping down sheets of plastic to protect the icons and stained glass, my father stood staring up at Jesus on the ceiling and said, "Ever think about iconography?" It would never end, I thought, and reminded the old man that I wasn't that kind of painter. My father said, "No, I mean as a *scholar* of iconography. With *your* background? You'd be *perfect…*" I didn't try to explain at the time—or at any time since—less because I was reluctant to confess to my father than because I wasn't sure myself—how these tired old images, most of them full-sized portraits of martyrs who all resembled each other, now seemed less important to me than the modern versions of Jackie Kennedy or Marilyn Monroe.

I tossed the spoon into the empty carton on the counter and

resumed searching the freezer. I pulled two Popsicles from a box in the back and held one up in its paper wrapper. The bishop seemed to be contemplating the back yard.

"Twin pop?" I said.

The bishop turned to see. "*Ti eineh aftoh?*"—What is it?

"Ice pop. Lime or Grape."

The bishop scrunched his nose.

I put the lime pop back into the box and closed the freezer door. I snapped the grape Popsicle in two, a wooden stick in each hand, and gave half to the bishop, who chomped off the steaming purple tip.

At last the bishop smiled. "One day you wake up, and you painted enough houses, and then what? You be like Zorba, jumping around, island to island, with no home. For eternity."

7
An Investigation of the Sublime

On the wall above my desk at home, Tug McGraw stretches toward the sky, elevated by the dirt mound beneath his cleats. The Phillies are World Champions. In a moment, Mike Schmidt will lead the swarm of celebrants. But in the immortal instant framed in the picture, carefully torn from the 1981 yearbook, it is as if Tug McGraw is God, reaching for God. At once one man and one city.

"Ya Gotta Believe!"

These are the words printed at the bottom of the page, just below the autograph the old man managed to procure simply by calling out these same words during pre-game batting practice. My father and Andrew blocked the view, but I could still make out his smile, hear his laugh, and for a moment thought maybe Tug McGraw and my father were friends, maybe they'd even played baseball together—impossible, I calculated later, back in my seat, gazing at the yearbook in my lap, recalling, as I would for years, that fall—that moment—the thrilling sense of being at the center of the universe.

Next to Tug McGraw on the wall above my desk is another icon, of Peter and Paul, First in Prominence among the Apostles, haloed, before a backdrop of gold, holding in their hands, between them, the church—literally—ahead of its time, in Byzantine style, domed, with a cross on top—the size of a large bird cage. Peter—*petra*, the rock, on which the church was built—had been Simon, a fisherman, who, Jesus insisted, in spite of Peter's protestations, would deny Him three times—a safe prediction if one considered the punishment the Romans had in store. One day Saint Peter would be crucified upside down, while, across town, Paul was being beheaded. Who could blame Peter for avoiding arrest? And who could be surprised when Peter came around, after meeting the risen Jesus, who forgave him completely and reaffirmed his calling? Who *wouldn't?*

Since the Saturday when my father told me to get a life—specifically, to get a place of my own, a nice Greek girl, a job I could be proud
of, et cetera—I had been carrying around in my pocket, rubber-band-
ed like a single team of baseball cards, a thin stack of blank three-by-
five note cards, the kind high-school kids used in the early stages of
research-paper assignments; in fact, I'd snagged the plastic-wrapped
pack from Sophia's desk drawer, above which hung three posters of
figures who inspired her—Bob Marley, Che Guevara, and Nike of
Samothrace. The winged goddess had lost her head, and once had
arms that held a musical instrument, her chest thrust out from tremendous wings—she'd descended from the skies to lead her triumphant
ship home. Sophia had been delighted by my comparison of her and
Winged Victory when I gave her the poster for her birthday last year,
so when I came for the note cards I was both pleased and saddened
to find her standing on her desk, scissors in hand, delicately slicing the
Scotch tape that held down its corners. "She's coming with me to
California."

Now that Sophia was gone, it would be all the more difficult to
buckle down on the matter at hand, not because I already missed
her—though I *did* miss her, and she'd been gone only since this morning—but because, in her, I'd always had an audience. She had been,
after all, the only person—since Dorothy—who had ever been wooed
by what I had to say about any of this stuff.

Last Saturday I had committed myself to a strict deadline and three
very reasonable goals: in two weeks I would put a dent in my art
book, at the very least by filling out two dozen note cards, and I would
speak to the cute blond from the rental office at Stone Bridge
Apartments. By accomplishing the latter goal, I would be both inquiring about apartments for bachelors as well as attempting to lay the
groundwork for dating a nice girl, albeit a non-Greek one.

The former goal should have been easy, since what I intended to
write down were ideas that had been merely lying dormant; it was
only a matter of sparking a light in those dark recesses of my mind. I
had once been inspired by Shepard Stillman, whom the Art History
majors called Saint, not Professor, when they weren't calling him

Shep—a name I had relished using, once I'd mustered the confidence. In the past week I had reread all my old papers from Shep's seminars, arranging them on my desk, culling the Philadelphia-related papers from the pile and creating categories—murals, architecture, sculptures—which would represent the major sections of my book—and sub-categories, dividing the sections into chapters, defined by era—pre-Anti-Graffiti Network, post-Anti-Graffiti Network; pre-City Hall, post-City Hall; and three eras for sculptures, demarcated by the Calders: the grandfather, Alexander Milne Calder—creator of *William Penn*—who begot Alexander Stirling Calder—creator of *Swann Memorial Fountain*, also known as *The Fountain of Three Rivers*—who begot Alexander "Sandy" Calder, creator of mammoth mobiles, such as *Ghost*, hanging in the Grand Stair Hall in the Museum of Art—the Father, the Son, and the Holy Ghost—three generations of monumental sculptures, all in a straight line extending the full length of the Ben Franklin Parkway, from the top of City Hall, to Logan Square, to Philly's own golden Parthenon a mile away.

I couldn't imagine that our magnificent boulevard, bordered with marble museums behind towering sycamores, was any less beautiful than theirs in Paris, the Champs Elysées, which had inspired Philadelphia's city planners, eager to merge art with architecture, and the city with nature—specifically with the largest urban park in the world, Fairmount Park, which William Penn had inadvertently named, observing, "What a fair mount," and which expanded from the grassy edges of the Parkway to the woodsy depths that stretched like fingers to meet the suburbs. In my senior year Shepard Stillman had driven an elite group of his loyal flock all the way out to Forbidden Drive, to the borders of the Park, where we left his van to scavenge the woods along Wissahickon Creek, to gaze—as he instructed—both *down*, at the ground beneath our feet—beyond, if we could—and *up*, at one high-arching stone bridge after another, the air silent but for the distant traffic and the crunching of branches and brown leaves. Shep said nearly nothing—he would just point—just as, in class, he would often let the projection of a slide glow for seconds that stretched out—the mad splatterings of a Jackson Pollock; the cracked-pot collage of a

Julian Schnabel; the inert darkness of a Richard Serra wall of steel, a colossal scar on a concrete plaza—the thing daring you to explain it, as Shep's own canvases did, his gigantic "ground paintings," swatches of earth raised up. We turned back for the van—then headed for the sculptures that lined Kelly Drive, our route to the city—only after trekking through Jody Pinto's anatomically correct *Fingerspan*, an enclosed bridge along a sheer hillside, nine tons of metal once descended from the heavens and threaded through the treetops by helicopter, its steel-skin walls filled with holes the size of eyes, windows to the gorge far below.

The art I liked best were the giant game pieces—tumbling dominoes; white pawns, black knights; Monopoly's silver wheelbarrow, the iron, the hat; blue bingo chips, B11, G59—scattered about the courtyard across from baroque City Hall. After a summer of obsession with the so-called Gnostic gospels, and the Nag Hammadi findings in general—three months in which I considered, less and less jokingly, that for my honors thesis I would edit and annotate what I would entitle *The Holy Appendix*—I wrote, instead, in the fall of my senior year, my best paper: "Lift Up the Stone, and You Will Find Me: The Gospel of Thomas and Plop Art: An Investigation of the Sublime in Thomas Paine Plaza."

As I read through the paper, albeit cursorily—as I'd been poring over my papers all week, rummaging through artifacts—it was hard to get a handle on what I'd been driving at back then, though I was impressed with the writing, as the editorial staff of Temple's academic journal, *Canto*, must have been when they made "An Investigation of the Sublime" the lead essay in the tenth-anniversary issue. I'd published a paper in the previous year's *Canto*, as well—"Turning the Church Inside Out: The Italian Renaissance Comes to Broad Street: Mural Iconography in Downtown Philadelphia." Celebrated in the paper was a seven-story mural—on the brick face of the old Girard bank, recently converted into high-end condominiums—modeled after Raphael's *School of Athens*, by the versatile Shep, misunderstood painter of leaves, who clarified his artistic vision: "With my Ground Paintings, I want to bring nature inside. With my murals I want to paint the students, the cab drivers, the Armenians who run the hoagie truck, not *as if* they are nobility, like Plato or Aristotle, but as the nobility they *are*, with their book bags, in their white aprons…. Painting murals isn't a shift in style for me, because I don't consider myself a nature painter, any more than I consider myself a muralist or a graffiti artist—all of which I've been—because context is everything. You don't impose your vision *on the world*, you *discover* your vision *in the world*, and the world varies with every step you take…. It's not just about self-expression; it's also about the world around you…. It's about having a point, and believing in it."

On the day of the "interview," I mentioned that I'd been considering a semester in Florence, expecting Shep to applaud my adventurousness. Instead, he asked, "Why?" and said there was plenty that I hadn't seen and done around here yet. "Have you been to the Guggenheim in New York? The MOMA?" He paused. "The *Museum of Modern Art*," he clarified, misinterpreting my frown. Shep had another apartment in SoHo. Here we were in his studio-office-apartment on Green Street. Suddenly, New York seemed as far away as Italy. "If you really want to learn about art, take a *studio* class. Try *making* something, instead of just writing about what *others* have made." Shep's famous unflinching deadpan either enhanced one's feeling insulted or confused one's feeling encouraged. In any case, I stayed put, and I took a studio class, an experience that confirmed my calling as something other than an artist.

Outside, the old man had revved up the Black & Decker, the cry of the chainsaw sounding, minutes ago, like any distant lawn mower. At first the muffled tapping had seemed inadvertent—my father's shoe nicking the plastic dome guarding the window above my bed—but then it came again, three knocks.

I pocketed my blank note cards and headed up.

The bishop followed my father along the walkway, the blue hem of his robe skipping at his heels on the white concrete, his hands clasped behind his back as though he were listening to birds singing, not to the old man shouting over the gassy, hacking-cough roar of the motor. From what I could make out, my father was complaining about

Theo's refusal to keep his aesthetic vision for the landscape confined to the back yard, where he'd been consigned since last summer. In an effort to create a more "natural" appearance, Theo routinely slashed at the right angles and rounded edges the old man so painstakingly maintained. The bishop nodded happily, though it was nearly impossible to hear what the old man was saying, until the motor stopped.

"...the last straw!" the old man kept shouting, "was when he unloaded all the grass clippings back onto the lawn! 'Natural fertilizer!'"

The bishop's shoulders bounced.

"Peter—ahh, you brought the rake," the old man said.

A small mountain of lush hemlock branches stood at my weathered Nikes.

"We need a trashcan—"

I plucked a still-folded Hefty bag from my back pocket, and let it unfold like a flag from my fist. My father set the chainsaw in the grass and peeled the bag open, as I stooped for the branches I sandwiched against the rake.

"Bravo," my father said. "I have more on the side of the house."

We made our way past my bedroom window toward snipped greens that led around the corner. The bishop drifted toward the white birches.

"Hey, there!" My mother chugged down the hill, pink-faced, in the final stretch.

The bishop waved, floating in the shadows toward the fence.

"Did you ask him to talk to me?" I said in a hushed voice.

"About what?" my father said. "No."

I raked the grass with my fingers. "I've got other ideas right now."

"I know. *Sigah, sigah*"—slowly, slowly. Then suddenly it was as if my father were rushing to squeeze more into the conversation, shaking the bag to settle the branches. "I keep thinking about your sister."

My mother was making her way across the yard, toward the bishop, in the shade of the trees.

"It's my fault, isn't it?" my father said.

"It's no one's fault," I blurted, wanting suddenly to relieve the old man of the weight he seemed to be hauling. "This will be good for her."

My mother was listening intently to the bishop, as they stepped out from under the canopy of the birches. The bishop might have been recapping our chat in the kitchen, or explaining how birch rods, like the one he swiped at the grass, were once used to beat, to *birch*, persecuted Christians. Or something else entirely, I realized, when my mother looked up from the bishop's hands, smiling, as something white, light—a fleck of skin from the tree—fell from his fingers.

8
Free LOVE Park

Every summer my boss, Eliot, hired a couple college kids—one of whom, five years ago, had been me—and took them into the suburbs to sand and prime shutters and drains while he manned the power washer and power painter. Eliot's bread-and-butter, though, remained the apartment complexes, whose units—each one comprising one or two bedrooms, a living room, dining room, kitchen, bathroom, and several closets—I could race through with masterful efficiency, almost as quickly as the young and upwardly mobile tenants seemed to move in and out of the places. After college I had wanted to get back to working with my hands; I'd seriously considered learning carpentry or plumbing. But you could get a job right away as a painter. In fact, you could be trained by the time your first lunch break rolled around; you could be an expert by the end of your first week on the job.

Just last week, late Friday afternoon, after coming all the way from Jenkintown to check out the finished apartment and lock up, Eliot handed over a ring of exactly five keys and said, "No reason for me to drive a half an hour every day now that you're pretty much my apartment guy." I was in the parking lot, packing up my truck for the drive home. As I hooked the five keys onto my key chain, I sensed that Eliot was expecting some expression of gratitude, as if my boss had just anointed me partner and granted me access to the safe in the office—not that Eliot had plans of sharing his business or that he had a safe or even an office. What Eliot had was a desk in the living room of an empty four-bedroom colonial in Conshohocken, a house that three years ago had been filled with his wife and three kids, who'd moved to Florida after the divorce. I had felt bad for Eliot, though the truth was I'd never been able to picture him as a husband or a father.

Eliot said he would be in Jenkintown again all next week, with the new guys, a couple of knuckleheads he had to keep his eye on, so he would check in with me now and then but certainly not every day. "When are you gonna get a cell phone?" he added. I didn't explain that if I had a cell phone, he wasn't the only one who'd be able to call me whenever, wherever—not that I was hiding from my parents in downtown crack houses or strip clubs. Still, I relished the little privacy I had.

As I did every Sunday evening, I assessed my inventory for the week, assembling in the corner of the garage what I needed for Monday. I envisioned myself, suddenly, in a nightmarish sequence of flashing images, in a year, ten years, twenty years, performing this same task, hunched over, back knotting up, belly bulging. In the morning I would back up my truck, open the hatch, and pile it all in—a five-gallon tub of bone-white flat paint, two cans of latex, primer, stain blocker, spackling paste, joint compound, caulk, caulk gun, roller trays, roller brushes, roller handles, brushes, mixing sticks, sandpaper, putty, scraper, tape, and drop cloth—before heading down the road to Stone Bridge Apartments, where I'd be painting another five units this week, at a pace of one per day, all by myself.

When I'd first gone job hunting after college, I'd been attracted to Eliot's impassive approach to daily life: I'm the boss, you're the employee; this is a paintbrush, there's the wall. Eliot was a man of few words, especially words of encouragement. There was no personal involvement—and no opportunity for vertical advancement—exactly what I'd been looking for.

But now enough was enough.

Slowly, slowly were my father's steady words of encouragement.

One note card at a time.

It dawned on me, the contradiction: the old man told me to take it slowly, slowly only when I set foot down the wrong path.

I knew what I needed to do, to light the spark. I'd wanted to have something to show for myself first, but tomorrow I would go see Shep—Saint Stillman.

"Good luck, Peter!" the bishop called out and ducked into his Buick.

The old man bowed at the bishop's open window, then stood as the Buick backed out of the driveway and headed toward Birch Hill.

My father crossed his arms, ruing the day, I guessed, that he'd set his mind on finding an assistant, or lamenting the fact that he'd be stepping down at all one day. I sympathized. The bishop had been right that I would get tired of painting houses; still, I would miss the job, just as I missed mowing lawns and being my own boss.

Now that I held the keys, I thought, there was no reason I couldn't at least *play* the self-employed man, no reason I couldn't drive down to the apartments tonight and set up shop for the week. After five years of playing the loyal employee, it was time to be my own boss again, or at least pretend to be.

The bishop's black Buick slowed down to a stop halfway up Birch Hill. I feared the bishop was having some kind of heart problem. Maybe he'd forgotten something—his hat or a wrapped plate of *kourampiedes*—and was about to back up. My father stepped into the yard, just as Freddy West swerved around the Buick and vanished into the pine trees that lined the Wests' back yard.

When the bishop's car continued up the hill, my father let out an exasperated breath and said, "That boy's going to kill himself one of these days, just like his brother."

I kept my mouth shut, not wanting to debate the matter. The old man had always considered Freddy a disaster waiting to happen, and now that Sophia was gone he must have regretted not tearing her away from the kid sooner. Freddy was the first boy Sophia had ever loved, or so she'd claimed, and he might have been the *last* boy, thanks to the old man, who'd done everything in his power to keep his daughter respectable. Now she would become as conspicuously uninterested in boys as was necessary to goad the old man into *begging* her to date a boy, even a boy without a drop of Greek blood in him, a boy with painted fingernails and purple hair that fell down over his eyes.

"Well," the old man said, stepping toward the house, "what are you gonna do?"—that rhetorical question again.

Only now I had an answer: "I thought I'd drive down to the apartments—set up shop for the week."

The old man seemed impressed, stopping in the grass. "Sounds like a plan." He gave me a firm pat on the shoulder and went inside.

As I packed up my truck, hauling the load from garage to tailgate, I thought about Freddy and his older brother, Brock, my best friend when I was growing up. Contrary to the old man's take on the West boys, Freddy was a good kid and Brock was more than just alive, having survived his ill-fated teens. Not unlike me, Freddy lived in the shadow of an older brother's reputation, though Brock's was a tarnished one. Freddy smoked cigarettes and rode a skateboard with a pot leaf drawn on it, but he wasn't a drug dealer, let alone a drug addict, nothing like Brock, whom most people—myself included—had been guilty, at one point or another, of writing off.

As a senior at Plymouth High School, Brock had gotten chased down for *garage-hopping*—stealing cases of beer out of his own neighbors' houses—a crime that might not have changed his life had he not run from the cops, empty-handed, through the Gimbles' back yard, slammed the trunk of his car, jumped in, and raced down Lincoln Drive and onto Kelly, getting almost to Boathouse Row before hopping the curb and skidding dramatically up to the edge of the river. During his attempt to avert arrest, Brock must have regretted having called attention to the fact that whatever he was hauling around inside his rusted-out Camaro was apparently worth risking his life for; he must have realized that no one in his right mind, not even a teenager hell-bent on saving himself from having a permanent criminal record, would flee the cops to ditch four-and-a-half cases of light beer. (The Kreiders claimed he'd lifted two cases of Miller Lite, the Brennemans one and a half cases of Coors Light, and the Gimbles one case of Bud Light—Brock must have returned to the Gimbles' garage for a second looting when he spotted the flashing lights.) In the trunk the cops found, all packed into the spare-tire compartment underneath the beer, several ounces of marijuana, along with a cornucopia of other popular drugs—random pills, as well as cocaine, acid, OxyContin, Ecstasy... The bust enlightened the local parents, as well as me, to the fact that the so-called popular drugs were all the drugs you'd ever heard of—and many you hadn't. The partying crowd at Plymouth was suddenly abuzz in the hallways and classrooms, well within earshot of teachers and out-of-the-loop kids, speaking openly, now that Brock's business was a past-tense thing—now that Brock himself might be a past-tense thing—as if it were cathartic to let out the secret they'd been harboring for so long: Brock had been the go-to guy, not just at Plymouth but throughout the neighboring districts and private schools.

Mythical versions of his arrest soon developed. The most agreed-upon theory about The Chase was that once Brock had found himself speeding away from red-and-blue lights, he'd decided to defect, to lead the cops back to the source in North Philly, strategizing that a white suburban kid playing Pied Piper might be able to win himself some points with the law, if not be celebrated as a self-appointed undercover vigilante (his light jail sentence later bolstered certain aspects of this story, namely that he was willing to point the finger); coming to his senses, he headed for the river, where he, along with the evidence, would plunge in, appearing, as he climbed the banks to safety, to be nothing more than a terrified, out-of-control kid, whose shitty old sports car, not to mention stolen beer, weren't worth recovering from the muddy Schuylkill. Of course he must have wimped out or he realized the river was shallow and so of course they would fish his car out and find his stash still dry and neatly packed in Ziploc bags and pill bottles.

I'd never suspected Brock of being a drug dealer—mystified, not to mention brokenhearted, as I'd been by the decline of our friendship. Now, I understood that Brock had traded me in for the money and adoration of local teenage junkies.

Lucky for Brock, he'd been only days shy of turning eighteen at the time of the arrest, so even though the identity of "the minor in question" didn't make it into the pages of the *Inquirer*'s Monday-morning local edition, the faces of my fellow students told the story: they appeared lost, some reflecting shock as well as sympathy for a friend and classmate who might be doing time instead of going to Middlebury, where he'd been admitted early-decision and had been planning to play lacrosse, some reflecting fear that Brock's shoes wouldn't be filled before they went into withdrawal and their symptoms began to manifest themselves.

Within a month, on house arrest—though not exactly home—Brock, tripping (literally, went the joke) on acid, launched himself from the second-floor deck of a friend's house and missed his mark, if his mark was the swimming pool and not the concrete surrounding it, though many speculated that the concrete *was* his mark and that these days he was as interested in going to college as he was in going to prison. Brock's model good looks and brooding, heroin-chic swagger helped elevate his legendary status, everyone, me included, imagining him, angelic, swan-diving into teenage oblivion.

The West boys had always been the adventurers. Brock had been the one with the dirt bike, the BB gun, the tree fort stocked with *Playboys;* he was the water skier, the motorbiker, the bungee jumper; the one who got stitches, chipped his tooth, broke his leg. He'd survived The Chase, just as he'd survived the acid-induced fall, just as he'd survived detention centers and rehab centers, just as he was surviving life in the world right now, wherever he was. His kid brother, Freddy, was no different, making a virtual living as a teenager who survived crashes, having landed a sponsorship from a skateboard company, who supplied him with free logo-covered stuff (boards, clothes, water bottles, stickers), which he, in exchange, sported in competitions—details that I'd picked up through Sophia's many tirades directed at the old man, who, having spotted her (allegedly) smoking cigarettes with Freddy, had forbidden her not only to go to the prom with him but to associate with him at all.

I heaved the tailgate shut and with two clenched fists launched my drop cloth, a blue tarp, over the packed truck bed. The thick plastic sheet ballooned and landed softly like a bedcover. I secured the sheet, weighing the corners down with paint cans and wedging loose material into gaps along the sides.

Halfway up Birch Hill I hit the brakes. Freddy had shot out once again from the Wests' driveway and was bearing down on my truck as if he were playing chicken—the kid's latest stunt? It was a wonder the bishop hadn't had a stroke. I waited for Freddy to swerve one way or the other. But as the kid gained speed, staring straight ahead—not looking especially determined or wearing a crazy grin—I began to wonder if Freddy was nuts enough to try to *jump* the truck, to lift off at the grill and then land on his trusty skateboard as it sailed out from under the rear bumper.

When our eyes met and Freddy crouched down, apparently poised to leap, I jerked the wheel to the right and gassed it.

"Freddy!"

I rushed from the truck toward the Wests' back yard, where the kid had disappeared, and, furious, hollered, "You're gonna kill yourself!" just as Freddy appeared through the trees, a flicker of tie-dyed T-shirt. I stopped fast in the middle of the street and bounded back to my truck. The kid was fine. Of course. Freddy had survived God-knew-how-many bone-crunching falls, one of them, this past spring, after colliding with our mailbox.

I rammed the truck's parking brake down with my right foot and leaned against the doorframe, still frazzled, waiting for the kid to show his face. Not far up the hill, still tucked in the shadows of the trees, was Daisy Diamond's Chevrolet, its tires nipping the lawn. Down at the corner of the Wests' property was the cluster of pines where the young lovers had been smoking—Sophia's unrelenting denial notwithstanding. And directly across the street was a plank extending curiously from a narrow gap in the trees, over a bed of brown needles, across the grass, and barely onto the macadam.

When I pulled back the branches, Freddy was standing atop a magnificent ramp, a gigantic version of the one on the driveway, three spray-painted stacks of red letters on its face: FREE LOVE PARK. Narrow, three-foot-wide arrangements of planks formed a path in the grass from the pine trees to the ramp. Freddy gazed down from the ledge at the top of the ramp, skateboard in hand, not admiring his creation but, it seemed, assessing a work in progress. The pale trunks of sycamores rose up behind him, their bony, leafy branches reaching out above his head, the ramp below splotched with shadows. Thin, toasted chips of bark littered the lawn. Two-by-fours lay crisscrossed in the grass by the patio, where, under the second-floor deck, two wooden horses straddled an electric saw.

The sixteen-year-old kid was building his own surrogate skate park.

Freddy let the skateboard fall from his hand. His foot trapped the board's lip against the ramp's ledge, and he flowed down the slope and onto the narrow wooden path. The wheels thumped at each groove, where one panel met the next. He hopped off and galloped toward tools scattered in the grass, as his skateboard skipped and flipped away. He picked up a hammer and a yellow box of nails.

"Peter." Freddy's hair fell in a plum-colored clump.

"Freddy."

Half of Freddy's stubby fingernails were painted black; the rest were just dirty.

"Nice ramp." I nodded coolly, disguising my awe.

"Nice hair." Freddy examined my head for a moment, before correcting my terminology: "It's a quarter-pipe. It's gonna be a half-pipe. Same thing on this side." The kid pointed to where he would build another ramp to mirror the one he'd completed, making—thus the name *half-pipe*—the bottom half of a giant wooden cylinder.

Freddy's earlobes were punched through with bright blue pegs that looked like bingo chips. His red-yellow-and-green tie-dyed T-shirt, picked up downtown at some march or rally to which he'd probably smuggled Sophia, displayed the familiar silhouette of not Bob Marley or Che Guevara but Philadelphia's famous death-row inmate, convicted cop-killer Mumia Abu-Jamal, whom angry teenagers like Sophia had come to idolize, or at least iconize, as a cult hero for the oppressed and falsely accused. It made no more sense for Mumia's face to be Rastafarianized on a backdrop of Jamaica's colors than it did for Che's, though I'd seen such shirts on kids of the same ilk.

I gestured with my chin toward the ramp. "How long this take you?"

"Since school."

It wasn't even July yet.

Freddy hopped onto the path toward the opening in the trees. "You start on the driveway," he explained, "get speed going and come in here."

I followed Freddy on the wooden path. The panels, rock-solid beneath my feet, were actually upraised on two-by-fours that must have been laid out first like railroad tracks and somehow imbedded in the ground. When Brock and I were kids, the cove within the pine trees had been the home of Blitz, Spud, Spit—ever-evolving games we improvised and renamed. I glanced up at Brock's old bedroom window.

"Heard from your brother?"

"Yeah."

Just beyond the trees Freddy dropped the box of nails into the grass and crouched down. *Free Mumia!* spanned from shoulder to shoulder. As the kid examined the boards beneath his feet, his hand rose to his mouth, where he went to work on his thumbnail, gnawing away at remnants of black paint. He wrapped his thumb in an angry fist, flicked his fingers, and cursed his habit, spitting through his teeth. The silver head of his hammer rose above his shoulder and came down in two swift punches. "Bitch of it's getting these angles. Getting the boards flush. It's gotta be smooth. Like concrete."

Like the concrete at the *real* LOVE Park, I thought. The *repaired* concrete—$60,000 a year in damage, I'd heard on the radio.

"When'd you hear from him?"

"Couple days ago."

Freddy tested the joints with the rubber tip of his sneaker, walking the plank toward the street. Apparently the kid wasn't interested in talking about his brother.

Two summers ago I saw Brock for the first time since high school. At first I hadn't recognized my old friend, whose beard and brimmed hat hid his face, though Brock had recognized me—or the truck— flagging me down with a wave from the driveway. "How goes it, mate?" he said, a convincing Brit, I thought, figuring he'd been living in London, until he dropped the accent to say he was practicing for Australia, where he was heading. "Catching a ride to the airport from the Professor." He winked at his father as he swung his oversized backpack into the trunk of the Volvo. "I miss you, brother," Brock said, surprising me with a cowboy-ish nod and tip of the hat. He spoke slowly and let his eyes rest on me, as his father waited patiently behind the wheel. I stuttered a goodbye, wondering if Brock's slow speech was a Southern or Midwestern drawl or a side effect of drugs. "Drop ya a postcard."

Since then, almost two years ago, I had received three postcards, the first from Australia, the next from New Zealand, the most recent from Nepal—all of which I had tacked to my bedroom wall. Brock's scrawled words never amounted to more than three sentences, but the arrival of each one made me feel desperate for the return of my old friend. In one, Brock had written, "You been a true friend through the thick of it, bro'," and I wished it were true.

Updates on Brock always came from my mother, who picked up what she could from Mrs. West. When I was in college, the gossipy snippets had always seemed overly optimistic: Brock was out west, giving skiing lessons in Vail; Brock was working with city planners in Seattle or Oregon, developing an elaborate scheme of converting SUV-drivers into bicycle-riders; he was in L.A., fetching coffee for studio executives, trying to make it as an actor; he'd met a girl, whose family owned a ranch, where he was working on a novel. One story I knew was true: after The Fall in high school the judge had agreed to cut Brock a break as long as his parents agreed to send him out west to a special rehab center for depressed teenage drug addicts.

"He's in Tajikistan," Freddy said. The name rolled off the kid's tongue as if he'd just said Miami or London or Paris. He added, nonchalantly, "Borders Afghanistan. Says there's all sorts of artists there." He'd suddenly adopted the amorphous locutions of his well-traveled brother. "He's getting way into photography."

In my mind, mountains rose up into blue skies patched with clouds, just under which Brock trekked along ascending jagged rocks, his six-month trip to Australia a distant memory, his giant backpack boiled down to a canvas satchel draped over his shoulder.

Freddy backtracked, first recalling some failed youth rally to free LOVE Park, then explaining to me that he—this sixteen-year-old kid—was now planning to meet soon with city government officials, to try to rally support for an idea Brock had written to him about while traveling in Europe last year—in either Amsterdam or Vienna—where the whole city was stocked with sturdy silver bikes no one stole because they were just left sitting all over the place, propped against light posts and lying in the grass, all of them supplied by the city, paid for with taxes, so if you needed a bike you just hopped on and cruised to the store or home or wherever and you just left the bike outside, and then somebody else could hop on and take it from there, and there were so many bikes that no one ever stole them because there was no point and you never had to bother with locks.

"Pretty cool," I said.

Freddy's hammer came down with a crack. He shifted the board to align it with the edge of the street.

"Think Philly'd go for something like that?" I said, circling Freddy.

"Worth trying."

I regretted sounding skeptical, so I changed directions, making my admiration obvious. "You could charge an entrance fee for this place. Who needs LOVE Park?"

Freddy slammed his rubber heel down on the joint where two boards met. One board sank slightly, becoming flush with the next. The kid's baggie nylon pants ballooned out when he crouched down to inspect the joints and pound more nails.

"This'll be even *better* than LOVE Park," I said.

As much as I admired Freddy, I also felt sorry for the kid, what with his utopian visions and an older brother bent on wandering to the ends of the earth. At the same time, though I had little in common with Freddy, I understood the kid's loneliness: not only had Freddy been kicked out of LOVE Park, along with all his skateboarding cronies, who were God knew where these days—probably stoned in their basements, playing the latest rape-and-pillage video game, killing time while their buddy here built them a skate park in his back yard— but he'd also been jilted by Sophia, *dumped for a chick*. That's how Freddy must have seen it. That's how his buddies must have razzed him. The poor kid had no way of knowing that Sophia had been forbidden to date—not just boys whose names didn't end in *-opoulos* or boys whose older brothers were convicted drug dealers, but *boys*. For better or worse, Sophia was driven to live by her own rules. No way in hell had she admitted to the kid that her decisions were not her own, that the old man had been the wedge that had driven them apart.

For years Freddy had zipped into our driveway and looped around aimlessly, while Sophia pretended to be raking leaves or sweeping. But the kid hadn't been deemed the forbidden fruit until this past Christmas vacation, when Sophia tested the waters by announcing he'd be her prom date. It was one thing just to be Freddy's friend, the old man had said, but if you go to the prom together people will see him as your boyfriend. "*What* people?" Sophia had screamed in the kitchen, and added, "What would be so bad about that anyway—if he *was* my boyfriend?!" She waited for an answer. "What about *me?* Ever think maybe *his* parents don't think I'm good enough for *him?*" "Don't say such a thing," my mother interrupted. The old man said nothing. "*I'm* not telling him," Sophia pronounced. "If I'm not allowed to go with him, then *you* tell him that he's not good enough for *you!*"

It was only after Freddy had become officially prohibited that Sophia's love became fierce, her romantic proclamations sounding like political rally cries—"I *love* him! Doesn't that *mean* anything to you?"—her threats to kill herself becoming more convincing, while she struggled to keep her self-diagnosed manic depression under control. She was able to stare at her food without blinking, until her eyes puddled with tears, which dripped into her salad and onto the table, well after the dishes had been cleared and the family had gone about their business of attending to their evening rituals, on several occasions remaining bug-eyed, hours after dinner, frozen there, despite my mother's pleading. Once, I found her sound asleep, in the morning, forehead on the kitchen table, a steak knife in her softly folded hand, poised to be spotted by a horrified parent. When I roused her, taking the knife, she said, "How long did it take you to forget everything that happened in high school?"

The old man had been biding his time, as it turned out, letting his daughter go on with these peaceful protests, as he carved into his chicken or pork, not bothering to say, "Enough is enough, Sophia." Finally, in January, Sophia had lured him into action, by making her cigarette-smoking obvious enough to be witnessed in the rearview mirror of the old man's car as he was backing out of the driveway. In his black wool overcoat, he marched across the street, huffing clouds of icy air, and pulled his daughter from the trees by the wrist. He drove her to school, and Freddy waited for the bus.

That night Sophia sobbed real tears at the dinner table but didn't bother putting up a fight—that is, until she realized that the reason she'd been grounded for a month was less for having been with Freddy than for *allegedly* having smoked a single stupid cigarette, a crime more unconscionable, you'd think, considering her punishment—she'd never been *grounded* before—than piercing your body like a pin cushion. Sophia shocked everyone when she brought a Bible from the living room, sandwiched it between her hands, and swore to God she hadn't been smoking. It was true that Freddy *used* to smoke, she admitted, but *she* never did, and this morning even *Freddy* hadn't been smoking, cigarette butts at their feet notwithstanding. "You just assume the worst about everyone," she accused the old man, and then finalized her tirade, with scientific precision—using the expertise one could expect only from an eighteen year old who was acing AP Physics and Chemistry—by reminding the old man that when warm air—in this case, *breath*, not unlike *his own*, when he stormed across the street, before he completely humiliated her—met cold air, the effect was *steam*, which resembled *smoke*.

Her punishment for swearing in vain on the Bible was an additional month of quarantine—she wouldn't be allowed out of the house until March. "I never go anywhere anyway!" she reasonably argued. Later, in her bedroom, I asked, "When are you gonna tell Freddy?" She turned sullen: "He'll figure it out."

Around Valentine's Day, her friend Veronica began to appear around the house more and more. At last, in the eyes of my parents, Sophia seemed to have matured beyond her obsession with Freddy, and we could all ease up on the suicide watch.

In hindsight, it seemed to me that Freddy had been excommunicated overnight, though, in truth, the complete purging from Sophia's system had taken months.

Freddy tossed the hammer into the grass and headed uphill. "This lady's fucking car's still here," he muttered, pausing alongside Daisy's Chevrolet.

"What lady?" I played curious. Skating yesterday, Freddy must have seen her sitting there for God knew how long before I showed up to play Good Samaritan.

"This lady was freaking me out yesterday, turning her car on and off." The kid eyed the car with scorn. "Then she just sat there for, like, fucking *ever*."

I knew how the story played out from there.

"It's an obstacle." Freddy kicked a tire. He looked up at the top of the hill, mapping out a path around the car. He cupped his hands to the windows and tugged at the handle of the locked door.

"Back off, Freddy," I blurted, but the kid just smirked at me.

When we reached the Wests' driveway, Freddy dropped his skateboard, trapped it with his thick-soled sneaker, and glided toward the ramp between the garage doors.

"Wanna try?" Freddy said.

I laughed a breathy laugh and shook my head, no way. "I used to have this old wooden job with red wheels and black sandpaper strips for grip."

Freddy made loops on the driveway.

"I went with Brock to LOVE Park a few times," I added.

"And *then* you ditched him?" Freddy braked with his front foot. The nose of his skateboard rose. A sticker, doctored with a black Magic Marker, read FUCK LOVE PARK.

"*What?*"

Freddy shrugged, the front wheels dropped to the pavement, and he went on coasting in silence.

"I never ditched your brother, Freddy."

Of course, it must have been hell for the kid, watching his big brother self-destruct, and so I wasn't about to give a history lesson. The kid needed a version in which the *world* ditched Brock. Still, Freddy must have known it had been Brock, not I, who had traded in his friends for the dope-smoking, tired LOVE Park crew that he started dragging back to the Wests' basement every afternoon. Meanwhile, I had gone on shooting baskets, reminiscing about elaborate Monopoly and Risk tournaments in the basement that Brock had turned into a teenage drug den, where for years we'd been content conquering an imaginary Atlantic City—Marvin Gardens, Boardwalk—lining the streets with green houses and red hotels, and an imaginary world—Urkutsk, Madagascar—barricading the borders with armies of candy-colored cubes.

Freddy rose up the ramp and came back down, making nonchalant arcs and semi-circles on the macadam.

"Is that, like, a family trait or something? You just *ditch* people?"

I gasped, "My sister *liked* you, Freddy. I happen to think she *still* likes you."

"*Liked* me?" Freddy skewed his eyes. "You don't know *anything*." He flipped his skateboard up and snatched it in the air.

"Listen, I just stopped to make sure you were all right…after you—" I gestured toward the street. "Forget it." I shuffled a few steps. "My father had his reasons, Freddy. I'm not saying they were good ones. But it wasn't Sophia's idea. You should know that."

"Out of sight, out of mind, man." The kid flicked his hand.

"Well, I really doubt she's gone forever. We all go through phases. Look at Brock."

"Eating pussy isn't a phase."

I pointed my finger. "Watch your mouth, Freddy."

"Brock always said you were a loser."

"Brock was too *stoned* to know any better, Freddy."

Freddy clenched his jaw. "You all think you're better than everyone."

As the kid's words sank in, I remembered the story of how the old man had snared Sophia from the pine trees. "These are not good people," he'd said, staring Freddy down, taking Sophia by the wrist. When Sophia relayed the story in her bedroom that night, I suggested that perhaps the old man had lashed out at the least threatening of the West males, instead of lashing out at Dr. West, the proud atheist, who for years had gone out of his way to corner my father wherever he could, relishing every opportunity to debate the existence of God, as though they were old pals, the professor and the priest. At the time I hoped that Freddy was as aloof as he acted, that he'd rolled his eyes at the old man, thinking, *Whatever, Father Pappas*, that the kid wasn't in his house, right then, brooding over the implications of just having been deemed "not good," damned by a priest, and then imitating his big brother by hurling himself from the second-floor deck. As far as I ever knew, Freddy had gone about his life without interruption, skate-boarding and smoking in the pine trees before school.

Now I wanted to say something comforting, but I'd been silenced by the kid, who seemed about to cry, as though my blank face some-how confirmed whatever horrible idea—about my family or people in general or Freddy himself—that might have been swirling around in his head.

"I wasn't even smoking," Freddy choked out, skating in circles.

"I know," I said, though the truth was I'd never believed Sophia's elaborate defense that day. Later, in her bedroom, she'd asked me my opinion on the whole swearing-on-the-Bible thing, asked whether or not she'd gone too far with the gesture, claiming that her own view-point was that the act, even for symbolic emphasis, was arbitrary and pointless in the first place, so she figured what the hell, it wasn't blas-phemous, because, after all, lying was a sin and you didn't need to be doing it with your right hand on the Book, in which the actual Commandment was printed, in order to make it a sin, and, moreover, if you didn't agree that lying was a sin in the first place or you just didn't care that it was a sin, then you probably didn't think much of the Bible anyway and so it might as well be *ten* Bibles or ten *diction-aries* under your right hand while you swore to God and lied through your teeth.

Of course, her philosophical rant hadn't shed a sliver of light on the question of her own truth-telling, but I wasn't about to ask her point-blank if either of them, Sophia or Freddy, had in fact been smok-ing. I was too afraid she'd accuse me of not appreciating the nuances of her reasoning, too stupid to understand that she'd sworn on the Bible to demonstrate that the question of her honesty had already been deemed moot by the inevitability of injustice.

"Freddy, I'm sorry, man." I knew I was fawning shamelessly now. "Seriously, I understand."

He was eyeing me down, sifting through insults that might be the final word. "My dad said your dad's a hypocrite," he offered.

"That's fine," I submitted.

Freddy wiped his nose on his shoulder, gazing toward the pine trees where he and Sophia had tucked themselves on their last morning together and on countless mornings before. He rocked his skateboard on its hind wheels, then coasted toward the garage doors, his back turned.

I headed downhill.

When Freddy had told his parents the story, they'd probably explained that the poor girl's father was out of his mind. Lucky for my father, Dr. West was not a violent man but an ex-hippie, who must have utilized the whole experience as a teaching tool, his unbelief bolstered by this ludicrous crusading priest so threatened by a boy with purple hair and no religion that he would scare him by insulting his "no-good" family.

But apparently Dr. West's insights about the hypocrisy of man had not been enough to heal Freddy's broken heart. Perhaps it was as hard for Freddy's father as it was for me to think of the kid as brokenhearted, let alone as being in love; it was even harder to think of Sophia in either state. I had always assumed she'd begun playing the tragic lover—contemplating daggers and poison (steak knives and antidepressants)—only after her prom plans had been quashed, only after her secret love had become forbidden, only after she'd been driven to announce—as a kind of declaration of independence—that Freddy was the love of her life.

I stopped at Daisy's car and leaned against the trunk. I wanted to go back to tell the kid that the prom was overrated, that he was lucky to have missed it, that he was too young to know that these girls—not just Sophia, but all of them, especially as they got older—sent mixed messages, pushing and pulling...

My prom date had been Eileen Stefanides—"Eye Lean," the other boys used to tease, back in middle school, tugging, nonsensically, at the skin below one eye, mimicking her lazy eye, which, by the time she reached high school, had turned completely normal. She drank like a gambler, at least on prom night, until she threw up on the gearshift of her father's car. She was the one Greek girl in the senior class—the one of the three—I had liked—even with the lazy eye; the problem was mild, really, the one iris sort of lagging when she looked sideways. But the defect was substantial enough, in the eyes of the boy population, that she'd been permanently written off years before anyone needed a date, lucky for me once the problem went away in high school.

Sparing her dress and the rug mats, she managed to get the door open, gracing the surface of the Country Club parking lot with a Southern-Comfort-and-roast-beef-marsala combination, not before asking me to swear, in the midst of heaving, tearing up, and sobbing heavily, that I'd never tell my parents about this, *please*, especially my father, the priest, *oh-my-God*, because if her parents found out, if anyone in the church found out, she wouldn't be allowed to go to Mills College, the all-women's college in Oakland, California (to which she did end up going and, not to my surprise, from which she never returned). She went on to confess—and this helped make sense of how things had always been between us—that she'd drunk so much tonight because she really wanted *to want* to kiss me, or even to do more than that, you know, not just because it was the prom, but also because she'd always liked me, *you know that, Peter,* and she always thought about it, and this was her last chance *to really see,* you know, because she was still holding on to this idea that maybe she was at least *bi*-sexual—*Jesus Christ, I can't believe I'm telling you this*—my stomach sank—but now she knew, *I mean, I've known,* of course, because you just know, in the same way *you* know you're attracted to *me,* Peter, and I'm *sorry* about that, I swear I am, but it's not *you*—I mean, it's not your fault—and I want you to know that this is why I can't go to Gettysburg or Ursinus or wherever my parents want me to go, that I have to go *far,* like, out West, where I'm going, no matter what, I swear to God, and I trust you with this, Peter, and it feels good to tell some-one, *you especially,* of all people, because I've known you since, like, Greek school and church camp and GOYA and all that bullshit, you know, and you've always been sweet to me, and because, seriously, I have always liked you and if it *had* to be a guy it would be you.

Freddy rolled lazily into the street at the top of the hill, wheels buzzing at his feet. I would tell Freddy that he shouldn't give up on Sophia, not if he really loved her, that he should tell her how he felt, that it didn't matter what my father had said that day, that it didn't even matter that she was in California, that there was nothing more powerful than the truth, especially when you wrote it down, and so he should write her a letter, because something written, see, it's always present, it's always happening right now, not like a phone call or even a face-to-face conversation, which you can just forget or change in your mind, but a letter, trust me, I know, you just keep reading it over and over, carrying it around with you, wishing you could change the truth into something it isn't, wasn't, and never will be, but you can't change it, you've always known it, from the day you first read it...

Freddy arced wide, nearly nipping the grass on the far side, and picked up speed as he homed in on the gap in the trees just down from the Chevrolet. I sidled alongside the car, playing pit-stop crew, clapping as Freddy sped toward me, crouched, focused on the wooden path up ahead. The kid was grinning, thinking of nothing in particular, it seemed—nothing but the gap in the trees and the giant ramp under the sycamores.

"All right!" I shouted, when Freddy shot through the trees, wheels thumping over the grooves like a rapid heartbeat. I followed him inside the wall of pines as the kid surfed the wooden wave to its peak, his feet, like a pole vaulter's, leading the way, his torso recoiling like a Slinky climbing the last step, but instead of landing, as he had the last time, he floated, frozen in the air, his back grazing the sycamore branches, and then, in slow motion, sank back toward the ramp—into the quarter-pipe—and, as if shot from a cannon—no mirroring quarter-pipe to catch him on the opposite side of the yard, not yet—sped back toward the street, toward me, as I leapt off the path into the grass.

I had expected Freddy to jump from the skateboard and somersault into repose or slide baseball style, but the kid was going way too fast to stop, and he kept going, apparently as planned, right back out through the gap in the trees where he'd entered, rocketing—*Jesus Christ, Freddy!*—right into the street and down Birch Hill, into the sunset, beautifully oblivious, I thought, as I leaned back against the hood of Daisy's Chevrolet, watching the kid sailing gloriously through space, past the rest of us, back here on earth, out of sight, out of mind.

9
When You Paint, Paint

Dorothy Maloney had summed up the secret to life in a single sentence, an adage she'd picked up from one of her pop-psych Buddhist-wannabe books: *when you wash the dishes, wash the dishes.* That's when you were doing it for God. I thought of her advice often, usually on the job, imagining Dorothy after dinner at a sink, steel-wooling a spaghetti pot, in no hurry. In the kitchen of her dorm I would stand and watch her, wondering what it was like inside her head, wondering if the only thought in there was of the soapy sponge that looked like a cloud, or if there had been a thought at all, and if such singular focus really did, as she used to claim, put you in the presence of God, where *everything of this world,* even the sponge, *falls away.* She had experienced this, she said; in fact, she was, she said—looking at me with her sorry blue eyes—beginning to experience it more and more. I'd understood: everything of this world falls away.

I sipped my Dunkin' Donuts coffee, gazing out from the second-floor patio of the corner unit in the H building of Stone Bridge Apartments, contemplating the rest of the day, the week, the years ahead. The two doughnuts I'd eaten hours earlier, each iced in patriotic July-Fourth-week red-white-and-blue, had given me a much-needed jolt after my three hours of unsettled sleep, but now I needed more than lukewarm coffee to get me through the day.

When you paint, paint, I thought.

In the middle of the night I'd sat staring into the flat blue Far Eastern skies of Brock West's postcards tacked to the wall above my desk. I'd read the backs—Brock people-watching in the Dubai airport, Brock catching a ride on the back of a pickup packed with grinning Cambodian kids—before plucking a worn piece of notebook paper, folded in a wallet-sized square, from a thin file marked IMPORTANT. I'd gone to bed, remembering the words I'd memorized long ago, having carried Dorothy's letter, masochistically, for over a year, the words I'd feared at the time would whirl in my head forever like a punishing mantra: *...you never really loved me...you've never really loved anyone.*

Beyond the parking lot where my truck was parked, between buildings L and M, a segment of the swimming pool shimmered, a slick triangle of brilliant turquoise. The sun shot through leafy trees onto the sidewalks, which were glowing like white sand. Three figures made their way along the path toward me. A young Indian couple— he in a blue suit and well-shined shoes, she in green hospital scrubs— were all geared up for the day—for the courtroom, for surgery; but presumably they wanted first dibs on the next available apartment here at Stone Bridge, where young urban professionals bided their time just inside the city line before making their final exodus into suburbia. I stepped back against the cool brick wall of the porch, into the shadows made by the leafy awning overhead. I didn't want to be seen as the weird painter-guy who was always hovering on a balcony, eyeballing the tenants—and especially the blond from the rental office— while pretending to sip coffee.

I'd dreamt enough of the morning away. It was time to get started, to do what I did best, to lose myself in the monotony of dragging a brush along the baseboards and joints where ceiling met wall and wall met wall. I turned toward the drop cloth, where my brush rested on the mouth of a newly opened can, beside a long-handled roller propped on the ledge of an aluminum tray. My left hand slipped naturally around the can, like a ballplayer's into his glove, thumb hooking the handle, pinkie reaching just under the bottom lip. I had the routine down pat, able to knock out a two-bedroom apartment by lunchtime, another in the afternoon, not that I was in a hurry. Eliot's contracts with three major apartment complexes in the area would keep me chasing vacating tenants—like a night janitor sweeping up, in and out before anyone noticed—for as long as I could endure the job.

As I jabbed the soaked brush into the first of the four upper corners of the living room and pulled paint into the three alleys of the intersection, I wondered if you could get *too* good at something, or, if, when you *did*, then it wasn't worth doing anymore, or it had never been worth doing in the first place. The first day on the job, five years earlier, I knelt at the baseboard, paint can set carefully to my left, dipped my brush, and bent over so that I could see the brush follicles getting as close to the carpet as possible without touching, determined to impress my boss, who was in the kitchen with the roller. No more than a minute passed before Eliot was standing there behind me, breathing over my shoulder, the tips of his white tennis sneakers in view. I figured the boss couldn't help admiring his new employee's meticulous touch, the way this newcomer, in just seconds, with no instruction at all, was already demonstrating a knack that inspired thoughts of destiny. The subject of such admiration, I didn't look up— I wouldn't gloat—but, instead, shuffled back on my knees, moving the paint can another foot or so, and resumed dragging my brush, even more carefully now, ever so close to the hairs of the carpet. "Give me that." No sooner was the brush swiped from my hand than Eliot, barely hunching over, slapped away at the baseboard, as if with a feather duster, and reached the other corner just as I pivoted on my knees to see my boss holding the brush out like an ice cream cone. "We're not artists, buddy," Eliot said, already forgetting—or, worse, disregarding, my name—that word, *buddy*, making clear I was anything but. I was an employee, another aimless punk fresh out of college, hired to do enough work to justify my seven bucks an hour. "You get a little on the carpet, you wipe it up with a wet rag. See that rag? Go wet it in the bathroom, and keep it by your side. Get up." I was still on my knees. "On your feet. Give me the can." I was about to be shown how you got the job done. Eliot grabbed the can like a football, dipped the brush, slapped it back and forth inside the rim, flung the brush, an extension of his arm, into the nearest crevice where two walls met, and in one giant swipe made a wide vertical stripe from floor to ceiling. "*Cutting*. You cut the edges and corners, and all around the windows, everywhere the roller can't reach. I'm on your trail with the roller. Go to it, Michelangelo."

Five years later I was as good a painter as my boss and, come to think of it, *had* been for at least a few years—which is to say I was as *efficient* a painter as my boss—but it was no major accomplishment to be a great painter of the interiors of apartments. *I saw the angel in the marble and carved until I set him free*, Michelangelo had said. "We're just giving her a fresh coat," Eliot had said, sweeping the roller across the wall like a push broom. "It's just white on white."

White on white on white.

Once you got good at this job, once you realized that there was nothing to it, that's when the real work started. Real skill was being able to pace yourself, day in, day out, to tune out, not to think about *white on white on white*—or, rather, to think *only* about *white on white on white*—not to think about how many times you'd done this before or how many more times you'd do it in the future, not to think about the fact that a monkey could do what you're doing, while you could be contributing something valuable to society. This job wasn't about proving yourself better than this guy or that guy. You're neither Michelangelo nor a monkey… All this I told myself when I first started out, and all this I continued to remind myself for the next five years: you never meant for this job to define you. In fact, that's why you wanted a job like this: because no job could define you. A job was a job. This was real work. Honest, noble work. Some of the greatest men had had ordinary jobs. T. S. Eliot had been a banker, Gandhi a lawyer, Jesus a carpenter—a poet, a prophet, the Son of God. You didn't have to become a priest, a monk, or a saint, you decided, never forgetting the J.F.K., Jr. obituary that claimed he hadn't wanted to be a great man, like his father, the president, just a good person. What *defined* you lay much deeper than what you did for a living. This job was a spiritual exercise, an exercise in detachment, an opportunity to practice humility every day of your life, to demonstrate that you didn't take yourself or your work too seriously, that you wouldn't be a better person if you were the boss or the guy who owned the apartments, that you were no better or worse than the guy who laid the carpet, or the guy working at the factory where they made the carpet, or the guy who shined the shoes of the guys who owned the factory and apartments.

I slapped the brush into the corner and dragged it toward the floor, where paint sank into the crevice between baseboard and wall. I drew a giant arc in the center of the wall, dipped my brush and drew another. The blue plastic drop cloth crinkled beneath my sneakers as I centered myself. The soaked brush, clinging to my loosely gripping fingers, twirled and smacked, traveled in figure-eights, an extension of the hand that held it, leaving glistening slicks in its wake, returning by itself, submerging in a flash, into the echoey insides of the can, where paint rose up, coming just shy of the metal casing that held the bristles together, and once again, and over and over, launching itself into the wall, which became three-dimensional and then—as the job fell away—*four*-dimensional. My legs were dancing on their own, my hands hovering—*à la* Jackson Pollock, only this wall of *white on white on white* was more pure than a Pollock, because it was not for the public to see. The need for an audience was what did Pollock in, made him drink, crash his car, kill that girl. I didn't need or want this to be seen or heard or known. This wall of *white on white on white* was not for anyone or anything—not even for myself—it was for *now*, for the *moment*, for the act itself. Everything was falling away.

I was floating, in the moment, detached from everything outside of myself, even from my own consciousness, except for the part of my brain that kept reminding me that these were the kinds of notes I should be taking down for the book I intended to write, a book in which I would describe the indescribable, describe, for example, what I was experiencing right now, describe a place where even Pollock had never gone, where the audience was irrelevant, where everybody had the talent to one-up the most important artist of the twentieth century, where I existed right now, as the sole witness to my own artwork, where I was experiencing internally the essence of art that Pollock had symbolized externally, where God was present, in my soul, where I was pure, where everything and everyone was pure, where we were all one, connected for eternity, not for eternity as in *for the rest of your life* or *forever*, but for eternity in the way Dorothy had explained it, where time as we understood it didn't exist at all, where time existed without beginning or end, non-linear time, time outside of time, where there was only *white on white on white*, where there were no answers to the questions or even questions at all. It was *that*—its holy, indefinite nature—that was the essence of art, defying, defiling, the question *why?* as only art in its purest form could, offering up no reason for itself, only being, for now, these shadowy drippings, this *white on white on white*, these wild, purged splatterings, my signature, to go forever unseen, to be destroyed by my own roller, by my own hand, the undoer of my own creation. I was a true original, or maybe not: but then, if there were a thousand, a million, like me, I was in holy company, a league of secret artists, connected in spirit, unknown to the rest of the world—as the wind blows a raked pile of leaves, the sun melts a shoveled bank of snow. This was not for nothing, but—I wanted to believe it—for *God*. Yet I knew deep down—not because I didn't *believe* it but because I'd never, in all the times I'd tried, including this one, *truly* lost myself, never come to a point where *everything of this world falls away* (always, inevitably, my thoughts interfered—I could never think of only the paint, let alone of nothing at all)—I was a faker, a maker of messes.

The moment the apartment door thumped open I imagined Eliot's dumbfounded face, his inarticulate castigation—*this is how you abuse the privilege of carrying the keys?*—his most loyal employee turning with paint-splattered arms and face, the mess on the wall dripping like a rain-drenched window.

In a flash I recognized the green scrubs. All three of them stood paralyzed in the doorway, bathed in sunlight, bug-eyed. I might have been drenched in blood, a murderer mid-stab.

"Sorry." The blond stepped back into the hallway, gently pulling the door shut.

"Wait!" I wiped my cheek on my shoulder. "Come in."

The door re-opened. Before ducking into a back bedroom, they nodded politely as if at a bum who'd peed his pants.

A puddle of white paint had formed at my feet on the blue plastic. I set down my can and brush and went to the bathroom, where I discovered, in the mirror, a white-freckled and frosted-haired psychopath. I washed my hands in the sink, thanking God for water-based paint, and rinsed my head under the faucet in the bathtub.

The blond and the Indian couple had already re-entered the living room when I returned, scrubbing my head with a towel meant for wiping up paint. They stood facing the wall—my magnum opus. I couldn't tell if their faces revealed delight or disgust. There was a moment, before I looked at the wall myself, when I hoped to discover, maybe from this distance, a truly inspired work of art, *white on white on white*, a sun-drenched image of beauty that could have come only from the unselfconscious expression of the human unconscious.

The wall was marked by grayish-silver slashes where the brush's wooden handle and metal casing had struck and gouged the plasterboard. There would be spackling and sanding to do. Meanwhile, rivers of white rushed toward the floor, where a half-gallon of paint was tumbling over the baseboard and dipping under the drop cloth.

I lunged for the base of the wall and with the towel damp from my hair began scooping paint. I peeled back the plastic sheet to find a thin stream between the carpet and baseboard. Veiny rivulets were finding their way toward my knees. Shuffling, I dammed the flow, pushing the paint back toward the wall where it belonged. Finally, I stood up and with a brush feathered out the remaining drips and wrinkles.

My audience had sneaked out without shutting the door.

As I wiped my hands on my shorts, a flash of embarrassment rushed through my arms and neck. I imagined firing the paintbrush, puncturing a hole in the plasterboard. Instead, I side-armed it through the wide-open sliding glass door, the thing spraying arcs of rainy dots as it somersaulted like a tomahawk, the wooden handle skipping off the railing, catapulting into the white glow of the sky, and dropping out of sight. I waited for a yelp but heard nothing.

I went out onto the porch. I sat down on the concrete slab and gazed out through the iron bars of the railing. The paintbrush stood in the grass, bristles up, stuck like a white flag.

I took out my wallet and unfolded the letter.

Dear Peter,

I'll be heading back to my parents' on Sunday, packing, then as soon as possible going south, to North Carolina (as planned). Ten days of silence might be exactly what I need. I only wish you were going with me. Somehow being silent without you seems impossible. You and me and a bunch of monks—remember? How easily we forget. It was going to be our secret journey. Now I can't believe I'm doing this alone, but the thought of not going at all makes me sadder than I already feel—if that's possible. Are you sure about this? You can just watch me leave your life? I've been imagining us on the road, and it's just hitting me now that maybe you were never really, seriously, going to come with me. Were you? Maybe you never really loved me. Maybe you've never really loved anyone. I don't mean that to be mean. I just mean, maybe you haven't, not really. I'm so mad and hurt right now, and yet all you have to do is say you want to come with me and we can go back to our plan. I've been thinking maybe I've never been open enough, maybe I just assumed too much, that how I felt was obvious enough in how I acted, but now I think I should have said some things out loud, like maybe I should have said: this is love…what we have…that's what this is. I know it's hard for me to say it…maybe because it sounds so cliché, and I want everything to be so original (I can't stand that about me! how do you make "I love you" sound original?), or maybe because of some f'd-up daddy thing, how he never said it and all that, and everything else I told you, but no excuses (it's hard for me to even write it now, here, can you tell? notice the quotes?). It's not because it's not true anymore—it is true. It doesn't go away just because the other person doesn't feel it (or doesn't know he feels it!). Okay, I'm rambling. I love you, there, I wrote it, I said it, I'm saying it: I love you! You're an idiot. Do you think I've ever written that to anyone before? If you think so, then you really are the stupidest smartest person I've ever met. Does this make any difference to you? Or will you just burn this letter and never call me?

I guess you're home with your family (that I never met—do you think I never noticed that you never took me home, when you live fifteen minutes from school?). I don't accept any of this, Peter. That's the main reason I'm writing this. I want you to know that this is unacceptable. I don't believe you don't want to come with me...I think you just don't know how...to just do something completely different from what you or anyone else ever expected. What good are your IDEAS? I'm not saying this because I want you to feel bad—I would never intentionally hurt you (or anyone?), but I let myself believe you were romantic and adventurous. You made me believe that by the way you talk about things. But talk's cheap (sometimes the cliché is the only way to say it, I guess). But you're the most cautious, conservative person I know (more than my own mother). Somewhere deep inside you I know you must be hurting, even though you may not even know it. And I hope for your sake your feelings stay buried inside you because I can't imagine how much it will hurt if they ever surface.

Or maybe it's just me—not me, I mean.

Dorothy

I imagined her in a tomato garden, skin golden, hair shimmering, naked kids, hers, a boy and a girl, traipsing about, dusty-white, dried dandelion floating in the air, a thin, fair-haired figure, her man, nothing like me, stabbing a pitchfork into the ground, unable to resist the beauty of it all, of his life, sweeping Dorothy behind low bushes, his tool's wooden handle wagging in the sun.

Of course, I could always hurl myself over the railing, but more than death I feared paralysis, which would land me home to convalesce with my uncle and grandmother.

I tucked the letter back into my wallet and went to the kitchen to check the clock on the oven. Almost eleven. Enough painting for one morning. Too early for lunch. The Dunkin' Donuts were still making their way down.

The regret was tough to swallow, the shame impossible.

Okay, so I was an idiot. I should have gone with her. Or maybe I just couldn't admit that Dorothy Maloney wasn't for *me*, that her dream wasn't mine, that I wouldn't have been able to fake it, driving to some *ashram* or whatever, and then what?

Dorothy Maloney was ancient history, I told myself. God knew where she was.

But Daisy Diamond was here now. And she was a woman who wanted a man. She wanted *me* to be that man, the man who pursued *her*. Any woman wanted that. I knew *that* much.

No time like the present, I thought, and then remembered the Gospel of Thomas, the Jesus no one knew: "What you look forward to has already come, but you do not recognize it."

I could come and go as I pleased here. I'd leave the porch door open, plug in Eliot's little white-speckled radio, and crank up KYW News so loud that anyone outside would assume there was actually a man at work in here.

I'd drive downtown and comb her neighborhood for salons. I'd ask if Daisy was in today, or pretend I had an appointment. I'd say of course I loved my haircut, but I wanted it even shorter. I didn't want to hold back this time. I'd go as far as she wanted to go.

Just as soon as I went to see Shep.

10

The Gospel of Shep

In Rafael Santi's *School of Athens*, the 1509 fresco painted in the Stanza della Segnatura in the Palazza Pontifici, in the Vatican, it is Plato to the left of Aristotle, the two of them robed, sandaled, peripatetic, yet frozen in a moment of philosophical communion, before a series of archways that recede into blue skies; all around them on the marble stairs are other robed and sandaled thinkers, including Apollo and Minerva, contemplating geometry, astronomy—and the liberal arts—acquiring truth through reason.

In Shepard Stillman's *School of Philly*—painted mural; old Girard Bank; Broad and Spring Garden; 1996—it is Jonathan Hughes and Heather Ware, instead of the Greeks, who are the central figures—donned in denim instead of draped in robes—Shep's apprentices at the time. From here—so close—across four lanes of Broad Street and the small parking lot beyond the sidewalk on the opposite side—giant brush strokes are whole body parts: a lemon-yellow S, tall as an apartment wall, forms the muscular groove from Jonathan's shoulder to his elbow; on a swatch of sky blue that would fill a gallery wall, a body-length slanted black stripe makes the shadowy fold at his thigh—*chiaroscuro* right there in his Levi's; a solid white line, pushed on with a roller, spills into a half-moon, fanned out with a brush—Heather's nose and forehead. Surrounding them are twenty-four Temple University associates, unknown to the general public—instead of Apollo, a security guard from the law school; instead of Minerva, the Armenian woman whose lunch truck sits outside the Liacouras Center and who makes the best fresh-cut-turkey hoagie in North Philly—all the figures immortalized on the *trompe l'oeil* stairway, rising as if from the sidewalk, the inner dome of the ancient breezeway making the old bank's real walls seem marble, the fair skies in the distance the actual heavens over Philadelphia. Up close, *School of Philly* is a miracle of mass-scale Impressionism; six blocks west, a masterpiece of photorealism—at any distance, worthy of a description that words couldn't seem to capture, not at the moment, anyway.

Shep's whole body of work—the seven murals, the countless ground paintings—not to mention Saint Stillman himself, deserved the proper treatment, a single book.

My little pencil, saved from a miniature golf game and dug out from the glove compartment, was poised at the blank note card pinned by my pinkie to my thigh. I remembered the night Jonathan Hughes, who had since joined the Mural Arts Program, came to speak at one of Shep's Art of Philadelphia seminars. In his paint-splattered overalls and bandana, Jonathan went on about the meaning of *School of Philly*, which glowed on the screen behind him. Crossing back and forth through the beam of the slide projector, he explained how Shep had been inspired by Rodin, specifically by the *Burghers of Calais*, in which a town hero and his five companions, who had all volunteered to die, were displayed not on a pedestal but at ground level, in order to demonstrate the common ground they shared with humanity. Shep was sitting nearby, on the surface of a female student's desk, wearing his black-denim getup and his ever-stoic, un-interpretable face. All the while, I couldn't help wondering if Jonathan had really been so hard-pressed for time, after working on whatever mural, that he couldn't spare a minute to change out of his overalls and bandana—or if he'd actually painted at all that day. I had done a paper on the *Gates of Hell* the previous semester, so the Rodin Museum was fresh in my memory; Jonathan's assessment of the *Burghers* was safe enough, but the analogy to Shep's mural seemed tenuous, not to mention irrelevant to his purpose as guest speaker, and so I was thrilled when Shep interrupted: "Tell them about the protective acrylic coat you applied." The purpose of the guest speaker, Shep had informed the class prior to Jonathan's rushing in late, was to provide firsthand knowledge of the *process* (erecting the scaffolding, priming the brick) and the *politics* (choosing the location, proposing the design) of creating a mural—two topics that bored Shep to tears, only slightly less, it seemed, than did his former student's impromptu comparative analysis of Auguste Rodin and Shepard Stillman.

When Jonathan once again began to stray from his directed mission, this time transforming not into visiting Professor Emeritus from Harvard but head recruiter for the Mural Arts Program—explaining with a sudden dreadful urgency that there was a backlog of thousands of requests, that the city's funding was insufficient to keep up with demand, especially when murals could cost over $50,000—Shep stepped in, subduing the dramatics, by instructing the class to sketch a human figure in our notebooks. We relished the opportunity to draw. When we looked up, happily, he said, "One of the few things in life that are free. Poverty is no excuse for not making art. In fact, it can be inspiring. Of course, the more money you have, the more paint you can buy and the bigger the picture you can make. But be grateful for every dollar. If someone gives you a nickel to make art, it is an act of faith." That said, he went on to enlighten everyone on the virtue of Philadelphia's Percent for Art Program, which, since the seventies, required builders to provide the city with art equal to the cost of one percent of construction—not chump change, when you considered the price of a skyscraper—no fancy window trimming pawned off as art, Shep said, rising to his feet now, getting as excited as I ever saw him, a detectable fluctuation in his voice, but *fine art*, like Claus Oldenburg's *Clothespin* in Centre Square, Jean Debuffet's *Milord la Chamarre* a stone's throw away; Robert Morris's *Wedges* in Fairmount Park—all of these we've seen—Tony Smith's *We Lost*, Liberman's *Covenant*, Oldenburg's *Split Button*, on Penn's campus; Theodore Miller's *Cubus Assemblage*, on the warehouse wall on Spring Garden—we would be without *all* of these if not for the One Percent program—Beverly Pepper's *Phaedrus* at the Federal Reserve Bank on Sixth Street, Sandy Calder's *White Cascade*, hanging inside; Fredenthal's *Water, Ice, Fire;* Leonard Baskin's *Old Man, Young Man, The Future*—Shep's favorite—which the class saw the day he led a tour along the Delaware River, from Isamu Noguchi's *Bolt of Lightning* at the Ben Franklin Bridge to *Old Man, Young Man*, in the courtyard of I.M. Pei's Society Hill Towers.

With only a profile view at first, I'd thought *The Future* bright, wide open, literally, the young man envisioning the rest of his life, the old man imagining infinity; the sculpture had seemed almost romantic, less modern than Shep was making it out—calling it paradoxical, both hopeful and harrowing—until I realized that a disjointed hulking glob of bronze, set off from the male figures and, as such, seeming to be an entirely different sculpture, if a sculpture at all, was actually *The Future*, a vulture-like bird staring the men down. Once I sidled up to get the *Young Man*'s perspective, I found *The Future* neither paradoxical nor harrowing, but plain terrorizing—the viewpoint seemed to be that of Prometheus, anticipating thirty-thousand years of literally gut-wrenching misery. What about the bird, exactly, seemed *hopeful?* I trusted that Shep saw something I didn't, as Saint Stillman went on about public art's capacity to enrich not only the physical beauty of a given environment but the soul of the passerby as well.

Shep's sermons, enigmatic as they often were, had been enriching to the soul; I wished I'd taken better notes, or even recorded the classes, though I knew Shep would have forbidden it. Shep's exact words were lost, but his *School of Philly* was still there, and it, too, was enriching to the soul, as was *William Penn* up ahead, atop City Hall, so towering from this angle. This was the best seat in the house, I thought, parked on Broad, facing south, gazing at these two great monuments that had never gotten their due respect. Alexander Milne Calder had blamed the architects for the botched installation of his sculpture, assembled unceremoniously, piece by humongous piece, and appearing in-full one day, standing askew, William Penn's back to the sun, his face doomed, for eternity, to his own shadow. What must have made the completed job all the more anticlimactic, not only to Calder but to every Philadelphian in 1901, was that, though the *sculpture* was the largest of its kind in the world, City Hall itself, at the apex of newly erected Billy Penn's hat, was not the tallest *building*—as it *would* have been, had it not been slow to finish, at least for a short, glorious time, until the Eiffel Tower and the Washington Monument inched it out. Equally anticlimactic was the unveiling of Shep's artwork. *School of Philly* was the city's greatest mural, its painter its greatest living artist, as far as I was concerned, yet the scaffolding just seemed to vanish one day, leaving in its wake another masterpiece,

whose creator had already returned to his studio, to paint his unas-
suming leaves. There should have been thousands of people dancing
in the streets at the unveiling of such a magnum opus, singing to the
music of the police band, drinking to the artist, the toast of the town.
If there was any justice in the world, some day in the not-too-distant
future—perhaps with some help from the book I was envisioning—
Shepard Stillman would become a household name in this town—in
certain households anyway, at least in the ones in which Calder and
Eakins were already familiar.

Perhaps I could shift gears—not that I was in a gear yet—and make
the book about Shep. *The Gospel of Shep*. But there was only so much
you could write about paintings of leaves.

For all I knew, Shep wasn't even living in Philly anymore, in the
same apartment, six blocks away. Maybe he'd moved to New York, to
his other home, where his wife, an ex-student, had lived when I was
at Temple; Shep would always be making it back just in time for whatever Monday night seminar. Or maybe Shep had found another student to marry and shipped out to Santa Fe or Austin, or to some new
hotbed. The ex-student wife I had known about had been Shep's second ex-student wife. By now there could be a third or fourth. There
had always been rumors about Shep with the undergrads, both male
and female, who made up his inner circle, which I had never cracked,
perhaps because I lived off campus or didn't smoke grass or wasn't an
artist—it wasn't enough to be a lover of art. The real Shep disciples
were painters, drawers, makers of odd, original sculptures and col-
lages, but they were also scholars and philosophers, artists who were
not so single-minded that they'd gone to an art school, like Tyler or
Moore, but artists who were thinkers first. Shep had studied geology
at a college that had remained nameless, in New Hampshire, and
advised students to "study what you want to learn more about" and,
later, to "do what you want to do." Thusly would read *The Gospel of
Shep*. He didn't teach studio classes because he had no interest in
teaching *technique*—a term for which he did not disguise his scorn—
nor in presuming (let alone doubting) anyone's talent, just because a
committee had found a portfolio promising. He was of the firm belief

that all people were artists and that it was only a matter of time before the so-called non-artists became sufficiently moved to make something lasting of their experience—for most people time just ran out. When I insisted I was a terrible artist, Shep asked if I'd "ventured past the point of humiliation." Still in the league of the so-called non-artists, I had fancied myself a kind of thirteenth disciple—though at times the most beloved disciple—winning the highest praises in Shep's Art History classes and then pretending to have my own good reasons for not stopping by the studio for a coffee and a smoke and, when I did stop by, for not lingering indefinitely, as did select others, for whom Shep's door seemed ever-revolving.

The most convincing rumors had been about Heather Ware, a graduate assistant the semester Shep talked me into taking a studio course. He'd convinced me that drawing and painting might inform my critical perspective, which he seemed to be grooming. "Where would the artist be without the critic? The *intelligent* critic," Shep said, and encouraged me to start with reviews in the local papers. Heather maintained Shep's studio, mixed paint, and projected slides onto blank canvases so that Shep could get right to sketching his leaves, and sometimes she got the sketches started herself. It was common knowledge that she slept there most nights whether or not Shep was in New York; students would stop by at all hours and find Heather, groggy, on the couch behind the desk. There was no crime in marrying your ex-students, but it seemed safe to assume that Temple had some policy forbidding faculty to jumpstart their relationships when their future wives were still undergrads.

Shep's status as employed full professor always seemed precarious to me. Thomas Eakins himself had been bumped from the top spot at the Academy of Fine Arts, after exposing the last of a male model's concealed flesh to an audience of female students. About a hundred years before that, Ladies Only were denied the sight of even female privates; on Mondays, the day the Academy permitted women to enter, the nudes lent by the Louvre were draped and made decent. Proof of impropriety was easy to find—or it was found inevitably, when someone was looking for it. And so, on a Thursday afternoon in the spring of my senior year, I was bracing myself for the knock on the classroom door, for the authorities to come, once and for all, for the legacy of Puritanism in this town to finally catch up with Shep.

The night before, at an optional, though well attended, figure-drawing instructional, twenty or so students were sketching a life-size wooden mannequin, when Heather Ware, who was overseeing the session, got up in a huff and made a phone call. No answer. She dialed again. "*Shep*," she hissed, and stretched the cord into the hallway. When she returned, she apologized to the group in vague terms and said she didn't blame anyone who wanted to leave, at which point several people closed their giant sketchpads. "Sign in before you leave—you'll still get credit." Those who left missed the opportunity to draw Heather, who, after another fifteen minutes, announced she was "just gonna do it myself." She explained, as she unbuttoned her jeans, that she'd modeled for two years after college, both here and at other schools in the area, and so the no-student-model rule seemed moot under the circumstances—assuming, she added, smiling as she unsnapped her bra, that no one minded a female model two weeks in a row. Of the remaining dozen devotees, no one seemed to mind. This was my first optional instructional, and it would not be my last, I decided. The remainder of the hour seemed to pass by in a flash. As Heather hiked up her panties, she said she'd really appreciate it if no one mentioned this to Shep, or to any of the faculty—to no one, actually. She wasn't concerned about herself, she said; she just didn't want Shep to catch shit for something she'd done on her own. The other students shrugged and thanked Heather on their way out.

Presumably, no one ever mentioned it.

I headed toward Shep's apartment, finally, cutting into the neighborhood by a narrow street off Broad. From outside, the old place looked the same, right down to the partly open white door atop the concrete stoop. Feeling suddenly relieved, invigorated even, I slammed, unintentionally, the door of my truck, and hopped onto the sidewalk, just as the white door opened wider and a young man with a curly blond mop of hair backed out, resting a heavy box on the railing as he locked up.

"Does, uh—" I got his attention. "Shep…ard Stillman…?"

"Yeah," the young man said, over his shoulder. When he turned around, he was smiling, elated, it seemed, as if affected by the atmosphere inside. "Just missed him." He gathered the box in his arms and stepped down. "You a student?"

"Ex."

"He'll be back about noon tomorrow. Just a quickie to New York. You know…" He grinned, hiking the box against his chest. "Do me a favor?" He gestured toward his red car, holding out his keys.

I took the keys, unlocked the trunk, and helped with the box.

"Want me to give him a message?" the young man heaved, happily.

"I'll come back tomorrow," I said.

"Thanks for the hand. Charlie Young, by the way." His hands free, he patted me on the shoulder as he shut the trunk and darted for the driver's seat.

Beaming, Charlie Young took off, as if there were someplace else out there in the world that could possibly make him happier.

11
Sheer Venus

Across town, a few blocks west of Daisy Diamond's apartment, was a corner spot with the hip, one-word name *Clean* displayed in neon-cherry cursive in the bay window, alongside a poster of a man with a thin beard I imagined sporting. Inside, I tried seeing beyond the front desk into the back room, where spirited men's voices whirred with the sound of dryers blowing, the whole place abuzz with a Saturday-morning kind of excitement. The receptionist, pink-skinned with sculpted golden sideburns pointing toward his grin, said they didn't have a Daisy—but they had a *Darin*, who was just finishing up his eleven-o'clock—I didn't want to be Darin's eleven-thirty, did I?

Two blocks west of *Clean*, passing Buddy's Back Door and a movie house boasting a double feature—*Better Than Bush* and *Probing Uranus*—I realized I'd made a wrong turn. I headed back in the direction of my truck, which I'd parked illegally on Daisy's corner, as I had during my brief stay on Saturday. I'd left the hazard lights on and lowered the hatch—evidence of a man at work—a strategy that had always proven effective back in my Temple days when I got desperate for safe parking in North Philly.

Picking up the pace, I turned arbitrarily onto Eighth Street, passed a jewelry store and parking garage, and came upon *Sheer Venus*. In the bay window a life-sized Venus stood in her shell, orange curls snaking down her body, the poster suggesting her need for a trim. Suddenly another slender beauty was greeting me at the door, shaking my hand firmly. "I'm Monica...Botticelli." The owner, I deduced, shared not only the Italian Master's last name, but also his Venus's long curls, albeit dyed auburn, assembled with wooden sticks poked through a piece of leather.

"I'm Peter...Pappas."

"Pleased to meet you," Monica Botticelli said, holding the door, and it seemed by her smile that she was in fact pleased to meet me. Escorting me to the receptionist's desk, she said, "Allison will take care of you," and added, with a detectable wink, "I have to check on my girls," before heading toward the back room.

Allison put her hand over the phone's mouthpiece, and said, "You're here for Monica?" just as Monica returned, beaming.

I said, "I don't have an appointment, actually."

Monica said, "Squeezing in a quickie on your lunch break?"

"Uh—" I looked down at my paint-splattered army shorts.

A hair dryer hummed in the back room.

"Have a seat, Peter." Monica gestured toward chairs against the wall. "Daisy can fit you in."

How many Daisys could be cutting hair in Philadelphia?

This was the place.

I could still make a run for it, say I forgot to feed the meter...

Instead, I took a seat and swiped a magazine from the table. Monica's heels clicked toward the back room once again. I leaned forward to see past the wall of shelves filled with bottles. When Monica glanced back, I bowed intently into the magazine on my lap, suddenly a connoisseur of hairstyles.

The hair dryer stopped in the back room. Monica escorted a petite woman digging through her purse to pay for the yellow-S hairdo that curved between her shoulders.

"She'll be ready for you in a sec, Peter."

I had rolled up the magazine and was rapping it against my thigh, imagining another version of myself, not the fidgeting one sitting here, but a sauntering figure who greeted Daisy with a gentlemanly hug and didn't balk when she felt his boyish throbbing.

"Peter?" Monica called.

I pretended not to hear a thing, reopening and riffling through the magazine, and, with a finger, scanning the haircuts like numbers in the Yellow Pages.

"Ready? You can bring that with you..."

I cursed myself for having let my imagination run loose even for a moment. I forced myself to think unsexy thoughts, first of baseball, of sliding headfirst into home and swallowing a mouthful of dirt. I could feel Monica's eyes on me. "*Peter?*" I would be doomed to this chair forever, the heads of well groomed men sprawled on my lap. My mind raced desperately, unwittingly, toward my own innocent grandmother—*Yiayia, forgive me!* I imagined her spread-eagle, sun-dried and white-naked in her bed. At once I was nauseated, filled with guilt, disgusted by my own unconscious default method of unsexing myself, this inexcusable, if effective, last resort, a shameful exploitation of my grandmother's undeserving, used-up flesh.

I set down the magazine and followed Monica back.

In the far corner was Daisy—*my* Daisy—her back to me, in black slacks and open-shouldered sweater, her hair thick curls today. She was standing between a sink and a back door, assessing combs and scissors on the countertop. Next to me, in a chair facing a mirror bordered with glowing light bulbs, sat a sleeping woman, whose hair was a glistening arrangement of greased tubes. Daisy turned and smiled, gesturing toward the chair at her hip. Anything but a sauntering gentleman, I waved from the doorway and took long, quiet strides, not wanting to disturb the sleeping woman.

"Hello, Peter," Daisy said. "What a nice surprise."

Sunlight through Venetian blinds streaked the hardwood floor.

"Hi," I whispered, twisting into the seat. The room was warm and quiet, insulated by pinkish brick.

"She can't hear us," Daisy whispered, teasing. "You're not happy?"

"Happy?"

A whiff of fruit mingled with the chemical smell of antiseptic. Daisy flicked my hair with a comb, waiting, I realized, for further instructions, getting right to business.

"I'm happy," I said. "I was thinking maybe shorter."

"Really?" Her fingers grazed mine when I reached for my hairline. "I wouldn't go much shorter."

"Okay. Whatever you think."

"*Peter…*" she chuckled, and set the comb down on the countertop. "Step into my office…"

And just like that Daisy opened the door behind her. The blinds shook, and I sat up, my eyes on the sleeping woman across the room. "Come," Daisy said, slipping out first, leading me down wood-plank steps and into a backyard area. A bronze-colored car was parked, this side of a narrow street, on a bed of matted-down grass mixed with stones. I followed Daisy toward the car, where I found myself backed against the driver's door.

"How did you find me?" She stood inches from me, hands on her hips.

"Well—"

"You're sweaty," she said, and, glancing down, added, "What are you *wearing?*"

"Sorry," I said.

My stomach clenched up as she reached for my shirt and pecked my unsuspecting lips. Daisy settled against me then, her arms draped over my shoulders. As I lifted my face back away from her rose-scented snakes of hair, she finger-tipped and kissed my lower lip. When I puckered to reciprocate, the tip of her tongue appeared in a flash and vanished.

"It's not *wet*, is it…?" She stepped back, looking down.

My shirt hung down past my belt.

"Your paint, on my slacks," she added, pinching material at my thigh. She pointed a finger, playing bully-cop, while I played squirming criminal, backed against the car.

I looked down. "It's water-based. It dries fast."

"Lucky for you." She straddled my knees, nudging me with her hands on my shoulders. "Get down here." My sneakered feet inched across the stones between her shoes. I reached for the side mirror to keep from slipping.

"I came from work," I said.

"Long lunch break. Your boss must be wondering where you are."

"I can do what I want."

"I'm sure," she said. "I can do what I want, too."

"What about the woman sleeping in there?"

"Aren't *you* the worrier…" She curled her fingers over my clean-cut ears. "She's Monica's. Besides, I told Monica to keep an eye out for you."

"For *me?*"

Daisy pecked my chin. "Come home with me."

"How'd she know?" I said. "Now?"

"For lunch. You know where I live." She pointed to the narrow street, a shortcut.

I pictured my hazard lights blinking outside her place.

"I should get back," I said. "You told her I might *come* here?"

"You can do what you want," Daisy teased. "Yes, I told her." She kissed my cheek.

"I know. I just— I'm in the middle of work."

"You have to eat, right?" She bit my ear lobe. "I was hoping you might come." Her breath shot to my thighs. "Or maybe you really came for a haircut."

"No, I'm hungry. It's just…"

She took my hand. "Listen," she said softly, "no pressure," and led me toward the steps. "You know where I live. You come when you want." She stopped and smiled. "Okay?"

I held on to her hand as she started up the steps and I stayed put on the ground. On the middle step she paused and looked down.

"I can't go *in* there," I said.

She stepped down, grinning.

I fluffed my shirt, eyeing the alley. "I'll go *that* way."

Daisy clenched my hand. "*That's* nothing to be ashamed of…"

I snickered and stepped back.

"But I understand if you don't want to come inside with it." All at once her hand slipped from mine and found the source of heat in my pants. "No one can see us."

My tongue melting beneath hers, I clenched with all my might, willing my imagination once again in the direction of a headfirst slide, and then, as I cursed myself, my grandmother on all fours. But it was no use. Daisy let out a moan—of pleasure, or disappointment?—her dark eyes retreating, her hand suddenly the only firm thing between us. My failure had already passed me by, unnoticed even by me in the midst of my desperate clenching, but unmistakable now as Daisy sank back toward the stairs and I sank back into myself.

"Go down the alley," she said quietly, "to the street." In a flash she bowed her head and disappeared inside.

In the alley I imagined Daisy rushing to the bathroom to gather her wits, reminding herself that she needed a real man.

Out on the sidewalk, in the sun, the coast clear, I inspected the thick fabric of my army shorts, where a faint dime-sized stain had emerged between the pocket and zipper, a dab of ink through a broken pen. I had been with a woman for the last time, I decided. Nothing was worth this humiliation. Maybe I'd missed my calling to be a monk. Or maybe this was God's sign that I ought to be one. There was no point in an abstinent house painter.

I tugged my T-shirt down to my thighs and walked steadily to the red light at the corner, where I waited for a cab to pass through the intersection, then began jogging along Eighth Street, past another garage, past a Wawa mini-market—I was hungry, I wanted a hoagie, but I sped up into a sprint, if you could call it a sprint. The air revived me as I picked up my pace, my damp flesh bouncing in my boxers, weighty against my shorts, gearing myself up for a life without women, not that such a life would be all that different from the one I'd been living.

I slowed down, raking my fingers over the bars of an iron gate, beyond which a parking lot sat barren and wide steps rose up to giant columns and dark bronze doors that seemed as though they'd been bolted shut for centuries. This was the old Greek church, I realized— St. George's—Daisy's neighbor. I imagined it dark and musty compared to my father's church—St. Peter's—sun-drenched through its pale-blue windows. Yet these days every church seemed to me as foreign and ancient as this one, as though the only people still making their way through those creaking doors were little old ladies wrapped in black. I considered testing the doors, perhaps to find a hundred *yiayias* swathed in mourning clothes, praying for souls like mine.

Just ahead, a red light throbbed, its source—my truck—just out of view behind the corner building at Eighth and Pine. In my mind I hovered above Daisy, mute, limp, pointless, her black sweater and pants peeling back on their own like the thin shell of a boiled shrimp, her pale, arched flesh revealed in segments—belly, breasts, nipples…

I slammed my truck bed shut and headed home, envisioning myself in a white frock, climbing rocky steps toward an ancient monastery on a cliff. Still, even as I climbed, I saw her: waist, hips, glistening tuft of hair. On second thought, I would pull into the emergency room at Jefferson Hospital to get a lobotomy. There was no point in a monk who spent his life lusting and repenting, lusting and repenting.

12
Male Bonding

My stomach whining, I drove down Provincetown Avenue, back to work. My lump of flesh felt as lifeless as an old man's, a wrinkled sack of stones. I'd been trying my best to revive it, all the way down Kelly and Lincoln, torturing myself with defunct fantasies, imagining myself with Daisy, in her bedroom, in my basement, in the church downtown, in the apartment where I was headed. Now she was sitting next to me, inching out of her black pants, thumbs at her waist, gesturing with her chin to the McDonald's up ahead, reading my mind, seeing that I was very much alive after all, directing me into the parking lot, into a discreet spot in the shade under the trees. It dawned on me that her retreating dark eyes might not have been *knowing* eyes but *un*knowing eyes, seeking assurance I'd been too dim to offer. In her eyes—in her hand—not only had I shrunken in my shorts, but I'd lost interest in her, come to my senses about this woman who was old enough to be my mother—her worst fear confirmed.

Tonight I would call her and play the man who had shown restraint, because God knew what we might have done right there on the steps in broad daylight.

I was a gentleman after all.

A wave of hope came over me, as I inched toward the intercom, contemplating which of the Value Meals I would order—the Big Mac, the Double Quarter Pounder With Cheese. Both. This was occasion for a feast.

Inside the McDonald's, beyond the giant windows, haloed by a golden arch in the glass, a man with wild white hair—*Theo?*—carried a tray in both hands, bowed his head and squinted, in spite of his glasses, apparently recognizing my truck. He stood there, frozen, in loose-fitting gray sweatpants, the shoulder straps of a book bag—mine from college—looping under the armpits of a raggedy oxford-cloth shirt. I waved, but Theo didn't respond, his hands full, his vision distorted, perhaps, by the glary glass. A small woman in a dress—his lunch date?—framed within the adjoining yellow arch, nudged Theo out of view.

The row of cars moved toward the glowing menu wall in the mulch bed up ahead. I followed, questioning, now, whether it had been Theo after all. Who could the woman be? Some homeless woman whom Theo had offered to buy lunch? Or some woman, considering Theo's appearance, who offered to buy *him* lunch? Was it possible, come to think of it, that the woman was the same "friend" from over a decade ago whom my parents had deemed a bad influence, referring to her as Theo's "street woman" even after she'd played nurse the last time he tried to kill himself? Probably the woman was just a friend from the library, or even the librarian, though it was hard to believe that Theo had a companion of either gender, not only because he avoided people in general, but also because he avoided regular show-ers, believing that Americans were over-bathed, over-shaved, conditioned by the West to hate their own natural smell.

For as long as I could remember, Theo had spent his days at the East Birch public library, just up the street. He trekked on foot around mid-morning, after breakfast and several cups of coffee, which he drank at the kitchen table, while reading giant books he'd signed out the day before, getting his juices flowing. He returned home by six o'clock for dinner. Typically he crammed a Tupperware container filled with leftovers into his vinyl book bag. He ate, he said, in the library, not wanting to interrupt his research once he was immersed in history. In the summers, as kids, Brock and I would incorporate into our afternoon activities covert operations that required sneaking into the library and spying on Theo, who, especially in the eyes of my cronies, seemed extraordinarily strange; he was either a CIA agent or completely insane, what with his electrified hair rocketing toward the ceiling, his head down, his concentration unflinching, even when struck by a well-aimed spitball from the bookshelves.

Nearly at the intercom, I was tempted to park and go inside to order. But, curious as I was, I decided my sixty-five-year-old uncle deserved to eat in peace with whomever he wanted—with whoever was willing.

I assembled lunch on the passenger's seat before pulling out of the lot, the Supersize Coke between my thighs cooling my groin. The salt-scent of Big Mac and fries thickened the summer air. My Double Quarter Pounder With Cheese—an appetizer—bloomed from the yellow wrapper spread open on my thigh. A Happy Meal for a new man. Settled in, I sank my teeth in and gassed it.

*

The fuzzy sound of KYW News escorted me into the apartment. I lowered myself onto the carpet, setting my drink down, for a five-minute siesta. Legs and arms out like a stuck snow angel, I closed my eyes and tried to think of nothing, not even the static buzzing beyond the voice of the anchorman, not the traffic or the five-day forecast or the Phils' five-game winning streak or the progression of cancer in Tug McGraw's brain or the jam-up on the Walt Whitman Bridge or the sweltering heat or the fire in Kensington or the shooting in South Philly or these unpainted walls surrounding me or Dorothy Maloney or Daisy Diamond or what she would have fed me for lunch instead of a Double Quarter Pounder With Cheese, Big Mac, Supersize fries and a Coke.

I was dozing, done for the day. What difference did it make if I finished painting the apartment now or if I waited until tomorrow? Five units by the end of the week—no sweat...

I scraped myself off the floor, and within ten minutes, after fighting off sleep, nodding off behind the wheel in a thick-headed fog, I was sinking, knees tucked, into my bed, hearing, in my mind, her whispering, *It's okay,* as I grew smaller in her hands and I sank deeper into darkness. I'm not hungry, I heard myself saying, insisting, I just ate, Mom, no, nothing's the matter, Mom, please stop worrying, Mom, repeating myself for hours, it seemed, floating, until I realized I was dreaming, or half-dreaming, and I was home, in my basement, and it wasn't my own voice I was hearing, but Andrew's—*Peter's a big boy now, Mom*—upstairs, in the kitchen, telling my mother he was sure I was fine, wherever I was.

One bite, Mom. Come on...

Andrew, stop it.

You're too skinny. I can't even pinch an inch.

Andrew.

One little bite.

I'm not eating it.

Show me one inch, anywhere.

Ow! Andrew... You liked me better fat?

You were never fat.

I sat on the top step, at the closed door.

Keep that away from me...

It seemed suddenly obvious to me, and so all the more embarrassing, that Andrew had always been her favorite; what was worse, she'd deprived herself of Andrew, attending to those who needed her. In my earliest memories of Andrew, he was skittish and rowdy, energized by fast-pumping blood, itching to dive back into the water or blast out the doors into the neighborhood. Later, on Friday nights, he and the old man would cackle at comedies in the living room, passing a bag of pretzels back and forth, even on the night ABC aired the documentary on the Shroud of Turin, the previews for which had both thrilled and haunted me all week. I had assumed the discovery would catch the attention of the world, let alone my father, who said he had enough proof. My mother watched patiently with me, on the ten-inch screen in my parents' bedroom, the two of us making the best of our choice, sitting up, with a spaghetti pot filled with popcorn between us, our backs to pillows, as laughter rose from the living room. As it turned out, after all the blathering of scientific and historical facts made credible by the deep-voiced narrator, the documentary's findings remained as fuzzy, in my mind, as the image of the ghostly Christ burned into cloth like charred marshmallow. Even at that age, I should have known better, particularly after *In Search of Noah's Ark*—the movie I'd dragged my mother to see, at the beach, several summers before—had led to a colossal mound of snow, from which an ancient wooden boat poked, dark fossilized planks exposed like pirates' treasure; again, all I'd garnered from the movie was the same tantalizing image that had lured me in the first place. That night, my mother and I caught up with Andrew and the old man, on the boardwalk, at some game booth, where they'd already won a stuffed monkey for Sophia by gunning baseballs at pins.

When I entered the kitchen, Andrew shouted, "Doc!" and, in a flash, recalling Saturday, I braced myself for a sucker-punch that would even the score. But Andrew kept clearing the table, his back turned.

"*Peter*," his mother gasped, her hands in running water. "I've been worried *sick*—"

"I'm here. I've been here—"

"Have you seen Theo, honey? It's almost seven-thirty."

I shook my head.

Andrew waved a fistful of silverware. "Hundred bucks he's asleep in the library."

A few weeks before, on a Friday, Theo had fallen asleep at his carrel and didn't wake up until after midnight, after the doors had been bolted. My parents were in Scranton for a youth-group conference and so my mother wasn't around to call the police. Theo stayed until closing the next day. Several times over the years, particularly in the dark winters, the library called to ask someone to come pick up Theo, who had fallen asleep and seemed too delirious to find his way home.

Andrew took three plates to the sink, grinning at the thought of Theo asleep in his books. Suddenly he did a double take and said, "Holy shit, Doc. Lookin' dapper."

"*Andrew*," my mother said. The language.

I reached for the ponytail that didn't exist.

"So what's up, Doc? We're due for some male bonding."

Andrew was certainly being jovial. This would be his way of making peace: dropping by for dinner, cleaning up, horsing around, saying nothing of the scuffle on the driveway or the Lexus or Melanie.

"You can help yourself, Peter." My mother flicked her hands over the sink like wet lettuce and turned for the garage, her light-blue Adidas pants pinched between her thighs. "I'm off. Yiayia's been fed.

Your father had a council meeting, so we ate. Help Theo with a plate when he gets in."

"*If...*" Andrew said.

She smiled and shut the door.

"...he gets in."

"He's a grown man!" I called out, scooping a steaming pile of toma-to-sauce-smothered pork and potatoes onto my plate. Andrew rinsed something in the sink. In the silence it dawned on me that maybe Andrew deserved an apology from *me*. After all, how Andrew spent his money and what he did with Melanie was *his* business. "Sorry, uh—"

"*Hey*," Andrew interrupted. "Don't." The water stopped, and, thwacking his hands together in a kind of referee gesture—game over—he started toward the garage.

I nodded, and Andrew went outside. The tinny sound of a basketball made its way into the house from the driveway. At the kitchen table I was shoveling steaming pork into my mouth, when Theo peeked in through the screen door.

"They gone?"

I swallowed.

Theo's book bag slid off his shoulders and landed on the desk in the corner.

"You won't tell," Theo said.

"Tell what?" I said.

Theo stared.

I shook my head, no, I wouldn't tell, and took another bite.

"*Say* it." Theo pulled out a chair and sat down.

"I won't tell," I said, my words garbled.

Theo grasped my arm as I forked a potato.

"Promise."

"Jesus, I won't tell anyone. What's the problem?" I bit the tip of the potato. "You can do what you want, Theo. No one can stop you."

"You promised."

"I'm not saying anything." I chomped away.

Theo eyed me skeptically and looked toward the garage. "What's that?"

"Andrew. Dribbling."

Theo looked over his shoulder at the front door, then said softly, "I've been thinking about my own apartment."

"That's good," I said.

"Not with *her*," Theo said. "She lives with her sister. I need a place to work."

"You don't have to explain."

"You think about getting your own place? Theo bowed to see my eyes.

I stabbed a chunk of pork. "I've been thinking about it."

Theo's stubbly cheeks sank suddenly. "You're *moving?*"

"No time soon," I lied.

Theo's sad gray eyes opened wide.

I pointed with my fork, sliding my plate toward him.

He took the fork and dabbed tomato sauce onto a potato. "I had a Big Mac."

"Me too," I said.

Theo scooped a mouthful. "I can afford a nice place. I've been saving—"

Andrew opened the kitchen door and displayed the basketball on a cone of fingers. "Peter," he panted, "I need a rebounder. Theo—you made it home alive." He shut the door.

"What's *he* doing home?" Theo said.

"Male bonding," I said.

Theo wiped his mouth with his hand and paused, realizing: "I liked the hair long."

"Me too." I gazed into the back yard, as Theo went on eating.

"She's my friend," Theo said.

"I'm glad," I said.

Outside, the backboard thumped.

"She saved my life," Theo said.

"I remember," I said.

Theo's fork scraped the plate. "You can go play if you want."

I waited a moment then scooted back on my chair. "I'm just the rebounder."

In the garage I rifled through a wooden chest of baseball bats and various deflated balls. Andrew pivoted and sank a shot, got his own rebound and put in a lay-up. Empty-handed, I flinched when Andrew pump-faked a chest pass.

I fielded a bounce pass and put up a two-hander that shot off the rim toward Andrew at the free-throw line.

"Ten in a row. Here we go." Andrew's fingers curled in the air. The ball fell through the net and skipped off the pole toward me. I lobbed it back. Andrew sank one after another, as I stood in position under the net.

"Five," Andrew said, eyes barely on the basket.

"You all right?" I said.

"Perfect." Andrew gathered and lofted the ball in a single fluid motion. "Six."

I jabbed the ball with a fist. "How's Melanie?"

Eyes on the basket, Andrew said, "She's got some shit to figure out."

"Seven." I held the ball until Andrew made a target with his hands.

"Women are complex, Doc." He shot. "Eight."

"Tell me about it." I passed the ball.

Andrew held the ball and grinned. "*You* tell me about it."

I grinned back. "Shoot."

"Who *is* she?"

I leaned back against the pole. "She's older."

Andrew sat down on the ball.

I gripped the pole behind my back. "She's the one who cut my hair."

"This is yesterday?" Andrew said. "What happened?"

"Don't tell anyone." I crossed my arms on my chest.

"Who am I gonna tell? How *much* older?"

"Thirty-something. Late thirties."

Andrew squatted and rolled the ball back and forth in front of him. "You ask her out?"

"No. Sort of."

"You get her number?" Andrew stood up.

I shrugged and stepped out from under the basket.

"Jesus, Doc…" Andrew shot. Nine.

I punched the ball back and hooked my thumbs in my pockets.

Andrew pressed the ball to his hip. "Call the hair salon, near the end of the day, when you know she's working. Say, 'I was in the neighborhood and I was wondering if you'd like to join me for a drink.'"

I laughed. "I don't drink."

"It's time you started."

"Why would I be in the *neighborhood?*"

"Why *wouldn't* you be the neighborhood? It's a big city, Doc. If a woman's interested, you think she's gonna be thinking about why you're downtown? Shopping, tell her. Looking for a watch. It doesn't matter. Ask her if she knows anything about watches, could she meet you. You could really use a woman's opinion, tell her—there you go. Flirt, Doc. Use your God-given charm."

"Right." I stuffed my fists into my pockets.

Andrew flicked the ball into a spin on his index finger. "Meet her at Tiffany's, so she can show you the ring she likes. I guarantee she's got one picked out already."

"Yeah." I laughed.

Andrew shot the ball and snapped his fingers. "How many is that?"

"Ten," I said, as the ball skipped away. "What would I be wearing?"

"*Wearing?*" Andrew walked toward the ball in the grass.

I lifted my arms, displaying my paint-speckled shirt and shorts. "I can't wear this. She knows what I wear to work. I wouldn't be all geared up for going out in the middle of the day."

"Jesus, Doc." Andrew scooped up the ball. "Say you finished early. You took the day off. She's not gonna be thinking about why you're not wearing your stupid army shorts. You still don't have a cell phone, do you?" He under-armed the ball to me under the basket. "Tomorrow we're getting you out of the Stone Age, Doc. You're not calling from a *pay* phone."

I sank a lay-up. "I don't want a cell phone."

"You still a member at the gym?"

"Technically."

"We'll work out in the morning," Andrew said, "and then get you a phone."

"I have to work," I said.

"So do I. I'll crash here tonight." Andrew flashed his hands up for the pass. "We'll rent a couple a movies."

I imagined Melanie sleeping alone, surrounded by unpacked boxes.

"Something mindless. Let's go..." Andrew drifted toward the Porsche. "Bronson or Dirty Harry." I rolled the ball into the trees, as Andrew dug his keys from his pocket and flashed a clever grin: "We'll bond."

*

In the video store Andrew stood before the James Bond section, examining his fingernails, or so I thought until I sidled up and saw the sparkling thing at his fingertips.

"She waits till we're all moved in—*everything*." Andrew kept his head down, eyes on the ring. "We're completely out of our old apartments, so there's nowhere to go."

I stared at the cases on the shelves—*Her Majesty's Secret Service, Live and Let Die*—the various Bonds, standing bow-tied and stoic, their shadowy-cleavaged playthings, in spandex and heels, leaping from exploding fireballs into the foreground.

"Just last night. I poured champagne—to celebrate. I'm thinking, here we are, our own place. And she says, 'I have to ask you something,' and I think, Oh, no. That's not good, when a woman says she has to ask you something. I'm assuming she's gonna ask me about other women, whether I've ever cheated or something. And I'm thinking, okay, *no*, which is the truth, and we'll move on. Or maybe she's gonna ask about what happened Saturday—not telling Mom and Dad about living together. Fine, I can handle that. I fucked up, I just need time, I'll tell them, et cetera, right?" Andrew looked up. "So you know what she says?"

I shook my head, picturing Melanie in pajamas, ready for bed, holding off on champagne.

"Guess." Andrew buried the ring in his fist.

"No idea."

"You have to guess." Andrew took *Octopussy* off the shelf and gazed at the case.

I shook my head again. In my mind Melanie was loosening her ring.

"'Would you *convert* for me?' This is what she says." Andrew's smirk broadened. He nodded furiously as if confirming my disbelief. "I'm like, '*Convert* for you? Where'd *this* come from?'" He flipped the case and scanned the back. "She says it again, 'Would you convert for me?' She's serious, so I say, 'Sure.' But she says, 'You're lying.' And she's glaring at me, and she's freaking me out now. And I'm like, 'Fine, you're right, but we've talked about this,' and she says, 'No, we've *never* talked about this. It's always just been assumed. I'm the one to convert for *you*.' And then she launches into this whole thing about how she doesn't *trust* me anymore, how I'm *selfish* and all this shit, and how if it came down to it she's not sure if I'd *sacrifice* for her, and I'm like, 'What *sacrifice*? What the hell are you *talking* about?' She's gonna tell me that converting is this huge *sacrifice* for her? They don't even go to synagogue or whatever on *holidays*. But she says, 'That's not the *point*.' And then she takes it and slaps it in my hand." He raised the ring onto his fingertips. "And she just stares at me and says, 'Leave.'" The ring dropped into his hand. "I'm the one that just paid the deposit on this apartment and the first month's rent and she's telling me to leave. I couldn't believe it."

"You left?"

"No, I drank my champagne. I told her she was crazy, and I turned on the TV. And then she stands in front of the TV. And then she turns it off and goes, 'Say it,' like she's giving me one last chance, and I'm like, 'Say *what*?' and she goes, 'I'm not even asking you to *do* it. I'm just asking you to *say* it.' I honestly have no idea what she's talking about at this point, and I go, 'Say *what*, Melanie?' very calmly, like I'm talking to a crazy person, and she goes, 'That you'd convert for me. That you *would*,' she says, and I'm like, 'What do you mean, *would*? If *what*?' and she goes, 'If I *asked* you to.'" He put *Octopussy* back on the shelf, keeping his cool. "I'm like, 'Are you *asking* me to?' and she says, 'No, I'm saying *if*—'" Andrew turned completely, wagging the ring at me, and I was suddenly facing him head-to-head, as Melanie must have been. Andrew proceeded in a barely restrained voice: "I'm holding this ring, which is almost two fucking carats, and she's asking me if I'd become *Jewish* for her. *If!*" I looked up the aisle. Andrew lowered his voice. "*If* she asked me to, which she *wasn't*. She's practically not Jewish *herself*. So I'm like, 'Melanie, put the ring back on.'" He shoved the ring at me, and I gestured for it. "You *know* I wouldn't convert, because you're practically not Jewish *yourself!*" Andrew jerked the ring back, and I flinched. "And she gives me this look and then locks herself in the bedroom." He put the ring back into his pocket and began nodding, staring straight through me, as if at the closed door. I braced myself for the inevitable kick or punch.

"Then you left?"

"No, I fell asleep on the couch. When I woke up, the ring's still on the coffee table where I left it. I knocked on the bedroom door. She's not in there. I have no idea when she snuck out, no idea where she went. Home, I guess. And she leaves this note on the bed, two words, *Please leave*." Andrew shook his head, staring at my belly—as if at the note on the bed.

"I can't believe it. Sorry."

"Don't say sorry." Andrew looked up and put a hand on my shoulder. "If this is the way it would be, fuck it."

"What are you saying?"

"Six years, and then one night in the same place, and *boom— done*—that's all it took."

"It's *over?*"

"What do you think I've been telling you here, Doc? She's the one who needed to"—Andrew made quotes with his fingers—"*test it out*."

I scanned the shelves, imagining Melanie clicking down the sidewalk, wiping her tears and catching her breath.

"How about one Sean Connery and one Roger Moore?" Andrew swiped two cases from the shelf.

I exhaled and caught up with Andrew at the checkout counter.

*

Near the end of *Octopussy*, Andrew's snoring woke me up. I'd fallen asleep in the beanbag chair, wrapped up in an afghan, my head back on the ottoman, while Andrew slept on the sofa, legs sprawled, his socked feet at my ears. After *Goldfinger* we'd sought to resolve the great debate: Connery or Moore. Andrew had said Sean Connery was cooler because he didn't give a shit. I had said Roger Moore was cooler because he was truly indifferent; he wasn't posturing to get the girl—"He's just as content *without* her. That's why he's never a dick"—while Connery was always turning his nose up—"It's all part of the seduction for that guy. He *expects* her to be under the sheets in the end. But for Roger Moore it's like a pleasant surprise when she's waiting for him—he's like, 'Oh, hello there.' It's a nice alternative to sleeping alone, but he'd sleep fine without her. Connery would be tearing the place apart if she wasn't lying there with her legs spread." Andrew was laughing, as I got caught up in the imitation, looking under the coffee table—under the bed—pouring on the Scottish accent: "*Where is that conniving bitch?*"

Right now, as Andrew slept, it was Octopussy who couldn't stand being dismissed, while the other, doe-eyed Bond girl was somewhere waiting patiently. I wouldn't wake Andrew, even to remind him of Sophia's empty bed. I understood that being on the couch in the morning was all part of giving the impression that he'd slept here only by accident, that everything was cool.

I crawled out from the afghan and stopped the movie.

In the basement I plucked the letter from my wallet and dropped it into the trashcan under my desk.

When I got into bed, Octopussy slipped out of a sea-green gown, pleasantly surprising me.

Tonight the *Sports Illustrated* swimsuit models would stay tucked away in the top drawer of my nightstand—these mermaids in my mind that had been expanding in number, issue after annual issue, ever since the time in middle school when I verified the truth about what happened at a certain age, as Brock had warned. Dr. West had been the one to tell Brock, who was as skeptical as I was when he relayed the fact that, while you were sleeping, "jelly comes out."

Imagining grape, I couldn't begin to guess what had motivated the professor to tell such a lie, which, he must have known, Brock would relay to his cronies. On the beanbag chair, I'd been riffling through pictures of ecstatic girls emerging from the ocean. Mindlessly, and with no intended dramatic effect, I was jiggling myself, as I did when flicking the last drops into the toilet, when I remembered handsome Mark Miller, at the urinal, not flicking but squeezing his like a tube of toothpaste, while boasting to another urinating friend of the number of fingers he'd managed to get inside a certain willing classmate he called his girlfriend. It was then—jeans at my knees under the afghan my aunt had woven for me—that I put two and two together, realizing that Mark Miller would know how to use it. My insides boiling as I squeezed, I imagined an explosion of blood and piss potent enough to flood the room and wake the neighborhood. But in no time at all I stirred up a moderate amount of the dormant stuff to which Dr. West must have been referring and which was not grape, though I could see why the professor had described it as jelly. What a relief when the evidence—as if in the hands of a nervous, hand-roiling magician—had vanished as quickly as it had come.

As I drifted into sleep, into dreams, a breeze came in from the balcony, as Octopussy said, Oh, Peter. Nude, in a field, Dorothy rocked her small hips, saying, Come away with me. In the back seat of her car on the hill up the street, Daisy hiked up her polka-dotted dress, saying, Come home with me, and then, on the carpet in a freshly painted Stone Bridge apartment, she hovered above me, saying, Let me feed you, as she lowered a nipple.

13
Hard for Your Woman

The next morning the old man sipped his coffee, eyeing my army shorts. "What's he have you painting these days?"

I hiked my gym bag higher onto my shoulder. "Same as always."

My mother, geared up for her walk, turned from the stove.

Andrew stood at the counter and stirred his coffee.

Theo spun on his stool, squinting and grinning. "Looks like you lost control of the brush."

I scowled at Theo: *I know your secret, old man.*

"Taking a change of clothes?" my father said.

I set my gym bag on the floor near the refrigerator.

"We're going to the gym," Andrew answered for me.

I shuffled over to the sink, milk carton in hand.

"No work today?" my father said.

I poured my Lucky Charms.

"They know how to reach me." Andrew tapped the cell phone fastened to his belt. "After the gym, we're finally gonna get Peter one of *these* babies."

Mid-munch, I glared at Andrew.

"You want eggs, Peter?" My mother tilted the pan to show four sizzling eggs, their yolks perfect yellow circles.

I shook my head, spooning my Lucky Charms.

"You're not working today, Peter?" my father said.

"Who am I making all this for?" my mother said. "Andrew?"

Andrew patted his flat tummy.

"*I'll* eat them," Theo called out.

"Too much cholesterol, Theo. You already had two. What are you eating, Andrew?"

"I'm still hungry," Theo said.

"*Peter*," my father snapped.

I swallowed. The spoon clanged in my bowl.

"I asked if you're working today."

"I go in when I want."

"Since when?" The old man set his coffee cup on its saucer.

I pulled the ring of keys from the giant pocket at my thigh. "I paint five units a week. He only comes on Fridays."

"That's a nice arrangement." My mother handed me a plate from the cupboard. "Sounds like he's giving you more responsibility."

I set the plate on the counter.

"I doubt he means you come and go as you please," my father said. "He's paying you to go to the *gym?*"

I filled my mouth with cereal.

Of course, no one was pressing Andrew for the details of *his* life, as he stood there quietly slurping his coffee, as if this were any other morning, bright-eyed after a night on the couch, dressed for work in his white doctor jacket and the same khakis and sneakers he'd worn the day before, enjoying the benefits of the Don't Ask, Don't Tell policy that applied only to him.

"Okay, Theo." My mother handed one plate to the old man, the other to Theo, who leapt from desk to table.

"Look at that." Theo lowered his face toward the steaming half-moon and yellow eyes.

"Where are your glasses, Theo?" The old man pierced an egg yolk and turned to me. "You can afford a cell phone?"

I drank the pinkish milk and set the bowl in the sink.

"You should be saving," my father said.

I picked up my gym bag.

"Are you joining us for breakfast, Olympia?" Theo said.

"Is that an invitation, Theo?"

"Absolutely."

"Eat," she said, "so I can finish the dishes and go for my walk."

"I may crash here again tonight," Andrew announced.

"You don't need permission," my father said.

"Sleep in Sophia's bed," my mother said.

"Olympia, more coffee?" Theo held up his mug.

"Are you offering or asking?"

"Asking."

The phone rang.

"You can see where the coffee is," my mother said, drying her hands on a towel.

Theo shuffled toward the coffee maker, his wine-colored slippers shushing the room.

My mother plucked the portable from its base on the wall. Her smile sank. "So*phia, hon*ey!" Instantly in her greeting there was a strange, dreadful tone she seemed to be echoing. "What *is* it, sweetheart?"

Andrew and I froze at the door to the garage. The old man had been walking to the sink, chewing while scooping the last of the egg yolk from his plate—he stopped, fork in his mouth. Theo slurped, then set his mug on the counter.

My mother stood in the middle of the kitchen, where the men surrounded her.

"Whatever you want, honey. Don't worry. It's fine, sweetie. I'll get you."

"Looks like I'm back on the couch," Andrew said.

My mother frowned at Andrew and went into the dining room, where she reassured Sophia.

"I'll be there, nine-thirty. Of course not, honey." She glared at my father. "No one is going to be mad at you," she declared, and then whispered her goodbye. When she clicked off the phone and returned to us, her face was rosy and damp. "She's very upset and embarrassed."

"Why would I be mad?" my father said.

"Has it even been two days?" Andrew said.

"She doesn't need anyone harassing her." My mother set the portable on the kitchen table and took Theo's plate from his hands. "She's embarrassed she's coming home already."

"Did something happen?" my father asked.

"She didn't want to talk about it," my mother said.

"Did you *ask?*"

"Of *course* I asked, Paul, but she said she didn't want to talk about it."

"So much for saving the homeless," Andrew said.

"She'll find plenty of people to save here," my father said.

"Stop it," my mother said.

"I guess the honeymoon's over," I let slip.

"*Peter*," my mother huffed.

My father, Theo, and Andrew all laughed.

"You *guys*..." My mother ducked out the screen door.

I had unwittingly allied myself with the men of the house. My father, still grinning, must have assumed I'd meant something like "Party's over"—our little Sophia was coming home—score one for the family. I ducked into the garage, ashamed to have just betrayed my sister, let alone my mother, though I was sure no one would consider the literal implications of my wisecrack.

Cackling, Andrew pounded me on the shoulder. "Good one, Doctor."

*

Andrew watched me set up shop in the unfinished Stone Bridge apartment. "Just in case," I said, flattening the drop cloth and turning the radio on in the living room.

"Not a bad setup, Doc." Andrew panned the place, arms akimbo, as if impressed by an office with a view of the city.

"It's not brain surgery." I shrugged, as I locked the door.

"I mean, you should take advantage of this place."

"How so?"

Out in the parking lot, Andrew admired the trees and the quiet neighborhood across the street from the parking lot. "You could have your own private *soiree* here. Who would know? You got the pool, your own private resort, Doc. Perfect for a young single man like yourself."

"Speaking of single men."

Andrew rustled his keys. "I've never *not* been single." He displayed his fingers. "You see a ring? Have you *ever* seen a ring?"

"So what's next?"

"Next?" Andrew aimed his keys. His car beeped.

"Have you talked to her?"

Andrew sank into the black leather cockpit of the Porsche. The engine moaned. "Let's get to work on that gut."

I smiled, patting my belly with two hands. I turned toward my pickup, as Andrew pulled into the street. In the driver's seat of the truck, I clenched handfuls of flesh at the edge of my belt. On the third turn of the ignition, the truck started. Behind some trees the little red car hummed patiently.

*

Andrew called out over the buzzing of the stationary bikes, which overlooked the swimming pool. Biking was a good way to get the blood flowing, he said, gazing down at the patio, where a smattering of bikinied bodies on lounge chairs were catching the first rays of sunshine through the gaps between the high-rise apartment buildings surrounding the club.

As we pedaled, I answered simple questions—"Where does she live?""Where does she work?" Yes, she'd been married—her husband died; no, she didn't have kids; yes, she was good-looking—*very*—yes, objectively speaking, not just in my eyes; to be exact, forty-three—"So she *said*," Andrew clarified, and added, "Let's say forty-five. How's her body?"

Then it was time to get our muscles pumped up before swimming. Andrew stood at the head of the bench, while I got comfortable with the bar. I'd cleared the bar free of weights in order to reacquaint myself with the motion first. Andrew stretched his arms lazily over his head. His gray Penn Med T-shirt rose up, revealing his shadowy grooved muscles, permanently distinct. His chrome cell phone and beeper, clipped to the waistband of his red shorts, gleamed like pistols.

I should focus on my upper body, Andrew advised, in order to counter-balance my thick trunk, which, even if subject to the swimming regimen he'd outlined for me, would not begin to shrink for at least six weeks, not until after my metabolic rate was completely altered. Remember, Mom had lost only five pounds in the first two months, but then ten in the next two months and so on.

"Success breeds success, Doc. Getting started's the toughest part. When was the last time you really worked out—not just *biked*, but lifted weights?"

"It's been a while," I said—not a lie, technically—though the last time had been in college. "I just do cardio usually," I explained. *Cardio:* Andrew's word for jogging or riding a bike. A one-hour workout, three times a week (twenty minutes of cardio, twenty minutes of lifting, twenty minutes in the pool)—that's all it would take, Andrew had encouraged me, back in January when he'd bought me the six-month membership—an embarrassingly expensive Christmas gift, which, I learned later, my parents had pushed Andrew to buy for me, because (my mother's rationale) it would give her sons a reason to spend time together and because (my father's rationale) I needed to start shedding some weight and just getting out of the house now and then.

"You been swimming?"

It was obvious that Andrew's gift had gone completely wasted. In my bulky getup—one of the many double-X, Beefy-T-brand T-shirts and lined bathing-suit-style beach shorts I'd picked up at Target with the intention of wearing to the gym—I was in worse shape now than I'd been in on New Year's Day, when Andrew sat me down in the living room, after we'd gorged ourselves, and devised the three-day-per-week workout plan.

"I don't mind the treadmill." I wouldn't confess to coming only twice since the new year began. I did the math: seventy dollars a month since January—six months—came to four hundred and twenty dollars. This was my fourth visit (including my introductory visit with Andrew), so each so-called workout had cost a hundred and five dollars.

"You gotta *swim*, Doc." Andrew might have been pleading with a patient. "When's your membership up?" He counted on his fingers—January, February… "This is it, Doc. Beginning of July is six months. You gotta extend it, or else you'll lose the membership fee, and then you'll have to re-pay it if you want to join again."

"Membership fee?"

"Two hundred forty bucks or something."

I adjusted the sleeves of my T-shirt, lifted the bar off its brackets, lowered it to my chest, and repeated the motion, calculating...

The value of each of my four workouts had just shot up sixty dollars—to one hundred sixty-five dollars. This had been the price for loafing on a treadmill while watching music videos on a TV hanging from the ceiling.

"Ya gotta get hard for your woman, Doc."

Andrew was right. This was it. I was making a promise to myself, yet another resolution: I would extend the membership, today, and commit to the three-day-per-week workout plan, including the swimming. I would make up for lost time, starting right now. This was the year, the summer, of new life.

"Ever been with an older woman?" Andrew's hands hovered, waiting to guide the bar back onto its brackets.

I lowered the bar again before returning it.

Andrew gripped the bar and stared down.

"Over forty?" I said, as if I'd been with women in their thirties.

"They know what they want. You could learn a lot."

We slid forty-five–pounders onto the bar, one on each side. A woman in black Lycra pants and a white sports bra slinked by. I recognized her braids from the front desk. I lay back on the bench.

"Ever take your coffee black?" Andrew's eyes followed the woman into the back room.

I made the connection and shook my head, no, contemplating the miracle of brothers with nothing in common but their parents.

Andrew guided the bar off the brackets. "How long's it been?"

I grunted, lowering the bar and pushing back up, no problem.

Andrew went on, "In the last few years, who's there been? You tell me nothing about your women anymore, Doc."

I couldn't remember *ever* telling Andrew about "my women." I got up and grabbed another forty-five-pounder from the rack.

Andrew mirrored me on the opposite side. "Don't tell me the chick from college, Doc. With the short hair and the sneakers?"

"Dorothy."

"You haven't had sex in *five years?*" Andrew gasped, turning toward the window and looking down. The sun shone onto his contemplative face. "You know I've never been with an Asian chick?"

I heaved the bar off the brackets.

"Never wanted to. Too boyish or something." He twisted to lend me a hand.

The bar was stable as it rose again.

"Two-twenty-five here, Doc. Thought you haven't lifted for a while."

I stared into my brother's eyes. "*Two—*"

"C'mon, Doc, you got it—"

Andrew nudged the bar toward the brackets, but I tugged back.

His eyes were wide open, his fingertips barely guiding. "Three..."

My armpits clenched like fists.

"*Breathe*, Doc."

The bench shook when the bar fell back finally.

"You're a *bull*, Doc."

I sat up, rubbing my shoulders.

"You'll be putting up three hundred by next week." Andrew flashed a smile, lowering his shorts on his hips. "Ready for a swim?" Above his waistline peeked the familiar white stars, pinkish stripes, and faded blue of an ancient Speedo. His smile vanished, and he said, "I just realized you're with a *widow*."

I got up and stood next to Andrew near the window. The word "widow" instantly grouped Daisy with lonely old ladies in black. I wanted Andrew to think of her as exotic, as I did.

"I've definitely never been with a widow," Andrew said—longingly or contentedly, I wasn't sure.

Outside, an Asian girl, about thirteen, in an orange one-piece and orange cap, clapped her hands above her head and dived into the pool. Just as she sank into the water, a thunderous crash came from beyond the club's property. The echo rumbled in the walls. Though I saw nothing out of the ordinary, I visualized an airplane penetrating one of the sky-blue towers in the distance. In the past year the familiar mental picture was often triggered by loud noises. Shoulder to shoulder, Andrew and I panned the empty sky. After a moment, I imagined an air conditioner falling from a window, a TV tipping off a balcony, a dumpster slipping from the arms of a garbage truck.

An orange-capped head popped above the water's surface. The girl slipped out of the pool and headed for the white slat fence bordering the patio. Forehead to the glass, I tried to follow her around the edge of the window sash. Three women on lounge chairs had propped themselves on their elbows, their hands visors.

When Andrew's cell phone rang, I flinched. The first signal of a disaster, I thought: Calling all doctors.

Andrew checked the caller ID. "Gotta take this. Meet you at the pool." Before turning his back, he added, "You swimming in that?"

I made my way outside, where I looked up at the empty balconies. There was no commotion. No crowd had gathered. The girl in the orange bathing suit plopped into the pool. The women on chairs were lying back, staring at the sun.

I tucked my sneakers under a chair and sat at the edge of the pool. I submerged my legs in the water, up to my knees. I aimed my face toward the sky, where, in my mind, a flickering box was still somersaulting toward the earth.

Andrew said, "Duty calls, Doc. Gotta run." He looked in the direction of my gaze, toward the top of the building across the street, and then at me. "You gonna swim or sit there with your T-shirt on like an old man?" He flipped open his phone, back-stepping toward the door. "The Verizon store's on Walnut. Get *this* one. Best reception." He smiled. "Call her," he said, demonstrating with his phone to his ear. "I was in the neighborhood...shopping for a watch...how 'bout a drink?" He opened the door. "I expect a full report later."

I sat at the edge of the pool, watching the girl in orange wiggling through the water like a goldfish, wishing I were more like Andrew, or at least more optimistic.

A woman in a club sweat suit walked out onto the patio and glanced at the apartment building. "Someone said someone jumped," she said—to me, it seemed—and went back inside. Beyond the glaring glass, by the reception desk, silhouettes of sweat-suited figures floated aimlessly. In my mind a woman stood at the ledge of her balcony, eyeing her tiny red-car target.

I put my socks and sneakers back on and got my gym bag from the locker room. I'd brought a pair of khakis and a short-sleeved, collared shirt, but I wasn't in the mood to change. On second thought, I pulled my khakis over my shorts; I wasn't about to go waltzing around the city in this crazy-looking bathing suit or my paint-stained army shorts, which were stuffed in my gym bag.

At the front desk employees whispered as I passed. Outside on the corner several people—employees in gym suits; a couple guys panting in running shorts; expressionless passersby, their shoulders sunken from the weight of shopping bags—stared silently down the narrow street at the sealed doors on the back of an ambulance, which must have arrived quietly.

Down the block I dumped my bag onto the front seat of my truck and rushed up Walnut Street. All the while, in my mind, a woman fluttered through the air.

Inside the Verizon store, I spotted, on the shelf behind the main desk, Andrew's phone. When the saleswoman asked what my needs were—family, work, long distance, roaming—I did not explain that I was buying the phone to dial a single number. "Family," I said. When she asked if I was interested in "the family plan," I answered, no, and asked if it was possible to block certain incoming calls.

Out on the sidewalk, thumbing the buttons, I lamented the purchase. Since college I'd taken pride in getting by without a cell phone, the Internet, or even a computer. But what choice did I have? I could not call her from home, lying in bed while my mother crossed the floor above me—let alone give out the home number—and I could not keep swinging by the salon.

I tested the three-digit number for information. When the digitized voice asked for a name, I said, "Diamond, Daisy." At the ring, I clapped the phone shut. I picked up the pace toward my truck, digging Andrew's business card from my wallet and wondering when and to whom orthopedic surgeons handed out such cards.

"You got it!" Andrew cheered.

"Same as yours."

"Now I have your number," he said.

Only then did I realize that calling someone meant giving up your number. I wouldn't be calling home.

"Don't give this number to anyone," I said.

"Who'm I gonna give it to? You call her?"

"I gotta get back to work. I'll call later."

"You're *downtown*. You gotta call *now*."

"She's probably at work anyway."

"Even better. Leave a message. She comes home later, hears your voice, she's sorry she missed you. It's why you got the thing."

"Fine," I said.

"Full report."

In my truck I contemplated the duffel bag in my lap. In my mind the falling woman never hit the surface of the car.

I changed into my button-down and headed toward Daisy's, telling myself, *You have nothing to lose.* Then I checked the time on my cell phone—it was just after noon—and I quickly changed direction.

14
Last of the Independents

The leaves are dark, wet with rain. One glistening gob of white, like a teardrop, sits at the tip of a diamond-shaped leaf. From a raised ridge of yellow, green rivulets fork, spreading life to the black outskirts, where the imagination expands. The painting goes onward and outward, beyond itself, just as it turns inward and goes deeper, into the shadows in the soil, dipping and descending into the brown bowels of the earth, deep beneath its own first layer, that magical plane that seems to hover at the canvas, just above it, impossibly, heavy with rain, yet about to touch down.

The smoke from Shep's Marlboro lent a certain musky authenticity to the painting.

"It's incredible," I said, glancing back.

Shep nodded behind a rising gray cloud. His beard had turned silvery, his cheekbones, in the pockets below his pale-green eyes, grooved like walnuts.

"What the hell have you been doing with yourself, Pappas?"

Sunlight poured through the wide-open doorway, onto the concrete floor, onto the white walls, onto the glowing surface of the desk before the door, and onto the curly-blond-haired young man—Charlie Young—who stood hunched with a pen and sandwiched the phone between his ear and shoulder.

"Storing up, I guess," I said. "I've been wanting to stop by."

"Storing up?" Shep said. "Are you a squirrel? I see you cut your hair."

"Just the other day."

"Nice of you to clean up before visiting. Cup of coffee?" Shep turned for the white cup on the chrome shelf behind him. "So what's in store? Have a seat." He gestured toward the worn red velvet couch with sunken cushions and headed for the big sink against the back wall. He dumped his coffee and refilled with the nearby pot.

I sat down. Shep stabbed his cigarette in a white plastic dish dotted with black scars. He sipped his coffee. He plucked the red pack of cigarettes from the breast pocket of his charcoal denim jacket.

"You still teaching Art of Philly?" I said.

"Of course."

"Still taking them out to Forbidden Drive?"

"As long as it's there, I'll be showing whoever wants to see it."

Wisdom! I thought. I'd brought my note cards in case inspiration struck. *Let us hear the Holy Gospel…*

Shep went on: "This is it, man. Two, three classes. Charlie holding down the fort when I'm gone. Wife and kids in New York. That's the gig. Tell me about *you.*"

"Kids? Wow…"

"Boy and a girl."

"That's great."

Shep jabbed a cigarette between his lips and walked to the desk, where he reached past his assistant, Charlie, for a framed picture. "The frog is Jack. The ladybug is Sarah." Shep handed the picture to me and set his steaming cup on the chrome shelf. "Four and two." He took a small box of matches from his jeans pocket. The match hissed as he leaned toward the orange flame.

"Your wife," I said. In the picture she bowed toward the kids, in a snow-white fur suit that covered her feet, her mittened hands on their shoulders.

"The rabbit," Shep said. "She had me in a bear suit."

The kids held empty plastic pumpkins. Shep's wife cleared a drooping ear from her face.

"Halloween," I said.

"Trick or treating in the Village, Pappas. You haven't lived."

I smiled. Shep took a thoughtful drag.

"So?" Shep said. "You?"

"I've been thinking." I set Shep's family picture on the shelf. "I have an idea."

Shep sipped his coffee.

"I'm coming up blank, though, when I try to find the words."

"You been thinking about this idea for long?" Shep said.

"Pretty long," I said.

Shep took a deep breath. "Nothing wrong with having an idea. Who says you have to find *words?*"

Again I thought of the note cards and the unwritten *Gospel of Shep*.

"Ideas have their way of working themselves out," Shep said. "I'm not saying forget your idea. Not that you could if you wanted to. It might surprise you one day, in some form you never imagined. Maybe you won't even recognize it."

Amen, I thought.

"In the meantime..." Shep raised his cup, toasting to that day, or to the time until then.

I sat up, gripping my knees. "Or I could quit my job and just do it."

"That's an option." Shep dropped his cigarette into his coffee cup. "You want to tell me about it? Your idea?"

Charlie, at the desk, hung up the phone.

I stood up and plucked the note cards from my khakis. *This is LOVE*, scrawled in pencil, was all I had to show for myself. I snapped the rubber band and wagged the deck. "It's all right here."

Charlie turned from the desk, tapping a pencil to his notebook. Shep was smiling, thumbing through my blank note cards, when Charlie broke the silence.

"Readers' Forum in Wayne just said they'll take a dozen. I'm gonna head out there."

"How's it going otherwise?" Shep asked Charlie.

I tucked my note cards back into my pocket and drifted toward Shep's leaves, leaving Shep and Charlie to their business.

"Still waiting on Head House in Queen Village," Charlie said. "The last of the independents. Joseph Fox is almost sold out. Jerry from *Philly* mag left a message, promised to save some space in August— two hundred words, with picture. I shot him the cover and a blurb, and he said we'll talk. I think when Borders and Barnes & Noble see that, they'll order. Meanwhile, now that we're on Amazon, it's a whole new ballgame. They'll have to run another thousand, at least."

"You should run for Senator," Shep said.

I stood with my back to the leaves, as Charlie bent over a box by the door.

"I want to catch them before they close," Charlie said.

"It's rush hour," Shep said.

"That's why they call it rush hour." Charlie smiled, a stack of books cradled in his arms.

"Leave one for Pappas," Shep said. "Sign it quick."

Charlie set the pile on the desk next to a laptop left open. He lifted the cover of the top book, took a pen from a mug, and scrawled something. He flipped the book shut and set it on the desk. He spun around and skipped off the stoop, out onto the sidewalk.

I followed Shep toward the desk. Shep picked up the book and handed it to me. The book was heavy in my hands. The photograph on the cover was magnificent: LOVE Park's pale-blue geyser in the foreground was a gushing-water mirror image of City Hall's thick tower framed in the background, those stacked red letters—LO/VE—on their steel pedestal, dancing magically in the middle ground, the book's title in matching red-letter font, *ART OF THE PEOPLE, BY THE PEOPLE, FOR THE PEOPLE: PUBLIC ART IN THE CITY OF BROTHERLY LOVE*— Charles Randall Young, with an Introduction by Shepard Stillman.

"Charlie's a hell of a photographer," Shep said.

"Yeah," I choked out, flipping through. I cleared my throat. "I'll say."

"He's also shamelessly self-promoting."

I shut the book and looked up.

"I didn't have anything to do with it," Shep said. "I let him use me— my name."

I held out the book. "You should sign it."

Shep set the book on the desk and found Charlie's inscription on the title page. "So what next?" Shep offered, hunched over. "This job you mentioned—you working *right now*, as we speak?" Shep turned and laid the book in my hands. "This is new for you, Pappas. Shirking your responsibilities. It may yield something good—something *new*, anyway. Don't wait another five years before you stop by again."

In my truck I opened the book on the passenger seat. On the title page Charlie had written, "Good Luck, Charlie." On the blank page to the left, Shep had written, "The best ideas of men have been left unrealized. Shep." That was Shep—he spun gold on the spot.

I coasted toward Broad Street, paging through the book, thinking it garish in its waxy colorfulness, vulgar, cowardly, virtually pornographic—wasn't it?—in its absence of text, but for the faint descriptions in the corners, noting only the title, artist, location, date, and materials—*School of Philly;* Shepard Stillman; Broad and Spring Garden; 1996; acrylic emulsion on stucco, varnished with acrylic gloss. Of course, Charlie's book would sell, while my book would be relegated to the coffers where the best ideas of men were left unrealized. The wrenching in my abdomen was not due to the fact that Charlie had beaten me to the punch—hardly. Nothing but pictures, Charlie's book was the antithesis of the one I had envisioned, but, as such—and this is what left me breathless, suddenly, sidled up to the curb, just as Shep's mural came into sight—it rendered me speechless, wordless, inarticulate as I was when gazing at the real thing. The truth was that every photograph, on page after brilliant page, was the next best thing to the original, as valid a translation as anything I could render into words.

Of course, I could still forge ahead and write my own art book, the inverse of Charlie's book, translating the untranslatable, mining the sublime for the words that would capture what the photographer could not comprehend in his limiting two dimensions. And then it dawned on me: these were all—my words, Charlie's pictures—feeble attempts not to do justice to the originals but to join the blessed realm of their makers. And so the likes of both me and Charlie were doomed, in any case, if not to obscurity then to misguided admiration. People would see what they wanted to see, if and when they wanted to see it.

Not much had changed since the fourth century, I thought, when those Egyptian monks risked their lives for posterity, burying the books ordered burned by a bishop, who had decided what was holy and what was not. At the dawn of the New Testament, monks were sealing up banned gospels in the side of a mountain, dreaming of a day when the whole truth would spread its light upon the earth. Could they have imagined that more than a millennium would pass before some unknowing soul, in 1945, perhaps a few years too late, stumbled upon their treasure, *The Gospel of Truth*, *The Gospel of Thomas*, *The Apocalypse of Peter*, papyrus pages magically intact, text still legible, translatable? When I first learned of the Nag Hammadi findings and of the Egyptian who had made the discovery, I thought it noteworthy that when the man's name was mentioned there was no need for clarification, to distinguish Muhammad Ali the boxer, from Muhammad Ali the villager, who'd discovered the so-called Gnostic Gospels, which, as it turned out, were deemed more heretical than ever.

The Greatest Story Ever Censored.

Ah, well, that *Gospel of Thomas* never deserved to see the light of day in the first place, spewing such blasphemous stuff, portraying a Jesus who was off his rocker, a delusional, channeling Buddha, yammering on about the Light in everyone, pointing to the Divine in everything, as if the Kingdom had already come, and God were playing hide-and-seek, and I was the seeker, and what the hell kind of a sign was I expecting, anyway?

15
Museum Without Walls

I dialed information and wrote the number on a gas receipt.

I typed D-I-A-M-O into my phone's directory and then deleted the letters. She needed a code name. O-C-T-O-P-U-S-S… I backed up. Octopus sounded like a buddy's nickname or some kind of hardware store. I rehearsed my lines, hoping to get her machine.

Hello, Daisy? It's Peter calling.

Yeah, I was in the area, but I have to get back to work…I was shopping for a watch on my lunch break…no, I didn't find one, so, yeah, the next time I go shopping, sure, I could use a woman's opinion…

Who was I kidding? That was Andrew talking, not me.

Who?

Peter. Peter Pappas.

I had the name of a cartoon character. I belonged in a nursery rhyme or a limerick. *There once was a man named Peter Pappas picked a peck of pickled peppers…*

Daisy. Pete.

I'd drifted all the way to the river. I clapped the phone shut and hung a hard right. I motored up Market Street toward City Hall, which sat up ahead, squat and grime-gray, a massive dead-end of baroquely shaped shadows. As I rounded the building, I told myself to keep circling the block, to head back in her direction—*left!*—or just to stop, right here, along the curb at LOVE Park. I pulled over, my heart racing, breathing deep, trying to relax. My truck's hazard lights clicked as traffic rushed past. If I called now, she would wonder: who was the hyperventilating stalker at the other end of the line?

Pappas. Pete Pappas.

Through the trees I saw the top edge of the LOVE sculpture and imagined Dorothy and me, at its base, resting after our self-designed walking tour, which we'd mapped out the night before. She'd taken photographs of all the outdoor artwork on our walk from Temple to the Art Museum, from Shep's mural to the potpourri littered about at Broad and Market—the bronze of Frank Rizzo, flanked for eternity by giant Parcheesi pieces and the towering Lipchitz the mayor himself had feared would tarnish his reputation as a man of good taste—to the dripping-wet orgy twisting from the roof deck of the T.G.I. Friday's just beyond the Four Seasons, to the Calders hiding in the trees along the Parkway.

That was the day Dorothy and I came up with the idea for the book about Philadelphia art, just the stuff outside—that would be the point: the city itself was "a museum without walls," she said, which we would capture throughout the seasons, the bathers in the snow, Billy Penn backlit by different-colored skies. She would take the pictures—starting with these, today—and I would do the writing. With extended arm, she held out her camera, aimed it toward us, tapped her red sneakers together at the rubber-tipped toes, and took our picture, the one for the book jacket, she'd said, the two of us at the base of the LOVE sculpture.

Once again I was getting caught up in ancient history.

I told myself that Daisy Diamond might like to take a walk around the city to look at art. Why not? She would think it romantic. I would pretend to be walking aimlessly, though I would know where I was going, and we would wander and laugh at pointless stuff, and she would be impressed when I told her to look closer, to see that the Clothespin's metal coil formed a "76"—the year of the Bicentennial, the year I was born; then I would tell her to look more closely, to see that the Clothespin was actually two people kissing, that the coil was actually arms embracing, and that once you saw the lovers you could never again see only a clothespin. Maybe that would be the moment she fell in love with me, the moment she would look back on and say that's when she knew…because I made her see the beauty in things, things she'd seen a thousand times but had never really seen…because I could transform simple things right before her eyes…

Suddenly there was a knock on the passenger-side window. A square-jawed, helmeted cop on a mountain bike gestured with a twirling finger to roll down the window.

I reached over and cranked the handle.

The cop lifted his chin above the edge of the glass. "Problem?"

"Uh." A steady flow of traffic wound around my truck. "I got lost."

"Ya can't stop here. Where you headed?"

"I got it." I held up my phone. "I had to make a call."

The cop thrust his thumb in the direction that I should get moving, and I sank into the traffic, toward the museum, where up ahead the road forked, looping left back toward the city and branching right onto Kelly Drive toward East Birch. *Pussy!* I cursed myself as I felt the pull toward home. *Left, God damn it!* I was going to live in my parents' basement forever and turn into the next-generation Theo, wasting my life, not knowing reality from fantasy, fact from fiction. My hands, still stiff on the wheel, had betrayed me. The rocky wall along Kelly Drive and the canopy of green above closed in, my mind, along with my truck, decelerating, a car horn blasting as it swerved.

I had to go back, but little white signs on the rock wall said no turns. I would wait for a clearing and dart into the parking lot of the next boathouse along the river. I came to a stop along the curving yellow lines, prayed my truck wouldn't stall, and floored it.

At the edge of the lot I turned off the engine and stared at the river, then at my phone. I was in the area, I would say, and, hopefully, she would take it from there. You *were* in the area or you *are* in the area? I could hear her asking. What *tense* should I use? How should I begin?

I could wait till tonight, when I could ask Andrew to call and pretend to be me.

I was incapable of even faking being cool. Then it hit me: I could offer—in fact, I *should* have offered already—to give her a lift back to her car. Right now, or later, or anytime.

I started the truck. The sound of the engine would make me seem like a man on the run, squeezing in a call. I sidled up to the curb so that I would have to holler over the cars humming by. I rolled the window down and pressed "send," praying once again for the answering machine.

She picked up after one ring and said hello.

"Daisy," I said.

"Peter?"

"I was shopping for a watch on my lunch break."

"I'm on the other line. Why don't you come by?"

"Now?"

"Sure. I just got home from work."

"Already? What time is it?"

"A little after three. I guess you didn't find one you liked?"

"Find what?"

"A watch."

"Oh. No. I need a woman's opinion."

"Are you hungry? Do you like tilapia?"

She would see me in a few minutes, she said, and when I clapped my phone shut I saw that I really had lost track of the time—3:16. If the blond from the sales office had brought any clients to see the apartment today she would have been suspicious of the blaring radio and the paintbrush propped on an open can. I would tell Daisy I couldn't stay long because I honestly had to get back to work.

As I headed toward the blue glass towers on the horizon, I pictured us embracing at the door, picking up where we'd left off at the salon. I considered taking a minute now, pulling over and parking far away from the runners' path this time, and relieving myself so that I would be one step ahead when I got to her apartment. But then I remembered the young cop on the bike and imagined him beyond the limits of his precinct, busting the same fat loser in the pickup, not for blocking the traffic this time but for assaulting himself in a vacant boathouse parking lot along the river.

16
Mr. Quiet Returns

All the doors of her apartment building were wide open, the smell of frying fish pungent even on the sidewalk. *Tilapia*, I realized, stepping into the living room, as Daisy called out, "Come in!" In the kitchen, clouds of heat curled toward the ceiling. I closed the door behind me, then reopened it, realizing she'd left it open not for me to enter but for the smell of fish to escape. The gauzy drapes floated before the screened square openings of the living-room windows. I waved to her in the kitchen, not sure if I should walk back to greet her. "That's for you," she called out from the stove. When she turned, head skewed, I saw the phone sandwiched between her ear and shoulder. She gestured with a spatula toward the coffee table, where on the corner an already filled glass of red wine sat next to a cork and a half-full bottle. I put my nose to the rim. "You'll like it," she said, and waited for me to sip. A single swallow warmed my cheeks and shoulders. "Monica says hi," she said, and smiled. "He says hi, too… *Ciao, bella*." I took a bigger sip, as she turned back toward the stove.

On the couch I felt a warm rush in my face, as I sipped and stared at the coffee table, set for one, a fork on a folded paper napkin. Stove knobs clicked off, spatula, pans, and plates scraping and knocking. "I'm coming in one second!" When the stove fan whirred to a stop, the apartment went silent. I turned off my phone, a faint trickling of notes in my cupped hands.

I stood up when she arrived. She set down the steaming plate and signaled with a finger to wait. She closed all the doors and huffed, "Okay," as she twisted around the coffee table and stepped out of her shoes, which tumbled to the wall. She sidled up to me, thigh to thigh, and beamed, "So did you change your mind?"

About lunch? About her?

"You're happy now?" she said.

I nodded, not sure exactly, but optimistic…

Her fingers flashed into my hair. "It looks good." She smiled and gestured toward the wine in my hands. "You like it?"

I sipped. I was no connoisseur—red, white, good, bad—so I would not fake having an opinion. The wine, my hair, the food, Daisy—yes, I was happy with it all. Happy not to be barraged by questions about yesterday, about our tryst behind the salon, happy that she seemed happy to see me.

"Mr. Quiet returns," she said, beaming.

"*You* seem happy," I announced.

When I heard my weird tone of mixed surprise and admiration, I vowed to remain Mr. Quiet for the rest of my short visit. It was about time I shook off my first impression of Daisy Diamond as a pill-popping manic-depressive who'd needed me only for a ride home on Saturday. To the contrary, she was a beautiful, intelligent woman who was not dependent upon me or anyone or anything else, perhaps not even Xanax.

"I'm happy you're here," she said.

My stomach growled—inaudibly, I hoped.

"Someone's hungry." She cut the fish with the fork and cupped her hand under a steaming bite.

"What about yours?" I said.

"My…?"

"Dinner—or lunch," I corrected myself, checking my blank wrist for the time.

"I ate." She blew softly on the fish. "Open." I opened my mouth. "This is for you."

When she clenched my thigh, reaching for my wine, I wished I'd relieved myself when I'd had the chance. Mid-chew was no time to be excusing myself to visit the bathroom, and Daisy's bathroom was no place to be relieving myself.

"Tastes good." I swallowed, as she held the glass for me to sip.

She pecked my wine-glazed lips, which I'd raced to seal in time. She licked her lips and smiled, amused, it seemed, and set the glass on the coffee table. "*Tastes good*," she grunted—mocking me, I realized, trying to coax me into articulating a complete thought, proving myself evolved beyond a caveman.

And yet I couldn't think of what to say or do to fake being civilized. I took another bite as she stroked the side of my head.

"You like it?" she said.

The fish? My hair? It didn't matter. I smiled, a fawning dog, back with the stick, ready for my grooming. I resigned myself to having nothing to say. She didn't seem to mind. Her chin rose as she scanned my head, Jane Goodall inspecting her chimp for ticks.

"What are you thinking about?" she said.

I'm thinking about how I'd cut off my foot—my leg—not to make a fool of myself again.

In my pants I was pumping like a heart.

Her knuckles drifted down to where my shirt opened.

If I faked diarrhea and bolted upstairs, I would insult her tilapia. I pictured myself hunched over the toilet, aiming pearls into the water.

These khakis, I lamented, would not hold my dreaded secret as my army pants had. Then I realized that I'd left my bathing-suit shorts on at the gym and that (God forbid I needed it) they would provide the protection of a pair of diapers (God was indeed merciful and worked in mysterious ways).

"Tell me something I don't know about you," she said.

She scratched my chest with a fingernail.

"Like what?"

"He speaks." She grinned. "I don't know. I feel like I've told you my whole life story. Tell me what you dream about."

"*Dream* about?"

"Yes," she said, and then, playfully, with trilled "r" and husky German-sounding accent, "tell me about your *dreams*."

"I don't know. Weird stuff," I said. "A lot of times…" This was the truth: as a boy, instead of envisioning sheep jumping over a fence, I envisioned myself running the bases in a perpetual homerun trot. "I just keep rounding the bases—on a baseball field—in slow motion—"

"I don't mean your *dreams, vreh!*" Daisy howled, clenching my index finger.

"What?"

"No, go ahead now, tell me your dreams. I like this…"

"You said *dreams*."

"I meant what you dream about *doing*—with your *life*."

She slapped my thigh, laughing, and reached for her wine glass. "This is more interesting. Tell me about running around the bases. You like baseball?" She sipped, eyeing me over the rim.

"No. Yes." I was King of the Idiots. It could be worse: I could have tried being romantic—*I dream of lying with you on a beach*—or sexy, launching right in with *I dream of you spinning on me, the two of us like a human pinwheel…*

"I like baseball," she teased. "Come *on*."

Grimacing, I said, "I want to write a book."

"A novel?"

"An art book."

When her eyes lit up, I believed what I was saying.

"About the art that's all around us—outside. Sculptures. And murals. The LOVE sculpture, stuff like that."

"That sounds wonderful. Like a coffee-table book?"

"*No*," I blurted, though she seemed excited by the idea. "I mean, it wouldn't be about the pictures so much as the analysis."

"The *analysis*. Hmm." Daisy smiled courteously.

The author in her presence was suddenly an aspiring writer of textbooks.

It dawned on me that Dorothy's pictures had always been what would sell the book; and now, of course, Charlie's pictures would sell Charlie's book. "I mean, it *could* be a coffee-table book."

"Do you have a title?"

"No. Unless," I said, realizing, "*Museum Without Walls*."

"That's *good*." Daisy patted the coffee table. "I'll put it right here."

I nodded, feigning gratitude. I could fetch Charlie's book right now and venture past the point of humiliation.

Daisy scooped another piece of fish onto the fork. "Here. Eat."

When I opened my mouth, she set the fork onto the plate and instead filled our wine glasses. "Tell me something else," she said. She handed me a glass and twisted to face me. "Cheers." She clinked her glass against mine. "What else?"

I sipped.

"Well," she grinned. "I'll tell you what *I've* been dreaming about, for a while, actually. Going back to Greece."

"That sounds nice."

"It won't be for a while," she said, "not till I sell the house."

"Sell the *house*? You mean you're *moving* there?" My stomach whined. My throat clenched up.

"Not for a while. I have the property in Athens." She touched my cheek. "*Look* at you." I must have appeared red as wine. She tucked her legs underneath herself, her knees against my thigh. Hot, heavy air spilled through the windows. "You can *visit*," she teased, and spared me from hearing, *Don't cry*, which she might as well have said.

Something was cracking inside of me, for real, I thought. I could feel something deflating in my chest—a pin piercing a lung. It was as if I were folding up, my head sinking into my shoulders, my ribs, like the fingers of fists, squeezing the air out, curling into the center of myself, as she went on about opening a salon in Athens.

"Sit back, Peter." She patted the couch's cushion behind me. She pushed the plate of fish to the edge of the coffee table, making room for my feet, which I kept on the ground.

I gulped the wine, which she held for me, my face swelling with heat.

"*Peter*—" She kissed my lips, swiping my cheeks with her thumbs, my tears merging with sweat. "*Hey*." She set both our glasses down. She said sweet-sounding things in her sweet-sounding voice, which was distant and fuzzy.

The air poured into me like molten bronze, heavy and hardening.

I wondered how I must have appeared to her—a stunned giant on the couch, my shoulders rising and falling. I couldn't muster the strength—or the generosity—to assure her I wasn't dying. I felt nearly nothing—only vaguely frightened, and fascinated, by my own strange inward retreat; in a flash, I thought of Theo, at twenty-six, on a train into Athens, his dissertation manuscript in a leather bag on his lap, his whole brilliant life ahead of him.

"Are you okay?"

I blinked—yes.

Daisy knelt beside me, feeling my forehead, kissing my eyes.

"Should I call someone? Do you need something? Was it the fish?"

I closed my eyes—no.

"Say something, Peter."

"A woman jumped from a building today."

"*What*, baby?" She stroked my face. Her leg stretched across my lap.

"She landed on a car."

"Where? When? This is *awful*."

"From a balcony. The building next to the gym. You could hear the crash."

"Why didn't you tell me?" She cradled my head in her arms.

I began to breathe.

She smiled and kissed my mouth. "Okay?"

I nodded.

"Okay," she whispered.

Her thighs formed a V that forked at my hips, her dress, snug, black cotton, curling back toward her belly. In the shadow below, black hairs curled out through a narrow path of doily-patterned pink. As she kissed my neck and face, she began moving against the buckled-up material of my pants and, underneath my pants, my bathing suit and, underneath my bathing suit, my obscure flesh, which seemed now to be more incomprehensible and powerful in its capacity to disappoint than anything I could imagine. Behind shut eyes, I contemplated the sin that had bloomed in my mind like a black flower: I had exploited the imagined death of a stranger to explain my sadness, disguising myself as a man in crisis, when what I was, I knew deep down, was a coward, dreading a lifetime of loneliness and inadequacy.

For now, to my growing relief, Daisy seemed indifferent to what I was harboring—or *not* harboring, as it were—between my thighs. Her arms enveloped my head. She was whispering my name. Her belly clenched up, and, suddenly, I was, I realized, in spite of my own unprecedented inertia, in the clutches of a woman in ecstasy. My body was miraculously lifeless between my thighs, and yet, considering her evident pleasure, I was relishing, for the first time in my life, a sense of potency, in spite of what was otherwise an excruciating mortar-and-pestle grinding. When she guided one of my hands to the soaked silk between her thighs, I braced myself as she moaned and gave a final jolt.

My hand remained sandwiched between my khakis and the damp veil cupping her flesh. She reached back for a glass of wine and sipped. She set the glass on the table and said, "Lie back." I twisted as she slinked down, unzipping my khakis, her tangle of black curls at first blocking the view to what must have appeared to be a ludicrous pair of boxers—canvas-thick cloth speckled with red targets. "Were you swimming?" Daisy grinned and tugged at the waistband, which, she discovered, was reinforced on the inside by a knot she picked loose easily before discovering, once and for all, the irrefutable evidence that I'd been faking interest in her all along.

I was limp as a wet towel; only the towel was, for once, dry.

"These things happen." She was holding the numb, inert extension of myself.

One should be grateful for getting such clear signs from God: I could reject my calling to be a monk, but God would have the last word on my celibacy.

"I don't know what's the matter," I said, as she climbed toward my face. "This never happened before."

"*Shhh…*"

I stared up at the sprawling map of gold-rimmed water stains, imagining the two of us nude on a beach I decided was Crete—white sand below a hillside of rubble—on a giant sky-blue towel resembling the Greek flag, some terrycloth job we picked up from a vendor on the walk from town—the two of us in this same position, chest to chest, her legs astraddle, my head on the cross in the corner, where, back home, the stars would be, in a night-blue sky, if we were dozing on a beach in New Jersey, her reassuring breath in my ear.

17
All God's Creatures

Beyond the floating drapes and screens, the day had dimmed. The brick façade across the street was purple-gray. Daisy's fingernails danced through the hair on my leg. My eyelids strained to open, and then I left them closed. My fingers sank into her nest of hair, which grazed along my belly, as she petted me like a sleeping Easter chick and took me into her mouth. Her patient incubation began to rouse me, and once I stirred I swelled quickly against the warm walls enshrouding me and—"Oh, God!""It's okay," she assured me, rising for a moment and descending again, realizing—I flinched like a stabbed fish and it was over.

I would do her the favor of keeping my eyes shut as I left, sparing us the embarrassment of having to say anything.

But she remained on me. Her wet warmth was crippling. I needed to cool off, air out. Was it possible she didn't know I was done? Did she expect me to rise again? I wasn't sure if it was pleasure or pain I was feeling, but I couldn't take it anymore.

"Sorry—" I blurted, squirming.

She rose to her knees, sweeping her hair back. "I loved that," she said—words I never expected—and in one fluid, shocking motion— shocking less because she was suddenly unveiling herself than because she was still progressing toward something—she criss- crossed her arms and peeled her dress over her head, tugged my bathing-suit shorts and khakis down to my ankles, and crawled out of her pink panties.

"What are you doing?" I whispered.

She smiled down at me, her breasts contained in a pink lace bra, her nipples like shadowy sealed eyes, and flicked the plastic fastener. Before I could get a grip, she lowered herself into my mouth, and, reaching back, scooped me from our shared reservoir of tangled dampness.

"I have tricks," she grinned, "to make you *come alive.*"

I looked up from her slick breast, smiling weakly. Dirty talk, I thought. My incompetence was about to manifest itself in ways I'd never imagined.

"Secret tricks," she said.

I couldn't fathom how to respond, not that I could utter a word. I turned my face to breathe. She sat up, her hand, down below, fondling my limp flesh, which felt bloated and heavy, embarrassing as a colostomy bag.

I wondered how to tell her, without sounding ungrateful, that I was a hopeless case, that I appreciated her effort and that I was sure her technique—whatever she was up to down there—was effective with normal men, but that, as she could see, I was no normal man, but a stagnant excuse for a man, who—if I was lucky, or *un*lucky, come to think of it, considering the unrealized expectations that came with my dysfunction—was doomed to an occasional burst of life that would serve as a tormenting reminder not only of what I was missing but also of what real men were experiencing in sustained intervals on a regular basis—

A fingertip—an accident?—at first the rigid edge of a fingernail and then a bit of round flesh, vivid as a thumb hooking a cheek, slipped over the edge of what seemed to be the other end of the universe...

I was standing now, my breath and vision returning. As the electricity dissolved along my spinal cord, I remained flaccid, a sagging sack of flesh between my legs, pants and shorts in a violent twisted bunch at my ankles, my feet having been unable to free themselves even as I'd bucked wildly. In my mind, I saw how I'd shot out from under her, and was grateful—thank *God;* I might have *killed* her—she'd slipped gracefully to the far cushion, where she sat, now, smirking, elbow on the arm of the couch, fingers curled in the air caressing an invisible cigarette.

I hiked up my shorts and pants.

"You won't be so surprised next time." She reached for a glass and swallowed the last bit of wine in it.

"*Next time?*" I gasped.

"Don't be such a prude." She set the glass down, grinning. Her foot lifted off the couch, her toes aimed at me. She was taunting me with her nakedness, but I kept my eyes lowered. "You didn't like it?"

"I guess I don't see the point." I pulled at my shirt stuck in the cushions. "I'm sorry."

"The point in *what?*"

I shrugged.

"This? *Us?*" When she reached for the floor, I stopped buttoning my shirt. Arching back on the couch, hips in the air, she pulled her panties up.

"I didn't mean that," I said.

"Because I said I'm going to *Greece?* I told you I have no idea when that's going to happen." Sitting up, she clicked her bra in front. "Honestly, Peter, what did you expect? Can't we just enjoy the moment?"

"That's not what I meant either."

"Are you still thinking about that woman?"

"*What* woman?"

Daisy looked at me, appalled.

"*No,*" I said, remembering. The mere mentioning of *that woman*— my *use* of her, let alone my forgetting her—sickened me—whether the story was true or not.

"Don't act insulted now." She stood up. "Is it about *sex*—your *penis?*"

"*Jesus,*" I gasped.

"You can *talk* to me, Peter. I'm on the Pill, you know. There's nothing to feel anxious about."

"I have to go." I sat down, plucked my sneakers from under the coffee table, and unlaced them on my lap.

"*Be* that way." She raised her empty glass—a toast—*to your impotence!*

She stood at the windows, staring through the drapes floating dreamily toward her. Her lips kissed the rim of the empty wine glass. Her fingertips danced along the drape's edge. I told myself to savor the moment: Daisy Diamond was the most magnificent thing I would ever see. I wanted to be standing behind her, pressing my body against her, rising into her. This had been my last chance to experience what men and women had been experiencing since the beginning of time, the glory that God, or Nature, did not deny to even the lowest life forms. Was it too much to ask? Outside, beyond the windows, in the dirt at the base of the stinking gingko tree and on its leaves and branches, ants and beetles and gnats were all fucking away; in the dog shit in the dirt at the base of the stinking gingko tree flies were fucking, and in the parks the dogs themselves were fucking and in the alleys the cats were fucking and everywhere the rabbits were fucking, far and wide all God's creatures having a great fucking time, and here I was lacing up, tying up, buttoning up, and zipping up once and for all.

Daisy turned from the windows, arms crossed, and said, "What's the point of anything, Peter, really?"

"I don't know."

"Honestly, I don't understand."

I sat there, looking up at her, dressed and ready. "Please don't get all depressed now because of me."

"Well, if there's no point in two people enjoying each other, you tell me what's the point in anything?"

"You're right. I have no idea." I looked at my blank wrist and at the walls and at the dark sky. "What time is it?"

"You want me to say I *like* you? Is that what you need to hear?"

"No—" I stood up.

"Sit," she said. I sat. "I *enjoy* you. I enjoyed *this*. You need to explain to me—"

"What's to *enjoy?!*" I gripped my knees.

"You didn't enjoy it? Okay. Don't do me any favors." She went for the door.

"Of course I *enjoyed* it." I stayed seated. "You're the most beautiful woman I've ever known. I just wish—I want *you* to enjoy it."

"You think I'm lying? Trust me, I wouldn't waste my time."

"I know that. I mean—*I* want to enjoy it. *More.*"

"You think you might enjoy it more with *men?*"

"God, no! I just want to be *good!*"

"Peter, look at me—" She paused, hands on her hips. "I don't know what you've done or experienced. I won't assume, so forgive me if I sound condescending, but you have nothing to worry about."

"I don't need to hear this."

"It can take a while for a man and woman to get to know each other, physically, to get comfortable with each other."

"You don't understand."

"I *do*."

"You *don't*."

"I'm a little older than you are—I don't have to tell you that. Maybe you've been with men—"

"I'm not *gay!* Why do you keep *saying* that?"

"Fine! It makes no difference to me. What I'm saying is I know how it can get when men get older. You're still young, but things start to happen. It's nothing to worry about."

I wouldn't tell her I'd been cursed since before I was sixteen. I stood up, feeling a rush to the head, digging for my keys, checking for my wallet.

"Next time will be different. I promise." She gripped the waist of my pants and tugged. "I have more tricks."

I grimaced.

She kissed my cheek. "You okay to drive?"

I nodded, only now realizing the effect of wine when all you had to eat was a bowl of cereal and a bit of fish. Still, I had to go. God knew if I went back to the couch, she would whip out her magic wand.

"I meant to ask if you wanted a ride to your car," I said.

She looked down at her half-naked body. "You'll have to come back for me."

I reached for the doorknob.

"Tomorrow's my day off." She put her hand on my chest. "I could help you pick out a watch."

"Maybe we could just go for a drink or something."

"Wine in the afternoon. I like the sound of that." She pulled me down by the collar and kissed my mouth.

"I could show you my new place."

"You have your own place?"

I nodded. "Out where I live—*used* to live."

18
Angel of Resurrection

Coming into view was the sour-yellow face of the clock on City Hall's tower. Nine o'clock. We'd slept on the couch for hours. Even now my dream of our lying on a beach in Greece had a lulling effect. I turned on my cell phone, half-expecting a dozen messages from Eliot, though, of course, my boss didn't know I was now accessible twenty-four seven. As far as I could tell, there was no message from Andrew, who must have been waiting patiently for the full report. I was eager to impress my brother with the highlights of a well-executed plan.

I wouldn't be lying when I told Andrew I'd gone back to Stone Bridge Apartments to wrap things up, to turn off the radio, close the sliding glass doors, and seal up the paint can. Inside, there was no sign, thank God, that the blond from the rental office, let alone Eliot, had been around. I peeled the veiny scab of paint that had formed around the grooved underside of the lid, a bulky string of gray flesh that wrinkled at my fingertip; I coiled it in my hand and flushed it down the toilet. Another day had lapsed and I had yet to finish a single wall.

What I wouldn't tell Andrew was that, swept up in my planning for tomorrow, I'd stopped at the Wawa on Provincetown Avenue and picked up a gallon of milk, a carton of orange juice, a bottle of Coke, a dozen eggs, a loaf of bread, three cans of tuna fish, a box of spaghetti, a jar of tomato sauce, a bag of Doritos, a *Philadelphia Inquirer*, a *Sports Illustrated*, and a broom—all of which would serve as evidence of my living here, or so I hoped, as I propped the broom in the corner of the kitchen, tossed the magazine and newspaper by the radio on the floor in the living room, displayed the food on the countertops, set the eggs in the egg slots on the refrigerator door, and arranged the beverages on the top shelf. Tomorrow I'd hit the liquor store for the wine.

At the door to the apartment, I lamented the expanse of bare carpet and decided that tomorrow I would smuggle lawn furniture and Andrew's old futon from home, along with wine glasses and toilet paper. I figured it wouldn't be difficult to convince Daisy I was still in the process of getting things together here in my new place. I could say I was saving up to buy good, permanent stuff—a bed, a desk, bookshelves, a wine rack—the things I would have for the rest of my life. A few more months of humble living and then I would really settle in. Before locking up, I headed back to the kitchen, where I pinched open the juice carton, swigged some milk, and ground an egg in the garbage disposal, leaving shell bits and slime to dry on the stainless steel. Grateful for this moment of insight, I split with a handful of Doritos, the bag open on the counter, evidence of a bachelor on the run.

When I got home and slinked through the kitchen, the light from the TV was flashing on the walls of the living room. Andrew shot up from the couch when I appeared, hovering above him.

"Doc," Andrew grumbled, and lay back down. "Where the fuck have you been?" His eyes fought off sleep. "You get laid? Just kidding." He zapped the TV off, and the room grew dark. Andrew's white-socked feet shone in the porch light coming through the bay window. His toes dipped under the afghan, which he stretched up to his chin.

"Where is everyone?" I said. "Sophia home?"

"Yes," Andrew said. "Everyone's exhausted."

"It's not even eleven."

"Late enough."

"Anyone ask about me?"

"No." Andrew sighed.

"Mom didn't call the cops?" I chuckled, only half-joking, wanting to know what I was up against in the morning—to prepare for questioning. Andrew shook his head. It seemed impossible to me that the night had passed without someone assuming I'd been killed by terrorists or, worse, brainwashed into joining them. "Seriously?"

"Go to bed." Andrew rolled over and muffled into the couch, "People have their own shit, Doc. They're not always wondering about how you might be fucking up your life. Sometimes they're busy fucking up their own."

*

In my dream I walked hand-in-hand with Daisy, under the canopy of trees in the concrete courtyard of City Hall, muttering something about lovers on a beach. Daisy's eyes fluttered, as she gazed across the street at the huge Clothespin. Fountains gushed red and blue water into the sky, and all down Market Street American flags jutted from apartment windows. Daisy and I imitated the two halves of the Clothespin. Her eyes retreated, and then she was gone. All I could hear was fabric flapping, the flags slapping in the wind, a dress sailing down through the sky, thousands of pigeons plunging from roofs and ledges, the air thick and gray with wings. The slow-motion swirl of red-white-and-blue moved up Market and down J.F.K. Boulevard, to Thirtieth Street Station and back again, around and around, an endless, desolate parade, leaving only me, balled up in Centre Square, on the steaming-hot lid of a manhole, beckoning the Archangel Michael, angel of Resurrection, who remained still, bronze, in the train station down the street, as I awaited the city's primordial breath to swallow me into its bowels, a fossil in the making, a chrysalis in reverse, all flesh and bones and nerves, the carved-out pulp from my own skin. Half-awake, suddenly, I inched back into what felt like a warm, hollowed-out womb.

"Peter." It was a whisper through a crack—Sophia, home, her face burrowing into my shoulders, letting out a cry that came from deep in her throat and sustained itself even through the single word she choked out when I tried to face her. "Don't." She pressed her T-shirted soft chest into my bare back, for a fleeting second her nipples like faint fingertips, her knees curling into the backs of my legs, which I freed up from the tangled bed sheet. "Let me stay here." The basement was as black as the backs of my eyes. I stared straight ahead.

"What happened?" I whispered.

As she went on sobbing, I wondered at her inevitable broken heart—and Andrew's—and my own cold witnessing of it all. I imagined Veronica in bed, grinning at the ceiling, and the head of a girl, peach-faced with flowers in her hair, rising up from the covers, just as

Sophia, newly arrived from Philly, frazzled from flying, entered the room with her suitcase and backpack. She must have stayed in California a day longer than she'd wanted to, just on principle, I figured—after all, she didn't go out there just for Veronica; she had dreams of her own, damn it—before calling for a return ticket.

"What did she do?" I muttered, half-dreaming.

"Who?"

"Veronica."

"Nothing."

Minutes passed, and Sophia began to breathe through her sobbing, her chest rising and falling against me, her face buried in my shoulders.

"Something happened, Peter," she said.

"Okay…"

"Something terrible." Her crying picked up again, and again I tried to turn toward her, but with a hand she blocked my cheek and repeated, "*Don't*—"

"What happened, God damn it?"

"I got an abortion."

"*What?*" In an instant my confusion turned to sickening sorrow, as an image of Sophia being raped, spread against a wall, flashed in my mind. She didn't resist my turning over now, though in the dark I still couldn't see her, as my hands rose to her wet face, and I said again, more gently, "What?" In my chest pity and rage swirled. "*When?*" I hissed, and then whispered, "Don't answer that." The details made no difference right now. She didn't want to answer questions. My anger surged for a moment, as I tried to erase—or *crystallize*—the violent image in my head—*I would kill him!*

"*Who?!*" I hissed.

"Don't get mad," she sobbed.

"*Mad?* I'll kill him right now!"

"*No*, Peter. *Please. Listen.* I couldn't *tell* you—"

"What are you *talking* about?"

"It was *Freddy's*. I wasn't planning on coming *back*—not *yet*."

"Freddy? *Freddy's?*" Her use of the possessive—*Freddy's*—was more deplorable than the name itself. She was *sharing ownership?*

"Who do you *think?*" She sniffed. "You can't tell him. He can't know. He hates me enough—not that he would have wanted it—"

"*Tell* him?" In my mind I was already smashing Freddy's little rapist head against his beloved backyard quarter-pipe.

"You can't tell anyone, Peter. Nobody knows. Just Veronica."

"*Freddy...*" I imagined the sneaky fucker in the Wests' basement, pinching a joint, eyeing Sophia, who was sleeping, wedged into couch cushions...TV flickering in the corner...beer bottles on the coffee table...as he crawled on top of her... "I'll *kill* him—how'd he do it? When did this happen?"

"*We* did it, Peter. It was *my fault*—"

"Don't *say* that!"

"It's true. He was always careful, and a couple times I just didn't care—I don't know why—we didn't have a condom, and I just let him—I *told* him to, I *wanted* him to—he was nervous—I didn't think—"

"A *couple times?*"

"I *loved* him, Peter—I *still* love him—where have you *been?*—and then I *did* that to him...I can't believe I *did* this...I can't believe what I *did*...I *hate* myself..." She was crying and panting, muttering into the bed sheet, a mantra of self-loathing: "I'm so disgusting...I'm so disgusting...I'm so disgusting..."

"*Shut up,*" I hissed, and she twisted away, turning her back. I touched her shoulder. "Sorry. Just—stop saying that." She scooted back into me, catching her breath, took my heavy arm, and pulled it into her chest like a doll.

I propped my head on my free hand and stared down at her, as if I could see her in the dark, and for a long time I listened to her breathing. I imagined her in the airport, master of disguise, wiping tears of joy as she made her way toward my mother, and then later in the kitchen, in my father's arms, this misery of hers, just as the old man had suspected, nothing more than homesickness, finally cured.

"Why did you come home?" The question had dawned on me suddenly.

"What *else* was I supposed to do?"

19
Philadelphia

My parents had quietly blamed the hijackers, until they'd found a more targetable scapegoat in Freddy. It was in the fall of her junior year when they'd begun to fear that their daughter was degenerating—frightened by her cynicism, short skirts and punkish jewelry, not to mention irritable bowel, which caused her to hunch unattractively. Of course, there were many players involved in Sophia's tragedy, none of whom deserved all the blame, let alone cruel and unusual punishment—even Freddy, who as an atheist had no reason to resist his natural urges, especially if Sophia was on a mission to liberate herself from my father. You couldn't blame my father because it was his job to enforce the rules that a girl like Sophia lived to defy. You couldn't blame my mother, who was all for women's liberation but couldn't help trying to lure her daughter back into dresses, which Sophia refused to wear and instead seized every opportunity to make a spectacle of her melancholic confusion, even on Easter Sunday this past spring, when she added to her standard black church apparel a red-yellow-and-green Rasta knit cap she must have picked up on South Street—when no one told her to take the thing off, she ended up leaving it on the kitchen table.

You couldn't even blame the hijackers, though you couldn't deny that it was that September when the metamorphosis began. As far as I knew, Sophia had never been to New York, but for weeks she wept in front of the TV while watching all the footage. At dinner she sobbed over a full plate, asking how anyone could possibly eat. What she couldn't understand was how those people did what they did, *knowing* they were going to die, *and for what?*—not the *terrorists*, but the firefighters and the police officers: the first tower had already fallen, so they *knew* the second one would fall, and they *still* went in there to help people they didn't even know. "*I* wouldn't do that," she cried. "I mean, I *know* I wouldn't. How am I supposed to live with myself, *knowing* that?"

My father was stumped. My mother was preoccupied by the prospects of her car being detonated at the grocery store. It was a quiet winter. Sophia took Theo's advice of writing about her feelings. He handed her a marbleized notebook, and she started right there at the dinner table, completing what she called her first collection of poems a year later, in the winter of her senior year, too late to make a selling point of her accomplishment in her college applications, too soon to make a selling point of her publishing two poems, the first in a March issue of one of the smaller city papers and the second in the spring issue of *One Love*, which she swore was a totally legitimate Lesbian Studies quarterly that Veronica's aunt, who taught at a college in New Jersey, co-edited. After missing her application deadlines, she announced she didn't need to go to school to be a poet and one thing was for sure: the reason she'd written a book of poetry, which Veronica's aunt said was totally publishable, was not to beef up her resume. She was sick of hypocrites who played sports or joined clubs, or, worse, did community service or got politically active, just because it looked good. And so she distinguished herself by not applying to college at all, becoming the official spokesperson for everyone oppressed, and transforming herself into the embodiment of self-deprivation—thin, pierced, ratty-haired, and dressed for a funeral. One night at dinner, Andrew asked if maybe she was taking the terrorists' message that Americans were gluttonous infidels a bit too personally, and she said, calm as a lamb, that Andrew didn't know what he was fucking talking about, that this was about saving strangers, to which Andrew responded, well, lah-dee-fuckin'-dah, I wouldn't know anything about that, would I?

I figured that Freddy West was the first soul Sophia was trying to save. But I should have known that there was more to their friendship than skateboarding and video games; after all, she was on a mission to love everyone she'd been *trained*—her word—to avoid. In one of her dinner sermons, she preached that just because you rode a skateboard or had a tattoo or a pierced eyebrow or even a pierced tongue or did drugs or even sold drugs or worshiped Allah or even no God at all or had sex before marriage with men or women or even both or shot a cop, even if it wasn't in self-defense…you weren't necessarily a bad person. When my father blamed the Wests for this kind of anarchic rubbish that got us into this mess, Sophia explained that Freddy and Brock, even Dr. West, were exactly the people who needed love the most—the lonely ones, the drug addicts, the non-believers.

What about neo-Nazis? Andrew asked. Psycho-killers? Love them too?

Everyone should just love everyone out in the open, Sophia said.

My father was hard-pressed to provide Sophia a convincing count-er-argument. All he could say, once she started yapping about Jesus and the lepers, was that she wasn't Jesus, who, remember, was the only Son of God, who was crucified for our salvation—and that he was still her father, and he didn't want her hanging around the Wests' house anymore, doing God knew what over there—and that was final. And so she became passionate about not only skateboarding, but, at some point down the road, sex with Freddy—an act of misguided unconditional love?

Sophia wrote not only poetry that winter but at least one article for the Plymouth High School newspaper, in which she reported that the Gay-Straight Union's posters, which had simply advertised their meetings, had been unfairly confiscated by the administration, who wished their group didn't exist. "We wish we didn't exist, too," Sophia explained to her readers. "The whole point of a group like ours is to promote a culture in which a group like ours would be moot. But we're not moot. Far from moot. That's why I joined. What is the point of a Gay-Straight Union made up of only gays? If everyone joined, the point of our group *would* be moot because we would all be a gay-straight union anyway. Martin Luther King said…." Sophia the Preacher. The Dreamer. My father must have been bracing himself for a crusade against the church's all-male priesthood, or maybe even a law-suit, if he refused, as he had years before, to let Sophia be an altar girl.

As the old man read Sophia's article at dinner, Andrew, skimming over his shoulder, asked if "moot" had been one of her vocabulary words that week.

"No, but 'asshole' was."

When the old man, rather than hang the article on the refrigerator and praise Sophia for her unconditional love, stuffed the *Plymouth Rock* in the trashcan under the kitchen sink and scolded her for being so brazen in the name of gay relationships—she was a priest's daughter for God's sake—Sophia took her mission to the next level, befriending Veronica, the founder and president of the Gay-Straight Union, a girl whom, on her first visit to our house, Sophia introduced proudly as "out," adding a new term to the Pappas vernacular, as if "bisexual" weren't enough, and proceeding to invite her home as often as possible, as if daring my parents to expel this polite, pretty, and, as far as they were concerned, confused, girl from their sanctuary of decent living, as if daring them to deem the girls' affection as anything but pure and wonderful platonic love, cozying up with Veronica under blankets, watching movies from the couch, munching popcorn. A gay-straight union, my parents could only assume.

The morning after Sophia's return from California, I lay wide awake in bed—my belly in the small of her back, my arm still clutched at her chest—imagining my sister with her legs spread, Veronica holding her hand as the doctor scoured her insides, black fishnet leggings folded over a chair in the corner. Throughout the night I'd contemplated ways of torturing Freddy, but resisted the urge to sneak into the Wests' house with a wire clothes hanger, the appropriate weapon, I decided, in lieu of the more sophisticated instrument the doctor might have actually used. Sophia shuddered momentarily and went on breathing quietly.

When the kitchen's sliding glass door thumped overhead—my mother heading out for her walk—I whispered, "You up?" thinking Sophia should sneak back to her own bed before our mother discovered her missing and reported a runaway or, worse, found her cradled in my bed.

I tried to shift away, but she hung on to me like a frightened little girl, and I was in no hurry to free myself.

The light came on in the basement—someone having flicked the switch at the top of the stairs.

I yanked my arm from Sophia's grip.

"Doc?" Andrew poked his head over the banister.

Sophia sat up behind me and touched my neck. "You cut your hair."

I braced myself for Sophia's interpretation of my clipped ponytail, a symbol of tyranny's continuing reign of terror, in this case of my acquiescence to the old man's incessant nagging.

But she smiled and said, "It's nice," her feet poking out from the sheet as she adjusted her sun-yellow T-shirt.

"Well, what do we have *here?*" Andrew folded his arms, pretending to be interested, but was already hovering over the dresser, snapping open my cell phone.

"It's called *incest,*" Sophia said, sliding off the bed. "Promise you won't tell."

"As long as you two keep it to yourselves," Andrew said over his shoulder. "I'm not interested." He fiddled with the buttons on my phone and set it down.

"You're not invited anyway." Sophia made a sour face and stood up.

"Three's a crowd." Andrew grinned. "Peter, I need a favor—"

"Did you *know…?*" Sophia waited for Andrew's attention. "That Philadelphia means brotherly *and sisterly* love? *Adelphia* means *siblings*—male and female—not just brothers."

"You're a genius," Andrew said. "Truly, a veritable fountain of worthwhile information."

Sophia curtsied, pinching her T-shirt into a skirt, and skipped away—my little sister, deflowered, scoured, her act intact. I was wincing, straining to play along, though my instinct was to run after her and wrap myself around her.

"She wants me outta there. Today." Andrew stuffed his fists into his pockets. "It won't take long, but I need you with the truck."

"You're moving out?" I put my hands through my hair.

"Don't play dumb. It's done. It's just a coffee table and some other shit."

"You got a new place already?"

"No. That's the thing. I've got nowhere to go with it. But I don't want Mom and Dad to know."

"How—?"

"We'll put it in the attic. I'll be into a new place in a couple days."

For a moment I imagined living with Andrew in our own bachelor pad, maybe at Stone Bridge, where I could play apprentice.

"I have to work." I poked my head into a clean T-shirt.

"Don't give me that. You're your own boss." Andrew lobbed my army shorts from the desk chair.

"I seriously have to catch up today." I stepped into my shorts and slipped into my flip-flops.

"It'll take an hour," Andrew said.

"Yeah, right." I unzipped my gym bag on the bed.

"What are you doing?"

From a drawer I plucked a pair of khaki shorts, my favorite Temple T-shirt, and a navy-blue short-sleeve button-down and displayed the ensemble for Andrew's approval before stuffing it all into my bag. "Flip-flops okay with this?"

"Where you going?"

I dug out my Nikes from under the bed. "I don't know—for a drink?"

"You're wearing shorts?"

"It's ninety degrees."

"Mom wants to have a cookout tonight," Andrew said.

"A *cookout?*" I said. "I'll say I have to work—which is true."

"Wear a belt at least. You taking her to McDonald's for milkshakes?"

"Belts pinch me."

"So lay off the Big Macs." Andrew checked his watch.

"She won't see it anyway." I lifted my shirt to reveal my empty belt loops, then scooped yesterday's wrinkled khakis off the floor and flattened them against my chest. "Better?"

"Pure class, Doc."

"Any other helpful advice?" I headed for the bathroom.

Andrew called out, "Let's roll. She wants me gone by the time she gets there."

He seemed to be carefully avoiding Melanie's name.

"What time's *she* getting there?" I collected a toothbrush, a tube of Crest, a comb, a bottle of Pert, a disposable razor, a canister of Edge, and, from deep in the cabinet under the sink, a long-lost plastic

Temple Owls soap container, inside of which was a wrapped bar of lemon-zest Dial. I rushed to the bed and emptied my hands into the bag.

"Are you planning on *bathing* with this woman, Doc?"

I hiked my bag over my shoulder, stuffed my pockets—keys, wallet, cell phone—and followed Andrew upstairs. "You need to tell me what wine to get."

At the kitchen table Theo guarded his pencil, glancing up with gigantic eyes, while my father, dressed for work, sipped his coffee, and spoke consolingly, it seemed, to Sophia, who stared at her folded hands. "Help out at the church…courses at Temple…" the old man was saying, and, amazingly, Sophia was nodding and even jotting notes on a piece of paper torn from Theo's notebook.

I dropped my bag by the refrigerator and went for my breakfast in the cupboard.

"No time," Andrew muttered and gestured toward the garage. "Take a banana."

My mother, hair damp from her shower, appeared from the foyer, carrying Yiayia's plates.

"Did Andrew tell you about the barbecue tonight?" She offered these words as an appeal to everyone, it seemed, not yet convinced she'd sold the idea, especially to Sophia, who might have been secretly planning her final getaway.

I hid my head in the refrigerator, looking for something portable, other than fruit. Andrew rapped a knuckle on the refrigerator door.

"Peter?" my mother said.

"I'm really busy, Mom." I looked up from a cup of yogurt I'd mistaken for pudding.

She gestured toward Sophia at the table. "It would be nice for us all to be together."

Let the healing begin, I thought: family-dinner therapy.

She turned to the sink. "An early Fourth of July picnic," she said.

"Fireworks!" Theo sang out.

She rinsed her hands. "I'll pick up hamburgers and hot dogs. Sophia, do you want anything special?"

"No, thanks," she said sweetly.

My mother wasn't about to trust Sophia's newfound agreeability—or my suddenly packed schedule.

"Why so busy, Peter?"

"He's got a date."

I shot a murderous look at Andrew, who was thumbing his cell phone violently.

My mother dried her hands on a towel. "You're dating someone?"

"No, Mom," I said.

"Is that why you got the haircut?" she said.

"What?"

"Who *is* she?" Theo called out.

"*Watch* it, Theo!" I spun from the refrigerator.

Theo's eyes blinked steadily, like hazard lights.

"You're behind at work?" My father had been distracted from his consultation with Sophia, who all of a sudden seemed to be watching from outside, from some newfound peaceful perch, her open-mouthed expression changing from curious to rapt—her legs, I noticed, in a long-lost pair of cut-off jean shorts.

"Peter, gimme your cell-phone number again," Andrew said. "I thought I had it here…"

"You bought a cell phone, Peter?" my mother said. "Write your number on the refrigerator, honey—"

"You oblivious *dick!*" I blurted at Andrew.

Andrew looked up, finally—*What?*—as I swiped my gym bag from the floor and headed for the garage.

"*Peter,*" my mother said, poised with the felt pen attached by a string to the whiteboard on the freezer door.

"You guys going to the *gym* again?" my father called out. "I thought you just said you were behind at work."

I stood frozen at the door.

"What's the matter, Peter?" My mother let the pen hang from its string and approached me.

"Honestly, Mom—" I clenched the doorknob. "I have a lot of work to do."

"It's fine, honey. Go ahead and do what you have to do." She patted my cheek and handed me a granola bar, which she pulled magically, it seemed, from behind my ear.

20
Exhuming Isaac

A still-unquenched longing born the spring the Winklesteins went on their three-week trip to Israel deepened my sense of connection to Melanie—and to her family: to her brother, Abe, who went ape-shit over my mother's *spanakopita* when he came for Easter dinner last year and whose supposed black-belt power, stored up within his lanky-geeky exterior, had always mystified me; to their maniacal Jack Russell terrier, Isaac, who before he died showed me a certain privileged affection, licking the sweat from my legs and lapping from the spout as I watered the plants around the house; to Dr. and Mrs. Winklestein, who'd left on the kitchen table not only the keys to all four of their cars in the garage but also three pairs of Phillies tickets, for the home-opening series against the Pirates, which they would miss while touring the Holy Land.

Dr. Winklestein had lured Andrew out of the city to the suburbs, by offering a taste of what life was like when you were one of the top surgeons in the region. But, after only a few days, living in the Winklesteins' house and even driving Dr. Winklestein's cars lost their appeal for Andrew, who would go crazy, he said, living in the boonies, commuting forty-five minutes each way on I-76, when his apartment was a three-block walk from Pennsylvania Hospital. I, however, was living at home and would benefit, Andrew predicted, from taking some time-outs from my arduous life as a scholar, reading all that Art History and Philosophy or whatever. Not to mention that I was the one more inclined to manual labor, what with my lawn-mowing business in high school. So skimming the leaves from the pool and monitoring the filtering system would be no sweat, nor would walking Isaac, especially since I was so much better with animals than Andrew was.

The truth was that I didn't mind taking over; I spent my days at the Winklesteins' house, tucked deep in an ancient nook of the western suburbs, where the world seemed pulpy and vital, washed mossy green by the air filtering through the leaves overhead. By the pool in the back yard, sunbeams streamed through the trees like lamplight through an afghan's stretched-out holes. I floated, reading textbooks spread open on my knees. The Winklesteins' garage refrigerator stocked canned beer, which I displayed in the pool chair's Styrofoam cup holder, though I preferred the taste of Coke and Dr. Pepper. After all, I was twenty-one now. Granted, I was anything but a partier, but I was a college guy, nonetheless, the kind of guy who could enjoy a beer while reading Sartre and Nietzsche; I was nothing like the guys who tumbled into the Existential Lit mid-term earlier that week, defending themselves to Professor Brophy, right there before every-one in the class, explaining with wry grins that, yes, they were aware of the responsibility they had to themselves and their classmates, that, yes, especially as seniors, who should be modeling good scholarship, they appreciated the weighty implications of their actions, and that, well, though there was no excuse for their lateness, the fact of the matter was that they tended to ace tests and write their best papers when drunk or hung over—and who was anyone to judge, really?

These were the guys who sat in the row behind Dorothy Maloney, whom at the time I had never spoken to, only glanced at, over my shoulder, pretending to be annoyed by the wisecracking jerk-offs behind her. The truth was that I was vaguely jealous of them, especial-ly when Dorothy—as well most of the class, including Brophy, and even me—couldn't disguise being amused by their weekly antics and vaguely relevant commentary on a given topic. I wished I'd had the guts back on the first day of the semester to move into her row before Brophy finished the seating chart. Brophy had said that once he learned all the names we could sit wherever we wanted, but no one ever relocated, and so I remained doomed to stealing glances—that is, until Andrew decided to have his little *soiree* at the Winklesteins' and I convinced myself not only that Dorothy was dying to talk to me about that last essay question on fate and free will, as she headed back to her dorm that Friday afternoon, but also that she was dying to go to a party with me out in the middle of nowhere.

Dorothy hadn't bothered explaining to me that one of the wise-cracking jerk-offs was her spiteful pothead ex-boyfriend from high school, whom she'd followed to Temple—a mystifying fact to this day—until after they sacked the party, running off with a bag of pretzels, a cheese plate, and two bottles of wine and then mistaking Isaac for a speed bump on the driveway. At first the dog had appeared to be on all fours, nipping at the bumper right up to the edge of the estate, barking insanely as the car vanished into the darkness. But as I approached, I realized that the thing was convulsing, its black-eyed head bobbing like a broken toy's, its white coat having been gnarled under tires.

Promptly joining me on the driveway was Abe's high-school-senior girlfriend, Jessica, who, for the first time in her life, had smoked pot, from a bong, which Dorothy's ex-boyfriend had charmed her into trying. Andrew had invited Jessica, he explained to me later, less out of courtesy than out of the admittedly not-fully-thought-out strategy that her being there would snuff out any theory—God forbid anyone should have cause to form a theory—that he was being secretive about, let alone irresponsible by, having "a few friends over for a swim." By the time the party had reached its high point—or low point, as it were—"a few friends" filled the living room, kitchen, and poolside. I had always thought Andrew's choice to invite his girlfriend's brother's girlfriend analogous to informing the cops of a robbery you hadn't yet committed. Upon witnessing Isaac's spasmodic expiration on the driveway, Jessica rushed inside to call the Winklesteins' hotel in Jerusalem, crying hysterically, boiling with pot-induced paranoia. But in his infinite ability to placate, Andrew managed to calm Jessica down—and calm Abe down too—explaining how in a panic he'd called Abe's girlfriend and asked her to please come over because he'd found the dog floating in the pool, not yet dead, and then how Jessica had stroked Isaac tenderly on the patio, whispering comforting words into his ear, escorting him into his long sleep, the poor thing now in the living room, in a milk-crate casket she'd lined with blankets. I'd watched in awe as Jessica's tears changed from mortified to merely sorrowful. Andrew's version had converted what she must have feared was partial culpability into saintliness.

But then there was the problem of Isaac's corpse, which was malformed by tires, not bloated from drowning—and whoever heard of a dog drowning, anyway?

On Saturday, on a detour from an already sickening ride to Veterans Stadium—they'd just announced plans for a new park and so the Vet was doomed to implosion—Andrew buried Isaac in the woods off Forbidden Drive, in spite of my protestations, not to mention Abe's instructions to keep the dog wrapped in blankets in the garage or boxed up under dry leaves in the back yard. Andrew had marked a fake grave in the back yard with the pool skimmer, grabbed a shovel from a hook in the garage, and hauled Isaac out in a black canvas duffel bag—not in a milk crate, let alone one lined with blankets—as if he were off to the gym. Andrew had insisted that we had no choice, that the dog's mangled body was incriminating evidence, no matter where it was buried. I had assured him that no one would insist on a coroner's report, let alone go exhuming Isaac to do an autopsy. "Better safe than sorry," Andrew had said, gassing Dr. Winklestein's Mercedes. "It's for the best. Trust me. No one wants to see their own dog like this."

Now, over five years later, I was lost in the past, choking back tears, as if *I* were the one breaking up with Melanie. I stayed silent in the liquor store, even as Andrew offered his version of an apology for the public announcement he'd just made back in the kitchen minutes earlier. "I didn't mean to mention your date, Peter—or your cell phone—it just slipped out. Everyone thought I was just joking, anyway…" As Andrew pointed at wine bottles, I nodded in approval at the reds under ten dollars and at one for twenty that looked like what we'd drunk at Daisy's—a Greek wine from Santorini. Amazingly, Andrew didn't press me for an explanation as we loaded a shopping cart and then two brown paper bags that filled the foot space of my truck's passenger seat.

The bottles rattled and the windshield flickered with green shadows along the river as I trailed the red Porsche, picturing myself and Andrew passing each other in silence to and from the truck bed and lugging a dresser, a bed frame, mattresses, boxes of clothes, computer,

TV, stereo, and the framed print of Eakins's *Gross Clinic*, a gift from me when Andrew graduated from medical school. In my mind Melanie watched from the stoop, wiping her tears, and Andrew asked whose was this decanter they bought in New Hope and whose was that watercolor they picked up in the Bahamas and there was no question, ha-ha, whose was the stained-glass Star of David in the front window and it was a good thing, wasn't it, that they'd never gotten a dog after all.

Suddenly, for me, the end of Andrew's relationship with Melanie represented the end of any chance for closure, the need for which—in general, I realized, as I entered the city—never presented itself fully until the opportunity to reach it was already receding into the past. The Winklesteins had never questioned, of course, Isaac's backyard burial location. In fact, when I was invited for dinner, in thanks for helping take care of the house, Abe and I marked the supposed gravesite by nailing to the nearest tree a framed close-up of Isaac, as well as a pewter-and-stained-glass ornament that marked the home of a Jew, a *muzzazza*, an ornament customarily intended for doorways, Abe had explained minutes earlier, as he pried it with a kitchen knife from the inside frame of the garage.

Now, fastened to the doorframe of Andrew and Melanie's first-floor walk-up was a similar *muzzazza*, and below it was a yellow Post-It, which Andrew stuffed into his pocket, just as I arrived on the sidewalk below.

"What'd it say?" I asked.

"It said you're late. Get your shit out of here A-SAP."

My truck blocked a hydrant at the corner, hazards on, hatch open, signaling, once again, men at work.

Andrew and I each carried a stack of empty drawers to the pick-up. Each waited for the other, then, standing guard on the sidewalk. Melanie had prepared boxes, all of them sealed with clear tape and Magic Markered: Andrew's sweaters, Andrew's T-shirts, Andrew's CDs and DVDs. I watched Andrew for tears, but only sweat moistened his face, as he panted and dropped off the next load. A lamp, a laptop, and small speakers went into the Porsche. The bed was hers, Andrew said, as was the sofa. Together we carried the dresser, which had been dragged, certainly not by Melanie alone, into the living room, tracks still in the carpet. There was the coffee table, a brown leather loveseat, and a nightstand—all of which filed neatly into the truck bed, alongside the dresser, the boxes, and the Eakins print of the bloody surgery. Not much else, Andrew explained, because they'd planned on replacing old stuff, which they'd trashed or left behind in their old apartments. "Final check," Andrew said, heading inside.

I leaned back against the passenger door of the truck and wiped my face with my sweat-soaked T-shirt. An oven-breeze swept by. When I was a kid, it had always been enough for the weathermen to tell the temperature, but now the meteorologists had a number for how hot the heat *felt*, the index, which for a week had been pushing a hundred ten. I couldn't remember humidity like this growing up, hot air that seemed to be teeming with pressure, each molecule a tear duct about to burst.

Feet shuffled on the sidewalk around the corner across the street. When I recognized the voices, my impulse was to duck inside the truck before they stepped into view. Abe, his pale limbs sprouting from dark socks and running shorts, carried a pizza box, and Melanie, in jean shorts, sipped from a straw. Halfway across the street, they spotted me. I faked a surprised smile, which I let morph into an uncertain squint.

"Peter." Melanie's smile put me at ease, while Abe's suspicious glance rekindled my long-harbored guilt about Isaac. "I didn't recognize you." Melanie reached for my hair as she stepped forward for a hug. Behind her, Abe opened the pizza box to display an untouched pie. Despite my drenched shirt, Melanie kept her arms wrapped around me, as my eyes rested curiously on the steaming pizza.

Lunchtime already?

"Roasted peppers," Abe said.

"Have some." Melanie let go and looked up at me. "We won't eat it all."

"Seriously." Abe slid the box onto the roof of the truck.

I kept my hands in my pockets and my eyes on Melanie, straining to return what must have been her sad, goodbye smile.

"You look so different," she said. "I mean, great."

"I didn't think you'd *be* here," I said.

"I didn't think *you'd* be here. He said first thing in the morning. I was beginning to think he changed his mind."

I mirrored Melanie's curious glance toward the apartment. "He's in there."

"I figured." She slurped from her straw. "I guess I'll go see." She disappeared around the corner and called back, "Save me some."

Abe was grinning, teeth clenched halfway toward the crust. He pointed to the pizza, and I gave in, granola skittering in my gut. I chewed quietly and nodded to Abe, who nodded back—*good pizza*—the two of us as if in a TV commercial, a couple of inarticulate greasy-lipped twits, who, if we kept our mouths full, wouldn't have to broach the topic of our respective siblings' sudden change of heart nor of long-harbored secrets regarding conflicts of faith or the vile death and bogus interment of family pets.

Our heads bobbing, Abe said, "Still painting?" and, clearing my throat, I said, "Still, uh—" gesturing with a flat-handed chop. "Karate?"

"Not karate." Abe grabbed another slice. "Tai Chi."

"Ah, Tai Chi." I nodded, though at the moment I didn't know Tai Chi from chai tea, let alone from karate. My mind was somewhere else. Abe might have been working in a gym or a Chinese teahouse.

He eyed me skeptically. "I'm still at the studio, if that's what you mean. Still an instructor. Just not karate."

I went on nodding, not about to admit my confusion. For the last six years I'd never fancied Abe a full-time instructor, with or without a black belt. I'd always assumed he had a regular job like everyone else—or like me. A carpenter, a cab driver. Now I imagined being trained by Abe, who, in my mind, hugged a kick bag I stabbed with my foot.

Abe glanced at the apartment. "Think they're all right in there?"

"I have to tell you something," I said.

"What's that?" Abe said. "Have another—" He pointed to the pizza.

"When you were in Israel…"

Abe looked up, mid-bite.

"It's not a big deal," I said. "I just think you should know."

"Know what?"

I laid my crust in the box and wiped my hands on my thighs.

"I mean, everything we said—or Andrew said—wasn't exactly true."

"What are you talking about?" Abe's jaw worked in slow circles.

"About Isaac."

Abe set the remainder of his slice in the box and swallowed. A lump moved down his throat like a rat through a snake.

"You wouldn't have wanted to see him," I said.

"Water under the bridge," Abe said.

"I don't know why—it seems idiotic now…"

Abe crossed his arms.

"We didn't bury him in the back yard." I braced myself against the truck, shuffling back a step along the curb.

"Then *where?*"

"Fairmount Park."

"What? *Why?*" Abe took a deep breath.

"We didn't want you to get upset. He was hit bad."

"*Hit? By a car?*"

For a moment I couldn't remember exactly how Isaac had died, the true story blurring with the one Andrew had invented.

"I'm really sorry," I said.

"*You* shouldn't be apologizing." Abe aimed his gaze down the sidewalk.

"It wasn't *Andrew's* fault," I said, my memory of the details returning. "It was some asshole at the party."

"*What* party?" Abe began to whistle as he exhaled, some kind of calming ritual, I suspected, the Tai Chi master contemplating methods of inflicting pain—chops to the windpipe, kicks to the shins. "Andrew had a *party* while we were in *Israel?*" Abe shook his head, self-reproachfully, it seemed, as if he should have trusted his worst suspicions from the outset. "I *knew* she was drunk, or *stoned*, or whatever she was that night—" He glared toward the apartment. "He was lying through his teeth—and so was *she*."

"Your *girlfriend?*" I kept my distance.

"*Ex.*" Abe started down the sidewalk.

"Abe, wait," I called, following. "What are you gonna do?"

"Don't cover for the asshole."

"*He* was covering for *me*," I blurted.

Abe turned at the wrought-iron railing.

"*I* killed him." I didn't know what I was saying now, pointing over my shoulder at my truck. "I put him in my truck, and I buried him." In this new story everyone was innocent but me. I sidled alongside the brick face toward Abe, who gripped the handrail. "He got away before I could get the leash on, and then I couldn't find him, so I got in the truck and he shot out from the trees. It was pitch black. I figured we could say he ran away. But then I told Andrew—the next day—and that's when he called your girlfriend and told her to come over. He didn't know what to do. He wanted to kill me. He was ready to go dig him up. And then your girlfriend went crazy and kept calling you, and that's when Andrew grabbed the phone." I stood sandwiched between flowerboxes, my back to the wall. "He figured drowning was a peaceful way to go, I guess."

"I never believed it," Abe muttered calmly. "Dogs don't drown."

"Exactly," I said, relieved for a moment, even as I anticipated a knee to the groin—some kind of closure.

After a moment, Abe nodded and grinned. "So how was the party?"

My mind went blank.

Abe added, "You don't even know what's true anymore, do you?"

A chorus of "Fuck *you!*" shook the windows. Abe and I looked up at the apartment door.

Abe stepped toward me and aimed two fingers at one of my eyeballs. "You're *both* nuts." His breath reeked of sour peppers.

"Go a*head*." I turned my cheek, anticipating the world going black, my gory retreat.

Gazing down his nose, Abe lowered his hand. "That's not what Tai Chi's about."

"Get out!" Melanie's command was followed by deep thumps—dropped boxes or bed legs—along with Andrew's refusal, "*You* get out!"

Abe kept staring into my eyes, even as Andrew emerged onto the stoop and blurted, "What the fuck are you *doing*, Abe?" Abe turned, finally, when Andrew's hand landed on his shoulder.

"Take it easy, Andrew," Abe said, still facing me.

Andrew muscled for position against the brick wall, twisting to face Abe.

Shuffling toward the stoop, I said, "This has nothing to do with you, Andrew."

"You think you're hot shit with your black belt?" Andrew hissed.

"I don't have a black belt," Abe said.

"Well, *now* the truth comes out," Andrew said, delighted.

"*Yes,* it *does,*" Abe said. "I just learned about your party a few years ago."

All at once Andrew's shoulders collapsed and his voice softened: "Jesus, Peter…"

I stood at the railing. "It was my fault, I told him. You had nothing to do with it."

Andrew sighed. "Look, Abe. I'm sorry." He glanced up at the apartment door and let out a resigned breath. "You know what? I should go—" he said, and turned face-first into the wrought-iron corner of a flowerbox holder, and crumpled over.

"*Whoa,*" Abe said.

I leapt from the railing and steadied Andrew to his feet, wrapping my arms around his shoulders.

"Doc," Andrew said, patching his eye with a hand. When he checked his palm, it was alive with rivulets of dripping blood.

"Can you open it?" Abe said.

Andrew didn't dare unclench the muscles holding his eyeball in.

Abe brought a handful of his own T-shirt toward Andrew's face.

"Don't—" I stretched my own sleeve to wipe Andrew's cheek.

Andrew's eyelid fluttered.

"It got the side," Abe said. "Can you see?"

Andrew nodded.

I took off my T-shirt, bunched it up, and presented Andrew with a white-cotton flower. "Press."

Blood spread into my shirt like drizzling syrup, just as Melanie screamed, "Abraham, you *nut!* What did you *do?*" and rushed down the steps.

"I didn't do *anything*." Abe took Andrew by the arm.

"Oh, my God—" Melanie stooped to see, as Andrew balanced himself against a tree. "What happened? *Andrew...*"

"I hit the flowerbox." He pointed.

"You *what?*" She peered into his open eye. "Do you feel queasy?"

Andrew pulled the T-shirt from his face.

"Oh—" Melanie cringed at the gash. "You want to sit down?"

"Doc, how do I look?" Andrew smiled.

I winced and crossed my arms. "Not bad."

"He shouldn't *drive*, right?" Melanie said. "You can't drive."

"I'm fine." Andrew checked his watch. "Doc, you should get outta here. Busy day ahead..."

"You sure?" I said.

"I'll get ice," Abe said, and turned to go inside. "Keep pressure on it."

"Abe—" I called. "I gotta go." I gestured with a thumb toward my truck.

"Oh." Abe reached out and shook my hand. "Peace, man."

"Bye."

"Oh, *Peter...*" Melanie took my bare shoulders and kissed my cheek. "No goodbyes, okay?"

I could hardly bear her sweet smile.

Andrew escorted me up the sidewalk, holding the T-shirt to his face.

At the truck I said, "I didn't mean to mention the party—it just slipped out."

Andrew nodded, wincing. "It doesn't matter. The whole thing's a mess. Go."

I rounded the truck to the driver's side. "What were you fighting about?"

Andrew laid an elbow on the roof of the truck, squinting. "I'm in debt up to here, and she wants me to pay half her rent." Slowly he lowered the shirt and opened his eye, grinning. "Doc, I've got your sweaty-ass T-shirt on my face. Here—"

"I don't want that thing," I laughed, and ducked into the driver's seat. I leaned toward the open passenger window.

The gash extended from the corner of Andrew's eye, purplish and frayed like tiny swollen lips.

"You all right?" I said.

Andrew bowed and put his hand out for a soul-brother shake. "My keeper." He dropped the wet, bloodstained T-shirt onto the passenger seat. His silver watch flashed.

Our hands clasped, I said, "Can I borrow that?"

Andrew unsnapped the wristband, and the watch tumbled into my hands. "Keep it. It's yours."

21
History of the Greeks in America

Theo hadn't yet made his way into town or even out of his boxer shorts. He raised the watering can to the hanging plant on the front porch. Stooping, he picked at a plate, his belly, white as feta cheese, drooping over his waistband. One hand on his waist, the noon sun blazing, he brought a glass of foggy liquid to his lips and surveyed the yard, as if he were the proud owner of acres of olive trees.

The coast would have to be clear before I could get all of Andrew's stuff into the garage, let alone into the attic. Midway down Birch Hill, I wondered if each day, while the family was out of the house, my uncle returned early for his own personal siesta, if in fact Theo had already put in his morning shift at the library and was home playing tycoon, opening all the doors and windows, stripping down to his boxers, sipping ouzo, spitting olive pits, smoking cigarettes, watering the land. From the grass Theo snapped up the hose, already gushing, and aimed it at the clean-angled bushes lining the front of the house, obviously in no hurry to get back to work on the History of the Greeks in America.

I pulled over to wait for Theo to go inside. Beside the truck, fallen needles, golden dust, and stars of waxy residue had stained the hood and windshield of Daisy's abandoned car. Theo made his way into the yard, freeing the hose behind him with a jerk, a mad cowboy rustling sheep in his underwear, his face masked in a cloud of smoke, a secret pack of Marlboros peeking over his waistband. He gunned an arc of water at nothing in particular, unless he was nourishing the dark circle of dirt and distended roots in the shadows under the birches.

Suddenly Theo whipped around, a sagging wave trailing in the air, and set his eyes on the dark figure in the window, Yiayia in a black dress, her fist rapping at the glass. Theo dismissed her with a splash and returned to the bushes and flowers, while Yiayia remained pounding the window, demanding that Theo do, or stop doing, only God (and maybe Theo) knew what—that he fix her TV or bring her some lunch or stop smoking cigarettes. The delayed sound of each flat clack reached me on the hill only when Yiayia's fist drew back. I anxiously awaited the explosion of glittery shards, Yiayia's hand cracking through, Theo's frazzled response, my own necessary intervention. Theo spun around, his back to the house, and showered the lawn. I sank in my seat, hoping Theo's thick frames would fail to magnify me into view. In a minute Yiayia's hand settled by her side, though she remained in the window as Theo exhaled a cloud of smoke and, reaching his arm out, tapped his ash into the green grass.

I was anticipating some violent outbreak. I'd been bracing myself for the inevitable meltdown for more than ten years, ever since Theo had proven himself unfit to live in a local apartment alone, let alone with a woman, the year Andrew moved to West Philly and I moved into the basement, vacating my bedroom for my uncle. The stories I'd overheard as a kid had prepared me for a certain clash that had never ensued. Perhaps Theo had come to fear his own lows and was determined once and for all to occupy his space peacefully: he managed his moods dutifully with lithium—or so he claimed; he sometimes broached, but then forfeited, arguments on the topics that fueled his passions—he might defend the sexual proclivity of the Commander in Chief, or lambaste the American people for their prudery, or call the church archaic and irrelevant, but he always stopped short of insulting the old man personally; he spent only a portion of his disability checks, on cheap journals and pencils, while he saved for his trip to Greece, where he would finish the work he'd started years ago—a fantasy my parents had been encouraging since Theo had moved into the house, as it kept him focused, his energy properly channeled, his money in the bank, not in the manipulating hands of his "street woman," who, my parents had claimed, didn't "know her own age." My parents had feared that the woman had been using Theo for sex, as if Theo had been an unwitting participant, or an oblivious donor of his seed—perhaps, God forbid, the woman had even wanted a baby, which my parents were convinced they would have ended up raising themselves. Clearing out Theo's old apartment, they'd found a sandwich baggie of marijuana as well as sex paraphernalia (details I'd barely made sense of, listening from the basement steps, as the rules-of-the-house had been laid down). Theo had argued that she was too old to get pregnant and that she'd saved his life: even after he'd threatened her with a kitchen knife and then gorged himself on tranquilizers, she'd called not the police or the doctor, who would have insisted on the straightjacket, but my father, even though she'd known that the old man thought of her as a homeless prostitute and that he would take Theo away from her once and for all.

When Yiayia moved away from the window, Theo turned back toward the house, having dragged the endless hose to the street, where he flicked his cigarette butt. Lassoing a coil at his side, he walked to the porch, picked up his plate and glass, and went inside. I drifted toward the driveway. The garage door was open, no cars in sight. As I lowered the hatch, a tidal wave of Greek crashed upstairs and then receded into the house. In a flash, I imagined Yiayia whirling about, a witch without a broom, spitting her untranslatable fury into the corners. When I heard a dropped glass—or a broken vase—I relished the perfect timing, the chaos distracting whoever was inside from my secret mission in the garage. When the walls and floors thumped and vibrated and the unknowable screaming went on, I cracked the door into the kitchen, just as Theo entered from the foyer. In the delirium of his own rage, Theo was hissing, "*Gamoh tin Panayia sou*"—Fuck your Virgin Mary—a string of wicked sounds I hadn't heard since the night Theo proclaimed that it was only a matter of getting my mother mad enough before she kicked him out of the house just as heartlessly as the old man had kicked him out of the church; he'd begged for mercy, then, when she pinched his ear and led him to the door like a dog. Right now, Theo went on cursing fearlessly, attacking the drawers, or so it seemed, until he swiped a saucepan from a lower cabinet—an unlikely weapon—and exhaling, trudged into the foyer and upstairs. I stepped lightly into the kitchen and then the dining room, where I stood with my back against the wall of icons. Out of her room, Yiayia trod around the third floor, her thick shoes clicking and thumping, hollering what sounded like a single

Greek word of countless syllables. I didn't dare expose myself, as Theo climbed the stairs, muttering unintelligibly, and the clang of the saucepan echoed off the walls. Suddenly Theo unleashed a burst of Greek as unrestrained as Yiayia's, though his seemed borrowed, not only for its barbaric quality but also for its surprising fluency, the outpouring accompanied by the striking of the saucepan against the banister, a storm of violence that finally compelled me to twist into the staircase.

Gripping the handrail at her waist and shaking her index finger, Yiayia cursed at Theo, who jabbed the saucepan in the air, taunting her, perhaps commanding her to cook for herself. I squatted on the bottom steps, stealing glances, my head out of view from Yiayia on the third-floor balcony, toward which Theo continued to climb. Yiayia, howling all the while, made her way around the banister that guarded the square stairwell opening—a boxing ring in reverse—through which from the first floor you could see the third-floor ceiling and over which, miraculously, no one in the family had ever purposely flung himself nor accidentally fallen—perhaps until now, I thought. When Theo reached the third floor he stood directly above me and directly across from Yiayia, who volleyed shouts, until a flash of silver turned her silent, the saucepan striking the wall behind her and clanging on the floor. I hesitated before rushing up the stairs to play referee, blind to their antics as I made my way to the second-floor landing, wishing I'd never come inside, realizing in the same moment, in a bittersweet rush of insight, that I should have taken—and still could take—*would* take—Andrew's stuff to my own makeshift apartment, just as soon as I escaped this asylum.

Something else had been thrown—a small, framed picture that flipped through the air and skittered across the second-floor landing. Theo mirrored Yiayia's walk, threatening to throw another picture he'd swiped from the wall, which provided an endless arsenal. They hollered back and forth, across the open space, Greek never before so distinctly their own language. Caught up in the dance, Theo didn't seem to realize—as Yiayia flung her hand like a handkerchief, surrendering to him or dismissing him or showing him he'd driven her to tears—that she was guiding herself along the handrail back toward her bedroom. The door latch clicked. Theo, in plain sight, stood in his pale-blue boxers. I couldn't predict my uncle's response but prepared to call 911. Theo gazed across the barred expanse, then lowered himself, along with the old photograph, and began to crawl, just above me, his hands peeling off the floor, one after the other, as he dragged himself toward the door.

22
The Miracle of Viagra

"I thought you'd forgotten," Daisy said on the phone.

"Something came up," I said, as I raced back to the city.

Locking the door to her apartment, Daisy said, "Beautiful watch."

"Timex," I said, nonsensically, as she reached for my wrist.

"Rolex," she corrected me, and stepped onto the sidewalk.

I shrugged, feigning modesty, and helped her into my truck.

Then we were standing in the Stone Bridge apartment. The wine glasses I'd taken from home were sitting on the marble coffee table.

"You have good taste," Daisy said—generously, I realized—as she turned a ten-dollar bottle of wine in her hands.

The moment she picked up the bottle from Santorini, I knew what I'd forgotten, and, standing there, I dreaded returning to face my doctor-and-lawyer Indian neighbors, who had also just moved in today and who, not without apparent suspicion, had lent me a hand with the leather loveseat.

"My neighbors never returned my bottle opener," I said.

Daisy looked up from her unzipped purse. "When you get back, I have a surprise for you."

I paused at the door, suddenly overwhelmed by a strange feeling of gratitude—alone with Daisy, as if in a hotel room that could be anywhere. When Daisy smiled, setting her purse on the carpet, gratitude swelled into what I believed, for the moment, was *true love*, such as I had never felt before—I gauged this feeling by the fact that I didn't know what surprise Daisy had in store yet felt unconditionally devoted to her and to whatever she might have planned. I would have left everything in Philadelphia behind, right that second, and followed her to Greece or wherever she wanted to go. Daisy's softly closed fist, surprise inside, awaited me on her lap. I mirrored her smile. It was all I could do to refrain from blurting *I love you*.

"What is it?" I approached.

"Open and see."

I sat down and, hooking my fingertips gently under hers, peeled her fingers all at once. In her hand was a sky-blue diamond tablet. I knew it wasn't candy. *Acid?* I'd never so much as inhaled someone else's marijuana smoke. But okay. With her thumb and finger she held it up to my mouth like a Valentine's heart with a message.

"*Pfizer?*"

She put it to my sealed lips. "Trust me."

I knew only that you needed a prescription.

"It won't make you Hercules," she said, "but it might help. Open—"
She opened her mouth to demonstrate.

"*Viagra?*" I turned my head.

"It's not what you think."

"That's the *last* thing I need."

"If you don't need it, then it won't make a difference."

"No way." I eyed the thing skeptically, pinching it from her fingers.

Daisy patted me on the knee, went to the sliding-glass door, opened it a crack, "For fresh air," she said, and slipped into the kitchen. The bag of Doritos rustling in her hands, she returned, licking her carrot-orange fingertips. I imagined her hours from now, lying there next to me, done, delirious. She perched an empty glass on her knee, and I slipped the pill between my lips. As I rushed downstairs, praying my neighbors drank wine, I gathered saliva and managed to swallow.

*

The drug's effect was instantaneous, I thought, when in the hallway I mistook the vibrating phone in my pocket for the miracle of Viagra. Coincidentally, I became anxious in the Indians' doorway when the wife went to the kitchen for a bottle opener and left me in plain sight of the husband, who couldn't disguise his disgust as he adjusted some shelves in the living room. I turned off my cell phone and kept a hand stuffed in my pocket.

It didn't take me long, then, to lose faith in the drug: the confidence that had come with my visions of endless Tantric sex on the living-room carpet vanished the instant I felt the familiar rumbling, Daisy's warm thighs secure around my hips—this in spite of the wine, which had numbed my pelvis like Novocain. There wasn't enough time even to dread the passing of what would nonetheless remain a momentous event in my life, let alone to revel in, or, really, even to consciously register the experience. It seemed instantly something of the past. I was afforded only enough time so that in the future I would be tormented by a (barely) informed sense of what I was missing in life. Daisy jerked—in disappointment, I assumed—as I began to pull away, but she hugged me against her, reminding me, "It's okay," and I relaxed, as much as one could relax, bracing my weight above her on the couch, her hands firm on my back.

"I thought I hurt you," I said.

"I came," Daisy said.

At once the two words invigorated and devastated me: my inadequacy was of no consequence to her. Just as I began to consider the implications of this fact, shrinking inside of her, she added, "We have something in common," and smiled.

I twisted to the other side of the couch. "I'm worse than an old man."

She laughed and crawled toward me. "It doesn't work that way. It helps to get it up, that's all. We'll just have to keep doing it over and over." Her hand slipped between my legs.

They hadn't bothered to make a drug for *my* problem. Everyone else grew out of it. You were expected to jerk off when you were sixteen, gain control when you were eighteen, and fuck like an oil rig by the time you were twenty-one. When you were sixty, maybe, you sneaked a little blue pill for a boost. I was alone in this—or I *would* be once Daisy was gone: no one else would be so easily charmed by me; no one else could ever charm me into all of this.

"Be patient." She was rolling me in her grip like a sack of marbles.

Should I be getting hard again already?

"I'm immune to *Viagra*," I muttered, chin against my chest. "It's no use."

She faced me on the couch and grinned. "What turns you on?"

Over and over again, she provided, with such grace, opportunities for my humiliation. What did I know of turn-ons outside of what I'd concocted alone in my own bed?

"What makes you *hard?*"

Was she serious? As if what she was doing right now wouldn't ordinarily do the trick.

"Do you like this?" Daisy asked.

I nodded. I liked it, of course, but at the moment only as one liked a back rub.

"What do you think about when you lie in bed alone?"

Somehow Daisy had come to know the world of my sex life, which took place alone in my bed, where reality met fantasy, where human contact—albeit with myself—did not mean instant disappointment.

"You," I said, a safe answer.

Her tongue entered my ear, a wet finger in a socket, my neck and ribs sizzling, as I remained inert in her hand—some electrical glitch. I touched her leg to let her know I was still alive.

"Relax," she whispered.

I clenched my thighs.

"You want me to kiss it?" she asked earnestly.

I smiled meekly. Yes. No.

"You want to do it yourself?" She took her hand away.

I squirmed. "No—"

She put a finger to my lips. "There's no rush." She poured some wine, panning the bare apartment. "You have some music?"

I envisioned against the opposite wall the stereo equipment stacked in the back of Andrew's Porsche. I went to the closet, where I dug through the hidden cans, drop cloth, rollers, and brushes; in the bedroom I plugged in Eliot's paint-speckled radio and found a jazz station. Perfect, I thought. An uninterrupted note from a saxophone escorted me back into the living room, where Daisy faced me on the couch, wine glass dangling from a hand, legs slightly open, one across the couch cushions, the other bent at the knee, heel against the coffee table.

"Let me look at you," she said.

The high note from the bedroom spluttered and faded.

A circle of red swirled at her fingertips. She sighed, stiffening, curling her leg on the coffee table.

I stood there, naked, beyond shame, something worse than a virgin.

There was silence for a moment.

I took myself into my hand. It was worse to stand with my arms at my sides.

A husky voice sang from the bedroom, "*Darn that dream…*," betraying my expectations of jazz as instrumental background music. The owner of the voice might as well have been playing here in the flesh, at a piano in the corner, winking over his shoulder.

"Tell me what you want." Daisy had inched down on the couch, both knees up.

"What I *want?*" I said.

"What you want to *do* to me."

I took a deep breath.

Her fingers pointed. "I want your hard cock inside me."

Oh, Jesus. I aimed my limp flesh in Daisy's direction. A bouncy saxophone interlude urged me to reciprocate with some flattering fantasy. "I want…" My mind was blank, unable to imagine even a moment beyond what I saw before me.

"I want you to straddle me…" She tilted her head back. "And come all over me." A hand lathered her neck.

Oh, God. In my mind, I thrust between her pressed-together breasts, the tunnel between them, even in my now lubricated imagination, instantly slick with my own fluid.

"That turns you on?" she said.

She grinned, suddenly, and I exhaled, relieved (mostly), forcing a smile, realizing this was only dirty talk, foreplay, designed to jumpstart me. Okay. I would play along. She hadn't suggested anything outside the boundaries of my own imagination, and obviously she knew what she was doing, observing for herself: I had begun to swell gradually.

The throaty serenade played on.

Daisy smiled. "I want you to fuck my tight ass."

"I want to," I said, ridiculously, firming up.

Daisy twisted, onto her knees, and looked over her shoulder, one hand sweeping hair from her face, while the other appeared, fingers ascending, between the two halves of her glorious, white back side. "When you're ready—"

"I'm ready," I blurted. I didn't want to rush, but I didn't want to wait too long.

This time I would last, I would.

"Okay," she said, grinning as I approached. "Use the bottle."

"What?" This was going too far—*wasn't it?*—make-believe or not.

"After you come."

I tested her with a smile.

Three bottles stood tall between us. She gestured toward the still-corked one.

Reality was carrying on beyond the walls around us, a spacey trumpet floating in from the bedroom, a door in the hallway squeaking and thumping—the Indian couple making another trip to their U-Haul—keys jangling and going silent.

Sizing up the bottle, as if it were my own, I rounded the table, grinning devilishly.

"Oh my," Daisy giggled, and buried her head in her arms.

I anticipated my imminent finish. Daisy's hand rose once again from below, this time gripping me like a tool and guiding me precisely. My shoulders bowed, my whole body softening above her, my hands out to my sides—one clenching the bottle—as if preparing for the familiar fall. But as Daisy eased back, I straightened naturally, and, just like that, I was up, for good, now, I knew it, I'd found my balance, and I was on my own. When Daisy looked back, smiled, and said, "That's it, baby," it seemed to me that this was all there was in the world and there was no reason why it should ever have to end.

Then a lock's bolt smacked in its metal socket, and Daisy whipped around as the door opened.

Eliot stood there, frozen as I was.

"Eliot!"

"*God,*" Eliot gagged and pulled the door before him, leaving a gap.

"What the fuck is going on in there, Pappas!"

Daisy slid belly-down onto the couch.

"Nothing!" I set the bottle on the table, considered my boxers on the floor, and rushed to the door instead. "This is *my place*, Eliot," I begged, pressing my shoulder to the door, praying for mercy, hoping Eliot would appreciate some unwritten man-to-man pact and go along with the story.

"You *know* him?" Daisy peered over the arm of the couch.

"I'm his *boss!*" Eliot wouldn't budge. He managed to glare inside, despite my shoulder. "Let me in, Pappas, or I'll call the cops…"

"Eliot, *please—*"

As Eliot rushed in to comb the place, he glanced at me. "Can't you control that thing? *Christ…*" He found his supplies in the closet and cooled down, arms akimbo, panning the living room. "Look at this…"

I hopped into my boxers and khakis. I thrust my fists into my pockets. Daisy, hunched over, stepped into her panties and swiped her bra from the carpet. She stood up, facing Eliot and me head-on, straightening her arms through the loops, the late-afternoon sun blazing through the glass doors behind her, her body shadowing her dangling breasts, her nipples the color of roses going brown.

"Don't you have any respect for women?" she said.

I bowed shamefully as she fixed herself inside her bra, less relieved than distressed when I found her stern stare resting on Eliot, who stared back at her.

"The keys." Eliot turned to me. "A half hour I'm giving you…"

I fished the keys from my pocket.

"…to get your perverted mess out of here, including your *whore*."

Daisy buttoned her jeans. "You mother*fucker*."

I braced myself.

Eliot struck a cowboy pose, kicking a heel up onto the wall behind him.

"You lonely men are all the same," Daisy huffed, buttoning her shirt, rushing into her shoes, hiking her bag over her shoulder, and meeting Eliot at the door. "You're so easy to identify."

"Yeah, how's that?" Eliot cocked his head.

"Every woman you want, you think is a whore."

Daisy disappeared, and Eliot stood there for a minute, working an invisible toothpick.

"Half an hour," he said, finally.

"Please don't tell anyone," I said, as the door clicked shut.

A horn fluttered and faded.

I slid down the wall, adjusting myself, as I descended, so that I wouldn't break against the waistband ceiling of my pants. Still, it hurt, as if it were continuing to expand. The little blue pill had worked, maybe too well. My heart was racing, and the wine seemed to be bubbling up in my chest. I waited a minute. I checked my Rolex—six o'clock. It felt more like three a.m. Feeling anything but imaginative, let alone aroused, I then—not exactly unconcerned—freed myself from my fly, stretched my legs on the floor, and went to work. Gray-purple clouds sank like ink in the sliding glass doors. Thunder rumbled, or was it the Indians tugging a picnic table onto the concrete floor down below? A cooling rain right about now would be too good to be true. From the bedroom a soulful DJ's voice announced that that was the great Miles Davis from *Kind of Blue*, that it was hot and humid and some kind of bad storm was brewing, and that the Phils had just blown their seven-game winning streak in the businessperson's special down at the Vet—business as usual in Philadelphia.

23
Look at Me

Daisy wouldn't turn to face me, even when I begged her to get into the truck. I'd been pleading alongside her since the McDonald's a half mile back. Only a block from Birch Hill at this point, she'd walked—in exactly this manner, I imagined, the whole way—her elbow deep in her purse, as if fisting a gun.

When we reached the plateau at the top of Birch Hill, she maintained her steady gait as she crossed before me toward her car tucked under the pine trees. So confident was her stride that there was no doubt her car would start, though I prayed desperately for a dead engine, just as my own truck went suddenly quiet.

At last, Daisy offered me eye contact—a smirk, over her shoulder—as she fanned out her keys.

I was already out of my truck.

A shout—my name?—from the Wests' driveway startled me. Sophia and Freddy, side-by-side, skateboards at their feet, shared the same puzzled frown. Mid-stride, I shoved an open hand in their direction, shushing them, keeping them back, as if for their own safety, though they were inching forward, too baffled to formulate a question but too curious not to watch.

When Daisy ducked into the driver's seat of her car, I called out, "*Wait!*" and dashed for the back door, which was locked. The front door remained open, and I realized, heaving, that Daisy was not especially in a hurry, her keys jangling and then, after a moment, her car starting.

She looked up at me with dully pleasant eyes, indifferent—or, worse, *polite*, as if to say (and then she *said*)—"May I help you?"

"I'm *sorry. Please*," I said.

"Ex*cuse* me?"

"*Come on.* Let me in."

"You need a *lift?*"

Hands on the steering wheel, Daisy glanced, merely curious, at my arm reaching past her shoulder for the back lock. I rushed for the handle, still anticipating screeching tires and my own scuffed face on the street, but I was already straddling the back hump, elbows in the front, when she casually pulled the front door shut.

"Where to?" she said, her taxi-driver eyes in the rearview mirror.

"Your place. Greece. I don't care. Why are you *doing* this? I'll go *anywhere* with you—" I grasped her shoulder.

The car bucked, stopped.

"Sir, I'm going to have to ask you to get out. You are *not* permitted to touch—"

"I *love* you!" I grabbed her face.

Her left hand circled around, catching my eye. "Get *out*," she hissed. "You think I don't have feelings?"

"We could *be* together." I clenched my eye shut.

Daisy's dead glare was locked into the rearview mirror.

"Why not?" I gripped the shoulder of the driver's seat.

The car drifted and stopped again.

"Be careful, Peter."

In the yard down below, Theo, hunched over, stabbed American flags into the grass along the border.

"I told you it was never my intention to hurt anyone," Daisy said.

"Who's hurt?" Slowly I opened my eye, blinking.

"Okay." Daisy nodded. "Let's go."

We inched forward.

"Where?" I leaned into the front seat.

"To tell your parents we're in *love*." Daisy's smile flashed in the rearview mirror. "That we're getting *married*, we're going to have *babies*…"

"Stop!"

The car bucked.

"You don't think we should tell them? You just want to *fly away*…to *fantasyland?*" Daisy's mock amused expression—mouth agape, eyebrows raised—hovered in the mirror above me.

I refused to answer her reflection and so muttered at her stubborn profile, "Look at me."

She sighed, "Oh, Peter..."

"No one has to know," I said.

"I thought you understood." Finally she turned to face me. "You weren't ready for this," she said, and added, just as gently, "You are just like your father."

I reflected, blankly, then uttered, "Fuck you."

Daisy began nodding. "Okay, *vreh.*"

I pulled back, dreading how she would prove me an idiot once and for all.

After a moment she began furiously snapping open the buttons of her jeans, loosening them around her waist.

Oh, God, not here.

"What are you doing?" I fired glances through the front and rear windshield: shin-high flags trailed Theo into the shade under the birches; shifty-eyed Sophia and Freddy pretended not to be watching, their kicked skateboards flipping in the air before them and crashing onto the macadam.

Her jeans spread open, she worked her panties down. What humiliating vulgar act did she have in mind next, to prove God-knew-what? The devil had gotten the best of me when I'd told her to fuck herself, so now here she was, administering my punishment, about to demonstrate for me the futility of taking me literally—or, worse, to demonstrate the ease with which she was able to do so.

She eyed me directly. "You know what this is?"

A pink ridge, a crease from fat she didn't have—a faint frown, from this angle, in the shadow of her open jeans, just above the seam of her panties.

"You never saw this?" she said. "Or you never asked."

What?

"A scar, *vreh.* I had three miscarriages with my husband, before he got sick, before you were in *high school.*" She touched the scar. "This one, a boy, your father's..." She was already buttoning up her jeans, her point proven, apparently, or at least the evidence in. "...Emergency C-section, in April. He was being strangled by the umbilical cord. I carried seven months." She gripped the wheel. The car seemed to exhale, and we began coasting down again. "Your father doesn't even know I was pregnant. When I told him I still wanted a child, he was finished with me."

We reached the bottom of the hill. I held my breath, my hands slick, unsteady, on the ridged vinyl, the ground moaning, it seemed, a sickening vibrating in my skin.

"You want to tell him?" Daisy's eyes directed me toward the Lexus entering the mouth of the driveway.

There was no reason for me to imagine the disaster intimated by my father's eyes. In an instant, his squinting lids peeled back to reveal what looked like the white flesh of boiled eggs; in the next instant, his gaze passed beyond me, to something larger than the trouble this woman might embody. A warning cry, my name, howled by my sister, streamed in over my shoulder, as I caught sight of her through the rear window. Mid-hill, Sophia was racing toward me, brushing past pine branches, until her accelerating legs lost out as if to wild invisible bicycle pedals. Chest thrust, she was momentarily lifted by wings, her whole body propelled not only by gravity and the natural force of her own weight, but by her desperate attempt to save me from the run-away truck beyond the reach of her outstretched hands. It was as if, had she been fast enough to catch up, she could have seized the truck's bumper and, like Wonder Woman, stopped it cold. On his skate-board, Freddy *had* been fast enough, latching on to the tailgate, as the truck bore down—*sounding its own horn?*—Sophia on scuffed hands and knees, shrinking in the background. I ducked and braced myself, praying the truck would lift off just in time—Chitty-Chitty Bang-Bang-style—or turn just in time, or, at worst, strike so that the car's trunk would accordion up and I'd thump against the front seat and that would be it. The collision felt far off—maybe, I thought, far off was how it felt when it was going to be fatal. And yet the car kept spinning and spinning, long enough for me to get my bearings and to realize I was safe, at the very center of it all, not really moving at all, only revolving, waiting to stop.

Freddy's was the first face to appear, gazing down at me, awe-struck. I was crumpled on all fours, staring up like a trapped animal, stunned, relieved, but not optimistic: where was Sophia, my father? My truck? It had had a mind of its own recently, dying and coming back to life how many times now? Maybe it had delivered the first blow and continued on a path of destruction. Maybe, at the center of it all, I had been unable to recognize the devastating effects of the tornado-car at the base of the hill. I remembered Sophia's body, airborne, then scraping, my father's eyes, helpless, and, now—or was I imagining this?—my brother's red Porsche, at the crest of the hill, crying out its own warning.

Daisy moaned—in pain, in regret, or in dreadful anticipation of what had now become inevitable. A maniac's hand—Theo's—stuffed with flags, scratched at the windshield. Theo flung the front door open and froze when my mother called from the front yard, some impassioned warning about necks and paralysis. Theo's hands, paralyzed themselves, hung delicately in the air, as he examined Daisy with the eyes of a little boy fascinated by the creature under the magnifying glass.

"*Dionysia*," I heard my mother say, and it was time for me to rise. "Peter." Seeing me well enough to sit up, my mother laid her hands on Daisy.

Theo had retreated, dazed by the blurry sight of me in the back seat—some trick in his mind, he must have thought, absolute proof he didn't think straight. When Andrew flung open the back door, I reconsidered my *own* mental state. When it was Melanie whose arms reached in for me, I knew I was delirious, dizzy, stepping out of the car, bracing myself, half-hoping, for news that would alter what I knew—or what I thought I knew—of reality. Beside Theo stood Freddy, arms crossed, skateboard at his feet. Beside Freddy stood Sophia, sobbing, blood-roses blooming on her knees. My apron-clad mother, smelling of mesquite, stooped, stroking Daisy's face, a grease-speckled spatula at her feet.

"They're on their way!" my father shouted in the front yard, so far managing to keep his distance, beyond the wrought-iron fence, raising a cell phone above his head, in triumph—having made the crucial call for help—and handing it back to his assistant, whose wife and sons lingered by the Lexus, their plans for a cookout on hold.

"She's all right!" my mother reported.

This burst of news kept my father at bay.

Hands on the wheel, Daisy whispered reassurances.

Andrew's eyes penetrated mine. His doctor-hands gripped my shoulders. He patted my cheeks and bowed toward Daisy.

My father looked at no one, containing his nervous energy by tramping small circles in the grass; then he headed for the Lexus, as if the next most urgent task was to clear the driveway. The assistant's two boys had returned to the safety of the back seat, where they watched from the windows.

Nauseous, head lolling, I spotted my truck, parallel-parked under the birches, the driver's-side door hanging open, apparently raring to go. I checked my pockets: I'd been conscientious enough to remove the keys from the ignition, but not enough to use the emergency brake.

Melanie kept her hand on my forehead, imitating my mother, who kept hers on Daisy's—crash victims struck with fevers.

A siren's leaking-balloon cry was winding toward us.

My father was performing forensic chores on the perimeter of the scene, a hubcap, presumably Daisy's—nonetheless as irrelevant as a Frisbee—tucked under his arm, his hands free to pluck from the grass more evidence that nothing more than a car accident had occurred here.

From the front door, already halfway across the lawn, quietly, cool-ly, Yiayia was about to enter the scene she must have been watching all along. She appeared majestic, in an unlikely outfit, one appropriate for the theater, a sky-blue dress cut just below the knee, matching heels she managed expertly through the thick grass, silver hair in a spiral pinched at the top.

My father looked up from a handful of green glass shards (a bottle-neck still intact) swept from the street near the mailbox, where he'd propped the hubcap. It wasn't until the old man saw his own mother that he started for Daisy's car, rushing to fill the space that, perhaps only in my eyes, he had been averting. No one but me seemed to be impressed, let alone suspicious, even when the old man blocked Yiayia at the gate, gesturing gently as if back toward the asylum. Yiayia raised a hand, from which my father magically backed away. I had begun to step away from the car, unsteadily, at first, eager to escape center-stage and to clear out for the paramedics, who had parked behind the car and were now approaching. But my grandmother's hands seized me, her palms warm and dry on my cheekbones, the firm ridges at the base of her fingers pressed into the sockets of my eyes.

"*Ta matia sou*"—your eyes. Removing her hands, she kissed the left and then the right side of my face, a slash of blood extending like stray lipstick from her mouth.

"I'm okay, Yiayia."

"*Pia eineh afti?*"—Who is she?

She understood I'd been in the car with her; perhaps she'd seen the crash or even the whole pathetic performance.

I backed up, into the fringe, alongside Freddy, Sophia, Andrew, and Melanie, our view blocked by the navy-blue-shirted men, whose backs filled the doorway of the car. My mother and Yiayia watched through the windshield. My father, his face as dull and inexpressive as his black suit, stood guard at the gate. The old man wouldn't dare look at me, even as I backed up toward my truck, past Theo, who was in the shadows, planting flags.

The whites of Daisy's eyes flashed through a crack between two dark sleeves, her mouth uttering, I was sure, words of self-reliance. The blue figures divided completely into two and, framing her, raised her from the seat. She stood, silent, and stepped away from the car, in my direction, though she gave no sign of seeing me. She shook herself free from the hands at her elbows, turned toward the house, and took another step, proving herself able.

I found myself anticipating—hoping for, dreading—her words, which I might not hear, standing by my truck, but whose effect I would witness: my father ridiculously cradling an irrelevant broken bottle, accused, shamed, damned.

I imagined a prelude of spit.

Raising her arms to her sides, displaying her quite capable body, rotating once, and, as if taking a bow and retreating from a grateful audience, Daisy dropped behind the door and started her engine.

24
In the Divine Moment of the Eternal Present

It was impossible to believe that I'd ever been small enough to fit between the side rails of the sliding board. I couldn't imagine that even the kids who went here now were small enough. The school itself—let alone the mulchy square containing the swing set, the horizontal ladder, the dome of scaffolding, the animals fastened to steel springs—seemed scaled down for an altogether smaller species. The grassy field that extended toward a second baseball diamond and that was outlined on the horizon by a cluster of trees, had seemed, then, to be infinite—or to run right up to the border of where infinity began. The trees—a forest then—had been spooked; in their black shadows balls got lost for good; there the worst kids were rumored to be doing unfathomable things. Now the feeble husks of the trees, no more than ten of them, I was amazed to see—black bones, all knobs and joints, in the gas-blue sky—seemed to be standing thanks only to the mercy of a grounds crew I imagined on riding mowers, skirting the moat of overgrown grass.

I had never felt a particular fondness for the place. The reason I'd come, now, on the brink of my journey, was to get one last look, just as they said a person got a last look at his life before he died. Even so, I wasn't going to get morbid. I wasn't going to punish myself or anyone else or even harbor grudges. I wasn't going to get sentimental. I certainly wasn't going to go combing the whole godforsaken county for the landmarks of my uneventful life, though it wouldn't take me long—the schools, the church—and I was ready for the drive, having just filled up at the Mobil station around the corner.

I was prepared to go it alone, all the way, to California or Seattle or—who knew?—Vancouver or Alaska, or to wherever my truck finally died, somewhere, I prayed, at least outside of the area code. I was thinking I'd head toward Pittsburgh, as good a place as any to start. It was possible—though I wasn't getting my hopes up—that Dorothy would be back home from whatever commune or temple she'd ended up in. I'd missed my shot, I knew—I would admit it. But now I understood what it was all about and maybe, I'd say, this was our second chance. *Mine*, at least. To get away from it all, to leave it all behind. I was already on the right track, I'd tell her: I was heading west, and I was empty-handed. Together we could be monks of our own devices, of the open range, worshippers of small towns and diners, where we'd shack up in motels and make enough money washing dishes to make it to the next town. We'd be mystics of the first order, art lovers devoted to the proliferation of ordinary, uncorrupted beauty. We'd expand our book to include all the towns and cities in America. We'd publish a *Museum Without Walls* series. We'd expand our definition of art to include key chains and postcards. We'd have pseudonyms.

Of course I would have to have a pretty good sales pitch when she told me that this was all a fantasy, that that was then and this is now. Dorothy had always had a stubbornly realistic side, as much as I'd loved her for, or at least envied—or marveled at—her ludicrous romanticism. Was it even romanticism? It was hard to say without knowing what she'd done since heading south. It had always been hard to imagine even her—let alone *me with her*—lasting more than a week on some farm, fending for ourselves, let alone sharing our tomatoes with strangers. Maybe she wasn't a romantic at all, but a fanatic, flitting from one religion to the next. How else to explain her interest in *me?* She'd invited me up to her dorm room, impressed with something I'd said in class—I might have mentioned my father was a priest, to give myself credibility. Her closet had appeared to be a shrine, or a mausoleum. She'd opened a shoebox-tomb filled with photographs of her ex-boyfriend, who lived in the adjacent building, as well as a giant Ziploc bag stuffed with two green fists of marijuana, all of which, she'd said, sniffing, were a testament to her discipline, as she sealed the bag and set the box on top of other boxes I'd assumed were filled with shoes though, come to think of it, might have stored the remains of other past obsessions. I wondered, now, if she had a shoebox for *me* and, if so, what she stored in it.

One night in the spring of our senior year, we'd taken the subway to West Philly to catch some photographs at the Annenberg Center, where one of the artists I had learned about in my Post-Modernism class, Andre Serrano—the great, young iconoclast who did *Piss Christ* back in the eighties—was premiering his latest work. I had told Dorothy all about Serrano on the way there. The camera around her neck turned out to be bait for the guy, who asked her if she was a photographer herself. He was tall and lean, in narrow black clothes, and couldn't keep his eyes off her the whole time I was trying to ask him about the flack he caught for making icons out of stuff like plastic-keychain crucifixes and his own bodily fluids. Finally I backed off, figuring Dorothy was safe, what with her vow of purity and all, and turned my attention to the giant brightly lit close-ups of nuns and cardinals, whose warts and nose hairs, I deduced, were, like the artist's urine, supposed to challenge one's perception of what was holy in this world. Later, when Dorothy bragged, as if I should have been proud of her, that she'd given Serrano her phone number, she asked, "Wouldn't *you?*" "Wouldn't I *what?*" At this point she wasn't talking about giving the guy her phone number; she had *plans* in her eyes. "If you met, like, Uma Thurman?" she said. "*Uma Thurman?* Why *Uma Thurman?*" I wanted her to say it—what she was planning, what she had already, in effect, pissed away. "I just mean, someone incredibly beautiful. I mean, you'd *have* to." Have to *what?* Of course, after that, I never asked—it didn't matter if she ever had or hadn't. She might as well have. That night—still a fuzzy memory—we probably went back to her dorm and then, when I headed home, pretended my not staying later indicated a turning point in our relationship, as if we'd ever had a prayer.

Leaning on the hood of my truck, the engine anxious, I plucked my wallet from my pants and Dorothy's letter from my wallet, the same godforsaken letter I'd dropped into, and retrieved from, God knew how many trashcans since the day I'd first read it. I opened the letter, as I considered ways of destroying it, wondering if the cigarette lighter in the truck worked and, if so, if it could ignite paper. Instead

I simply opened my hand into the wind.

The letter cut through the air and landed at my feet.

Life wasn't getting any easier out on my own.

I could sell the Rolex if I got desperate enough, I thought. And then, ashamed, I vowed never to sell the Rolex, seeing myself rummaging through restaurant dumpsters and sleeping on park benches before pawning my most prized possession.

I scraped the letter off the ground and, crumpling it, walked toward the trash barrel at the corner of the school. I imagined some fifth grader finding it at recess and laughing with his friends at lunch, calling me, or "Peter," the addressee by that name, a "douche," their new word for the day—"What a *douche!*" "Who is this *douche?!*"—then passing it around in class until forced to hand it over to his teacher, who would turn out to be my old teacher and, as such, would instantly recognize the addressee as the same Peter—Pappas, wasn't it?—the priest's son, who'd gotten in trouble for proselytizing at recess, threatening the girls who were known kissers and the boys who kissed them with the eternal flames of Hell.

I'd been such a fanatic myself. It was a wonder I'd had any friends. The truth was that, other than Brock West, my friends hadn't been friends so much as students I'd shared classroom space with over the years—maybe even Dorothy had been one of those people. That might explain why, growing up, I'd spent so much time at church, where, alongside my father, I'd felt a heightened sense of importance, if not popularity, whether or not the other altar boys and Sunday-school kids recognized me as a friend. My silver cross, once on a chain around my neck—for years, now, hooked to my keychain, sharing space with a sterling Phillies "P" my mother had bought me at sixteen, pleased my name shared the first initial—had become, along with the "P," the kind of relic that marked the time and made you wonder what, really, you had to show for yourself—for your *life*—and who you really were.

Already even the letter in my hands seemed to be a memento from a life lived by another person, a person I couldn't imagine having been, and a memento of the agony I'd put myself through—and *her* through: God forgive me! After all, Dorothy *still* would have taken me with her!

In the future, something would remind me of who I was now. I was, I realized, already, at that very moment, standing there on the playground of my old elementary school, a past-version-of-my-future-self, whom my future-self would recall pityingly, thinking myself—this future Peter—more fully evolved, more enlightened, the memory of this moment, of this whole godforsaken week, triggered by some found object I would look upon with condescending scorn.

I couldn't decide who was the bigger idiot: me-now or me-in-the-future, who would, inevitably—in spite of this moment of insight—look back and scoff.

What a joke it all was, I decided. We live our lives, "growing," we tell ourselves, remembering of the past only the details that make us think we've suffered nobly and changed for the better.

I folded the letter into my wallet—what difference did it make?—and headed for my truck, which puffed and coughed, shaking its shoulders, gearing up. The keys, the cross, the "P," all twirled on a finger and smacked my palm.

Fuck Pittsburgh.

The engine hummed, for now. I would catch the Turnpike, aiming myself in a straight line west. When my truck died—and it would, of course, soon—I would snag the next ride, and then the next, and I'd be gone, a man without a plan, without a past, existing in the divine moment of the eternal present, detached from all earthly possessions, and not giving a *shit*.

I would shave my head the first chance I got.

Man, I was going to be one bad, bald Quaker-Buddhist motherfucker, of my own denomination, born again.

My truck was cooking. The exit wasn't far ahead. God, this was easy! That I could have split a week ago!

But the past was the past. And it was *all* in the past now. Now there was only *now*.

I expect nothing. I fear no one. I am free.

Free to live by my own rules and to be my own judge.

It wasn't *my* problem that my father wanted to live his life fancying himself a propagator of morals, while he pranced around in a robe, spreading his message of love in whatever form he found permissible. I wouldn't call the old man's followers fools—who was *I* to judge? It was my father's right to live the way he wanted to live, just as it was everyone else's right—*responsibility*—to live the way he or she wanted to live. Just as it was Daisy's right to live the way *she* wanted to live. Just as it was my right to live the way *I* wanted to live, to do what I felt was right, to make a little detour, right now, not to go so far as to cast spray-painted aspersions across the wall of icons that kept the congregants from the altar, but, I figured, to type up a newsletter—nothing libelous, just the truth—which I would then photocopy on official St. Peter's Greek Orthodox Church letterhead, a hundred or so, right there in the old man's office, and slip into the Liturgy books in the pews.

Almost eight o'clock on a Wednesday night. I prayed that a Bible study group or a youth group was meeting, so that I could slip through the back doors. Not that I wasn't willing to break a window.

I would not be surprised if, pulling into the parking lot of the church, which sat tucked into a neighborhood not far from where the Blue Route met the Turnpike, I found my father sitting in his Lexus, awaiting my arrival. After all, once the ambulance and Daisy had left and my truck and I had gone missing, everyone would have devised a theory and strategy: Sophia would have assumed that I'd been too embarrassed to answer questions about how my date had gone; Andrew would have assumed—secretly, I hoped—that I'd gone to meet her at a rendezvous; my mother would have assumed I'd been delirious with a concussion, her flair for the tragic intensifying, imagining that my accident-rattled brain was, by now, alight with a fireworks display of bursting aneurisms, or that the mysterious facts that had led to the crash must have been pushing me to suicide (*Oh my, it would finally dawn on her, was Dionysia the woman Peter had had a date with?*); my father would have had no choice but to go searching, not only because my mother would have been urging him, frantically, but also because the old man could no longer deny the truth, any more than I could deny it myself.

When I entered the parking lot, Stavros—thank God—was spraying Windex on the windowpanes of the French doors that were the side entrance. Stavros's wife, a plump immigrant in a peach dress, waved her rag from the concrete steps as if to the boat entering the harbor. Beaming, Stavros stuffed a rag into his rear pocket and hobbled toward me, as I slowed down to a stop.

"*Yiasou*, Peter!"

Stavros, in a red lumberjack shirt and similarly rustic heavy black boots, thrust himself through the window, all arms and head, his slap-happy greeting—hands, in a flash, making their way from my cheeks to thighs to ribs to ears to neck—culminating in dry lips—a doughnut of damp stubble—pressed to my forehead. Stavros stood back, shaking his head in disbelief, as if the Prodigal Son had at last returned.

Little did he know.

"Eh, look—!" Stavros's yellow corncob teeth spread wide across his face.

I jerked, glancing over my shoulder, for a moment thinking the Lexus had pulled in behind me, until Stavros's hands burst in again, this time for my head—a long-lost soccer ball—his thick fingers sinking into the seams. I couldn't get over the happiness the guy felt and for a moment wondered if maybe Stavros mistook me for someone else, someone he could have recognized from church. "You looking for your father?" I averted another lusty grab. Stavros's eyes danced playfully, as if the two of us were now into a game in which I tried to dodge his punchy fingers. "He's no here. He take Father Chris and Sendee, and the boys, to your house for, eh, peek-neek. You no go?"

"No, I go." I gestured for the door and Stavros stepped back. "I have to do something first."

"Ah, for your father. What you need? Stay here, I get it. Stavroula! *Ela tho!*"—Come here!

His wife bounded toward us, eager to participate.

"Get something for Peter!"

"No, no." I tried opening the door, but Stavros's hand came down onto the base of the window frame, his back turned.

The engine idled.

Stavros's wife smiled, nodding. "*Neh?*"—Yes?

Stavros turned back to me, gesturing for me to stay seated. "What you need?"

"Thank you. I can get it. Thank you." I nudged the door and managed to get a foot on the ground.

"She'll get it," Stavros insisted.

His wife smiled sweetly. "I get it."

I would have been better off wrapping my fist in my shirt and punching in a window. Or I should have come back after they went home, *if* they ever went home.

"I'll get it myself. It's *okay.*"

"Ah, it's *okay,*" Stavros repeated. "Well, you get what you need. You know where everything is…" He didn't disguise his disappointment or his insinuation that I was going to be screwed without his help. Stavros tossed his chin into the air. "Close the door when you fee-nees."

"Thank you," I said. "I will."

Stavros headed inside, and his wife followed. She shook the horizontal bar, making sure and then demonstrating for me that the door would stay open. She waved from the orange-lit hallway. When the light went off, the church went still.

Finally, I got both feet onto the surface of the parking lot. I'd have to work fast. I'd leave the truck running. Better to burn the gas than to trust the transmission. On the other hand, I might take a while in there, and some bored neighborhood kids would have nothing better to do on a summer night than to take my truck out for its final joyride. I killed the engine.

The church door stood open. I was free to enter.

The far doors thumped, and Stavros and his wife reappeared, heading home through the parking lot. She hooked her arm through her husband's, as she did every night, I imagined, as they sank into the shadows beyond the assistant's house, which sat dark and inert in the trees.

On the near wall of the church, reflecting the evening sky, the panes of stained-glass windows—shapes ordinarily distinct in color, outlined in black wrought iron—circles of grapes, ovals of bread—were all, in the shadows of the setting sun, some plum-ish shade of wine.

Communion, I remembered my father explaining, could never be taken alone. That is, the priest couldn't give it to himself, any more than a congregant or an atheist could give it to himself, whether in the church with the chalice, wine, and bread or in a prison cell with a Dixie cup, Welch's, and a Saltine. You needed a witness to consecrate the sacrament. The same with Confession: you couldn't do it on your own—not even a priest. You needed a witness to make it real. The same sort of logic applied to the sin, I was thinking, and the old man knew it: I was the witness to that which, until now, had known no reality outside the world the old man shared with Daisy for God knew how long. What my father didn't know was that Daisy had a son, my brother, who, had he lived, might have been the witness instead of me, or who might have harbored the truth, to protect the old man, a better son than I was. But the boy hadn't lived—a twist of fate, literally, his life source snaked around his neck; and, now, as Daisy packed her bags, my own seed might be incubating—it wasn't impossible—if it had managed to get far enough on its own.

This was all my father's fault. And the old man had no idea. He might be at Daisy's house right now, telling her she couldn't leave the country soon enough—or would he be pleading with her to stay? For the last five years, I couldn't stand the thought of my father spoon-feeding them all, not after learning that he was using Confession to screen for the Communion-worthy. Now I couldn't stand knowing what they didn't know, knowing what *my father* didn't know.

If and when the old man tracked me down, I would be up-front with him, give him a chance to disrobe—right there at the vestment closet, where I would show him the stack of newsletters ready for distribution—to expedite his retirement, to go ahead and hand over the reins to Father Chris, who could hardly wait. Or maybe I'd wait by the altar, gripping the staff with the giant cross on top, the one I'd led processions with as captain of the altar boys, and dare the old man to take it from me, or, better yet, dare him to take the chalice, asking him who, after everyone knew the truth, would take from his spoon, who would be the witness to make it real.

Either you tell them or I'll tell them—that was how it had to go, before I went anywhere else.

As I took my first step, and then shot out toward the church, it was as if the hinges had been triggered by the hand of a guardian angel— mine or my father's, I wasn't sure—or triggered by a vibration from around the corner, in the wake of Stavros-and-his-wife's backdoor exit, a vibration that had traveled slowly through the walls and had just reached the open side door, which was falling softly back into place.

Now the bar that could open the door was but a broken window-pane away. Teeming with adrenaline, I cocked a fist and braced myself for the worst of today's lacerating collisions. I held back for a moment and tried to examine the latch, which was invisible in the deep shadows of the thick door. The seal was so tight that my laminated gym-membership card wouldn't fit through, that is until I pulled on the handle just enough so that the card, wedged momentarily, tipped over the latch and onto the tile floor. I might have jammed a screwdriver in there or taken a window out with a hammer, if not for the fact that my tools had been stored in the closet with the paint supplies, all of which, by now, Eliot must have confiscated along with Andrew's furniture.

Below the stained-glass windows, in the mulch around the gardenia shrubbery, flat stones, as white as the flowers, made a path toward the water spigot. The dirt was wet around a coiled hose where Stavros must have been watering. The glistening green leaves left my sleeves damp. The plate-sized slab lifted easily out of the soil.

At the door I rehearsed a two-handed stab, and, suddenly, without further deliberation, I punctured the glass, like egg against egg, then carefully plucked triangles, one by one, from the pane's groove, stacking them in my free hand as though I were planning to salvage the window with glue once my business was done.

When I turned, finally, to lay down the broken glass—the rectangular border now ready for my wrist's safe passage—my father was standing in the grass by the curb, arms at his sides, his expression mysteriously impassive, behind him the Lexus parked head-to-head with the truck.

I hadn't heard a thing.

Startled, I skipped back from a piece of glass that clanked at my feet.

"I thought I'd just watch," my father said. "If you don't mind." He crossed his arms. "You go ahead. I won't bother you."

"You're in no position to be sarcastic."

"What position would you say I'm in?" The old man's hands sank into his pockets.

"Not one to be asking the questions."

"I assume you've got some."

I glanced at the small pile remaining in my hand.

"What do you suggest we do?" my father said. "Forgive me—" He raised a finger to his lips. "No questions. I should say, *Tell* me what you think we should do."

"That's the best you can do?" I toed the piece of glass toward the grass. "If you're not asking questions, you're giving orders. For all your preaching about humility..."

The old man bowed, offering his open hands. "I am your humble servant."

I glanced back at the door.

"May I suggest," my father offered, "we take this conversation inside?"

"No. Just— We're not having a *conversation.*"

"Whatever you want to do, Peter. You're in charge." He paused. "I don't know what you're thinking, or what went on between you and Daisy Diamond—"

"*Don't* say her name," I snapped. "*Me* and—?"

"Okay. Relax."

"The question is what went on between *you* and her," I heaved. "There's *no* question," I corrected myself. "I *know*. More than *you* know."

"Let's..."

I rocked in place. "Don't tell me what to do."

My father held out a hand. "Let's just go," he said. "Somewhere..."

"I could *kill* you," I hissed. Something deep within me had driven me to say it, something not exactly me. Still, it had sounded true, *still* sounded true, hanging out there.

"I can see that." The old man was holding out his ring of keys now. "You drive."

I stood stock-still, until a jangling smudge was sailing toward me and I was swatting hopefully at the air, glass clattering all around me.

25
Absolution

Andrew was thirteen or so—lying in the bathtub, as I brushed my teeth—when he demonstrated to his little brother the phenomenon between his legs. "Look." The thing moved without assistance, flopping over magically, and stretching itself out like an arm when you yawned. "You just think about a naked girl or something." His voice had more than just promise in it. With lucid foresight I anticipated following in my big brother's footsteps—every one of his footsteps—envisioning myself plowing through pool water, head and shoulders like the prow of a ship, boiling the Communion wine and handing off the silver cup to my father, transforming my boy-body into something tremendous merely by using my imagination, lamenting only, even then, that I'd have no little brother of my own to pass the secret knowledge on to.

Long before Andrew started medical school, I had known I would become anything but a doctor, though only God knew what. By the time Andrew was a high-school record-breaker, I had discovered myself to be anything but an athlete, lucky to stay afloat long enough to be saved by lifeguards, who hauled me in from beyond the break in the waves, about twenty yards out from the family umbrella. By then I'd also resigned myself to—in fact I'd relished—pats on the head from the girls Andrew brought home from school and the local pool and, to my amazement, introduced to my parents as girlfriends: "This is my girlfriend Beth," "This is my girlfriend Stephanie"—"Nice to meet you, Beth," "Nice to meet you, Stephanie." They would disappear into the basement, hiking their book bags or gym bags over their shoulders, and I would be left in the kitchen, Andrew's ally, forking meatballs into my mouth, straining to appear oblivious, beginning to understand that the trick to keeping secrets was believing you had nothing to hide.

Within months of beginning his freshman year, Andrew quit the Penn swim team, much to the dismay of my father, who'd relished going to high-school swim meets, or at least sharing newspaper clippings from the pulpit, often managing to segue from the sermon to the sports page. More time for the books, Andrew explained, and then for the next four years barely made it home for the holidays, as if he were going to school in Boston. It wasn't going to be easy getting into medical school, he panted, dropping his bags onto the kitchen floor, and who could argue? His fraternity brothers, he reassured, were providing plenty of support, and the housemother fed them heartily.

By then I'd been serving as an altar boy every week, though the schedule required the normal boys to serve only once a month. The old man had taken to calling me his right-hand man. "How's my right-hand man?" I couldn't wait until Sunday, couldn't wait to be behind-the-scenes, to see the ushers preparing the soundboard, adjusting the microphones, filling the candle bins, couldn't wait to see my father nonchalantly donning a robe from a hanger in the closet, instructing the altar-boy captain, who would be me not-soon-enough, and, later, his back to the people, pouring the steaming wine into the chalice, crumbling the bread, which fell from his fingers, pressing his fingertips to the altar cloth and rubbing them over the chalice, tonguing the holy crumbs from his dry, clean palms, sipping straight from the cup, before all the others took from his spoon. He would gesture ever so slightly with a hand, and just like that, their clothing would shift, and everyone would sit, or kneel, or stand, whatever he commanded, and he would whisper, only loud enough, it seemed, in spite of the microphone, for me to hear, "My brothers and sisters, forgive me," not that he needed forgiveness for anything. I couldn't wait to see, after the service, the ladies, my mother among them, in the back offices, quietly arranging piles of money from the offering baskets, couldn't wait to see, as I held a basket of bread for the throng flooding toward me at the exit, my father at the opposite end of the center aisle, greeting the parishioners, who kissed the giant silver cross in his hand and often the hand itself. I couldn't wait to be captain, to carry the cross, to instruct the younger boys (how to carve the bread and then to stand with the basket at the exit), to hold the Communion cloth while my father held the spoon, couldn't wait to learn the secrets behind the icons, to learn the secret language of the Liturgy, to become my father's right-hand man for real, and then to take over the reins.

All that was a long time ago, long before I would have had the nerve to give the old man the silent treatment, driving God knew where at this point, the highway having transformed a while back into two lanes that had continued to narrow toward what had appeared be the edge of the earth. And so I'd taken the next exit and was soon sealing up the windows to keep out not only the light rain that had started but also the smell of manure. It was difficult to fake knowing where you were going when the road was lined on both sides with walls of corn, which seemed to be rising as the rain came harder and the night got darker. I retraced the maze in my mind. I'd hooked a left, away from the Turnpike, abandoning the route for my solo journey, and gone south, instead, on the Blue Route, and then west, after all, not wanting to find myself on 95 North, looping back toward Philly. I'd been surprised when the glowing fountains up ahead had turned out to mark the entranceway to Longwood Gardens, which I hadn't thought about since I was a kid, when such magical places, like Hersheypark and Great Adventure, had seemed not only to be located far far away but to exist outside of time altogether. Still, I had no idea where I was. By now we were deep into Chester County, or Lancaster County, heading south, or west. Or north. So what if we were lost anyway? That might have been my plan all along, to force my father to speak, if only to bark out directions. But the old man remained quiet, gazing at the changing landscape, hands on his thighs, even when the rain had turned the windshield into a black blur and I still hadn't found the right knob for the wipers.

Rain was pounding the roof and hood. Intermittent waves seemed to tear at the metallic shell encasing us. A milky cloud, where two glittering beams merged in the near distance, led the way into endless darkness. My instinct was to stop, though there was no shoulder, only a grassy lip and then the corn. We would have to brace ourselves in the middle of the road, in the intolerable silence.

"Why don't you stop?"

The old man's first words tightened my grip on the wheel.

"The next intersection," the old man said. "Let's wait it out."

I shot a quick glance at the old man clawing at his knees.

Suddenly, we were driving through an illuminated waterfall.

"Enough's enough, Peter." The old man reached toward the wheel.

I swiped at his wrist. "It's *not* enough!"

"You can't see where you're going—"

"I *see*."

The yellow lines flickered beyond the blazing-white rain.

"Let's stop and we'll talk." The old man spread his hands on the dashboard.

"*You* start talking, and *I'll* stop." The speedometer needle hovered above zero.

"It was a sin. We all sin."

"Don't bring everyone *else* into it," I snapped, and then realized, "You *admit* it."

"It was a long time ago, Peter. I've confessed it. I'm still ashamed. I'm sorry you had to find out, especially the way you did."

"You confessed to *who?*"

"Peter, pull over here, *please*."

A stop sign flashed in the headlights. I inched along the roadside and stopped. The old man pressed a button, and red light pulsed all around us.

"I confessed to God—"

"That's not good enough."

"Maybe you're right—"

"You need to tell Mom. And while you're at it, everyone at church. You're a priest. Jesus Christ—"

"Hey—" The old man put a hand out. "You wanted me to talk, let me talk."

I took a deep breath and stared into the dark wall of corn.

"Your mother knows—"

"*What—?*"

"Your *brother* knows. He figured it out, somehow, when he was at

Penn—this is years ago—I don't know how long he knew. But he told me it had to stop, and he was right. I didn't make any excuses to *him*, and I won't make any to *you*, now. I promised your mother it was over, and that was it."

I kept my eyes aimed over the black ridge of the old man's shoulder. "That was *it?*"

"That's it."

"You're lying."

"It's the God's honest truth."

"Not *all* of it."

"You want *details?* Let's at least allow the woman *her* dignity."

"Aren't you cutting it off a bit short? Andrew went to Penn ten *years* ago. *Six* years ago if you count medical school."

"I was thinking of his residency, to be honest with you. I remember him in his white hospital coat. So, okay, three years ago." His voice softened. "It was on and off, Peter."

I turned away. "I know you were with her *last year*—last *fall*, to be exact." I two-fisted the steering wheel. "You don't think she *told* me? There's *evidence*."

"What evidence?"

I shot him a look. The old man's eyes cracked. I clenched my throat and twisted in my seat.

"It was just once," the old man leaked.

"I *know*, God damn it!" I swung around, eyes blazing.

"You want to hit your old man? Go ahead!"

I held my fists to my ribs.

"This I've only confessed to God, Peter. You don't have to believe it. It was over. For a long time it was over. And then *once*, yes, last year."

At the corner across the street a tree's black branches spread out into the sky, the headlights, through the dazzling rain, outlining its silhouette, which sank into the landscape and reemerged, barely there.

"*Why?*" I said.

It was silent, but for the crushing rain overhead, in the wake of the unanswerable question, the last word—*why*.

Beyond the shimmering glow, in the brief moments between torrents of red, splotches of white—rocks? or the rain, playing tricks?—shifted and flashed by the tree. I focused, filling the blanks between illuminated shapes, when a black dot stood out, somehow, in a sea of black dots, stationary, slippery, appearing as an eye, staring back, a marble hovering like some mystical orb. I wondered if the old man could see what I saw, this cow, or cows, crouched in the flood under a tree. There was nothing left to say—or nothing left for *the old man* to say. Perhaps it was enough. And yet it felt incomplete. Or maybe *too* complete. As though everything that there was to say had been said, and now there was nothing at all left to do but drive home.

The old man choked out, "She made me feel—"

"That's *enough*," I snapped, just as I remembered, with a kind of sickening sweetness: *You are just like your father.*

The old man was waiting for me to look at him. Did he want absolution from his son? I forgive you, Father. Your sin is our secret. That was how it was supposed to work. No penance necessary. Only contrition. He was a forgiving God. Christ suffered so that we wouldn't have to. Still, I thought, there needs to be balance. Justice.

Suddenly, I was in awe of God's forgiveness: He was the Great Balancer; He absorbed it—and that was it. After that, you only had to forgive yourself. I had never felt so far away from God as I did right now. I understood that what I was about to say was something deeper than Confession, closer to justice, or retribution—the opposite of forgiveness.

"I fucked her."

The old man gasped.

I looked right at him.

"I'm still your father."

Outside, all around me, black tunnels offered safe passage, in every direction away from there.

"I wasn't going to say anything," the old man said. "Out of respect for *you*. You disrespect *her* when you speak that way—"

"*Disrespect her?*" I grumbled. "Don't—" I twisted for the door.

"Peter—!"

The door thumped open, as the old man's hand landed on my

shoulder and I whipped around to face him.

"*I* wasn't going to say anything out of respect for *you!* She was *pregnant!* You had a *son!* He was *dead!*"

The rain was spraying my neck and seeping through my shirt. I reached back and pulled the door shut. Enough was enough. The old man pressed the hazard button, and a faint clicking I hadn't noticed stopped. The last red pulse sank slowly into the shining blacktop, a signal to head back where we came from. The car was quiet, in spite of the rain that hadn't let up.

I had never seen my father crying. The tears were invisible, but the thin skin under his eyes glistened. He was crying, I imagined, not for a dead son, but for a living one, for what I had become.

26
The Promised Land

I tried to maintain the rhythm, the slow rising and falling, the push uphill into the rain and the rush down, but without the yellow ribbon that, now, I realized, had been my lifeline, the road flashed like film running out and we were hurtling into blank space. I brought the car to a stop, as I had several times since making that fatal right turn, east, I prayed—not wanting to retrace the long route that had brought us there—and, feeling the weight of the earth beneath the tires, I accelerated again. Slowly, slowly at first, and then the car rose up again and fell down again, the illuminated rain swelling like stardust.

A flicker of pure white, a bursting flash—in my mind?—in an instant I am blind, and breathless: it is an implosion, the weight on my chest is immense, and I can feel us being thrust back, as if through time. The moment passes and the weight has been lifted. Air wells up quickly, and I am facing my father, who mirrors my gaze, our breathing synchronized, our shoulders rising and falling together. Blood forks on my father's forehead like lines on a palm. The pale sacks from the dashboard expire like punctured lungs, as a drizzle of yellow from the left headlight sinks out of sight. For a moment everything seems outlined in the same jaundice-yellow, until all I can see is what I imagine, like my father grinning when I whisper, "Cow."

The engine starts, but the headlights are dead, not that the light would do more than reveal the mud spinning beneath the tires. I kill the engine. I flick on an overhead light and mention my father's blood, then turn off the light, to conserve the engine battery. In the afterglow, my father raises his fingertips to his forehead and insists he's not hurt. I take the cell phone from my pocket and turn it on. The little bit of light it exudes reveals my father's exhausted eyes. I tell him to rest. At first the illuminated square of green seems heaven-sent, but there is no connection. Okay. I tell my father not to worry. The phone will be my lantern.

It is only arbitrarily that I finally step upon macadam, after expanding my circle around the car, slogging through shin-deep mud, finding a wall of hip-high cornstalks, and dragging my fingers as if along the posts of a fence. I aim the drowned-out green light toward the ground, sliding my feet on the gravelly surface, moving forward, slowly, slowly, until I slip over the edge and then head back toward the middle of the road. I keep thumbing buttons to keep the light alive. Soon, I assume—I have no idea when—the phone will lose its power (an intermittent siren-like bell has ceased to warn me); I have not charged the phone, and I have not read the handbook. No sooner do I draw this conclusion than my hand blinks out and I slip off the edge of the road, grateful, when I catch my fall, that I haven't twisted an ankle. The phone, however, has slipped from my hand, and I comb the surface of the road until my fingers stumble upon it. I test the power button, and to my surprise the square of light materializes in my cupped hand, the phone reverting to some reserve of energy, which I quickly decide to keep stored-up, in the event that I find myself back in civilization or close enough to it that I'm able to make a call.

In complete darkness I am falling off the asphalt ledge again, this time crawling, finding, at my fingertips, the outer wall of what I hope, at first, is a house. Beyond the edge of the wall, I enter an open, roofed area—about the length of my body, I realize, if I were to lie down, though I don't lie down, not yet. I get a feel for the place, for the corrugated-metal roof, the concrete floor, the three wood-paneled walls that block the rain falling toward the open roadside—a blessing. I find a wooden crate in the corner and place it upside down against the center of the rear wall. A vegetable stand, I think, sitting back, just to rest for a minute, soaked through, relieved to be out of the rain, though it makes no difference at this point. The people who sell corn here—how far away could they live? There is nothing in sight. Even in Amish Country you'd think you'd find at least a candle in a window.

A black-box carriage with giant spoked wheels has emerged from the purple sky, and for a moment I believe, as one believes in dreams, that this is the chariot that has come for me in death. I am strangely at peace with the idea and wonder if I will be lifted up or if I must stand up on my own. The clip-clopping of hooves—an afterthought—continues in my mind, though the muscular haunches of the silvery-brown steed rest, stationary, before me, and it is then that I lift my head and understand I am alive and this is now, and *this* is now, even as my watch—my brother's watch—on which my ear has been pressed, measures out the passing seconds. A white face is looking down from under the wide brim of a straw hat, and in the instant the young man smiles crookedly the orange sun peeks over the dark earth in the distance, in the east, and a blood-watery thread stretches along the horizon.

"Where you heading?" the young man says, as if this were a common scene, a strange man covered in mud, crawling out from a vegetable stand, a hitchhiker thumbing a lift from a horse-and-buggy.

I am on my feet.

"We had an accident. We hit a cow, I think."

The young man nods and looks down the road. I follow his gaze and see only the road and endless green fields. In the far distance silos sprout like mushrooms near a white barn.

Finally I understand that the young man is waiting for me. I am amazed by the strength of the young man, who grasps my forearm and pulls me up. I twist into place and bow my shoulders, filling up most of the carriage.

"My father is with the car. We are stuck." I enunciate as though the young man speaks another language. "I walked forever. I have no idea where he is. Where the car is."

"Can't be too far."

The young man's hands are enormous on the leather reins, which leap and slap the horse lightly. The horse trots, and I am surprised by the smoothness of the ride. I am surprised, in particular, by the cushioned seat. These people have not lost sight of what matters, I think. The young man is silent. Just the necessary words. Simple: the white shirt, suspenders, black pants; no cell phone, car, electricity—fewer disappointments in life, I think, or at least less complicated ones. Washed clean of desire, like the Buddhists. Still, they allow themselves simple comforts, like a cushioned seat or even Timberland boots, whose logo of a tree is visible just below the cuff of the young man's pants. I imagine the young man, on a typical morning like today, filling a wagon pulled by three horses, by lunchtime hauling in enough corn and other vegetables to fill the Acme or Weis truck that comes once a week. When the truck drives off, he pockets the check that will feed the family and buy the essentials, not for a second envying the life of the man driving away in the supermarket truck. What's amazing is that the young man has *chosen* this life, even after cutting loose, as I imagine him, not long ago, at sixteen, testing a cigarette, gunning an old Trans Am down one of these endless roads, *Stairway to Heaven* blaring out the sunroof. The Amish have a word for it, though I can't remember it—*rumpspringer?*—the time when they explore the outside world before devoting themselves once and for all to this one. What faith! They're pushed out into the world, and then they return to be baptized, having seen what they've seen. They have eaten from the apple, made their exit, and returned to the garden. The rest of us are nailed down, I think, before we know our own names, out of one womb and into another, purified in the baptismal tub long before we need to be washed clean of anything. And then we're dried off in our mother's arms, and we hold on for dear life…

The young man has taken a right turn, and for a moment, rising slowly toward the crest of a hill, I wish the horse would pick up the pace. I'm not sure if this is terrain I've traveled. No footsteps in the mud or trampled tunnels through the corn indicate my presence. We might trot around for hours. The grass off the lip of the road glistens as the sun comes up behind us. I hope my father has managed to sleep. I hope he'll laugh when I hop out of an Amish buggy—not exactly a Triple-A tow truck. You walk all night and you bring back Amos Stoltzfus and his trusty stallion? Maybe Amos will take us home to Philly, my father leading the way, the old man in black on horseback, returning to the Promised Land.

The vision I have at the top of the hill is stunning, at first for its beauty: sun beams splintered as if by invisible trees stretch out across a world of green; clouds of mist, hovering just above the earth, float up into the light and vanish. The green shell of the car is awash with the same silvery coating that lights up the valley floor for miles. What draws my eyes is the shadow carved out where my father's door is open. For fresh air, I think, until I see, across the road, at the wall of corn, what appears to be a scar in the earth, my father's broad, black shoulders where his head should be, his back humped and twisted as if the fall stopped him for good the instant he hit the ground.

I am out of the buggy and running toward the old man, who appears tremendous in death, lying there, legs buried in corn, fallen in the wake of his son's idiotic trail. The grass is slick under my knees. In the rush, I slide and sink into the cold earth, seizing the old man's collar, just as my father calls out my name and steps into the light outside the car. Stalks of corn bow over the crippled legs of the cow, whose greater part remains dignified under the cloak at my fingertips.

"I'll be back."

As I twist around, the buggy is already shrinking in the distance, moving at an astonishing speed, the red triangle on the rear of the carriage blinking out when the horse makes a sudden turn into what must be a road hidden in the corn. My father is standing above me now, extending a hand to lift me to my feet. We step out of the soft soil, onto the road, where we stand in silence. I lock eyes with my father and mirror his pose, hands folded, head bowed. The old man's lips begin to move, but it's not until his pinched-together fingers rise toward his forehead that I realize we've been praying.

We're standing shoulder-to-shoulder on the roadside when a white pickup emerges from the corn and barrels toward us. It stops and spins back toward the nose of the Lexus. An older, bearded Amos, in a white shirt and black pants that match his son's, hops down from the passenger seat and taps his hat with a finger as my father and I approach. Young Amos—not exactly Amish, all of a sudden, but Mennonite or some denomination in between—is already wrapping a chain somewhere underneath the grill when I make my way around the Lexus. Lush sod has attached itself halfway up the tires.

"Give it some gas?" Young Amos says.

I nod and get in. The truck towers over me. Young Amos jerks himself up into the cabin, stretches his arm out, and grins over his shoulder. Dodge Ram, motherfucker. When he nods, I barely get my foot on the gas pedal before the Lexus is up onto the road. Older Amos has my father's black suit coat under his arm and is gesturing toward the corn. I get out. "Breakfast," older Amos says. Young Amos leaps down, beaming. "We'll get you some clean clothes." He's pointing toward the white house in the distance. My father shakes older Amos's hand. "Thank you." Older Amos holds on firmly, escorts my father to the car and into the passenger seat, then opens the back door and lays the folded coat into the foot space. My father lowers the window and shakes older Amos's hand once more. "We're so sorry." Older Amos nods and steps back. "Get home safely now, Father." Young Amos is standing at my window. I lower the window and shake his large hand. "Sorry. Thanks." Young Amos keeps a firm grip, as older Amos circles the car for his son. "Nice truck," I add. Young Amos smiles. "I could show you the motorcycle."

Driving off, I wonder what must be going through their minds when they see "ZEUS" on the license plate, assuming they know something about mythology—what kind of crazy ancient-Greek religion...

Breakfast would have been nice, sitting at their table, even wearing their clothes. We should have stayed, I think, as my father stares at the green corn whipping past. We're not getting any closer—to each other, let alone to God—the Amish, the Orthodox, the old man and I, right now, as we head home, still, after all these years, like stars falling from the center. I have no idea where I'm heading—in general, in life. I know that. I want to ask the old man, right now, how he has soldiered on, knowing—he *knows*, doesn't he?—that his is just another myth that will transform and fade away; I want to ask how he musters the enthusiasm—the mental strength, the *creativity*—to mesmerize them from the pulpit, not skirting but working in the facts, a priest asking for trouble, preaching in his own way about free will and evolution so that even the children, who don't know Choice from Adam and have never heard of Darwin, feel triumphant in their complicated but holy progress, while entropy, which is stronger than sin, keeps working its invisible force.

The old man somehow gets them to believe not just in *one God,*

Father Almighty…and the life of the world to come but in themselves, now, in their power to determine their lives with the free will God has granted them, and their destiny with Faith. I want to believe it all. But it seems to me that from the moment we're thrust into the universe our lives are predetermined not by a Divine Plan but by the arbitrary trajectory that sets us in motion. I will return home, and I will eat at my father's table, but I don't feel like my father's son, much less like a child of God—more like an orphan of Fate, alone, as we all are, alone-together, together-alone, the space between us expanding, slowly, slowly. It is one of the laws of the universe, after all, everything forever breaking apart…and yet we keep crawling, clawing our way back into the current, back toward our place of origin.

"I have to ask you a question," my father says.

In the daylight the labyrinthine road is essentially straight and wide and smooth. In no time at all, it seems, we have returned to Route 1 and are heading north. The old man is waiting for a response.

"Okay," I say.

"Were you careful?"

As if either of us has demonstrated the slightest bit of precaution. As if knowing the truth could possibly make any difference at this point. Must every sordid detail be accounted for? Still, it is a reasonable question, I must admit—for a father to ask a son—despite the stinging effect on our dignity, what remains of it. This is it, our first sex-talk. I will tell him yes. Trojan, I'll say, a convincing detail, and over time I will try to convince myself as well, shielding myself from the truth. That she said she was on the Pill is, of course, anything but comforting, when I consider what I now know. There is one other detail after all, I realize, that hasn't been mentioned—and won't be (keeping my mouth shut feels something like restoring dignity or even like forgiving): the Viagra, the other pill, my father's pill…

"God help us," the old man says, interpreting the silence, which lingers, until the phone buzzes in my pocket.

We have returned to civilization, as it were. The line is dead, though, and I realize that the buzzing indicates a stored message, or, as the androgynous digitized voice informs me, seven unheard messages:

the first from my father, who asks, could you please swing by the church to pick up Father Chris and his family and bring them home for the barbecue and also, Peter, I know it seems I'm asking you this all the time and I don't mean to burden you, but if you get a chance, please talk to your sister, God knows she'd die before she tells me what's the matter; the second from Andrew saying, seriously, thank you for taking all my shit home and hauling it into the attic and, seriously, Doc, the watch is a gift, I feel bad about giving you shit last night, we're brothers, we should be closer, seriously, I've just been crazy with all this shit with Melanie; the third from Andrew saying where the fuck did you go, you fucking idiot, now Mom's freaking completely the fuck out, and what am I supposed to tell her, that this woman is the reason you've been acting like a fucking idiot for the last week; the fourth from Andrew saying okay this isn't even funny anymore, now Dad is going out to look for you, and I have a feeling I know where he's going to find you, of all the women on the planet, Doc, all the beautiful, amazing, young women on this planet, my God, would you answer the fucking phone, what was the point of buying it anyway?; the fifth from Andrew saying he just got back and it's raining like a motherfucker, even the Porsche was hydroplaning, and we can only hope you're with Dad, since your truck is at the church, and we're seriously thinking of calling the cops if we don't hear from you soon; the sixth from Andrew saying they called the state police and Triple-A to ask if they've heard anything about a green Lexus with the Pennsylvania license plate "ZEUS," but no, and now Mom is asleep on a chair in the living room, it's after four, we're just assuming you're waiting for the rain to pass, I can't believe it's still coming down, I can't sleep, I'm just sitting in the kitchen, Father Chris and Sandy and their sons are asleep in the basement, they were worried and it was pouring and it got late, and I don't know if you're even getting these messages or what, but Melanie's here too, asleep on the couch in the living room, I told her I'd convert, not that it would ever come to that, but fuck it, if that's what she needs to hear, enough of this shit already, call when you get this; the seventh from Andrew saying the sun's up, Doc, and so's everyone else, except for Theo, who's been asleep forever, Yiayia actually went for a walk with Mom, slowly, just around the block, with Father Chris and his wife and the little kid on the Big Wheel, to get their minds off all of this, and they just got back and it was weird, Mom said they prayed and she knows you're okay, she can feel it, so now everyone's in the kitchen, drinking coffee, all the women are making breakfast, we're waiting for you, to hear from you, or just to see you pulling in the driveway...

The phone buzzes in my hand again, and it takes me a moment to realize an actual call is coming through. It is Andrew, ecstatic, announcing our safety to the mob in the kitchen. They howl in delight; for a moment it sounds like a party, to which the guests of honor are finally on their way. My concise explanation—entirely truthful if a bit lacking in detail—is sufficient to appease them: we got lost in the rain, we had a minor accident, we got stuck.

In the mirror on the visor, the old man is rubbing away a dry-brown crack that extends from a wrinkle in his forehead into his hairline. "It looks like we were wrestling in the mud."

Suddenly the city appears in the distance like some magical glass utopia. I am happy to think of it as home, though I don't technically live there. *Yet*, I decide. Signs for Philadelphia have brought me here, to 95 North, though it dawns on me that I should have taken the Blue Route to the exit for the church, where my truck awaits me like a sad old dog whose time has come. I know it, as a mother knows her son is dead or alive. I won't bother to test the engine—out of respect, I think, imagining myself at the wheel. Why force the old guy to cough up his last breath? Just let him lie there for now. Still, I head for the church, in spite of my father's directions home...

When at last we enter the neighborhood, the coast is clear on Birch Hill. From the driveway my father and I remain quiet for a moment as we watch, almost mournfully, Theo, muttering beyond the fence on the far side of the house, plucking American flags from the ground and plunging them back in. For a moment I think Theo is only now completing the job that yesterday had been interrupted, until I realize that he is spacing the flags out, resetting them, pacing a certain number of shoe lengths and inserting the little flagstaffs just off the edge of his toe. Suddenly from the garage Father Chris's son bursts out, skids, and spins a hundred eighty degrees. When he looks over his shoulder, I say, "Keep it. It's yours," but the boy is suddenly uninterested in the Big Wheel. Instead, he is mesmerized by the man he knows as Father Pappas, who is dressed up in jeans and sneakers and an old gray T-shirt. A smile grows on the boy's face as he recognizes the old man as someone who has come to play. The boy digs the basketball from the shrubbery. The old man scoops the feeble pass and waves the boy into the garage to follow, but he stays outside.

At the stove my mother is folding mounds of bright-yellow eggs with a rubber spatula. Pink-faced, she looks up, waits, but the old man is speechless. Sophia, Andrew, and Melanie sit cradling mugs at the kitchen table, observing my mother's silence. At the screen door, Father Chris and Sandy offer a respectful smile and, as if minding their own business, at least for the moment, turn their gaze back to their older son throwing a baseball to himself in the back yard. The ball makes a faint pop when it hits the mitt. Yiayia appears in the doorframe of the dining room, still in her sky-blue dress, sugar bowl in one hand, creamer in the other. Back into my army shorts, I feel idiotically dressed alongside the old man, the two of us in college T-shirts, Temple and Holy Cross, our hairlines still damp from having washed up in the church bathroom. Yiayia wears a dead expression as she examines the old man's grass-stained sneakers and torn neckline. The dining-room table is set with her fine china, thin white porcelain cups, saucers, and plates laced with pink roses, out from behind the wire-webbed glass doors of the locked cabinet; this is a special occasion, but we are anything but guests of honor. That we are safe and sound has not washed away anyone's resentment—they have had a hellish night; and, despite their glazed expressions, the explanation they want has nothing to do with the college-boy outfits, though my father's wearing what might as well be a Halloween costume—Superman or Darth Vader—can't be helping to quell anyone's curiosity. My instinct is to retreat if the old man doesn't say something in the next second or so. But I stand by him as he remains silent and Yiayia ducks by and busies herself at the counter.

Chairs rumble out from the kitchen table when my mother walks a large bowl of scrambled eggs toward the dining room. She pauses before me and turns her cheek for me to kiss; when I bow down, she whispers, "I love you," into my ear, as if imparting another secret, which I can hardly bear. She adds, almost inaudibly, the single word, "Forgiveness," and I understand: it is more than a secret; it is *her* secret, her secret power, with which she can conquer anything. Forgiveness is the way out, she is telling me, or, rather, it is the way *in*…

As if taking the cue from her future mother-in-law, Melanie takes the broiler tray from the oven and pinches the bacon like wet socks over paper towels that Andrew spreads out on a serving tray. Then they are standing there before me. Melanie kisses me gently on the cheek and says, "Hey, bro'." Andrew grins and says, "Welcome home, Doc." Sophia takes the coffee pot from the coffee maker and follows Yiayia, who returns to the dining room with the filled creamer and replenished sugar bowl. Father Chris pats the old man on the shoulder before stepping into the dining room and standing behind the chair to which Yiayia directs him. Sandy steers the boys, who have dipped in through the screen door; she hoists them into their seats and takes her place beside Yiayia at the head of the table.

Melanie has set down boxes of cereal—Corn Flakes, Raisin Bran— at the center of the table. The older boy slams his fist into a box of Lucky Charms, which the wild-eyed younger boy tries to wrestle away and which Sandy seizes, shushing them. Theo barges through the front door, calling out, "Peter! I've got a proposition for you!" and stands there stupefied when he sees that breakfast has nearly started without him. Yiayia hisses—"*Skaseh, vreh!*"—Shut up!—and points to the empty seat beside her. Coming from another room is the wailing cry of a baby, about whom I have forgotten completely, until Sandy exits and the rubber wheels of a stroller meet the carpet in the dining room. My father and I are still standing in the doorframe when Sandy takes her seat next to Yiayia and does something with her hand that makes the baby go quiet. We step inside, finally, an empty seat remaining on each side of my mother, who mirrors Yiayia with bowed head and folded hands at the opposite end of the table.

I am staring at the steaming eggs, anticipating a prayer to end this dreadful silence, when my mother nudges me with her elbow. She nods, smiles—forgivingly, or longingly—but I am numb, dumb. I follow Yiayia's glare to find my father's eyes clenched shut, jaw muscles trembling, fingers so tightly intertwined at his ribs it seems he may be having chest pain. Eyes flash from bowed heads. I want my mother to take my father's hand, to soften the grip he's got on himself. Instead, she leans toward me and whispers, "Peter": the old man isn't going to utter a word, and it isn't Father Chris who should be stepping in.

"Our Fath—" I choke out, but I can't go on. I haven't said enough to set the Prayer in motion—in fact, what I blurted sounded vaguely like "Oh Fuck—" as though I were suddenly possessed, cursing, or speaking in tongues—and so it remains silent. I lack the breath even to utter, "Amen," and I don't dare inhale. It's all I can do to keep from crying like the baby. They are merciful not to look. Their heads are bowed. If their eyes are open, they are staring at their folded hands, even the boys, who must be frightened by the strange silence, which feels nothing like prayer. Still, I raise my right hand toward my forehead, slowly, slowly, hoping this does the trick, and, thank God, it does...their hands rise up, first the younger boy's and then Melanie's...somehow they sense the shift, from the silence to the cross.

"I have a proposition for you, Peter," Theo begins, reaching for toast as he sits.

"*Ah, vreh*," Yiayia grumbles, waving in disgust, but Theo continues, as everyone sits.

"I've decided to go to Greece—"

"*Skaseh, moreh!*"—Shut up, idiot!

"Ma!" Theo points to the stairs, as if threatening her, and then dips his head to see me. "It won't cost you a thing. You just have to take off work for a couple months."

"A couple months?" Sandy says.

"That won't be a problem," I say.

Sandy adds, "I would love to go to Greece for a couple months," plucking a Cheerio from her plate and turning to the baby.

"All expenses paid," Father Chris adds. "Not bad."

"I've got a lot of research to do," Theo says, fueled by the interest. He leans onto his elbows. "You can't tell the whole story unless you start from the beginning."

"You ever been to Greece, Peter?" Father Chris asks.

Theo answers for him, "Never been to Greece. None of these kids—" He looks at Andrew. "Thirty-two years old, he's never been to Greece. And Sophia, Peter..."

This is an attack: that the old man's kids have never been to Greece and don't know the language... I look at my father, who is chewing slowly with sealed lips. According to Theo, the old man has raised them improperly, without a sense of real tradition, of pride in their Greek heritage, *in spite* of the church. My father's head is up now, and his eyes are open. Theo must be waiting for the old man to tell him to zip it. That's when he knows when to stop.

"Kimon was born there," Father Chris says. "The boys have been there several times. Sandy and I met there, actually."

"You see that?" Theo says. "That's what I'm talking about. Real Greeks." Theo leans toward the younger boy and blurts something in Greek.

Instantaneously the boy leans his head back and gargles a reply through a mouthful of cereal.

Somehow Theo has understood, lifts his fork like a joyful conductor, and sings, *"Bravo!"* and asks the boy something else, to which the boy replies, "Panayioti," his name.

"Panayioti!" Theo hails. "That's *Peter's* name too! Do you know Peter?" Theo points for the boy, who nods. "He's Panayioti too. And So-*phi*-a..." He exaggerates a Greek flair, emphasizing the accent, and then proceeds, down the row. There's not much he can do with "Melanie," though he enunciates with broad Greek-sounding syllables, "*Meh*-lah-nee," and, finally, with dramatically trilled r, "Ahn-*dray*-ahs."

Andrew winces.

"So what do you say, Peter?" Theo says.

"About?"

"Greece, *vreh!*"

"I'll think about it," I say.

"What's there to think about?"

"Why not take Andrew or Sophia?" I say.

"Andrew's a doctor and Sophia has school."

Sophia looks up, but keeps her mouth shut.

"And *you?*" Theo adds, eyeing me. "Tomorrow you turn twenty-seven years old and you have nothing."

I nod. "It was a rhetorical question, Theo."

"Myself, I was finishing my dissertation when I was twenty-seven, in Greece. The best year of my life—"

"*Siopa!*"—Be quiet!

Yiayia's command stops Theo at last.

The room is silent.

"I'll go," I say.

For a moment Theo is too stunned to speak, his eyes expanding to fill his large lenses. "To Greece?" he utters, terrified, it seems, that I don't mean what I've said—or that I do.

The others have resumed eating, and I wonder at our lonely progress. At last, I have joined them.

"Yes," I say, and I have lifted off.

Ah: yes. I am already somewhere beyond the word, where anything and everything is possible.

"Peter…" Yiayia puts her fork on her plate and finishes chewing. Her eyes rest on me. "I tell you a story. I tell everyone a story…" First, she corrects Theo: "Not *Panayioti*," she says, and looks at the real Panayioti. "Peter is his name. Not the Greek name, the American name." The boy follows her eyes back to me, but before she goes on she glares at Theo and says, "Listen, *vreh*. Write *this*." She turns to me. "Your *papou* was very happy when your mother was pregnant. She had a child, Andrew, but you were special because he counted the days. Nine months—July four. He loved his country. America. He came here as a boy and became a *great* man. This was wonderful, his grand-son to be born on this holiday. He was so happy when your mother goes to the hospital. July three, nineteen-seventy-six. Bicentennial. Everybody is celebrating. Two hundred years this country. For independence. Papou goes to the store, and he buys flags. *Micro*—" Small.

She shows the size between her thumb and forefinger.

"I know the flags—" Theo interrupts.

Yiayia swipes at Theo, who flinches.

"I *have* them," Theo says.

Yiayia's eyes widen.

"In a box." He points up.

"*Pahmeh*"—Let's go. Yiayia sweeps her hand in the air. Theo leaves the room and stomps upstairs.

Yiayia continues, "No cigars. Small American flags. He gives to the nurses, doctors, in the hospital…"

Theo is back, panting, presenting a small, gray cardboard box in his open hand. He sits down, watching Yiayia slide the cover off like a box of matches. She plucks out a flag and hands it to Andrew. She plucks out another and hands it to Sandy, who hands it to Panayioti. One by one the flags make their way to my parents and me. There are enough flags for everyone. They are tightly woven cloth, not paper. The little flagstaffs are wooden but not toothpicks—they are strangely dense for their size, rounded on the ends, and finished with a waxy coating.

"You come too early!" Yiayia announces. I look up. "One minute. Your mother goes into labor. Now Papou gets worried. He's telling you wait. You remember?" I look at my mother, who fingers her flag and smiles ambiguously. "Eleven, eleven-thirty," Yiayia goes on. "And then, you know, they have the strict records, they write down the weight, the time. Peter comes eleven fifty-nine—"

"*No…*" Sandy says in disbelief.

"July three he's born," Yiayia says. "But your *papou*, he gives the nurses and the doctor the flags, he says what difference does it make, July three, four, and so they put July four, twelve o'clock. He convinces them."

"They *lied?*" Sophia breaks her silence. "On his *birth certificate?*"

"The horror," Andrew says.

"No *lie, vreh*," Yiayia says. "Just one minute difference. Maybe the clock is wrong. Papou has this way. Charming like this. He gets what he wants."

Sophia blurts, "So Peter was really born on July third—*today.*" She tears at a piece of bacon, irritated. "Would they *do* that, Andrew? On official records?"

"They do a lot worse than that."

"Have you seen *The Verdict?*" Melanie says.

"Great movie," Andrew says.

"Where this nurse," Melanie says, "is forced to change a one to a seven or something and there's this whole big case. Paul Newman finds her hiding out, teaching in a Catholic school—she quit being a nurse because she felt so terrible about it—and she finally agrees to testify."

"*Star Wars!*" the older boy calls out, mistaking the direction of the conversation.

Panayioti recognizes the title and, with a mouthful of eggs, cheers, "*Skywalker!*" thrusting his fork into the air.

"They love these movies," Sandy says.

Suddenly utensils have become characters that fight and fly, and Father Chris is handcuffing wrists to the table.

In the midst of the commotion, Sophia whispers, "Happy birthday."

I prop my little birthday flag against my glass of orange juice.

Then Sophia announces to no one in particular, "I'm going to the fireworks tonight at the Art Museum, with Freddy."

The old man sets his coffee cup on its saucer and swallows.

Sophia grins daringly.

The old man and I share a glance.

My mother says, "I don't want you downtown alone."

"I said, I'll be with Freddy," Sophia says.

"I don't want you on the train at midnight."

"I'll *drive*," Sophia says.

"Sophia, you are not driving—"

"*Mom...*"

"I'll go," I say.

"Peter," Sophia says, not sure what to make of the offer, if that's what it is.

"Yes—I want to go," I say.

No one seems especially happy, but there's nothing more to say.

After breakfast I pack up the *Star Wars* action figures sprawled on the basement floor. I place each one into its own tomblike compartment in the official plastic case and out on the driveway consign it to Kimon, who holds it at his side like a gentleman and gives a single nod, indicating he understands the weight of his responsibility. Still, Sandy reminds him to say thank you and then whispers to me that these are probably valuable, aren't they? or they will be. She adds that she's not sure she wants Panayioti to be riding around in the church parking lot, though on its side with the handlebars tilted the Big Wheel fits into the trunk of the Lexus, and I remind her that they won't be living at the church forever. My father fingers a tiny star in the corner of the windshield, perhaps checking for hairs. Andrew examines the grill and the chrome around the headlights, peering at the old man, who attributes the damage to a stop sign and then declares it was dark and raining and maybe we hit something else, a curb or a bench or God knows what. Andrew takes the keys and tells the old man to give it a rest.

My father and I fall asleep on the Adirondack chairs in the front yard. For a moment, when I wake up, I'm not sure if it's dawn or dusk. Freddy is standing there and gives me a hand. Sophia is asleep in the living room, stretched out on the red couch, her knees wrapped in Ace bandages. My father strokes her hair in his lap and puts a finger to his lips, though Freddy and I haven't stepped beyond the carpet inside the doorway. The only sound is the sweep of Theo's pencil rubbing away at his desk in the kitchen. Still, Sophia awakes and sits up.

"That was nice," she says. When she sees Freddy, she says, "Be right back."

She returns from her bedroom wearing her Rasta hat and boots that buckle up to her knees. The bandages peek from under a red skirt that falls just short. My mother follows Sophia down the staircase and stops before the landing.

"This is a motley crew," she says, and adds, "You don't mind a chaperone, Freddy," not quite a question, though the kid shakes his head no, he doesn't mind.

We agree to meet at the LOVE sculpture at midnight. We can catch the train home from Suburban Station, right on J.F.K. Boulevard, where we just got out. Sophia and Freddy want to get as close to the museum steps as possible, so they head toward the Parkway. I decide to loop around and head toward City Hall, where the Clothespin's silhouette is enhanced by spotlights shooting up. I discover Papou's *kompoloi* in my pocket. I thought I'd dreamt it—Theo sneaking up on me, asleep in the front yard. I take out my note cards and sit at the base of the LOVE sculpture, my back to City Hall. I contemplate the three words I've written—*This is LOVE*—and thumb the blank deck. I watch the Ben Franklin Parkway flood with people from both sides, like the parting sea in reverse. Twenty-seven years ago tonight I was born just across the river, not far from where some practice rounds are popping in white bursts above the Art Museum, visible over the tip of the fountain gushing pink water from the sunken pool just below. Twenty-seven years ago tonight the highest point of the city was the hat on the head of William Penn, standing on the tower just behind him, the Quaker's dream of a Greene Countrie Towne still honored by gentlemen-builders delaying their own dreams of skyscrapers; there was something honest and muscular about a city that refused to grow vertically, something stubborn and lovely about keeping the people close together on the ground. Twenty-seven years ago tonight, bruised kids on skateboards were sailing off steps and crashing onto concrete, looping endlessly, wheels thumping and thumping on the cracks between the slabs of stone. Twenty-seven years tonight feels like eternity, not like forever, not like a long time, but like time outside of time, without beginning or end, time for a whole magnificent city to rise up all around you, time for your whole life to be your life at this very moment as you ooh and ahh at symbolic bombs bursting in the air and you remember lying on a blanket in the grass of the elementary school, your mom there with a plastic bag of pretzels and grapes, your brother off somewhere else, having refused to come along, though your mother pleaded and you wondered what he would rather be doing than watching fireworks on the Fourth of July, your birthday, and you couldn't imagine ever being as old as he was, and you never would be, you were happy to know, just as you were happy to know you would always be older than your sister, who was sitting at your feet, staring at the black sky, fingers in her ears, and who seems okay today, but you still can't help picturing her drugged up and dumped in a parking lot in North Philly, so you give up the best seat in the house, leaving your note cards on LOVE's pedestal, and head for the museum, though you know you won't find her and Freddy in the thousands of people in the street, not yet, not until midnight, when you'll find them curled up in the same spot where you curled up that day with Dorothy Maloney, in the spot where she held her digital camera at arm's length and took the picture that was meant for the dustcover, the picture you trimmed down and carried in your wallet before you carried the letter that like a masochist you're still carrying right now as you dig the old Instamatic from your front pocket, the camera you found tonight in a dresser drawer before rushing to catch the train, the camera the old man got you for your ninth or tenth birthday, the camera your mom used to take the picture Daisy Diamond laid on top of the old man's jeans in the paper bag you never forgot about, the camera you haven't used since college when you must have shot the first seven pictures on the roll still inside, the roll you're only half-hoping hasn't been storing pictures of Dorothy all these years, the roll that will produce the picture you're going to send to Brock West, who sent you a postcard that was just a photograph with a stamp on it, the postcard that must have arrived yesterday and that your mother must have set on your dresser, the postcard that in a rush you slipped into your pocket so you could look at it now, the first chance you've had, under one of the streetlamps along the Parkway, where every country in the world has its own flag on a pole, and you hope, as you look for the sign with the name, that the country whose flag you're under is India, where Brock mailed this postcard from, this picture-postcard of him sitting in a field, bare knees peeking over the tips of golden grass, grinning, head shaven, wearing a white linen shirt, his note scrawled in tall letters on the back, "Nicest people in the world, bro', don't know if they'll ever let me leave, or if I want to," beside a return address you can only hope is where he'll be when you send your reply, maybe the picture you're taking right now, sitting in the green grass, where you've found a gap in the crowd, timing the next explosion, fixing the camera on your knee, knowing if you're lucky this picture will be a smear of light in the night, though you will explain, "Fourth of July, bro'…" and it will seem like some kind of Zen thing, your version of a self-portrait, your version of America, of you and me, where we are right now, where I'm still thinking of the old man and what I can't get out of my head, not what he did before but what I did this morning, though I'm trying hard just to be here now, in the moment, and I know he forgives me, but I don't forgive myself, though I want to, and maybe that's enough, to absolve me, for not letting go, for going to the church instead of just going home, for going out to the truck while the old man washed up and then handing him the bag, silencing him, in brief, silent ceremony, letting the old man read this as penance, watching him peel off his black shoes and his black pants and shirt, handing him the jeans and setting the sneakers at his feet, stuffing the black clothes and shoes into the bag, which I folded and kept tucked under my arm, as though I were the last keeper of secrets, the final judge, even as I set the pictures on the shelf and led the way outside, even as I turned my key and remembered my truck was dead, even as I ran after the old man, who stopped for me, even after I showed him I hadn't forgiven him, not yet, even as I entered the house, anticipating their mouths agape.

ACKNOWLEDGMENTS

I am very grateful to so many friends who have worked with me along the way, reading drafts and sharing their wisdom and encouragement, especially Robin Black, Bob Huber, Jonathan Rubin, Dennis and Dorothy Baumwoll, John Bonaccolta, Matt Hartin, and Elisabeth Weed. Thanks to the Warren Wilson M.F.A. program, especially Wilton Barnhardt, Adria Bernardi, and Debra Spark. Thanks also to Mike Fitzgerald, John Fried, Alex Lyras, Nick and Georgia Lyras, Helen Papanikolas, Meghan Cleary, Heather McElhatton, Thom Didato, Curt Smith, Marc Bookman, Marie Dicandilo, John Pritchard, Kevin Maness, Dan Rottenberk, Dave Stango, Sharon Sweeney, Felicia Quinzi, Winnie Host, Holly Baker, Kyle Farley, Tricia's Book Club, Jeff Ayars, Christi Bailey, Lindy Litrides, Victoria Miller, and Dean Fournaris. Above all, thank you, Pete Turchi, Dan Loose, Del Staecker, Nan Wisherd, John and Trish, Sue and Niko, Mom and Dad, and Vana.